D0362633

# ENES SMITH

# COLD RIVER
# RISING

### A NOVEL

To Sara

Enes Smith
9.19.14

# COLD RIVER RISING

Enes Smith 2006

This is a work of fiction. Names, characters, places, and incidents either are the product of the author's imagination or are used fictitiously. Any resemblance to actual persons, living or dead, events, or locales is entirely coincidental.

COLD RIVER RISING. Copyright 2006 by Enes Smith. All rights reserved. Printed in the United States of America. No part of this book may be used or reproduced in any manner whatsoever without written permission except in the case of brief quotations embodied in critical articles or reviews.

Cover design by Road's End Films
Cover text by Kent Wright

For additional copies, go to Amazon.com

ISBN 1453750959
EAN-13 9781453750957

Library of Congress Control Number: 2006904613

Printed in the United States of America
Enes Smith Productions edition June 2006

## AUTHOR'S NOTE

I am a Šiyápu, a white man, and as such, any mistakes I have made regarding Indian tribes, peoples, customs, and culture are mine alone. This is a work of fiction, from a Šiyápu looking in from the outside, and any relation to persons and events are from the author's imagination, and not related to real people or events.

## ACKNOWLEDGMENTS

There have been many people who have contributed time and kind words, without whom Cold River Rising would have never happened:

Nancy Spreier, friend, consummate researcher, and constant believer, owed more than I can write - thanks to her husband and family for putting up with bibliophiles; Annie Hausinger, for the journey of friendship; Tom Jones, fellow cop and most talented man I know; Michelle Jones, friend who cares enough to force me to write when I've lost the way; Barbara Lambert, for editing and suggestions on the early manuscript, and introducing me to horses, large dangerous animals that don't like humans (according to Larry McMurtry).

For Tony, Melissa, Maddie, and Dani

and

Hunter, Halle, Samantha, and Justin


All my love

# **P**rologue

Monday, May 6
10:02 a.m.
Portland, Oregon

Martin Andrews had come to terms with evil in his life, and he thought he had seen most of what man could offer. Until the school this morning.

He went to the school because he had to. He thought later that his willingness to drive into harm's way was explainable only to those who had been in police work or the military or firefighting. In twenty-three years as a police officer, the last eight in homicide, he had been in the rank rooms of death, touched the waxy, shiny, tenebrous skin, and smelled the foul breath of people long dead. He had seen the stark lost hope in the eyes of prostitutes and druggies, street people and the homeless, in many ways more depressing than their death. He knew the dark side, could sometimes see it in his sleep. But until this morning, he had struggled and managed to remain above it, clinging to a thread of hope that good existed with evil.

Martin lost the thread this morning.

He drove the unmarked Ford through the bright sunny streets of S.E. Portland, checking residential addresses. He was looking for a witness to an old case, an easy way to get through the day. His radio was down low, a mutter in the background, but he heard the call go out just the same.

"Seven twenty one, unknown problem at the Nora Westley elementary school."

As the patrol unit answered, Martin realized he was just a block away. Closer.

"The caller was cut off - sounded like," the dispatcher hesitated. "Sounded like a gunshot or loud noise."

Martin drove the block to the school, slowing, turned his unmarked car into the parking lot. He told the dispatcher that he would assist, meet patrol at the front. It was quiet in the lot, the teachers' cars sitting alone in a group, as if they had been sent to parking lot detention. He parked next to a Volvo wagon and stood beside his car, watching. He grabbed his jacket and portable radio and studied the front doors, then walked across the lot, the school windows looking to Martin like big accusing eyes.

*Where have you been?*

Martin heard a loud noise from the inside of the school and he stopped in the lot, thinking that this was a stupid place to be. What was that noise? A shot?

As he reached the sidewalk in front of the entrance, the glass door to his right burst open and several kids ran out, their legs pumping as they ran across the lot and away from the building. A woman ran after them, carrying a small girl. She glanced at Martin, stopped, pointed inside, and ran after the kids.

The voice came over his radio, excited now "..shooter in the school, confirmed, repeating shooter in Nora Westley Elementary. . . all units. . .."

"Forty seven fourteen's in the front door, waiting for the first unit."

Martin entered through the glass front doors and looked around for the office, holding his Glock down by his leg.

"Seven twenty one's at the school."

Okay, now I have some help, Martin thought. The lessons of Columbine have not been lost on us. At a school we don't wait for S.W.A.T., the first units at the school just go to the trouble.

Must be between recesses. Quiet in here. He stopped inside the door and waited for his eyes to adjust to the florescent lighting. Something didn't look right, didn't smell right, silent alarms going off inside Martin, and then an internal voice screamed

*There's a body down the hallway, to the right in a pool of blood*

The blood glistened on the floor, trapping the body in its redness. Martin moved his gun up and covered the hallway, the skin on his face and neck tightening. As he reached for his radio he heard a noise behind him and whirled, his gun coming around. A uniformed officer, Terry Gordon, he thought, came in behind him. Martin pointed at the body and they both started as a series of gunshots blasted from somewhere down the hallway, a scream cut off by the last shot.

Officer Gordon spoke quietly, urgently into his microphone

clipped to his shirt.

More shots and shouting.

Martin held his Glock up in front of him, moving fast on the balls of his feet.

"Here," Officer Gordon said, and Martin peeked around a corner and saw bodies, a teacher and a kid, down the hallway by some gray lockers.

A kid screamed, muffled, cut off by a shot.

Another shot, close, two doors down. Who's doing this, a kid?

Gordon stood beside the door and reached for the doorknob as Martin stood to the side. As Officer Gordon's hand touched the knob, the door opened suddenly, thrown back against the wall and a man stood there, must be a teacher, Martin thought, and then the man shot Terry Gordon in the face. The blast from the gun sounded impossibly loud to Martin, the muzzle just inches away, the blood from Terry's face spattering, and Terry staggered back into Martin and dropped

*He's not a teacher, Martin, he has a gun, he's*

and Martin shot from five feet away, the bullets hitting the gunman, must be hitting him, but he's firing back, and why isn't he falling, and...

Martin fired again as a puff of wind hit him in the left arm, high up in the bicep, feeling the bullet snap on the bone, twisting him around, and then the gunman was gone. Martin stood there, swaying, his ears ringing from the muzzle blasts. He heard someone crying in the room. A kid. Where's the gunman?

He leaned in the door and saw him down on his back, up against a chair. His eyes were open, staring at the *Big A, little a* on the wall above the chalkboard. He wasn't moving. As Martin walked toward the gunman he saw a head and the bright eyes of a girl, about six years old. She followed him with her eyes as he leaned over and picked up the gunman's pistol and tucked it in his belt.

Kids were starting to peek up over their desks. Martin tried to wave his left arm at the girl but it wasn't working. He rocked back against the wall and slid down, pressing his shoulders against the blackboard, sliding slowly at first, and then he fell heavily from a crouched position, his Glock clattering on the floor.

"Ow." He yelled before he could stop the sound. He rocked over to sit, his feet splayed out in front of him. He fumbled for his Glock and jammed it into his holster. He looked around the room.

"Where's your teacher?"

The girl with the bright eyes pointed.

"She okay?"

"She's dead," another little voice said from the back of the room. The girl with the bright eyes crawled around her desk and moved toward Martin, leaving a trail of blood on the tile. She had been shot in the leg, more than once, Martin thought, the wounds pumping out blood in small spurts. When she reached him he put his right hand on her leg and put pressure on, pulling her into him.

*Ohmigod what have we done to our children*

Martin looked around the room, looking at the aftermath of a crazy man.

"He got the wrong room," a little voice said. "He said he was looking for Mrs. P, but she's next door."

Some of the kids were standing, staring at the shooter, others crying. A scream from down the hallway.

The girl said her name was Claire. She had her right thumb in her mouth and spoke around it. She pointed with her little finger, not letting her thumb out of her mouth.

"Mishsush Carter," she said, gave a little hitch, and continued to suck her thumb.

*Dear God, what have we done*

Martin held her and waited. He had heard sirens earlier, and now they were a constant background noise. Claire turned into Martin and nestled her head against his chest. Her face was pale, her eyes closing. Martin felt himself slipping and he gripped her wound harder.

Slipping.

The medics and police found them like that, and when they checked her he heard one of the medics say that she was in shock.

"Why did that man do this?" She whispered to Martin, and then "tell my mommy..." She was lifted up and placed on a gurney, the medics working fast, talking to each other in their own special language. Martin lurched up and followed Claire, trying to grab her hand as it fell beside the gurney.

The morning was still bright with sun as Martin came out and sat on the curb, feeling woozy, not wanting to feel, the parking lot a surreal scene of activity - jumbled police cars, S.W.A.T. vans, ambulances, parents arriving, police running to the school. He watched the ambulance as Claire was being loaded. As the medic shut the

doors, he looked at Martin and shook his head.
And the thread of hope ran out for Martin Andrews.

Later, sometimes at night, he could feel Claire's breath on his face.

Four years later . . .

# DAY ONE

# **C**hapter **1**

Cordillera Blanca Mountain Range
Central Peru

As the morning mist burned off the western slope, the woman with no feet waited on the ground, facing south. She was in a meadow, away from the rocks, and would soon be in full sunlight. Her eyes clouded with the milky opaqueness of death. Had she been alive, she would have been cold until the sun touched the meadow. She wore a purple and brown robe, the traditional dress of the Quechua Indians, or Seranos, People of the Altitude. Long pampas grass and yellow and red wildflowers pushed up around her.

Although she was watched from the surrounding rocks, she was alone in the meadow. As the air warmed the flies found her, and a trail of ants wound through the grass toward the body. A bird of prey circled high overhead, riding the thermals.

Others would soon join the circling bird. The woman wouldn't be alone for long.

Her attackers watching from the woods heard voices on the trail above the plateau. They heard laughter, a woman's voice.

They waited.

On the morning the woman died, Tara Eagle stood at the edge of the meadow and shrugged to relieve the pain in her shoulders, her shirt wet in a v-shaped stain under her pack. She was slender in blue jeans and hiking boots, her long black hair gleaming in the sun. She closed her eyes and listened to the other hikers as they came up behind her. She couldn't explain how, but she suddenly knew there was a body in the meadow in front of her. She could see the color of the woman's clothes, the slack and uncaring face, feet bloody like bright red shoes. Tara started to shake with cold, the skin on her arms going tight and bumpy, and dropped the pad and pencil she had been carrying.

When she opened her eyes, there was nothing but grass in the meadow.

*This will be the worst day of my life. Death follows me.*

Pedro, their Quechua guide came up beside her and she had other thoughts, more chilling and frightening

*You're to blame for this, Tara. You'll never get out of Peru alive, any of you.*

She glanced upward, hoping to shake the image of the body as the rest of the hiking group crowded up behind her. She looked past the group of students and then at the jagged mountain peaks of the Cordillera Blanca rising behind them. In front of her the mountainside spread out as if it would go on forever, down the slopes to the Pacific Ocean, fifty miles away. Tara had been okay until now, thinking only of a hot shower after a week of hiking. They visited pre-Columbian ruins in the Andes, a group of nine Native American students and one professor, and with their three Peruvian guides, they had only one more lunch stop, then on to the bus at Huaraz.

*Maybe I'm not to blame, but I can't get away from death, and that's the same thing . . .*

Tara jumped as Steve approached her from behind, laughing, saying something to the group of hikers. He grabbed the pad and pencil and examined her sketch. Tara snatched it back and flipped the pad closed as her two friends, Delores and Sabrina, panted to a stop beside her.

"Hey, sports fans," Steve said, "you're blocking the trail."

Tara glared at him, annoyed at his constant joking. If only he would be serious.

"Hey, Tara," Steve said, grinning, "my jokes too much for you?"

Pedro put his finger to his lips, motioning for the rest of them to be quiet. Her fear crept up her spine, her left knee buckled, and she straightened it, shaking. She hoped she had imagined the body in the meadow below them, for she had seen bodies before that hadn't actually been real. Her legs felt weak.

"Que es?" Steve asked. He was the only student in their group who spoke Spanish.

Pedro turned around, his eyes large. He glanced quickly at the rocks and then the meadow. He licked his lips.

Oh God, he's scared to death, Tara thought.

Pedro replied in Spanish, rapidly, his voice getting higher at the end. Tara waited for Steve's translation.

"Pedro, donde estan Mario y Ruppert?" Steve asked. She recognized that much – *where are Mario and Ruppert?*

14

Pedro pointed down the trail. The rest of the group crowded up behind them.

"Is it lunch time already?" Sabrina asked. Steve held up his hand.

"Pedro, call to Mario and Ruppert," Steve said in Spanish.

Pedro called.

There was no answer.

Mario and Ruppert, their other young Indian guides, had gone ahead to prepare a lunch.

It's too quiet, and now Pedro is scaring me, Tara thought. She shook the image of what she knew was in the meadow. All morning the hillside had been alive with bird and insect noise, and now she could hear nothing. Keeping her eyes on Pedro, she moved off the trail. The others followed in a tight group as they passed through a rock outcropping and stood at the edge of the meadow. The group huddled behind her, as if they were cold, the early banter gone. She squinted toward the meadow where Mario and Ruppert stood.

"Sendero Luminoso," Pedro whispered. He glanced from one to another, his hand shaking as he wiped his face with his shirt. Tara felt her scalp go tight; sweat trickled down the middle of her back. She knew what Sendero Luminoso meant. They all did. Sendero Luminoso - The Shining Path. Peruvian guerrillas dedicated to a violent overthrow of the government. Legs braced, Pedro appeared to be ready to bolt. Tara placed her hand on his shoulder. He tensed, but she felt him trembling.

When she was ten years old, she had seen a gopher caught in a leg-hold trap. She had been with a friend, taking a shortcut through a field, and they heard the gopher before they saw it. The animal had been chewing its leg, an atavistic attempt at survival and the leg was almost severed. As they approached, the gopher hissed and clawed, pulling on the chain. Tara had been as scared as the gopher, and now when she stood next to Pedro, she saw a frightened man, as trapped and as afraid as the gopher.

He was already chewing on his leg, and he didn't know it.

His eyes jerked to meet hers.

"Shining Path," Tara said quietly. "They told us in Lima that they were all in jail or dead, and with the search around the world for bad guys, we thought they were all gone." She lowered her voice to a whisper. "After nine eleven, it was supposed to be safe to travel again."

15

Pedro nodded. Delores and Sabrina leaned in closer to her.

She watched Steve start across the meadow toward their guides.

Tara glanced at the others and then followed Steve, the short grass reminding her of the high meadows on the Cold River Indian Reservation. The sun was warm on her face, comforting, as she left the rocks. Up ahead, Steve reached Mario and Ruppert, and stopped. As she came up behind him she knew at the last instant there would be a body there, as she had dreamed it, the odor of blood and the swarm of flies telling her she didn't want to look.

But she did.

Clasping Steve's arm, she stared at the body of the Indian woman. She took in the milky eyes of the dead woman. Flies that formed a black writhing veil where her face had been, the bloody, foaming mass where. . *Her feet, oh Christ she has no feet.*

Tara stepped back, her mind furiously attempting to deny what she had seen.

*The woman has no feet, and I did this to her. I must have, 'cause death follows me.*

She shivered. Her mouth went dry. She had seen violent death before. You didn't grow up on a reservation and not see it, or in the city for that matter. But this, this time . . .

Tara heard sounds of someone retching. Gretchen stared at the body, her hands over her mouth; then she turned and vomited, bending over at the waist, her glasses sliding down her nose and dangling crazily from one ear. Tara caught the sunlight glinting on the silver frames. The sounds of the retching jolted her stomach, yet she couldn't leave. The others came up quietly and clustered around the body in a curious half-circle, as if they were going to have to take notes and be held accountable later. For once, Tara thought, the professor didn't have anything to say. Maybe he was just catching his breath.

Standing to one side, Mario and Ruppert looked back across the rock formation they had just walked through.

What do they see? Tara thought.

Pedro said something in Spanish. He was shaking now, his fear a visible thing, affecting all of them. Tara lay a hand on his arm.

"Pedro, why did this happen, what's going on here?" She turned to Steve, wanting him to translate when Pedro answered.

"She wouldn't join, she ran away," he said in Spanish. "They killed her as a message. It's starting again." He glanced wildly around at the mountain, the meadow, as if he were picking where to run.

Steve translated for them, somber, his earlier laughter gone.

Pedro suddenly shielded his eyes and scanned the sky, then down the mountain toward the coast. Tara heard the unmistakable sounds of a helicopter rotor. She knew a helicopter this far up in the mountains in Peru meant army, either the Peruvian Army or U.S. Army advisers.

The helicopter came up on the meadow from the south and below their line of sight, hidden in a lower valley. It popped up over the rim of the meadow suddenly, as if it were the clever deception of a magician's trick, a deadly rabbit bristling with guns. The helicopter crabbed sideways to slow down, slowing and turning, the speed carrying it over their heads. Tara spotted the helmeted pilots and the gunners in the open doors, the helicopter and the men in green, a clattering metallic thing, an intrusion on the dead woman's privacy.

*The dead woman with no feet.*

The speed carried the helicopter to the far side of the meadow. It hovered there, just inside the rock formation. Tara froze. It was like one of those dreams where you couldn't run, couldn't make your legs work when they had to.

*Run. We should all run for the rocks.*

Tara turned to Steve, opening her mouth to tell him to run. The helicopter moved toward them, slowly, at 100 feet, sideways, the side gunner covering them.

No one moved.

"Steve, we've got to -"

An explosion shook the craft. It dipped a few feet closer to the meadow, a trail of smoke coming from the rocks they had just passed through. Smoke poured from the open doorway. Tara caught more flashes from the rocks and realized that people were firing at the helicopter. She watched in horror as the plexiglass windshield shattered, the pilot's body jerking with gunfire, holes appearing in the side of the helicopter, the crewman with the waist gun firing wildly over them, and then his body went limp in a spray of blood, the machine moving closer toward them and passing overhead, the turbine trailing black smoke. Figures leaped up at the edge of the meadow, firing at the 'copter.

Tara watched as the other pilot fought for control of the craft as it careened overhead. She ducked instinctively, turned and stared as the helicopter roared by. Out of the corner of her eye, she saw Gretchen and Myoko still standing, Myoko wiping Gretchen's face, as if they were on a picnic, unaware of the death above them.

The helicopter rolled on its side as it neared the rock formation they had just left, and then it flared up like a wounded bear on its rear legs, in a final defensive, defiant stance.

The figures across the meadow were still firing.

The craft rose up and suddenly looped upside down, the blade striking the closest rocks, the rotor disintegrating as the helicopter exploded in midair, slamming to the ground.

"Get down!" Steve yelled, and he hit Tara hard across the chest. She dropped, going down on her back in the grass as the world around them exploded. As she fell to the grass, she saw Gretchen blinking in the sun without her glasses, and then something struck Gretchen and she dropped, limp, in a shower of blood. Professor Bauchman stood, upright and curiously untouched amidst the flying carnage around him, a bewildered look on his face.

Another explosion shook the ground and Tara felt the heat from the fire as debris rained down on them.

"Jesus Christ," Steve muttered in Tara's face. He rolled off her and she struggled to get up, but his hand came over her and pushed her down again.

"Crawl," he said. "Anything that stands is dead, either from the copter or whoever shot it."

She nodded, her face inches from his, wondering as she crawled how a career college kid knew such things.

They moved through the grass, away from the fire, slowly, using the heat as direction. Steve led, working his way to Gretchen. Tara watched as he gripped the girl's hand, held it a moment, then slowly placed Gretchen's hand on her chest. Tara crawled past, not needing to look.

She heard a scream, followed by loud moaning. Tara raised her head enough to see Myoko laying on her side, clutching her chest, a bright arc of red around her, her legs moving slowly, as if she were trying to crawl. Keeping low, Tara reached Myoko. She lifted the young woman's head and cradled it, listening to Myoko as she tried to breathe. She put pressure against the wound, Myoko's shirt slick with blood. As Tara tried to stop the bleeding a twisted piece of metal poked up through Myoko's shirt.

Tara sat up, found Steve and the others who crawled with him.

She shook her head as Myoko went limp. "She's dead," Tara said matter of factly. "She and Gretchen were standing . . ."

She stared at them. Steve and Delores and Sabrina, Robert and Carl. The professor had finally dropped. Kneeling in the grass, he looked wildly around at the rest of them. Tara gently placed Myoko's head down.

They sat there and no one said a word. Tara heard Delores crying quietly behind her. Then the ammunition from the helicopter's guns cooked off in the heat from the fire, popped and crackled loudly, sounding as if a string of firecrackers had been thrown in a campfire. Tara pressed her face in the grass, the blades sharp against her skin. She raised her head slowly, and glimpsed men with guns slowly walking toward them, searching the opening in the rocks and the area around the helicopter.

"Stay down," Steve said, and nodded toward the approaching men. Tara caught sudden movement off to her right, and Mario and Ruppert jumped up and ran for the other side of the meadow. Tara wanted to reach out and grab them, hold them. Mario's straw hat blew off and it hung there, suspended as if it were a child's kite.

*They're only boys, playing tag in a meadow, and this isn't really happening, a woman with no feet, a helicopter burning up, people with guns. . . .*

The man nearest them swung his AK-47 and fired a long burst, shooting at the two guides as they ran. Mario dropped immediately, his life ending in mid-stride, crumpling to the grass and out of sight. Ruppert ran with blood pumping from his shoulder, limping now. The others in the meadow fired at him, his body jerking and spinning as he went down. Tara stared at the man who fired first, watching as the rifle shook, the long distinctive banana clip protruding from beneath it. The shooter had short-cropped black hair beneath a straw hat. He wore a dirty white shirt and black pants, as if he were a waiter sneaking a smoke in the woods behind a lodge. She noticed dirt on his hands and then he spotted them.

He held his rifle up high over his head and yelled, "Alto!"

The others then continued to fire, long after Mario and Ruppert had dropped to the grass. One by one they stopped and looked at the man with dirt on his hands.

"Tara." Carl grabbed her shoulder and leaned in close, their heads touching. "Tara," he whispered, "they see us now. We'll never all make it away from them. I'm going to try to slip away and get help."

She nodded, grabbed his hand. "Carl, you must let them know, let my *tila*, my grandfather, know what has happened. Get to a phone somehow."

"Yeah, if I can."

"Call him," Tara whispered fiercely, her throat tight. He had blood on his clothes, his hands. It must be from Myoko, he didn't seem hurt. She released her grip on his wrist and he calmly wiped his hands on his face, the blood making hideous streaks. It reminded Tara of mourning, and she knew in a way it was . . . the death of their new friends and their innocence. Carl slid away on his stomach, worming his way backward toward the rocks twenty feet away.

The men with rifles strode toward their huddled group. The man with the dirty hands yelled something directly at them, but Tara didn't understand.

Still sitting, Steve threw his hands in the air. Tara slowly lifted her hands and watched this man who appeared to be the leader.

She counted about a dozen men in all. As they walked across the meadow they pointed their rifles at them.

*There's nothing we can do. They're gonna kill us.*

Tara flinched, expecting to hear shots when the gunmen discovered Carl, but none came. Their little group was surrounded.

The man nearest, the one who had shot Mario and Ruppert, the one with dirty hands, moved his rifle barrel up, motioning for them to stand. Steve got to his feet, spoke to the man evenly in Spanish.

"We're students, we mean no harm."

The man swung his rifle into Steve's head, the barrel connecting with a crack that made Tara jump. Steve staggered back but didn't go down and stood there swaying. A thin stream of blood rolled down his scalp.

Tara rose, her legs shaking until she thought they would buckle. Dirty Hands scanned her and then the group.

She gazed past him to the meadow, the heat from the helicopter bright on her face. She saw the cloth from the dead woman's purple and brown robe, and further over, a flash of white from where Mario lay.

*Grandfather, Tila, don't let this happen.*

Steve flashed her a slight smile, and she stared at Dirty Hands as he turned the assault rifle toward them.

And suddenly Tara knew that all was lost. After her parents died, she still had family. She had a Tribe.

*Save me, Grandfather.*

*But Tila is old, and his power is for the reservation, and like the woman in the meadow, we're all going to die here. Die away from home. Die here with no feet.*

*This will be the worst day of my life.*

As Tara waited with the others, waiting to be shot, she glanced down and saw her pad on the ground in front of her, the pages blown open to her latest sketch, a sketch of a woman lying in tall grass, a dead woman with no feet.

*I have always known about death before it happens. I'm afraid to tell my best friends, my family. Maybe this will not be the worst day of my life.*

*Not by half.*

*Death follows me.*

# Chapter 2

Carl burrowed in behind a large rock at the edge of the plateau, rolled up into a tight ball and pulled his knees into his chest, breathing hard. His heart thundered louder than the shouts coming from the clearing.

*If they look at me I'm dead.*

He was sure the others were dead, or would be soon. *Jesus, they blasted our guides, shot the shit out of them.*

He heard a sudden shouting in Spanish on the other side of the rock. He crouched, thinking they had him. He closed his eyes. More shouting came from the meadow.

Feet pounded on the trail as people ran toward him. An explosion shook the ground and he slipped to one knee. Carl drew his knees up to his chest as the first figure ran past him. *They're right beside me!*

Two men carrying rifles ran past him and entered the path in the rocks, followed by a very scared looking Delores. She stumbled to her hands and knees, and then was up and running again, her eyes flickering wildly around, looking at Carl and not seeing him.

Steve came next, his head bleeding, and it seemed to Carl that Steve winked as he ran by, as if it were all a big joke. If that were so, then Steve was a pretty cool guy indeed. Steve had seemed like a party guy, a black dude from Miami and some little Indian tribe there, a guy who never took anything seriously. Tara was next, and then the professor and Robert. Several men and women carrying rifles ran past, with Sabrina in the middle of the group.

A small man wearing a Chicago Bulls hat stopped and swung the barrel of his rifle toward Carl, his neck and chest shiny with sweat. All Carl could think of was, *bad choice for a hat.* The man wore a sweat-stained t-shirt that had once been white. The bearded face on the shirt glared at Carl with the hatred of a fanatic.

*Ohmigod*

Carl's breathing stopped and he tried to get up. The face. That Al Qaeda dude. Osama bin fucken Laden himself. But what the hell was he doing here in –

The rifle barrel moved away and then looped down fast, and

22

before Carl could throw his hands up a bright flash of pain exploded in his head. The gunman ran after the others. Blood ran down Carl's face and into his mouth, hot and sticky, the salt sharp on his tongue. He opened one eye.

The terrorists and his friends had disappeared up the trail. The canyon walls shimmered, looking to Carl like a giant mouth, a mouth from a bad dream that had swallowed them all and taken them to a place of horror.

They had all vanished, and he was alone.

Carl wiped at his eyes with his shirt, the blood slowing to a trickle. He reached up and moaned when he touched the cut in his scalp, a large goose egg already forming.

*Except for the dude with the Chicago Bulls hat, the Osama t-shirt, no one saw me. Except Steve, he saw me, and he's gonna be dead soon.*

*We'll all be dead.*

*Every last one of us.*

He curled up behind the tree and hugged his knees. His head pounded and he was sleepy. As he drifted off he realized he might have a concussion and then he knew with a certainty that the terrorists were on their way back to kill him. The concussion wouldn't matter after all.

He slept.

Tara ran, stumbled forward, lurched upright, trying to keep her feet, her breath coming in short gasps, as much from the terror as from the flight. They finally stopped a mile from the clearing. Their captors quickly herded them under a large overhang while a helicopter screamed over the top. The rotors were so close Tara thought they would hit the rocks. She looked up and her head was pushed rudely down and into the rock wall.

She was more frightened than she had ever been in her life, and she knew she needed to get a handle on it or she would be worthless. She heard ragged breathing, and then a whooping gasp. Delores was behind Tara, her hands on her knees, her body shaking as if she were freezing. Her cheeks were shiny with tears.

As Sabrina, Steve, and Robert pressed up behind Tara, she knew she had to be strong for Delores and Sabrina. It's my fault they're here, she thought. There was sudden movement from back down the trail. Three guerrillas jogged up, carrying rifles, the last a girl in her late teens or early twenties.

She had close-cropped hair, and she might have been pretty if her features weren't spoiled by her addiction to a cause. She had a banker's permanent scowl, and wore a faded blue work shirt. Her gray pants were baggy and muddy from the knees down. In fact, all of them had muddy leggings.

Tara knew then what most revolutionaries never knew - that when you were a *guerrillera*, you didn't get a hot shower until the struggle was over- and that usually meant never. To be a *revolutionario* meant nothing more than living in the mud and hiding in caves.

The girl spoke to the leader, speaking quietly in rapid Spanish. Tara leaned forward, trying to follow what she had said. The girl thrust her rifle in front of her, angry now, and they turned and looked at Tara.

"Buenos dias, amigos," Steve said behind her, his voice low and firm.

*He's as calm as if he were at the student union,* Tara thought. She held her shaking knees. *It's as if he were talking to friends. Who is this Steve person? Certainly not the clown I thought he was.*

They turned to look at Steve. The angry girl started forward with her rifle, her face red and twisted. The leader, Dirty Hands, held his right hand up. The girl glowered at her leader, and slowly lowered her rifle.

Tara strained to hear, to understand as Steve spoke quickly, holding up his hands in supplication. She thought she heard the word for "student."

*He seems so calm.*

Tara understood part of what he said. He was trying to talk their way out of this mess. This war.

But who is he?

Carl sat up and yelled, his voice covered by explosions from the meadow as a string of ammunition cooked off in the wreckage behind him. Tracers screeched past the rock in frightening patterns of red streaks, as if the dead crew of the helicopter were after him, gunning for him, saying, "Hey, come on Carl, death, it's not so bad, Amigo."

A helicopter raced overhead and was gone, it's rotors tearing at the sky on it's own mission of revenge for the burning Huey in the meadow.

Carl trembled as he stood and stepped out from behind the rock.

More ammunition exploded and he sat down on his pack and wondered just what the sweet hell he was going to do next.

He had gone to Peru as a lark, a way of getting out of class. His spring break would start the week he got back. He was the first of his friends to go on to college, only now as he sat on his pack he wasn't thinking of the University of Washington. He was thinking of his friends on the rez, playing basketball in the Indian League, eating at Taco Bell, and when the cops were otherwise busy, street racing their cars down the highway. In high school, he had a sticker on his Honda that proclaimed, "Custer was a Pussy."

At the University he was known as Carl. On the rez, to kids and adults, he was "Shooter." At a young age, Carl found that he could throw a basketball up from somewhere near half court with uncanny accuracy, hence, "Shooter."

His dad used to come to the games, and if they were scheduled early enough, he would be sober. When Carl "Shooter" would make a long shot, his dad accepted high fives from people sitting around him and grin, saying, "That ain't right."

Carl was good in the Indian League, hell, he was a legend on the rez, but at five feet four he wasn't exactly a hot prospect as a walk-on for the University squad where the guards were at least a foot taller.

Shooter, the Man From Three Point Land, once made eight three's in a row in a tournament, in front of the home crowd, people screaming his name with each basket.

Shooter! Shooter! Man from three point land!

Carl would run up and down the court, his braided hair flying, feeling like a giant.

When he went to Seattle from the rez last fall, he cut his hair. He wanted to be like the other kids, to fit in, to start a new life. He drove the one hundred fifty miles to the rez each weekend last fall, traveling I-90 up over Snoqualmie Pass, on down to Ellensburg and then to Yakima and the rez. On a good day, with few WSP troopers, he could make it in two hours. After the first trip, he got rid of the Custer sticker. That one had cost him dearly when a trooper didn't see the humor in it.

Carl was making the trip far less frequently now, and he knew that it might just come down to going home on breaks. He was changing, going to class, making new friends (who called him "Carl") and he found that he *liked* college. He didn't have a major yet, but his vague ideas about the future would become goals, and goals were in short supply among his friends on the rez. Scab, Gopher, Cricket. There was an unspoken distance growing between Carl and his lifelong friends, and it worried him. But he was fitting in at college, and since there were no five feet four basketball players on campus, he would have to be a giant some other way. For the first time in his life, he struggled with his identity. Maybe he wanted to be more like Whitey after all.

And now, with blood on his face, with people trying to kill him, he wasn't thinking of his dorm room at the university, he was thinking of his friends, his car, and the love he felt when his people screamed, "Shooter!"

The sun was low in the sky when Carl lifted his head and looked cautiously around. The air was warm, the quiet more unsettling than the earlier noise. He didn't know which way to go. He reasoned that trying to find the others was futile, if not suicidal. He needed to get to the embassy. He leaned back against the rock, feeling its warmth.

His head snapped up and he stared wildly toward the path in the canyon.

Something made a sound, something close by.

A footstep.

He heard it again. Another footstep.

*Someone is on the other side of the rocks.*

A brown foot in a hemp sandal slid around the rock, inches from his leg, and he bunched up, ready to jump and run. He stared into the face of a Quechua Indian.

*Pedro! He was alive.*

"Pedro," Carl croaked, finding his voice.

Pedro nodded, and put his finger to his lips. He touched Carl's shoulder.

"Carlos, rapido mi amigo," Pedro whispered.

"I've never been so glad to see someone in my life," Carl whispered. Although he understood very few Spanish words, he did know the words for hurry. Arriba. Rapido.

"Pronto," Carl said, getting to his feet, pain shooting through his cramped legs. "Arriba, that's fine with me, Dude. Let's get the fuck outta here."

Pedro held out a water bag and Carl drank, the water warm and wonderful. Pedro unbuttoned his shirt and poured water on the tail, then wiped Carl's face with such tenderness that Carl felt like crying. I made fun of the old guy, Carl thought, and now the old Indian man came back for me.

Pedro held out a handful of small, dried roots.

"They look like worms," Carl said, and picked a single root the size of a French fry from Pedro's hand. He would rather have had a Burrito Supreme from Taco Bell, but he took the root just the same, chewing on it as he followed Pedro through the canyon, up the trail, following the footprints of the others.

I couldn't wait to get off the reservation, and now I'd like nothing better than to see it, Carl thought.

Carl Twoshoes, otherwise known as Shooter, the Man From Three Point Land, a tribal member of the Yakama Indian Nation, and a freshman at the University of Washington, wondered if he would ever see the old rez again.

# Chapter 3

Cold River Indian Reservation
Oregon

On the day they got the news from Peru, Chief of Police Martin Andrews stared out at the Bureau of Indian Affairs Agency from his office window in the police administration building. Jail inmates played basketball in the fenced courtyard one floor below him, the players a blur of movement and energy, as if their bodies knew they would be locked down for the next twenty-four hours. From where he was watching Martin could imagine the smell of sweat and fear of jail as they played. A man drove toward the basket, elbowing his way through a crowd of opponents, his black hair bouncing as he jumped. He made the lay-up and pumped his fist, sweat running from his chest. He was tall, taller than the rest, the one known as Firemaker, Martin thought.

The wire mesh screen that closed the top of the basketball court had a panel missing, an escape route Firemaker had used twice in the past two weeks. Martin told the jail commander to leave it open. If there was one thing Martin had learned, they were, after all, on the rez, and escapees had no place to go. Firemaker stole the ball and made a difficult jump shot as the others closed in on him. Too bad he wouldn't be out in time for the season.

What was once the old BIA Agency was now a thriving town, with stores, restaurants, service stations, housing subdivisions, a medical clinic, and schools. Cold River the town was spread out along the river, surrounded by hills of lava rock and sagebrush. If Martin twisted just right, he could see Mount Hood rising up out of the forests on the north side of the rez. Storm Breaker. At least that's what Captain Johnson called it.

The Cold River Indian Reservation of Oregon was established in 1855 by a treaty with the middle tribes of Oregon and the United States Congress. The reservation was home to the Cold River, Wasco, and Paiute Indian Tribes. The northern boundary of the six hundred square mile reservation was sixty miles southeast of Portland. The reservation from the slopes of Mount Hood included timber lands, high mountain meadows, and the high desert lands of juniper and sage brush, rim rock and rivers with an annual salmon run.

Martin had been here a few weeks now, and this morning it seemed a lot longer. He had a funeral to attend.

He had arrived here with nothing more than a little hope – for *something* to go well for him again. He wanted to put the good yoke of work on again and forget the past, or to make a little sense of it just for his life. He'd been on the street too long to believe that Claire's death would make some sense of the world.

Four years ago when Martin was released from the hospital he left his job as a police detective, thinking that he could never go back.

He was now in his third week on the reservation as tribal police chief, and he wondered just what the hell he was doing here.

Police chief. Yeah, right, Martin thought. And I'm not even an Indian.

"Chief Andrews."

"Huh?" He looked up from the window. The basketball game was ending, the inmates slowly filing back inside. His secretary, Janie, was at his door. She had a round face and wore her typical uniform – a t-shirt and jeans.

"We need an officer to play McGruff at the children's pow wow at the Agency Longhouse this afternoon, after the funeral."

"Where's Hawk, have him do it."

"Don't know, Boss. The doggy suit's in the squad room."

"You know Janie, how can we run this place if we don't find these things out until the last minute?"

"Indian time, I guess, Boss. You're still on white man's time."

Martin moved toward the door. An officer walked by, young, female. Something passed between the two women, some communication that Martin didn't get. He watched her move through the administrative office. What was her name, Lori something? Janie was looking at him, grinning. "Don't you be looking at that, Boss."

"Janie."

"Yeah, Boss."

"Don't call me Boss."

"Okay, Boss," she said, and laughed, a harsh laugh that shook her entire body as she walked to her desk in the reception area. Martin followed.

29

"Get that officer, the one who walked through here, to play McGruff."

"Lori?" Janie made a show of dropping her jaw. She suddenly looked nervous.

"Yes, Lori."

Janie laughed, slapped her thigh, looked around at the other secretaries, and Martin gave a little laugh with her. Janie leaned close to Martin and lowered her voice. "Boss," she said, "not me, Boss, no I'm not going to get that Lori person to play McGruff." She looked at Martin as if he were a pure fool. "That's your job."

He felt like a pure fool. He found a box labeled "McGruff" on top of a locker in the squad room and placed the dog head on the table. The outfit was complete with a tail, dog feet and hands, and a large tan overcoat.

There were two people in the room when he entered - a reporter from the local newspaper, and Lori. Lori stopped talking and watched as Martin got the box down and removed the McGruff dog head and looked for the battery pack. He looked over at her.

"I need someone to play McGruff in an hour at the long house for a kids day pow wow. Want the job?"

Her eyebrows arched up and she moved closer, inspecting the dog. "I would love to play McGruff," she said softly, and stroked the fur.

"Great, the job is yours." Martin smiled at her.

"But I can't," she said.

"Why not? If you're assigned to another detail, I can change that."

"I was told that I could not be McGruff."

"What?" Martin peered at her. Maybe it's a tribal thing.

"I was told that I could never be McGruff," Lori said quietly.

"Who told you that?"

"The last Chief."

"Look, the last Chief is gone, and I'm Chief now, and if you want to be McGruff, you will be McGruff. In an hour."

Lori continued to stroke the dog's fur as if it were alive, just sleeping, an old and faithful pet that was taking a nap.

"I was told that a man had to be McGruff, that McGruff doesn't have TITS." She spat out the word as if it were something evil, enunciating the "T's" sharply, as if they had an awful taste. When she said "tits" Martin jumped back as if he had been struck.

"And, I'm a woman." Lori arched her back and pulled herself up straight, thrusting her chest out. The gold badge on her uniform shirt bounced.

The reporter raised his eyebrows and grinned at Martin, his bored look gone. They both stared at Lori. Martin hoped that this would go well – he didn't want to get sued or fired for something stupid.

"What do you mean, McGruff can't be a woman? That's ridiculous. I'm the Chief here, and you will be the dog!"

The reporter laughed and Martin flushed, realizing just how corny he sounded.

"Anyway, the fan seems to work okay," Martin said, putting the battery in place. "Will you do it? Play McGruff?"

Lori grinned. "You mean it?"

Martin nodded.

"You REALLY mean it?"

"Yes, you are McGruff, at one p.m., at the Longhouse."

Lori shook her fist in the air, twisting around. "YES!" She brought her fist down and then pumped it again.

"YES!"

Martin had a vague uneasy feeling.

"I love kids," she said, "I love kids and I'd love to be McGruff for kids." She shook her head, still grinning, stroking the imitation fur on the dog's head.

"Lori, thanks," he said, his mouth tasting like acid reflux. "I'm counting on you to take care of this. I'll leave word with the watch commander to have an officer drive you to the Longhouse and lead you inside."

She grinned at him. Martin smiled back, and left for his office. It's nice to resolve something so easily, he thought, and to resolve it so quickly. In just an hour and fifteen minutes, he would have given a lot to take back his decision, to force someone else to play McGruff.

As it turned out, Lori couldn't play McGruff.

But then, Chief of Police Martin Andrews wasn't an Indian.

Janie said something to the others in the office as Martin walked through on his way to his car. They laughed and she waved as he left the building.

Not only am I not Indian, I don't even look Indian, Martin thought. He wore a gray suit, white shirt, and burgundy tie, was of medium height, had close cut salt and pepper hair. He looked as if he

31

would be more at home in a bank or an insurance company. There were those in the Oregon State Penitentiary over in Salem who had discovered too late that Martin's easy nature could be deceiving.

Even though he was the first non-Indian police chief in the history of the sixty-member department, with his twenty-three years of police experience, he thought he could handle almost anything. Now, after three weeks on the reservation, he wasn't so sure. People would have thought him insane to leave a hole in the mesh on top of the inmate's basketball court. Here, it seemed to make sense. One of the times Firemaker had escaped they found him passed out in a tree within sight of the jail. On the rez, it wasn't just a small world, it was the *only* world.

The Presbyterian Church reminded Martin of the Methodist Church he had attended as a kid – red brick and stained glass. The brick matched the other buildings constructed during the days the BIA ran the reservation. One block over, the old administration building housed the tribal court, Parole and Probation offices, and the store. The grade school was across the street, with identical government-issue red brick.

Martin parked on a side street, got out and stretched, looking around for Hawk. He found his Captain and second in command on the lawn in front of the church. Captain Johnson was known as "Hawk," and Martin doubted if anyone knew his real name anymore. Hawk was not tall, but large, and gave the impression of an immovable object. The first time Martin saw Hawk move he was surprised that something so massive could move so gracefully, so easily. Hawk had a large face, no neck, and slab-like shoulders and arms. He wore a police uniform with shoulder-length thick black hair.

The grass was wet with an early morning rain, and now the sun was out and it was getting warm. Martin stood next to Hawk and smiled at some of the people he knew.

"Why are we waiting here?"

"Friends of the family will bring the casket here," Hawk said.

The gathering grew until the lawn in front of the church was covered with people. The funeral was for the brother of one of the tribal police officers. In the crowd Martin saw tribal police uniforms, suits, jeans and work shirts, and traditional tribal dress. An old woman walked across the lawn, the crowd parting as if she were Moses battling the waters of the Red Sea.

"Uh-oh," Hawk muttered.

She wore a dark blue dress and held a purse of white buckskin out in front of her body like a shield. She marched up to Martin and stopped in front of him, her face inches from his. He had a sense of being reprimanded and she hadn't spoken. He was aware of the silence on the lawn. People had stopped talking and were watching. Hawk moved a few steps away.

"What are you," she said, drawing each word out until the "you" was a snarl.

Martin flinched.

"Are you some kind of wanna-be Indian?" She yelled, the Indian sounding like "In-din."

"Uh, Martha, this is Martin Andrews, our new police chief," Hawk said.

"Nah, he's the new *white* police chief," She said. "Šiyápu."

"Chief, she's Martha Coeur d'Alenes."

She stepped back, looked Martin up and down with a look of pure disgust and turned and headed for the church.

"Wanna-be In-din," she said. The crowd parted for her again. Martin stared after her, feeling foolish, wondering what that presentation was all about. She called him "Šiyápu." The literal translation was "white man," but it could be said in many ways. Softly, like a lover, with a tender inflection, or with anger and disgust. Old Martha had used the disgust tone, Martin thought. Lower than a dog. An ambulance turned the corner down by the school, emergency strobe lights flashing.

"We use it as a hearse," Hawk said. "We just don't tell the live ones who ride in it."

The ambulance backed up to the sidewalk. Officers opened the doors and pulled a plywood casket out. The family of the deceased walked behind as the procession entered the church. Martin saw a little boy in a cub scout uniform, a little girl wearing a buckskin uniform holding his hand, a blend of cultures that no one thought strange. Martin and Hawk found a seat in the last pew. The family huddled in front with their public grief.

The ceremony, in both English and Sahaptin, lasted for two hours.

At the end, they reversed the order. The ambulance was already moving, a procession of cars strung out behind it as Martin got to his Bronco. Martin had never been to the burial grounds, but he knew he needed to be there. Hawk drove, following the procession up the highway toward Mount Hood. Halfway up the grade, they turned off onto a dirt track that wound up through the sage and juniper trees toward a basalt ridge. Martin found that the burial ground was not the white man's idea of a cemetery laid out in the usual square. The burial ground was linear, with grave sites on the side of the dusty road as they curved up the hill. They passed a small area of headstones and markers, and then drove through a wild area of juniper trees, as if they had left the cemetery.

"Each family has it's own burial ground," Hawk explained.

They drove in and out of the shade of the cliff. Each time they came to a plot Martin thought that the burial ground must be coming to an end. They had already driven a couple of miles. They passed a fenced in plot the size of a basketball court. Dusty headstones peered through sage and buck brush, aging witnesses to their passage.

Hawk pulled off the road behind a line of cars and they got out. Sage and wild flowers covered the hillside overlooking the valley. From here the Agency buildings looked like red blocks. The housing subdivisions were spread along the river like scattered, forgotten toys.

People clustered around a fresh grave, dirt and rocks piled in mounds on either side. Along with most of the officers in the department, there must be two hundred people in all. Some wore old shirts and jeans and stood at the foot of the grave, holding shovels.

"They dug the grave for their friend's brother," Hawk said. He pointed to the surviving brother. "He dug the grave for his brother with his friends this morning."

Sometimes at night, I can feel Claire's breath on my face, Martin thought. The beauty of this, the simplicity, the rightness. We hide our death and our grief as if we are ashamed of it. How good was this, a man attacking the ground with a shovel, preparing a place for his brother.

"Chief Andrews."

Martin turned and saw Pastor Michael approaching, his black smock billowing in the breeze. The Pastor stopped in front of Martin, perspiring heavily, blowing his cheeks as his chest heaved.

"You must say something to the family," Pastor Michael said.

Martin's stomach clenched. I don't know what to say, he thought. I'm an outsider, a Šiyápu. I don't even know these people.

"Uh, Pastor, I don't even know these people, I don't know what to do. . ."

"You don't understand, Chief, you *have* to. It's expected."

"Get Hawk."

"No, you," Pastor Michael said. He pulled Martin forward until he was standing shoulder to shoulder with Martha Coeur d'Alenes, in front of the grave.

"You must say something to the family."

What the hell am I going to say, Martin thought, I don't know these people, I'll probably say the wrong thing. The wind blew his coat. He held it closed with one hand.

He waited.

*Why doesn't she get on with it?*

Martin was hit with a blow to his side. He didn't move, but glanced at the Indian woman. She curled her mouth downward, toward him, and growled, "The man speaks first."

As he started to speak, he realized that the contempt was gone from her voice, and while it was not altogether friendly, it sounded respectful. He talked about family and friendship, about the friendship that he had seen in the department, in the community, and about the death of a loved one, a child, a brother. He talked about how the traditions of the personal digging of the grave, the sharing of grief, were important and the mark of a people who were to be admired. He stopped talking. The silence drug on and then a thin high wailing sound came from the woman beside him, turning into a beautiful soprano voice. Martha Coeur d'Alenes sang about the family, the brother, the man, the life, in a haunting singing voice, in Sahaptin. As she sang, she picked up a handful of dirt and threw it on the casket, and then moved away, back into the crowd. She turned and gave Martin a short nod, and then was gone.

Someone handed Martin a shovel and he threw a mound of dirt into the hole. The shovels were passed around and the grave was soon filled, the dirt packed, and mounded. Martin stood and watched. He felt like crying but didn't know exactly why.

*Ah, Claire, I should have died that day, not you.*

Hawk glanced at him as he drove them back down the hill. Neither of them spoke until they reached the tribal police department. Hawk turned off the engine and didn't move. He had something to say and Martin waited. Martin knew that Hawk thought that the job of police chief should have gone to a tribal member, and not to a Šiyápu.

"I will help you," Hawk said quietly. "I want to learn from you, so that one day I will be chief." He stared at Martin and held his hand out. Martin grasped the large hand and found that he couldn't let go.

"You know," Hawk said, "when I was a kid we played Cowboys and Indians." He opened the door and waited for Martin on the steps. He had something to say and Martin didn't rush him, knowing by now that the big man often took his time to talk, to carefully choose the words he used with the new Šiyápu police chief.

"I always wanted to play one of the cowboys," Hawk said. "They always won."

Martin watched Hawk's face, looking for the cue that he needed so he wouldn't mess up his response, serious now, and then the big man's face lit up. Hawk threw back his head and laughed. The loneliness of Martin's day fell away, his earlier indecisions and frustrations left him as Hawk reached out and put his arm around Martin's shoulder.

Cowboys and Indians.

Martin tried to picture Hawk in chaps and a cowboy hat, and he couldn't. The image just wouldn't come together. He gave Hawk a high five and the Šiyápu and In-din laughed together.

*What the hell am I doing here?*

# **C**hapter **4**

Huascaran National Park
Peru

Tara woke up and cried out, reaching blindly in front of her in the darkness. Her heart pounded and she gasped, the dream so real, so, just so - bad. She reached out again and then down and felt the damp ground. The others were asleep around her, thrown together in a small mountain hut.

She had been dreaming of her parents again, and when such dreams ended, they left her alone and frightened. Sometimes her dreams were dark and twisted journeys that never seemed to end, black soap operas with a continuing cast of creatures and a storyline that started again each night.

The first day with their captors was a painful blur of running, hiding, and constant threats. They had finally stopped at a deserted village in the late evening after running uphill for what seemed like most of the day, stopping twice when they heard helicopters.

After a meal of what Steve said was pampas root, they had been ordered into the hut, and had been forced to sleep on the dirt floor. Steve and Tara lay in a row with Delores and Sabrina. Robert was at the back of the hut. The Professor was next to him.

Tara sat up and strained to see in the dark.

"Tara," Steve said softly.

"I'm okay."

He reached out and touched her shoulder. She felt his movement as he sat up beside her. Parts of the dream came back to her. She shook her head, trying to banish the thoughts of her family.

When Tara was eight, both her *ila* (mother) and *tuta* (father) were killed in an automobile accident. When she was tired she would remember her last sight of her parents with a keenness, a clarity, as if she were looking through air that had just been cleansed with a fine spring rain. Only then it had been winter.

She could see herself now, sitting in the middle of the seat in her father's pickup, her mother beside her on the passenger side. On that last day they had driven to Dave's store on their way to the reservation school. The store was busy at a quarter to eight in the morning with the people stopping for coffee and a sack lunch before they had to be to work at white man's time of 8 a.m. Snow covered the sage brush and juniper trees beside the store, the snow dirty and brown in the parking lot. Tara watched as one of the store dogs urinated on a pile of snow, slowly looking up at them as they passed.

They drove the three blocks past the store to the Bureau of Indian Affairs agency school. Tara brooded as she sat between her parents. Her father would have called it pouting, but to Tara, it was brooding. She had been arguing, pleading with her parents since the night before, pleading to be allowed to go with them, and now they were taking her to school! Her mother was excited about their annual Christmas shopping trip to Portland, and Tara knew that she should be going. It was just so unfair.

"*Tuta*, why can't I go with you, shopping to Portland? I can skip one day, please, oh please *Tuta*."

Her father shook his head.

No.

"*Tuta*, please?"

Tara's mother leaned over and kissed her, smiling.

"How can we shop for you, buy Christmas presents if you are with us, you cute girl?" They stopped in front of the red brick building (Tara had wondered more than once why the buildings at the agency were either white wood or red brick) and her mother got out of the pickup, her breath forming a cloud in the clear, cold sunny morning. Tara kissed her father and got a hug from him, then slid across the seat. She hugged her mother beside the truck. The schoolyard was filled with noise and kids. Her best friend Delores waited inside the cyclone fence, holding her books, patient with her friends even then.

Tara turned and looked at her father again, one more time, hoping he would change his mind, knowing he wouldn't.

He smiled, and when he smiled it was always as if he knew some great secret that she wouldn't be told until later, when she was older.

"Remember to go home with Melissa," Tara's mother said. "We'll pick you up after supper."

Tara held her books and watched the blue pickup turn toward the state highway. Her mother looked back once and waved. Tara had been called out of class an hour and a half later, her grandfather standing at the door of her schoolroom, looking sad, and old, even then. Her parents had been killed, he told her in the hallway. Some trouble on the grade, a big wreck on the hill, six people died in all, he said. And now, she would have to be a very brave girl.

The next day she had gone to live with her grandparents. Her grandfather was on the tribal council even then, although he was not yet the chairman. The day after the funeral, she awoke in the quiet of her grandparents' house on the reservation, and felt the cold wetness of the sheets. She had wet the bed again. She felt the shame, the embarrassment, and she cried for her *ila* and *tuta* to come and take her back to the safety of their home. But they were dead. Tara's grandmother made the bedwetting their secret. She had never told anyone or said anything to Tara, and in some ways it made it worse.

Tara wet the bed for almost two years. She bore it with a silence that she and her *kala*, her grandmother, shared to this day. And now she was in an abandoned Quechua Indian village, her parents dead for sixteen years.

She whispered with Steve in the dark, careful to not wake the others. She knew they would need what sleep they could get to make it through the day. They whispered about their chances of rescue. Steve was upbeat and positive, and for that, Tara was grateful.

"They can't afford to feed you," he whispered, his breath warm on her neck. She could tell that he was grinning, and wondered again what he was really about. There was a lot more to Steve than that of a clown, a professional college student. She decided she liked the reassuring feel of his hand on her shoulder.

"Thanks," Tara whispered.

"For what?"

"For being here, for . . . for being you."

He squeezed her shoulder and Tara lay down, moving slightly to find a comfortable position. It was hours before dawn, and she was determined to sleep. She lay on her side and put her hands under her head.

"Help me *tila*," she whispered. "Help me to be strong."

She had hoped for a sleep without dreams, but yesterday had been a day with too much death. She slowly drifted off to sleep, her body too tired and sore from the panicked flight up the mountain.

In her dream, Tara was waiting in the driveway of her old house, the one she had shared with her parents. It was a ranch style house built in a subdivision on the heights above Cold River. From the driveway Tara could see across the town of Cold River to the hills dotted with sagebrush and juniper trees. To many it would appear desolate. To her it was beautiful.

It was dusk. The sun had just gone behind the hill above her house. The glow in the sky gave a strange tint to the driveway and the street in front. A pickup truck approached and turned into the driveway. The driver's door opened and a tall figure came toward her, striding purposefully in the dim light.

*Tuta!*

And then she screamed her father's name and launched herself at him. She threw her arms around him as tears streamed down her face, making a large wet spot on the sleeve of his buckskin shirt.

That this couldn't be happening didn't seem odd to her as she stood in the driveway, smelling the familiar tobacco smell of her *tuta* as she held him. He was 35, as he was when she last saw him in the same pickup, sixteen years before. A twenty-four year old Tara held her father and cried.

He kissed her hair and then gently pushed her away, holding her at arms length.

"Tara cute girl there are things you must do."

"Yes, *Tuta,*" she said, and then she was eight years old again, her father's arms around her, his name for her on his breath.

"You must be strong, because Delores and Sabrina are not. You must remember the lessons your *tila* and your *kala* taught you, and especially the lesson of the Cold River Indian and the *spilyay* (coyote)."

*"Tuta?"* Tara looked up at him.

"Yes, my little cute girl."

"Where's my *ila?*"

He removed her arms and turned to the pickup. Tara noticed that he was in full ceremonial dress, with beads sewn as a breastplate on the buckskin shirt. He moved to the open doorway of the pickup and leaned over the seat and grunted, pulling something Tara couldn't quite make out in the now near darkness. As he wrapped the bundle in his arms and stepped away from the door of the truck, dark hair fell down his shoulder.

*Ila!*

She cried, tears falling again as she ran up to touch her *ila,* her most beautiful, wonderful *ila*. Her mother's hand, cold, lifeless, dangled down beside her father's thigh, the fingers brushing the buckskin lightly as he walked.

*Tuta, what's wrong with her, she's*

*Tuta, why won't her eyes open*

Tara, now the eight year old Tara, whose parents had gone away and never returned, looked down at her *ila's* legs.

*She has no feet*

*Ila's feet are gone*

Tara cried out and sat up suddenly, still in the dream, reaching out for her mother in the dark hut.

Steve was awake, beside her, touching her arm.

She felt the slightest trickle between her legs where she had almost wet herself. The old embarrassment of bedwetting came back, and she hugged herself, wanting desperately to go back to her dream where she was eight, to see her *tuta* and *ila,* to be with them again.

And then, in a hut with a dirt floor in the Peruvian Andes and with the people outside carrying guns, for the first time since the killing began, Tara bent over in the dark and began to sob.

# Chapter 5

After the funeral Martin worked on numbers, budgetary allowances, boring, necessary work, filling time, waiting for Hawk.

"Chief."

Martin dropped the report he was reading.

Janie started into his office, glanced back over her shoulder, and then took two steps in.

"No, come over by the desk."

She walked up tentatively, jumpy, as if she were ready to bolt at any second.

"Hawk's here for you, he's waiting outside."

"You and me, Janie, we're gonna run this place."

"You and me, we are, huh?" She laughed. Janie always laughed, even when the topic was serious.

"Yeah. Hawk and I are going to Portland this afternoon to meet with the U.S. Attorney. We'll be on cell phone and pager. I want you to call me for anything."

"Okay, Boss."

"Call me Martin."

"Okay Boss."

Martin shut his briefcase. "I'd better not keep Hawk waiting."

Janie moved to the door. Martin knew there was something she wanted to say. "Don't worry about that Hawk, he's toe brainy."

"Toe brainy?"

"Yeah, you know . . . dumb. Toe means the opposite of the word it's used next to. On the reservation we say 'toe brainy'."

Martin Andrews thought he might make it on the rez after all. *Toe Brainy?*

"One more thing, Boss." Janie stood in his doorway, as if she were afraid Martin would bolt and not return. "There's a prisoner, name of Firemaker..."

Martin nodded. The basketball player.

"Firemaker is talking around to the tribal council through his relatives. He claims he is being held in the jail against his will."

Martin laughed. "Hell, Janie, every prisoner here is held against his will. Have the lieutenant look into it."

When Chief Martin Andrews left, Janie returned to her desk and giggled. She thought the new boss was nice enough, but he *was* certainly toe brainy to let that Lori woman play McGruff. Janie then told the rest of the office staff, and soon they were laughing and shrieking about the new Šiyápu boss who made that Lori girl McGruff.

Again.

Janie called her mother, and then four other relatives, all cousins. The other three office workers each called relatives and friends. The dispatcher, who was listening in, called six people in fifteen minutes, putting calls for police service on hold. Two jailers, listening at the lobby window, heard the story. They made calls. With each call, the story was accompanied with laughter and shouting.

Crazy white man, they said. Letting that Lori play McGruff. This new Šiyápu Chief is nice enough, they said, but he sure is toe brainy.

Letting that Lori girl play McGruff again. Wasn't the first time enough?

Martin and Hawk entered the highway from the Agency (so named for the old Bureau of Indian Affairs Agency) and started up the hill to the high plateau that led to Mt. Hood and Portland. Hawk drove the Bronco quickly, deftly moving into the passing lane, the speedometer passing seventy.

As Martin watched Hawk drive, he was content with the knowledge that he had made some decisive moves today. It was not going to be so hard after all to police an Indian reservation. In fact in many ways it was a lot like police work in other departments.

"Oh, who did you assign to play McGruff?" Hawk asked.

Martin knew that Hawk was still nervous around him, even with the connections they made today, and that a lot of the officers in the police department thought that Hawk should be chief, or at least that the job should not have gone to a Šiyápu.

"McGruff? Oh, Lori."

Hawk jerked his foot from the accelerator.

"Lori. You're kidding, aren't you."

"No, I asked Lori and she said she would do it."

The Bronco slowed. The Captain was pale. His hands trembled slightly on the steering wheel. Hawk hit the brakes and pulled to the right so quickly that Martin's shoulder harness locked. Hawk put the

Bronco into a sliding turn in front of a green Chrysler minivan, the driver slamming on his brakes and swerving to miss them.

They flew down the grade toward Cold River, the Bronco passing cars, Hawk driving like a man possessed. Martin was used to high speed driving, but now he was nervous. His uneasiness grew as Hawk turned on the siren.

"Captain Johnson, Hawk, wha-?"

Hawk waved him off. They passed a car on the right, the speedometer of the Bronco pegged at eighty-five.

In the Longhouse, the powwow was starting. The Longhouse was a room larger than a basketball court, with bleachers and chairs on all sides. The bleachers were full, with parents, elders, and teachers in attendance. A drum began a slow steady beat, and a group of boys in blue Cub Scout uniforms entered the arena.

They were led by McGruff, the dog who was about to take a bite out of crime.

With the overhead lights on top of the Bronco flashing and the siren howling like a crazed beast coming down from the hills to feast on the innocent, Hawk and Martin slid around corners, working their way through the streets of downtown Cold River, heading for the Longhouse.

"Getouttatheway," Hawk screamed, waving his arms at slower cars.

"Boss," he said, his voice sounding strangled, "you couldn't have picked Lori, you didn't, tell me you didn't. We've got to get her out of there. This can't happen...Boss what were you thinking of to make Lori wear that McGruff suit?"

They passed a station wagon, throwing gravel over the road as the Bronco slid around a corner at the administration building.

Two blocks to go.

Martin's fear of Hawk's driving was now replaced by a new dread.

"Chief," Hawk said, "couldn't you have asked Officer Lamebull or Officer Cornelious? Either of them."

Martin thought that he must have violated some Indian custom, putting a female in a dog suit. Hawk is frightened, and his driving is scaring the shit out of me.

"What were you thinking of?" Hawk said aloud as the Bronco

screamed up the hill to the longhouse. "She cannot be McGruff."

"No need to be sexist about it Hawk," Martin said. "I asked Lori to be McGruff, and she said that she had been told by the former chief that since she was a woman, she couldn't be McGruff..." Martin shut up, knowing how lame his reasoning sounded.

"Nononono," Hawk said, shaking his head, slamming on the brakes, sliding to a stop at a side door of the Longhouse.

"So I told her," Martin said, "I told her that McGruff can have tits..."

"Oh no no no, that's not the issue," Hawk said. "We could have any of the female officers or employees be McGruff. Just not Lori." He threw open his door and looked at Martin.

"She suckered you on that one, Boss." He ran to the door and threw it open, stopping just inside. Martin bumped into Hawk and tried to look around him.

"I hope we're not too late, or we're gonna be in some deep shit," Hawk muttered.

Hawk put his hand on Martin's arm. They were in a narrow hallway, the sound of drums and chants loud in the closed space.

"Lori has been McGruff before," Hawk said, "and we were told that she could never do it again." His voice rose above the drums. "She, uh, well she went a little crazy last time." They walked forward and stood with bleachers rising on either side of them. An Indian woman wearing a T-shirt that said "Rez Girl" gave Martin a hard look. In the arena three Indian boys danced slowly to the drums. They wore leggings and breastplates. Across the arena Martin could see a group of Cub Scouts and Boy Scouts standing in an uneasy huddle, watching McGruff.

Several images came to Martin at once.

McGruff was also dancing, Hawk's face was white, and everyone in the Longhouse (except for the three high school dancers) was watching McGruff.

McGruff had opened the trench coat and pulled the dog suit tight around her breasts, and to Martin's horror, the McGruff suit accentuated her already ample breasts.

And they were jiggling.

Her dance reminded him of the time he went with some buddies to a stripper bar in Portland. In fact, Lori was dancing as if she had put a year or two on the floor of a strip joint on McLaughlin Blvd.

Behind McGruff, the elders, tribal council members, and other tribal leaders were seated at ground level. As Martin watched in horror, McGruff danced over and turned around and thrust her backside up to within a few inches of the face of a tribal chief. Lori (McGruff) wiggled her body and bent over and looked at him through her legs, her breasts dangling, moving to a dance beat of their own. The chief leaned back into the person behind him, scrambling to keep away from the dog suit.

McGruff suddenly jumped up and whirled around, shaking her body, looking at it as if she were seeing it for the first time. McGruff spied a young man of about twenty in the second row, and she repeated the performance, pushing between two elders, bending over and shaking her body in the young man's face.

If anything, Martin thought, Hawk's color had changed from white to a pasty gray. By this time, most of the elders and tribal leaders had stopped watching McGruff and were staring at Martin and Hawk.

Glaring.

They really don't like me, Martin thought. He wondered then if he would make it out of there alive.

McGruff jumped down and moved toward the Cub Scouts, and they moved away from her like a frightened school of fish, moving together, staring at her. She shook her rear at a couple of them and then she waltzed off the floor, giving her chest a final thrust as she left. She stopped and looked across at Martin, gave him a little wave and blew him an exaggerated kiss. She pointed her large paws skyward as she made it through the exit.

*Oh...my...God.*

The drumming stopped. The silence was complete and total, as if a giant vacuum had suddenly sucked all of the air out of the Longhouse. A man stood up from the bleachers across the arena from Hawk and Martin, a short man with long gray braided hair. He stared at Hawk, and then pointed at the captain with his index finger, bending it, motioning for Hawk to come. He pointed to the end of the longhouse. From where he was, Martin could see the veins in the man's neck stand out, and his jaw was working. Martin recognized the man as Bluefeathers, the chairman of the tribal council. A man with the power of God in this sovereign nation.

Martin felt weak. Stupid.

And for the third time today, he felt like a complete idiot.

Bluefeathers walked to the far end of the Longhouse, slowly stepping on the wooden floor with all eyes on him. He didn't look at Martin or Hawk.

Hawk had such a look of despair and immobilizing fear that it scared Martin even more. Hawk looked as if he was about to be executed.

"What does he want," Martin croaked, already knowing the answer. He wanted blood, and now, not in an hour.

Hawk started moving, a wooden shambling walk, catatonic. Martin trailed behind, passing in front of the closest bleachers.

"Do you want me to go with you?"

"No." Hawk said. "Wait for me in the Bronco." He hung his head down and walked forward again, toward the end of the Longhouse where Bluefeathers waited.

As Martin walked out, a man got up in front of the microphone and began talking about the recognition of the Cub Scouts. He wore Levis, boots, and a western shirt, with long braids and his hair pulled tight against his head. He has on Buddy Holly glasses, Martin thought in wonderment. Thick black frames. Martin walked to the Bronco.

Hawk came out in minutes, his shoulders slumping as if his bones had somehow been bloodlessly removed. He got into the Bronco and let out a stream of air from puffed up cheeks. He shook his head and started the Bronco. They drove slowly through town.

Hawk didn't speak as they entered the highway and started up the grade.

Martin couldn't stand it. "What'd he say?"

Hawk shook his head. He idled up the grade, a line of trucks and cars passing them. Hawk smiled, a thin smile that worried Martin.

"This is not the first time Lori has been McGruff," Hawk said, glancing over at Martin. "Lori saw you coming and worked you wonderfully. She wasn't told that McGruff couldn't be a woman. Hell we're as liberated as any community. The women here will tell you what the hell they want, we're almost a matriarchal society." Hawk stared at the road, quiet.

Martin squirmed.

The Bronco was going ten miles an hour when they topped the grade.

"Lori has played McGruff before," Hawk finally said. "She horrified the elders and Cub Scouts and parents alike. She shook her butt, her boobs, her crotch in every face here, and I personally think she was looking for a man. That's why she was told that she couldn't ever be McGruff again. It's not about women Boss. It's about Lori. She got you, Boss."

Hawk drove faster. He passed several cars at the top of the grade where the road narrowed to two lanes.

"What'd the chairman say to you?"

Hawk shook his head, slightly, as if he didn't want to say.

"Is he gonna fire us?"

"No."

"Is he gonna fire you?"

At this Hawk smiled. He shook his head. "No, Boss, he won't fire me. He's my uncle."

"What about me, is he gonna fire me over this?"

"No. He knows you're the new guy."

"What'd he say," Martin asked again.

Hawk started chuckling. "He say, crazy fucking Šiyápu," and with this Hawk let out a laugh with such force the Bronco rocked. "He say, he say crazy fucking Šiyápu, don't he know McGruff don't have no tits?"

Martin glanced at his captain and then began to laugh. Hawk threw his head back, pounding the steering wheel with his fists.

The Bronco shook. They slowed. Cars backed up behind them. Horns blew.

"No tits," Martin laughed, and then he shrieked.

"No tits."

They laughed until Hawk had to pull over to wipe his eyes, cars streaming past them, people looking at them as if they were deranged.

They made it to the slopes of Mt. Hood before they were called back.

"Chairman wants you coming around right now," Janie told Martin on his cell phone. "He said right now," she added.

Hawk turned the siren on, looking grim. If Martin had learned one thing during his first three weeks as police chief of a tribal police department, it was that the officers used their sirens for just about everything.

At the administration building, Chairman Bluefeather's secretary smirked and waved them past.

"Close the door." Bluefeathers glared at them when they entered. He had the television on, the blinds pulled.

"Chairman Bluefeathers, we-" Martin said. He stopped and looked over to his right. Lori was sitting in the corner, staring at a spot between her knees, the McGruff suit and ridiculous dog's head in a pile on the floor in front of her.

Bluefeathers held his hand up. He pointed to the television.

"Watch."

The CNN news loop was returning from an advertising break.

"This is Richard Noble with CNN News. Our lead story this hour...U.S. military advisers to the Peruvian armed forces have found a grisly death scene in the mountains of Peru. A CNN camera crew, riding with U. S. Special Forces to film our drug eradication efforts, were at this scene earlier today. For more, we go to our camera crew in the highlands of Peru."

Chairman Bluefeathers stood with his arms folded and stared at the screen. Martin watched as the scene switched from the Atlanta newsroom to a mountain scene. A Huey UN-1 helicopter was in the background, it's rotors turning. The camera panned through the meadow.

"This is David Franklin, CNN News, in the central mountains of Peru, with the U.S. Special Forces Drug Eradication team. The team was called in today to examine the crash site of an army helicopter."

The camera angle widened, showing the blackened and twisted metal of the downed helicopter. "Over here," Franklin said, pointing to the middle of the meadow, "there are the bodies of five people. The bodies of the helicopter crew remain in the wreckage. We have been told that three of the bodies in the meadow have been identified as Quechua Indian, one woman and two men."

"According to what we have learned, the Peruvian Indians were guides for a group of U.S. college students who have been hiking in the mountains. The other two bodies in the meadow are female, and quite possibly American."

The scene faded to the newsroom in Atlanta. Noble looked up into the camera.

"CNN News has learned that the students were on a trek to visit pre-Columbian ruins in Peru. There has been a preliminary identification made of the students' bodies, both apparently from

Berkeley, California. There were six other students and one professor in the group, all from the United States. The whereabouts of the remaining students are unknown, and it is feared by the military that they may have been taken prisoner by the Sendero Luminoso, or Shining Path. The Shining Path, a leftist terrorist group, is dedicated to the violent overthrow of the Peruvian Government, and has recently been linked to the Al Qaeda terror network."

Chairman Bluefeathers reached over and turned the sound off, leaving Noble to pantomime the rest of his message. Bluefeathers stared at the figures on the set, then pointed, his finger jabbing at the screen.

"Tara is with those people," he grunted, each word a staccato burst of anger.

"Tara?" Martin asked.

"His granddaughter," Hawk said. "And my niece," he added softly.

The chairman jabbed at the digital recorder. He held his hand out and grabbed the disc as it ejected. He handed it to Hawk and slumped in his chair.

"My granddaughter is with those people in Peru, went hiking there for her spring break in college." He looked at Martin. "She's there with Sabrina Gordon, and her other roommate, what's her name Hawk? You know, Bill TiWee's daughter?"

"Delores."

"Yes, Delores." He looked up at Martin.

"I want you and Hawk to find out what happened to them. They're tribal members, and I want to find out what happened. Right now. And if you can't find them or learn what they have done with them, I want you to go to Peru. Take Lori here with you."

He waved them away, a dismissal.

Martin looked as he left the room. Bluefeather's stared at his desk.

"Okay," Hawk said. Lori gathered up her suit and followed them out, holding McGruff's head up in front of her.

"Either of you have a passport?" Hawk asked

"Yes." Martin said.

Lori mumbled yes.

"The man meant what he said, I know him, you don't. He'll have us in Peru tomorrow if he thinks it will help his granddaughter."

Martin had two thoughts at once. These people *are* crazy, and for the fourth time today, *what the hell am I doing here?* He opened the door of the Bronco and held the McGruff suit for Lori as she climbed into the back seat.

"Did Bluefeathers really mean that Lori would go to Peru," Martin asked, knowing she would be listening from the back seat.

Hawk grinned. "You speak Spanish, Boss?"

"Pocito," Martin said, holding up his thumb and forefinger.

"Lori speaks fluent Spanish. Her father's a Mexican national, her mother a tribal member here. That's why the chairman said she was going, and," Hawk said, looking back at Lori, "she's Bluefeather's niece. My cousin."

"Chief?" Lori spoke for the first time.

Martin turned around in his seat and looked at her.

"Can McGruff go?"

# Day Two

# Chapter 6

Cordillera Blanca Mountain Range
Central Peru

Steve lay on his side, listening to the camp come awake. It was first light, the beginning of their second day with the terrorists. At twenty-eight, he had spent much of his life in harm's way, often wondering if he would see the next day, the next minute. It seemed so long ago, but he had been in Baghdad months before the Third Infantry Division arrived. The first year Steve was in the army, he learned that he was a tribal member of the Mashantucket-Pequot Tribe, a group of Indians who were banished to Haiti hundreds of years ago, and recently received federal recognition. They proceeded to build the world's largest casino in Connecticut, on traditional tribal land. Foxwoods. Go figure. Hell, he thought his parents were from Haiti. He was black. When he got out of the army, he thought war was behind him. He checked out the tribal enterprise, and was offered a college education. He took them up on it. And now, what the hell was this, back into war, and these new cousins from the west needed him. Oh, boy did they ever.

*You assholes outside with all the guns might be in for a surprise. I've done this shit before – against a better enemy.*

Steve felt a strength, a stirring inside with the challenge to protect his new friends, and he knew he was up for it. He raised his head and saw the shapes of the others huddled on the mud floor. Delores whimpered in her sleep; the professor mumbled. Tara snuggled and clenched Steve with an arm, her eyes twitching rapidly in troubled sleep. Sabrina was close on the other side. Delores, Robert, and the professor lay along the back wall.

The grass and stick hut had a thatched roof. Dusty pots stood watch in the back corners. Steve thought the terrorists were in a larger building next to the hut.

*Pedro, where are you now, my man? This hut must belong to your Quechua relatives.*

The fact that Pedro their guide had disappeared, had melted away after Ruppert and Mario were gunned down, was not lost on Steve. During the last four days, Steve had talked at length with Pedro, especially since Steve was the only one in their party who spoke Spanish. He grew up in Miami and went in the army, *before* he knew he was Indian. You didn't grow up in North Miami and not speak Spanish.

Pedro was a survivor. He grew up in these mountains. And the terrorists didn't find Carl, Steve reasoned. Carl wasn't with them, and they had heard no more shooting as they ran up the mountain from the meadow.

Pedro and Carl, the kid from Yakama, the kid who was always talking about his car, his friends, and his girlfriends. Well, Carl, Steve thought, we make it out of here, your car somehow won't be as important as it once was. Running for your life has a way of doing that to you.

Tara moved, moaned, clenched her fists, and relaxed with her eyes closed. Steve looked around at the sleeping group. Robert raised up and stared at him with black eyes.

Steve nodded.

Robert, the Jicarilla Apache. Small, wiry. Out of their group, Robert (and possibly Carl) was the only one who could pass for a Peruvian Indian. Steve knew that Robert was a student at Arizona State. Other than that, he knew very little about the young man, but he seemed calm, confident.

Robert would be a warrior, Steve thought. He had a strength, a wisdom about him. Steve pictured Robert riding a mustang horse at full speed, yelling, screaming. It was probably a T.V. image, but he thought it an accurate one.

Robert nodded back.

They heard a loud bang and voices outside the hut. Robert's eyes never wavered.

Two bright black holes.

"Robert," Steve whispered.

Robert's eyebrows flickered.

"Robert, what do you think, amigo?"

Steve saw a slight smile on Robert's impassive face.

"It's very simple," Robert said quietly. "We protect the others." He looked around. "And take the guns away from the bad people."

"What if they don't want us to take their guns away?" Steve whispered.

"We only need to start with one, then we have something to argue with."

Steve smiled. A warrior. That makes two of us. Maybe that is one of the things that makes us different, he thought. We are not very politically correct. We are proud of our warrior heritage.

"I know about your Apaches," Steve said. "Warriors."

Robert looked at Steve, then at the opening.

"I'm a twenty-four year old college kid. With my people, a hundred fifty years ago, I would have been a warrior ten years now. I would have been tested in battle. I would have a family - horses, all that. I'm maybe a few years late, but I have the genetics to be a good warrior." His eyes remained steady.

Steve moved his shoulder, not wanting to wake Tara until they had to. Here we are, he thought. Enjoying ourselves in the outdoors, on a hike, with bad ol' terrorists all around. What fun. As for Robert, he seems to be enjoying himself well enough. When the time came, and Steve knew it would, he would count on Robert.

Tara lingered in that place between sleep and wakefulness. She wanted to stay in her dream, the dream of her parents, however painful. She knew on some level she was with them. Her dreams were often a mixture of fantasy and fact, of hurtful things left unresolved. During the early years with her grandmother, Tara often sketched the things close to her, the faces of those she loved, her animals, her grandparents. She gradually became better at it, her sketches maturing faster than she did. She often sketched her mother from memory. Never her father. In her dreams, Tara could see him, his face, his hands. When she would awaken, she didn't have a picture of his face. She couldn't see her father.

In that time before her parents died she hadn't really thought of herself as a separate being. It didn't occur to her that she was any different from her friends, or whether she was pretty or pleasant to look at. Her parents told her so. As a secret bed wetter, she was ugly, a child apparition of shame.

When she wet the bed the inner voice that spoke to her was an ugly Tara troll, and the voice took on a physical image, a little withered doll in a diaper. The Tara troll sat on her shoulder and told her, *"You're ugly Tara, just like me."*

The imaginary Tara (and she didn't know what else to call her) would spin around on her shoulder when she awakened to wet sheets and scream in her ear, *"You're worthless Tara."*

Her troll stayed with her even after she stopped wetting the bed, appearing when she was down, never coming 'round when things were going well. To send the troll away, Tara would sketch the troll and then tear up the paper, going on to sketch something pleasant, a hillside, a friend, throwing her energy into her Berol Prismacolor pencils and her sketch pads. Only two other people knew about the imaginary Tara troll - Sabrina and Delores.

As she was growing up, Tara kept an easel in her bedroom, often sketching before she went to bed. She kept sketches of her mother, her grandparents, her best friends, and several of her father, a bright oval emptiness for his face. His face eluded her and the sketch never came together. She had tried it from dozens of different perspectives - in his pickup truck, his favorite chair, camping - and it never came to her.

Only in dreams.

The troll was gone as the dreams faded, but she knew as sure as the sun coming up each morning that the troll would be back.

She gradually became aware of several things - she hurt, and she hurt everywhere - her legs, her back, the pain sharper now as the dream faded. She felt an alarming sense of dread, and then was comforted by the body pressed up tight against her.

Tara opened her eyes in the gray morning light and moaned. She tried to swallow and her mouth clicked, dry, her lips cracked. She moved and the cold wetness from her pants made her shudder. She wanted to go back to her dream, even if it was a bad one, a dream with her parents, and as her eyes opened, she didn't have that moment or two of disorientation that comes with awakening in a strange place.

She knew immediately where she was - on the mud floor of a grass hut in the Andes Mountains, held captive by teenage killers, wearing jeans - that she had almost urinated in during the night. And she was sore. Every muscle felt as if it had been ripped, strained, and torn during the flight.

She closed her eyes and saw her father's face, and then blinked open fast, looking at Steve's form next to her. *I can see my father, his face, his hands!*

With her eyes open, she could still see her father's face, could see the eyes, nose, the lines at the corner of his mouth. She would sketch him, and soon. In the Andes with death all around, she saw her father's face.

But first, she knew that she had to be safe. She was hungry, cold, wet, miserable, and her bladder was full. The shower she had longed for yesterday now seemed impossible. She wasn't going to pee in her pants, no matter what waited for her outside, and she sure as hell wasn't going to pee in the small hut with Robert and Steve and the professor. She rose up on one elbow and looked around.

Robert was watching her. She had the feeling that he hadn't slept, that he had somehow stayed awake all night and kept watch. She heard a noise from the outside and looked at the door. Robert shook his head as if he didn't know what to make of it.

Tara squatted beside the door. Steve sat up behind her and touched her arm.

"What's up?" he whispered.

"I'm going outside, gotta go," Tara whispered back without turning around, her face flushing. She pushed the door open and crawled outside. She stood and slowly stretched, looking for their captors. They were in a small clearing, circled by rocks, with a larger hut, more like a warehouse on the other side, probably where the terrorists or whatever the hell they were, had slept. She looked over at the rocks behind the hut and slowly started that way, wanting at least a little privacy. As she started around the hut she heard a yell from the other side of the warehouse.

"Alto!"

Tara froze, not knowing whether to drop to the ground or to return to the hut. She didn't have to wait - it was decided for her.

"Just stand still," Steve said quietly as he came up behind her.

Tara resisted an urge to put her hands in the air. She heard more shouts and sounds of running and she thought for a second she was going to lose her bladder in front of everyone.

"We're just doing our morning business," Steve said, raising his voice so he could be heard without turning around. "We mean no harm." Tara could feel his breath on her neck. A young girl ran around in front of Tara, holding a rifle in front of her, the barrel pointed at Tara's head. She looks younger now in the morning, Tara thought, maybe fifteen or sixteen. Just a child, although she was a deadly one.

*Don't ever forget that baby rattlers are more deadly than the big ones.*

The girl had dark, shoulder length hair pulled back with a red cloth tie. Her features twisted with an unfocused hatred. Tara had seen her the day before when they ran up the mountain, but they hadn't talked. The girl looked to the side and lowered her gun a little, the barrel still pointed at Tara. Tara risked a glance over her shoulder and saw the leader striding toward them, tucking a shirt into his peasant pants. Dirty Hands, that's what Tara had called him yesterday. As he approached, Steve was talking, saying something about el bano.

"Y esta Tara," he told Dirty Hands, "Y este Steve."

He's telling them our first names, Tara thought, making us human. Her estimation of Steve just went up another notch. Steve touched her shoulder, turning her toward Dirty Hands. Steve introduced her again, his voice pleasant, as if they had just met travelers on vacation. Tara nodded.

"Just go behind the hut and do whatever you were going to do," Steve told her quietly.

"Easy for you to say," Tara said, but she started moving anyway, the pain in her bladder too strong. She walked slowly, expecting a shout at any moment. She heard Steve say something to Dirty Hands, and then laugh. Tara flushed as she rounded the corner of the hut. When she was out of sight, she didn't waste any time.

Delores and Sabrina were talking quietly inside the hut. The jumble of rocks was about twenty feet from the rear of the hut. Tara thought about running, keeping the hut between her body and the terrorists, but she knew she couldn't leave the others. Never. Delores, Sabrina, and the others depended on her. They would stay together.

When Tara walked back around the hut the others were outside. Robert stood beside Steve; Delores and Sabrina were next to the door. The professor blinked and looked cautiously around. He had been talkative for much of the trip, pontificating about this and that until the others tuned him out. Now the professor was quiet, looking around as if he didn't remember or comprehend what was happening to them. He had brown hair and a small brown moustache, and was, Tara thought, somewhere in his mid forties. And very much used to being in charge.

The camp was coming alive. There was a cook fire in front of the large hut. A few of their captors were standing around the fire.

"Looks like we're gonna talk," Steve said.

Tara stood with Sabrina and Delores, touching their shoulders. Sabrina's lower lip was trembling and she was shaking. Tara put her arm around Sabrina and then pulled Delores into her, standing in a little group a few feet away from Steve and Robert. Dirty Hands began speaking to Steve and he pointed to Tara and her friends. Steve translated.

"He's telling us the usual Marxist bull," Steve said. "His name is Eduardo. He's the leader of this group, a splinter group of the Sendero Luminoso, or Shining Path. He says that we will be taken further up into the mountains, and then they will find a way to return us to the government, for an exchange of course." Steve looked at Tara and the others. Tara was staring at one of their captors at the edge of the group. A slight person wearing a grubby baseball cap.

"Steve," she whispered, tugging on his arm. She nodded at the gunman. "Steve, is that?" She suddenly wasn't hungry.

"Yeah, that's our ol' friend, Osama himself on a t-shirt. We figured," he said. He didn't add to that and Tara didn't ask.

"Eat," Eduardo said, and made a motion toward the cooking area. He started over to the fire. The girl with the rifle glared at Tara and followed Eduardo. Tara saw five of the terrorists. Yesterday, she had counted at least twelve. Where were the others?

"Wait a minute," Steve said quietly. He motioned for Tara and the others to come closer.

"Eduardo also said that if we tried to escape or harm them, they would immediately kill all of us. And he also said that if we are discovered by the government troops, that the army will try to kill us."

Steve walked toward the fire. Tara caught up with him and grabbed his arm.

"Why would the army harm us?"

Steve stopped and looked closely at Tara. Professor Bauchman came up between them and spoke. "Because you are students," he said, "and Guzman, the founder of the Shining Path was a professor, and many of his followers were students, and the army ultimately won't trust us."

"But we're American students," Tara said, "we're Americans. Surely the army knows that, and they will try to get us out." They'd better.

"Whether we like it or not," Steve said, "some of our tribes in the United States contributed money to the Shining Path a long time ago when the terrorist group first started. Probably seems a little foolish, given where we are. But you can bet the army knows this, and I think we need to find a way go get out of here. Both sides of this conflict may ultimately want us dead. But, hey, for now they are feeding us, so let's eat."

*What a great breakfast*, Tara thought.

"I think I can help with that," Bauchman said, "but I guess we should eat first." He looked at Steve. "Remember, when the time comes, let me talk to them." He looked around the camp. "Some of us know how to do that."

Steve grinned at Tara and put his hand out.

"I'm glad you think it's so funny," Tara growled at him.

"Oh, I don't think this is funny at all," Steve said. "But I want Eduardo and the others to think that I am a joker, a comediante, and then we may be able to get away from them after all."

Tara stared at the gruel as the others talked.

"What's that?" Delores asked, pointing at the cooking pot.

"Pampas root," Bauchman said.

Delores gave him a look reserved for fools. "No," she said, pointing to a plate of fried meat. "What's *that?*"

"Paca," Steve said.

"A large rodent," Bauchman said. "Actually it's quite tasty." Delores held her hand to her mouth and shook her head.

"Look," Bauchman said, raising his voice. "Let me talk to them. I'll at least know what to say to these revolutionarios, more than any of you. Some of us know how to do this." Steve glanced at Robert and shrugged. The professor's an idiot. He thinks he knows these people, but he isn't acquainted with sudden violence. And that's what they were all about.

Steve picked up a wooden bowl and dipped his fingers in and ate some gruel. He smiled at his new friends. "Haven't had pampas in a long time."

Tara dug traditional roots each spring with her grandmother, and maybe these locals from the south knew something besides Marxist theories and guns. Maybe Eduardo had someone who knew how to cook root. If he didn't, well, she could show him a thing or two.

"I'm not eating that stuff," Sabrina said, wrinkling her nose, and then she picked up a bowl and began eating.

"You gonna write about this?" Tara asked Sabrina. Sabrina was a writer, and a good one.

"Yeah, sure, if we get out of here. I think I'd rather imagine my scary stories than live them. This is a little too close, if you know what I mean." She glanced at the people with guns.

Delores looked sick, touching the bowl with her finger, as if it were something rotten, putrid. Tara wanted to hug her. Poor Delores, poor, scared out of her wits non-complaining Delores. Delores would do anything for her friends, including going to Peru with them. Delores would have never gone to Peru or any other country on her own accord. She just went because Tara and Sabrina were going. What Delores wanted was simple and uncomplicated, and she told them often enough. She wanted a husband who worked in the tribal mill or drove a log truck, a house full of warm Indian babies in the new housing subdivision in Cold River.

Here we are, Tara thought, eating gruel, slurping it up as if it were fry bread, standing around with people watching us and pointing guns at us. She shivered, suddenly cold and afraid. None of them touched the fried rat.

Eduardo stood behind his group with his arms folded across his chest. Tara began to sketch him in her mind. His face was older than the others, in fact a lot older. She sketched deftly, adding age, knowing the changes that were the inevitable result of time and gravity. Because of this, hundreds of surgeons were able to afford planes, vacation homes, and keep Mercedes Benz dealerships in the black. Time and gravity. Sun and wind. Smoke was the worst. Smokers developed scales. The face loses fatty tissue as it ages, particularly around the eyes and upper cheek bones. Jowls droop, but the eyes, the eyes showed age the worst. Wrinkles appear first around the corners of the mouth and eyes, and as the fatty tissue goes away, the eyes have a sunken look. She sketched, concentrating on the eyes until she got it right. The nose grows fleshier with age. Hair recedes from the head and grows faster in the ears and nose.

Eduardo was a lot older...more articulate than the others. Something about him didn't fit here. Tara stopped her mental sketching and looked around. She counted five others with him. They looked young, dirty and half starved. Well, we're even, she thought. We're young, dirty and half starved, but they are the ones with the guns. Tara still had her Swiss Army knife in her pocket, but she knew that it was never a good idea to bring a knife to a gunfight, at least that's what her grandfather had always told her. She finished, not quite so hungry, and put her bowl down beside the others.

Professor Bauchman stepped up between Tara and Sabrina, put his bowl down and looked directly at Eduardo. He cleared his throat and held his hands out. Tara looked back at Steve and he put his arm on hers, pulling her gently, slowly away from the professor.

She put her lips to Steve's ear and whispered. "This isn't going to go well, is it?" She had an image of the professor on the ground and she pushed it away, not wanting to see it, to deal with it. If she couldn't see it, it wouldn't happen.

"No," Steve mouthed. He moved her back another foot.

"Some of us know," the professor said with a warm smile, "some of us know what you are going through. We're not your enemies." He continued to smile. Eduardo stepped around the fire and came up to Bauchman.

"I have studied your ideals, have taught them for years, and some of us know we're brothers. In fact, I have organized rallies for world socialists and against the oppression you feel."

Eduardo nodded and smiled, as if he meant for the professor to continue, and Bauchman started again in earnest. Tara held her breath and slowly took a step back, carefully pulling Sabrina and Delores with her.

"Some of us know, and I'm certainly one of those who do, that I can help you, I can raise money and consciousness for your cause, just as soon as I get back to the United States, and I..."

Boom!

Eduardo pulled the trigger so suddenly that the professor was shut off in mid-word, the bullet striking him in the forehead, the sudden, sharp explosion causing Tara to jump. The professor's head snapped as if it had been slapped by a large hand, blood spraying back on Dirty Hands and on Sabrina. Sabrina held her bowl of pampas root, now a red bowl, away from her body, dropped it and screamed, her face in rigid agony.

A red mist was suspended in the air where Bauchman's head had been as he dropped, as if his string of life had suddenly been cut. Delores put her hand over her mouth and began to shake. She moaned, a loud keening sound, and leaned against Tara. Tara dug her fingernails into Steve's arm.

Bauchman's face had a wild grin, as if he could tame the savage beast with a smile, and Tara saw with a feeling of horror that he carried the grin with him as he dropped. It wasn't always true that you grimaced when you died. Bauchman had that same silly grin, as if to say, "See Tara, death ain't so bad, once you get used to it, and maybe there will be someone to bullshit here on the other side."

She felt a crazy giggle coming up, and knew if she started laughing she wouldn't stop until long after it turned into a scream. Sabrina was frozen at her side, staring at Bauchman. Delores continued to moan and shake.

Eduardo turned and pointed his rifle at Tara, his smile still there as he swung his gun to cover them. Tara flinched, and she could sense Steve and Robert tensing behind her.

*We're gonna die here, and it's my fault.*

*Death follows me. Oh, God...death follows me. I saw Bauchman on the ground.*

"As you can see, I don't respond like a typical college freshman," Eduardo said in English. "Come to think of it, I don't have the usual collegiality normally reserved for the pedagogue." He laughed and waved his rifle around, pointing it at each person of their small group. Tara didn't move, didn't breathe.

"Now," Eduardo said with a wry grin, "who among you would like to take over and be the spokesperson for your group?"

They didn't speak.

His smile disappeared. "Okay, then, I suggest you get ready for travel."

They started off, the girl in the lead with two others and then the stunned group of students following, and further behind, Eduardo and the last two terrorists. Tara looked back once as they climbed out of the camp and saw the professor's crumpled body in the spot where he had fallen. She had a sudden image of the professor standing in the middle of the plateau just yesterday - upright while people were being killed all around from him. Such is the way of war - the something that you can't train for or count on, something that the best equipment can't overcome. And she knew then the great secret of war - that anyone can be killed at any time, that there was nothing they could do about it.

"Help us Grandfather," she murmured, "or we'll die here." But the help better come soon, or it wouldn't make any difference. She started up the trail, with Steve and Robert talking in low tones behind her.

"That guy, Eduardo, needs some sensitivity training," Steve said.

"At the very least, anger management," Robert agreed, his eyes still shining as if this were his moment, his time.

"Aggression displacement therapy," Steve added. Tara saw them exchange a look. If they were going to do something, she hoped it worked.

"Bauchman was such a pompous asshole," Steve said.

"Yeah," Robert responded, "but so few of them ever get shot."

Sabrina laughed, a high soft sound, as if she were looking for control. Tara walked.

Delores cried.

"Robert," Steve said quietly, "before this is over, that Eduardo guy is mine. He killed the professor to make a point, nothing more. Just to make a point, to show us how dangerous he is." Steve walked behind Tara. "I can be spectacularly dangerous myself," he muttered.

*Maybe you'd better come for us today, Grandfather*, Tara thought.

Tara prayed for him to come for them soon, but as she was praying, she didn't think he would come soon enough.

She put one foot in front of the other and was suddenly with her parents on their last day, sitting between her mother and father in the pickup truck, humming, her face bright with a smile, for they had driven past the school and were taking her to Portland, going up the grade out of Cold River, the snow deeper here on the slopes of Mt. Hood, sparkling a bright white on the side of the road. She looked at her mother and snuggled into her warmth and safety. She glanced at her father and saw how carefully he was driving. She thought that maybe she had been truly happy for the last time in her life, sitting between the love of her parents.

In the Peruvian Andes, Tara Red Eagle put one foot in front of the other. She tried to push away her thoughts.

Someone else will die today.

*Death follows me.*

# Chapter 7

On the previous afternoon when Tara and the others were being run up the hill and hiding from helicopters, Carl and Pedro had been running as well, but most of their flight was downhill. Once, in the late afternoon, Carl heard helicopters, and he waved his arms. Pedro pulled him down until the rotor noise faded.

"They shoot," Pedro said, and pointed his finger in the universal sign of a gun, and went, "bam bam bam bam bam bam!"

"I get it," Carl said.

They began their wild day by running down the hill, hiding and then running again. As a college freshman, Carl was used to dorm food, but knew he would never make fun of it again. His empty stomach screamed for McDonald's and Taco Bell. He hadn't been running much since high school, but he was young, and when they settled into a mile-eating jog, he found he could keep up.

Carl and his rescuer spent a cold night in the mountains and began again at first light.

They got to the main highway into the Huscaran National Park sometime in the morning, having covered more miles than Carl had thought possible. They hid beside the road and waited. Pedro let the first four trucks pass and then stood up in front of a truck that looked to Carl a copy of the first four. It was a large cab-over diesel, black with oil and mud. Carl couldn't tell the make or model, except it seemed old and large and it rattled and belched smoke as it idled in the middle of the road. The truck had wooden stakes on the sides and was covered with a dark, greasy canvas. A truck from hell that would take them out of the mountains.

Down the hill to Lima and the U.S. Embassy.

The truck was loaded with crates of chickens, wood, some hemp, and bins that put forth a variety of odors that made Carl not want to investigate further. The heavy odor of wet chicken shit clung to his clothes, his nostrils. He tried to not breathe. His stomach lurched as he crawled back between the chicken crates and put his shirt over his mouth. He found that if he stretched out, he could lie down. Between the noise of the chickens and the roar of the truck, talk was impossible.

According to Pedro, the truck was heading for Lima. Carl tried a couple of times to talk with Pedro, and then quit. He dozed for most of the trip.

He woke up as they entered Milaflores, a large suburb of Lima with a million people. They slowed behind a line of cars and idled along through the city until they reached the city limits of Lima.

When they got to Lima they came to a stop, and Pedro leaned out of the back of the truck. Carl joined him and looked to the front. There were cars, trucks, and collectivos (vans) stalled in front of them for blocks. They inched forward. Carl stood on the tailgate and breathed in deeply, trying to rid his nostrils of the chicken droppings. Traffic jams were nothing new to Carl. He lived in Seattle.

"We go," Pedro said, and grabbed Carl's arm and pointed. About two blocks ahead, he could see the turrets of several military vehicles, some kind of tanks. Carl jumped off the tailgate and followed Pedro.

"Let's go," Carl said, motioning toward the army vehicles. The cavalry had arrived. This time they were the good guys. Pedro grabbed Carl's arm.

"No!"

Carl stopped. "Okay, amigo, we'll play it your way, but why for chrissakes not the army?" Why not?

Pedro wouldn't let go of his arm, and finally, Carl relaxed.

They weaved through the line of cars and got to the roadside and Pedro struck off onto a side street. Carl's stomach growled as he followed, and he looked around to see if he could spot a Taco Bell. Hell, even on *his* reservation there was a Taco Bell, a McDonald's and a Burger King within minutes of the convention center. What kind of country was this?

Pedro found an empty taxi and motioned for Carl to get in. American steel, Carl noticed, a Ford Crown Vic. They passed small, run-down shops. Pedro spoke rapidly to the driver, gave him some money, and they headed toward the roadblock.

"Uh, Pedro, what are you doing. We don't want-"

"Embassy."

Carl nodded. Now we're getting somewhere. His stomach growled. "Pedro, is there a Taco Bell somewhere? On the way?"

Pedro nodded and spoke to the driver. Carl went through his pockets and checked for money. His pack with his passport, his tourist card, his money, had been left in the plateau. When they left the mountain, Carl was too nervous to look for it. He pulled an old pocket knife out of his pocket, an "Old Timer" with one broken blade. He held it up to Pedro.

"No." Pedro waved it away. Carl tensed as they approached the roadblock, but the cab continued slowly through. A group of soldiers lounged next to a tank. The tracks loomed up above the car and Carl had a sudden thought of opening the door and running. It would give the soldiers something to do, and he wouldn't feel so trapped. And then they were through the roadblock, and within a minute their speed picked up and they were into the city. The cab turned off into a residential area and the driver stopped beside a small house. Carl had been on this side of town before - it looked poor, like parts of the reservation where he grew up. The cab driver came out eating a sandwich and handed a paper sack over the seat to Pedro.

Carl began eating what he thought was shredded pork (he didn't care if it wasn't - it was delicious) wrapped in a flour shell, and he didn't stop until the sack was empty. Pedro ate one, and waved off the others.

Carl looked up from his eating as they passed through each roadblock, and the cab driver must have been known, because they were waved through each one. As they got closer to the center of town, the streets were wider, cleaner, and there was even more traffic. The downtown business district, as modern as any North American city, was a striking contrast to the poverty of the suburbs. When they turned onto Embassy Row, he spotted more tanks. Helmeted soldiers with tinted goggles stared like impassive green bugs from a science fiction war movie, the turrets thrust out in front. They arrived in the late afternoon and Carl felt safe. There was a little patch of America just a block ahead.

The driver slammed on the brakes at a cross street as an Armored Personnel Carrier flashed past in front of them. He stopped across the street from the American Embassy. Carl saw two guards in the dress blues of the U.S. Marine Corps.

*Honey, I'm home.*

Carl got out of the cab.

"Pedro my man, I owe you my life. But if something happens and I don't make it inside, call this number and ask for Chairman Whanaman. Don't speak to anyone but him and keep trying." Carl paused as Pedro nodded. He pressed the paper into Pedro's hand and then reached in and grabbed Pedro's shoulder. "I'll find you, amigo, when this is over. You come see me in my country." Pedro nodded again and smiled. Carl stepped out and walked across the street. When he got to the other sidewalk he turned to wave at Pedro, and walked up to the Marine guardhouse.

The U.S. Embassy in Lima is an imposing building in the middle of a walled compound, on the Avenida la Encelada. Embassy Row. Carl knew that the staff was responsible for the U.S. mission in Peru.

Carl didn't give a rat's ass how many people worked there as long as he made it inside. He just wanted to get past the walls and into a little piece of America, and leave as soon as possible on the next plane home. He approached the marine guard at the gate, glancing over his shoulder at Pedro, who was now leaning against the fender of the taxi. Beside the guardhouse a metal gate crossed the driveway, shutting out the drive to pedestrians and automobiles. He was going to have to get past the marine guard to make it inside.

"Hello," Carl said to the nearest guard, a young marine who wasn't much older than Carl. The guard looked at him.

"What can I help you with?"

"My, uh, name is Carl Twoshoes, and I am an American citizen and I want to see the ambassador."

"Can I see your passport?"

"I don't have it with me, I lost it in the hills yesterday." The marine's eyebrows flicked up.

"Lost it in the hills - where?"

"Uh, up north, now can I just -?" Carl stopped when he saw a reflection of himself in the window of the guardhouse. He looked like every other street person he had seen in Lima. He was dirty, had on a shirt that Pedro had given him the day before, and in fact he looked like a Peruvian Indian, not an American Indian.

"Anyway," Carl said, looking at the Marine, "I was part of a group of students, mostly American Indian college students, and we got caught in a war between some terrorists and the Peruvian Army. Terrorists man, like Osama bin Laden, you know, that fucker? Some of us were killed and I hid and made my way here, and I...just want in so I can get home without being killed. God, Dude, just let me in."

"Hold on." The Marine went inside the guardhouse and spoke to his partner, a Marine with sergeant's stripes. The sergeant came out and looked at Carl.

"We're calling the duty officer inside the embassy. The duty officer will alert the ambassador's staff, and they'll let us know. We're on alert as well, with the attacks across the country - and we have orders to not let anyone in without proper identification. Sorry for the delay."

He didn't look too sorry to Carl, but then the Marine could go back inside at any time. Carl leaned against the guardhouse and waited. He looked around. The cab was gone. Pedro sat beside a tree across the street and down the block, his head down. He waved a finger at Carl, as if he could see him from that position. Carl just wanted to get home, to go to McDonald's, Taco Bell, and be anywhere in America now. Get some American food. Hell, he'd even eat some fry bread. Go to class when he got back to campus. His legs trembled, and for the first time since this began, he felt like bawling.

From his second floor window, the duty officer saw a young man in rags talking to the Marines. Hell, he couldn't save every peasant who wanted to go to America, and besides, he had a date. He would get rid of this one himself, as he had to go out anyway. Come back tomorrow. Manana. He straightened as the ambassador approached with his assistant. They looked out with him.

"What's this, another campesino wanting to go to the land of the free?" The Ambassador shook his large face.

The duty officer nodded. "I'll take care of it," he said, and walked to the stairway.

Carl was trying to be patient, but people had been killed, and he was about to start yelling. This was bullshit. A man wearing a gray suit marched up to the gate, and looked to Carl as if he were a military person. He didn't look at Carl, but came up to the guardhouse and spoke to the sergeant. Carl couldn't hear what he was saying but something about it didn't feel right. The Marine came over to the sidewalk and held his hands out, palms up, as he approached Carl.

"Hey sorry, man," the Marine said. "We are, as you know, closed. The ambassador's staff apparently said that you should come back in the morning. We open at eight."

"Look," Carl said, trying to keep his voice even, failing, his voice rising into a shout. "I've been shot at, and have been running around trying to find the fucking U S of A, and you've got to help me."

The Marine glanced at the guardhouse and shrugged at Carl.

"There's really nothing I can –"

"Forget it, and thanks for nothing," Carl said as he turned away. He might be as well off with Pedro. He looked across the street. Pedro was gone. He turned away, shaking his head, tired, hungry again, and as he got to the curb he almost stepped in front of a car that was pulling up fast. Two men in suits, two Peruvian men Carl thought, got out of the car, one from the front passenger side, the other from the back. The back seat dude left the door open and walked over to stand behind Carl.

Carl half turned to look at him, taking in the scars on his face that the suit did nothing to ameliorate. Carl's skin started to tighten, and his face itched.

"Get in, please," the front seat suit said in English.

Carl stood there, not moving, not wanting to move. His feet refused to move. Hell, my body knows to not get in with these KGB looking dudes. His left leg trembled again. He shifted his weight to make it stop.

"Get in!"

This couldn't be happening to a nineteen year old college student. Right dudes, get in, my ass. He tried to keep his lip from trembling. He looked quickly around and didn't see the Marines at the guardhouse. He took a step that way and the suit behind him pushed up close. He turned to run and the man shoved him toward the car, and the driver got out. A Humvee came up fast and two soldiers got out, their assault rifles slung behind them. Carl looked over at the gate and glared at the windows. The Marine came out.

"Thanks a lot man," Carl said.

The Marine started forward and waved at the men on the sidewalk. "Hey fellas, maybe we should just talk to your commander." The sergeant pointed to Carl. "He says he's an American."

"He's with a terrorist group," one of the suits said, "and they will say anything."

Carl looked for a way to run, believing in his gut that they weren't taking him to the Holiday Inn, when a hand fell on his shoulder, heavy, gripping him hard. He spun, suddenly in a zone, fronted the two soldiers as if they were an opposing basketball team's defenders, threw his hands up as if to shoot, their weapons coming up, and Carl ran around the back of the Humvee and into the street, hearing the shouts and men running, catching a glimpse of the marine running for the guardhouse.

Carl sprinted, looking wildly around as he accelerated to his top speed, his feet pounding the pavement on the wide street. There were large white houses on both sides of the street, embassies, no doubt, the next corner a half block away. He made a sudden cut to the left as a rifle on full auto went off behind him, the sound louder than the string of firecrackers they used to light on the Rez.

*Oh shit, they're shooting at me*

He pumped his arms and legs, the roar in his ears louder than the rifles behind him, and he ran full blast into a hedge and his momentum carried him out the other side, stumbling onto a lawn, and then he was around the corner and out of sight of the pursuit.

His speed had taken them by surprise, as it always did his opponents, but he knew that these guys were gonna seriously fuck up young Carl Twoshoes if they got him in their sights. He made it to the corner of a house with a courtyard, running full out, pumping his arms with a sprinter's grace, and a flurry of shots came from behind him. Bullets streamed by him and slammed into a brick wall across the street.

*I'm gonna make it!*

He looked down the street for a place to hide, and knew at once that hiding wouldn't work. The side street off of embassy row was like an upscale neighborhood in the states – large houses, manicured lawns, and expensive rolling stock in the drives. The wind streamed through his hair and he felt a wave of guilt come over him, running for his life and he missed his hair.

*You need your pigtails flying in this death dance.*

Carl sprinted around a silver Mercedes that blocked the sidewalk, the driver giving him a startled look. He moved to the middle of the street and concentrated on the next corner coming up. The windows exploded in a car to his right, glass raining on the street like angry crystals. He felt as if he could fly, determined to make the corner, wishing sorrowfully that he still had his hair.

*Just why did you cut it, you dumb shit.*

And then he could hear the chant of the crowd again.

Shooter! Shooter! Shooter! And then Downtown Man! Downtown Man!

As he got to the corner and decided to sprint to the right he caught a glimpse of an olive drab armored personnel carrier on his left, racing up the street, the soldier in the turret swinging his rifle to bear on Carl.

He saw a low rock wall across the street and angled for it when the first bullet caught him up high in the shoulder, spinning him around.

I've felt worse pain, Carl thought, staggering back around facing the wall. He tried to pump his legs and threw himself toward the low wall, driving for the basket with the crowd screaming his name, his legs not working now, but he was Shooter, the Downtown Man from Three Point Land, and he hit the wall and fell on top of it as the next bullets took him all at once. He rolled over the wall and fell onto his back on a lawn. He lay there, blinking as warm blood trickled into his eyes, thinking that he must be all right. The shoulder hurt like hell, but he couldn't feel anything else, and why was the lawn red, he couldn't feel . . .

*He was dribbling the ball again, a short, quick dribble, and he danced around a defender, smiling to himself at the surprised look on the defender's face, and he was dashing for the basket, his friends Scab, Gopher, Cricket in the stands, screaming his name. His dad was there with them, only this time he appeared to be sober, smiling, accepting high fives from people around him, saying, Carl was sure, "that ain't right."*

*Yeah, Dad, it ain't right. It ain't.*

Pedro watched the events from behind a row of bushes at the Japanese Embassy down the street. They killed Carlos.

His new young amigo from Norte America was dead. I never should have taken him here, he thought sadly.

He left through back alleys, a middle aged man in the clothing of the People of the Altitudes, fingering the piece of paper in his pocket. He knew where there was a phone where he could make the call. He would at least call the young amigo's people and let them know what had happened.

Young Carlo's own people gave him up to the secret police and the army. Pedro thought that maybe he didn't want to go to Disneyland after all.

# **Chapter 8**

*Disgusting little prick,* Captain Jack Nelson thought, as he watched the Peruvian Colonel pick his way across the meadow. Colonel Miguel Hernandez wore a tailored uniform, the pants stretched tight, making him look to Nelson as a bad actor in a low budget movie.

Colonel Hernandez stood in front of the smoking hulk of the Huey UH-1 helicopter, holding a light blue scarf to his nose. The toasted remains of the pilot and crew were of no consequence to him. He suppressed a number of conflicting emotions, his face a rigid mask. He did allow some of the anger he felt to show through, as it would do the men good to see it. But the anger was controlled, a conscious act for display.

The downed helicopter had been on an interdiction flight, checking routes of processed cocaine over the Andes and into Columbia.

This wasn't the work of the drug runners. They were capable of such an attack, but unless they were bothered, they would avoid army patrols. The message of the woman with no feet was unmistakable - the work of Peru's revived terrorist group, not too different from the socialists that had been trying to get the people to rise up for the past twenty years. They hadn't had much success, but this time it would be different.

He stepped back from the heat of the helicopter and allowed himself a small smile. The little bastardos who shot down his helicopter (and he knew who they were) had given him the perfect excuse for a fight and to unleash his troops. One thing about the terrorists in Peru, he thought, they keep coming back, and they justify my command, and that's why I have to help them.

Forty yards away, the rotors of his command helicopter were turning, ready for an instant departure if it was needed. In the plain beyond his Huey were two more helicopters – both from the United States Special Forces troops, with a Captain Nelson in command.

Nelson had a camera crew on board, and Hernandez would have to deal with that later. As he stared at the wreckage, it occurred to him that the camera crew might be useful after all.

"Colonel." Captain Nelson came up and stood beside him. "Colonel, I believe we have located all of the bodies that are left in the area."

Hernandez followed the captain through a rocky fissure and up onto a grassy plain. He saw the body of the campesino woman, the feet plainly severed, and he walked over and stood by the body, his head bowed, his hand to his eyes. Hernandez looked up from the body and then to the meadow, where Mario and Ruppert had fallen. He walked over and squatted in front of Mario's crumpled body. This one almost made it out of sight, Hernandez thought. He poked the sandal with his swagger stick, and then stood. This one was a guide with Quechecan dress and sandals. He turned and looked over the scene, the littered bodies, the smoke from the helicopter, and the men he had deployed. In truth he had grown tired of chasing the drug runners, of catching some and letting some slip through in exchange for making him a very wealthy man.

The drug runners would always be here. They had established a symbiotic relationship with the army and the politicians. In a sense, they helped each other, and who really cared if the estupido Norte Americanos wanted to put the white powder up their fat noses. He walked with Captain Nelson to the cluster of bodies in the middle of the hillside and took his time looking at each one in turn - Myoko and Gretchen together, their small day packs still on their backs. A few yards away from the bodies, he found two more small packs.

He picked up the packs and opened them, examining the contents. Lotion. A small compact. A woman's personal hygiene items (which still embarrassed him for some unknown reason) a tablet, pen, and a rolled up rain jacket. A nylon billfold with a woman's driver's license in it. He looked at it and handed it to Captain Nelson. Tara Red Eagle from the State of Oregon in the United States. A student, with an address of Cold river, Oregon.

"What is this town, 'Cold River'?"

"It's a town and an Indian reservation in the middle of the state," Nelson said.

"Indian, like the Quechecas?"

"Yeah, I guess, but many of them live together on reservations."

"Not a bad idea, putting the Quechecas on reservations," Hernandez mused, smiling at Nelson.

"It happened a long time ago," Nelson said. Hernandez nodded.

He knew of the American history with the indigenous groups.

We're not so different after all, you and I, Captain Nelson of the Special Forces, Hernandez thought. You just think you're better since it didn't happen on your watch. But we have all treated Indians the same.

They gathered the packs and identification, not finding any on the guides and not expecting any. They had identification of four people, with two bodies.

"Students," Nelson said, examining the I.D.

"They were most likely on a trek. They aren't dressed for mountain climbing."

"Drug runners?" Nelson asked.

"Terrorists," Hernandez said. He smiled.

"How do you know for sure?"

"Drug runners don't kill people and cut off their feet. That's something the Marxists have been doing for the last couple of decades. They want us to know who they are." Hernandez had known the terrorists were here. In fact, he had placed one here. He smiled again at the thought. He looked around again at the hillside as he removed a small radio from his belt and spoke rapidly in Spanish. An officer, a lieutenant, trotted over and saluted the Colonel.

"Any terrorists?" Hernandez asked. He already had his own answer, but for political reasons, he wanted Captain Nelson to hear this.

"As far as we can tell, any wounded or dead combatants have been carried from the immediate area, but we have found a dozen separate piles of brass, AK-47 brass." He showed a handful to the Colonel.

"Any blood, did we get any of them?"

"Doesn't look like it."

Hernandez turned to Nelson. "The others, and there may be a dozen or more students in the bush, didn't just run off. The terroristas," and as he said this he sneered, the word coming out harsh. "The terrorists took them hostage."

"Colonel, we didn't find any passports in the packs," Nelson said.

"The passports were probably taken by their captors, or are on their bodies."

"We'll help where we can, Colonel," Captain Nelson said. "With your permission, I'm going airborne to search the immediate area for more bodies or survivors."

Hernandez looked at the captain and then back at the bodies, wanting the Green Beret to leave the area but not wanting him to be the one to find the terrorists.

"Captain, ah, thank you and please thank your men for me for your assistance. But, I don't want you to get into trouble with your superiors, since your duty is for drug interdiction only, and not to assist us with our domestic issues." He put his hand on the captain's shoulder. "Not that your help wouldn't be appreciated, Captain, it would indeed. If you should come across a group, call us immediately. We'll be ready to go in about twenty minutes, and if you would meet back here and accompany us back."

"There is one more thing, Colonel."

Hernandez raised his eyebrows at Nelson and smiled.

"Since we are missing several students, U.S. citizens, we will be making a report to our command. We will assist in their recovery in any way we can."

"Let me ask you this, Captain, as officer to officer. Is there any indication that the missing people left voluntarily, or that they were forced to go with the terrorists, or whoever they are?"

"What do you mean?"

"I mean that we know that the revolutions that seem to arrive in this country every few years have traditionally come from the university, and that there historically had been some support from your country - from people also in the university." He looked at the captain, his face taking on a harder edge than he had planned.

"Colonel, *these* people must have been on a trek, probably from Huaraz or Yungay, and I doubt-"

"Of course, Captain Nelson, I am sure that is the case, but I was just trying to cover all of the bases." He smiled and clapped Nelson on the shoulder, having done exactly what he wanted to do. Place some doubt in the captain's mind, let it work on him. There *was* a historical precedent for his statements, and he now knew that he could use this to his advantage, however it came out. If he rescued the students (and, of course, killed the terrorists) he would be a hero. If the students were killed by the terrorists, so much the better. If the students were killed by his men, he could blame it on the terrorists.

Hernandez watched as Nelson walked to his helicopter, joined by two of his NCO's. It was about time he got the chance to once again show what he could do, to show that he was far and away above the other full colonels in the army, to show that he was destined for a general's position and one day to lead the army. It might work just as well if he killed some people in the countryside and blamed it on the terrorists, especially if he could find the students. But he would have to kill all of them, and he would hand pick the troops to accompany him. He had time, he had the troops, he had the equipment, and now he had the perfect excuse to propel his career to the top of the army.

*El Presidente would take notice.*

He stepped over a body and smiled.

Colonel Miguel Hernandez of the Peruvian Army couldn't lose. All he had to do was kill some students from the United States, and he sincerely hoped the terrorists didn't beat him to it.

He called his staff to meet him at the bodies. There was evidence here to collect, and who knows, it might be useful later on.

In fact, he was sure of it.

Captain Nelson signaled for his soldiers to meet him between the helicopters. The squad guarding the perimeter ran to meet him, their rifles ready. Most of them had been together in Iraq. Nelson looked at Hernandez as the colonel shouted at his men. Master Sergeant Stevens stood with Nelson and they watched the scene.

"Fuckin' embarrassment as a military man, huh, Cap'n," Stevens said, and spit.

"Roger that," Nelson muttered. He had never made any secret with his men of his loathing for the Peruvian Colonel.

*He's untrained, undisciplined, untrustworthy, and unprofessional, a political appointee of the worst kind, one who ruled by fear.*

"Okay, listen up," Nelson said. His squad moved closer.

"Things are going to get interesting, folks. That little butt hole," he said, gesturing toward Hernandez, "that little butt hole is in the middle of something, and I don't trust him. You know how he operates – he won't try to sort out hostages, the students have more to fear from him than they do the terrorists." He pointed at his intel officer.

"Rob, when we get back, figure out where the students might be, where they are likely to be going. We'll want to be there. It's a long shot, so God help'm." He pointed at the camera crew. "Let's get them in and get outta here."

Nelson thought about the students.

*God help'm, cause if He doesn't, they'll have to do it all themselves.*

They flew low over the smoking helicopter. It reminded Nelson of a scene from a village in Iraq – a burned out Humvee and a bus, locked together in a smoldering embrace.

*Gonna be another busy decade for warriors.*

# Chapter 9

Cold River Indian Reservation
Oregon

Martin Andrews walked through the administration area and the secretaries stopped talking. Lori followed, with Hawk in the rear. She was still carrying the ridiculous dog's head, the dog suit looking more preposterous than ever, the tail wagging as she walked. Martin unlocked his office door and turned to see Lori holding McGruff's tail in her right hand, twirling it like a tassel. Janie laughed and slapped her leg. Lori gave the tail one more small turn as she entered Martin's office.

"O. J.'s jury coulda picked a better McGruff than you did, Boss," Janie said as she came in. Martin could hear the laughter coming from the outer office.

Hawk entered, swung the door shut and grinned at Martin as the laughter grew louder from the outer office. Martin sat heavily behind his desk and swiveled in the large chair, the back rising above his head. On his first day he had wanted to replace the chair and get one more useful, but he hadn't done it and now he knew that he had to keep it. It was the biggest chair in the building, and appearance was important for the chief.

During Martin Andrew's first week as Chief of Police, he met what must have been half the families on the rez. Janie would come in and announce that a certain family was outside to see him, and she would give him advice and the history of each family. In each case, she would tell Martin, "Don't see them Boss, it's a waste of your time." Martin would see them anyway, and in keeping with the political correctness of his former life, he thought that he was being sensitive by coming out from behind his large desk, getting off the ridiculous chair and sitting with the families in front of his desk.

It made them uneasy.

"Boss," Janie would say, "Boss, the Smith family has come 'round to see you, but don't see them 'cause they are a bunch of Navajo dogs. They live over on the hill, and want to know what happened with the bicycle they had stolen about two years ago, have we found it and all. Don't talk to them, Boss." Martin had learned from the first day that Janie called everyone and everything she didn't like a "Navajo Dog," and he guessed that someone from the Navajo reservation had once been hired or promoted over Janie. Some of his best officers were Navajo.

Martin would see them anyway, and it would be like Janie said, the woman would talk with the kids sitting there, the man sitting and watching, saying nothing. And the hell of it was, Janie was usually right. They would talk about their family, and after about thirty minutes, the woman would ask if the police had found the stolen bicycle yet?

After the first day Martin realized that they were coming to see the new Šiyápu chief.

Hawk stared at a map of the world on the wall. Lori was sitting at the table. Hawk continued to stare at the map and put his finger on the country of Peru as Martin spoke.

"This is crazy, isn't it? Going to Peru?"

"Yeah, it's crazy."

"We gonna do it?"

Hawk kept his finger in place and turned.

"Yeah, at least I am. You, on the other hand, don't really *have* to go, but will be expected to. You can walk out of here." The intercom buzzed. Chairman's on the phone, Janie told him.

"May I put you on the speaker, Mr. Chairman? Hawk and Lori are with me."

"I've been in touch with the good senator and the state department in Washington," Bluefeathers said. He was crisp, angry. "I've been in touch with our good senator *and* the State Department in D.C. The senator was okay, but the State Department is treating me like a blanket-assed Indian. I'm leaving for Washington and will be there this evening, late, and plan to talk with these people. They keep talking around telling me, blah, blah, diplomatic channels, and they aren't doing a damned thing. You be ready to go to Peru. Do what you have to do." The speaker went silent.

"Boss." Janie pushed the door open a few inches. "Boss, that Martha Coeur d'Alenes woman is here to see you. Shall I tell her to go?"

He should say yes, get her out of here, but he knew he couldn't.

"Give me a minute and then send her in." Martha Coeur d'Alenes is probably here to yell at me again, Martin thought.

Now on the day he was ordered to go to Peru, Martha Coeur d'Alenes was coming to see him, coming to his office for more of the same and he steeled himself for the verbal assault that was sure to take place. He knew he couldn't refuse to see her. She would be "talking 'round" to everyone on the rez that the chief was too busy, too important of a man to see her. Janie stuck her head in again.

"You ready, Boss?" She sadly shook her head.

"Ten seconds." He looked at Hawk and Lori. "You two be ready to leave for Peru within the next twenty four to forty eight hours. Tomorrow morning we go to Portland to see an old friend. Hawk raised his eyebrows.

"An old friend named Dennis Underwood," Martin said. "He was once in Peru with the DEA, knows the country." Hawk and Lori walked to the door and started out.

"And Lori," Martin said. "Put the McGruff suit back on the shelf, and you were right, you can't be McGruff ever again." She smiled to herself and walked out around Martha Coeur d'Alenes. Coeur d'Alenes smirked as Lori walked by, and when Coeur d'Alenes entered, Lori stuck her tongue out at her back and then walked away. The secretaries laughed, and Martin wondered for the eighth time that day, *What the hell am I doing here?*

Martha Coeur d'Alenes looked around his office as if there were a rancid odor somewhere and it was up to her to find the source. Finally, she sat on the edge of the chair in front of his desk.

"You got any In-din in you, Chief?"

Martin shook his head. No.

"I thought maybe you was some kind of apple, that's why you are here. You know what an apple is, Chief Andrews?"

Martin nodded. He'd heard it his first day on the reservation, a term that was usually reserved for a derogatory comment for Indians who acted like they were white. Red on the outside, white on the inside. Sort of an Indian Uncle Tom. An apple.

"No, I'm not an apple. Just a Chief of Police."

Coeur d'Alenes leaned forward. "Then why you going to Peru with Hawk and that Lori girl?" Martin looked up at her.

"How did you -?"

"The whole reservation knows it by now. One thing In-dins are good at is spreading the latest rumor. That true? You going to Peru?"

"I guess I am."

"You sure that's in your job description?" She said it crisply. Job dee-skrip-shun.

Martin laughed. "I'm not sure what my job description is, but yes, here on the rez, it probably is in my job description." Coeur d'Alenes leaned forward and looked at him, as if he were a specimen who would morph into something hideous in front of her. Finally she spoke again.

"I think maybe you're up to it, Martin, helping us out. But you take care, Martin Andrews. Not all are going to make it back." She nodded at him, a curt nod, got up slowly, and walked out of the office.

Janie entered before Martin had much time to think about it.

"Larry Morrow here to see you."

Morrow was an F.B.I. agent out of Portland, assigned to work on the rez, mostly homicides. The F.B.I. had jurisdiction on Indian reservations for homicides and most major crimes.

Larry entered, looked at Martin, and shut the door. He was nearing retirement and didn't fit the mold of the typical agent, particularly when he worked on the Rez. He wore cowboy boots, jeans, a flannel shirt. He looked to Martin like an old biology teacher.

"I need some time off," he announced. "Can you believe that?"

Martin slid his phone across his desk toward Larry, and as Martin busied himself with a list of things to ask about Peru, he heard Larry ask his supervisor, Agent Markum, for the time off. He put the phone down.

"You be careful down south," he told Martin. "I'm going to my cabin on the Metolius for a week, starting now. No phone, no pool, no pets. Boss said he'd do the paperwork when I got back. I'm outta here." He shook Martin's hand, shook his head, and laughed. Martin could hear him laughing with Janie and the others as he walked past.

In Portland, Supervisory Special Agent Markum (one of the old F.B.I.) hung up the phone and wondered if the tingling in his arm meant he would have to give up racquetball. He dropped heavily in his chair. The pain ran up his arm and slugged him in the chest. He thought of how lucky Larry Morrow had been to work most of his career in the field, in the beautiful mountains of Oregon, instead of in an office in New York, L.A., or Miami.

He wondered what Larry's cabin looked like, there on the

Metolius, and the pain fairly exploded in his chest. He clutched his arms in front of his body and quivered, knowing that he was forgetting something, that he had missed something important, one thing he had to do…

*Oh yeah, I'm the only one who knows where Larry was going.*

He didn't hear the medics come in and try to jump start his heart.

# Day Three

# Chapter 10

Huascaran National Park
Peru

On the morning of the third day Tara didn't think she could keep up. She didn't remember hitting her knee, but her left knee was swollen and ached. Her clothes were stiff and she smelled. They trudged in a line up a hill, all banter gone now. By mid-morning they entered the ruins of an old village, their captors entering ahead, wary. In the early morning Tara saw what might have been another party of hikers in the distance. She looked at Steve and he shook his head, so she didn't say anything.

The constant threat of death had weakened her, sapping her energy and her ability to resist. Since the professor had been shot Tara knew that they were totally at the mercy of the terrorists. She thought that Robert and Steve were planning something, but they didn't say, and she didn't ask.

Their captors were proceeding more cautiously now, and for that, Tara was thankful. It was as if they expected something to happen, an encounter, or a fight with the army. The leader came back through the village and signaled a stop. Tara dropped amid a jumble of stones, many of them covered with grass and brush, the village given over to nature. She absently ran her hand over a stone as the others came up around her and dropped down as well.

"It's pre-Columbian," Steve said.

"What?"

"The stones, the village. Pre-Columbian."

"Oh." Tara pulled her hand back and turned to Steve.

"Well, that's what we came here to see," Tara said bitterly. "For God's sake, pre-Columbian."

The hillside and the view of the mountains would have been beautiful under different circumstances. The ruins were on the top of a ridge. The peak of Nev Huscaran was a white shroud in the distance. As she looked around at the ancient stone-work, Tara ran her fingers over the crumbled stone, lightly, as a blind person might read, searching for meaning in the last two days, as if the rock knew something, could tell her it was all over, but the rock couldn't help. It remained as it had for centuries, a silent and uncaring witness to untold violence and cruelty.

She sat on a stone step, not caring about anything other than her feet and knee. Maybe a shower. Delores sat down next to her and leaned into her shoulder.

"Do you think we will stop here for the day?" Delores asked quietly.

"No," Tara said. "I think we will go on until we've forgotten about everything but our poor feet."

She heard a noise coming up from the canyon below, a sound she knew but she couldn't quite place, the sound diffused in the mountains. A mechanical sound, a buzzing, drifting up and then it was gone, and then Tara knew what it was.

*Helicopter.*

There was a helicopter out there, probably closer than she thought, if she could hear it. She glanced at Steve. He shook his head, no. As Tara started to get up, she saw movement on the trail, and Eduardo came running toward them, motioning with his rifle, herding them off the trail and into the brush. Tara had a flash of fear, sharper than the underlying fear of their morning hike. The hike (and that was how she thought of it) had been uneventful since the professor's death, and then she remembered how the exploding helicopter had killed the girls.

The young terrorist came over with her gun and waved them down under some bushes. They waited on the ground until long after they could no longer hear the sound. They moved on, steeper now, the trail steep enough now that Tara had to grab rocks and brush to move up. Behind them toward the Pacific, and to the north and south, the peaks of central Peru pushed up through the mountain fog.

As the trail leveled off, Tara and the others caught up with Eduardo and three of his terrorists. Eduardo crouched on the trail. He turned and looked at Tara, and motioned for them to get down. Tara lay in the path, with Delores right behind her. With her face pressed into the rock, Tara smelled smoke. She lifted her head and looked around.

"Delores," she whispered. She turned her head around and looked at her friend.

"Be quiet, I'm sleeping."

"You smell that?"

"All I can smell is your feet."

Tara rolled on her back and saw a haze of smoke over the lip of the hill above her, obscuring the blue sky. The girl with the AK47 came back and waved her gun at them, and then ran back up the trail. When she was gone, Tara sat up and looked around. Steve crawled over and leaned against a rock and faced Tara and Delores. Sabrina crawled up to them. Robert took up a position behind them, facing down the trail.

"This could be bad," Steve said quietly.

"What do you think it is?" Tara whispered.

"Government troops own the helicopters, and I'm sure they have been looking for us. The smoke is probably from something they torched . . . while they were looking." He raised up and slowly looked around. "We sure got caught up in a hell of a mess. If we escape, and we will have to try soon, everyone will be looking for us, and I mean everyone. But, it looks as if, for the moment, we are alone."

"Where do we go?"

"The American Embassy in Lima, I guess, if we can get there. Maybe Ecuador to the north."

"When?"

"Now." He touched Tara's shoulder. "You guys get ready, when it happens, it will be quick."

Tara heard the sounds of running, sliding on the trail above them, and a shower of small stones rolled down on Steve. One of the younger boys burst into view, looking wildly back up the trail.

Tara heard a single shot, and then a fusillade of shots, explosions, and yelling. Somewhere up above a furious fight was in progress.

A scream came down to them and was cut off, sudden, with a single shot.

Tara winced.

Delores whispered, mumbling.

The terrorist, a young man about twenty, probably a Campesino conscript, clutched his rifle, his hand shaking, his eyes bulging and flickering. Sweat stood out on his face. The gunfire diminished, and then stopped.

Steve moved so suddenly that Tara jumped, Steve coming up behind the terrorist, grabbing his hair, jerking his head back and slamming his arm around the terrorists throat, violently pulling his feet off the ground. Robert darted in front, deftly catching the AK-47 before it hit the ground and pointed it at the trail above.

*But we're just college students,* Tara wanted to shout.

The terrorist's sandals beat a spasmodic drum roll on the dirt, dust swirling around his ankles as Steve held firm, the face in the crook of his arm turning colors, purple, blue, and then the feet stopped moving.

*He's done this before.*

*Steve's too quick, practiced. Confident.*

Robert quickly searched the terrorist, removing a knife and extra magazines for the rifle. Steve rolled the body off the trail, out of sight behind some brush. He stood and looked over the little group, and then caught Tara's eyes. Tara turned away and pushed herself up.

*Until now we were just victims. Captives. Now we've done it, we've killed someone in a foreign land. Death follows me, and it isn't over yet.*


Steve led, with Tara, Sabrina, Delores, and then Robert. Smoke billowed ahead of them, bringing with it a mixture of smells - burning wood, grease, and something sharp, pungent, and Tara instantly knew what it was. She had been to several house fires on the reservation, first as a kid watching, and later, as an adult who fought fires. Not everyone made it out of a house fire on the rez. She had never forgotten the smell of burning flesh.

Walking through the Peruvian Andes she smelled it again, and it brought it all back to her, the smell, as if it was just hiding out in her brain, in her nose.

Humans were burning.

Someone had burned human flesh.

Tara looked back at Sabrina and Delores. Robert gave her a slight nod. He understood. Tara remembered hearing him talking to Steve a few days ago (what now seemed like a lifetime ago) that he had worked on a hotshot fire crew during the summers, out of the Forest Service crew over in Prineville. But that was Oregon, and now here they were in Peru, in the mountains, where people were trying to kill them and now there were burned people up ahead. Tara walked up to join Steve, the others following.

"Might get bad up there," he said.

She just nodded, and stepped toward the smoke.

As they got closer, Tara realized they were alone. Their guards had disappeared. They moved up a slight rise, the trail now wide enough to walk beside Steve. She touched his arm, looking down the trail to a clearing. They were now on level ground, with brush and scrub trees on either side of the trail, and it was as if she were looking through a tunnel toward an open area beyond.

"Do you think they have left us?" Tara asked, looking at the smoke ahead.

"Don't think so," Steve said. "This is going to be a pretty large village, at least large for this area of the Andes. Must mean that there was a mission here, a school. That's the only reason the Indians came together in this large of a group. There might not be much left, after an attack by troops."

"They're looking for us," Tara said softly. "What do we do now?"

"Let's see what the village has," Steve said. "The troops might be there, and we'll have to assess what to do if they are. Be ready to drop to the ground or ready to run. If we can, we'll meet here. If we get separated, let's meet for the night at the ruins where we stopped for a rest, about two miles back down the trail."

Tara crouched as they approached the clearing. As they got to the opening in the brush, Steve stepped off the trail and behind a large rock. Tara stood behind him, looking around his shoulder to see into the clearing. In the center, about fifty yards from where they stood, the remains of a building were smoldering, the roof and walls had fallen in and were burning. It had been a large building for the mountain tribes, probably a school or church or both. Behind the building in a semi-circle there were several huts, and they too had been torched. The last two on the right were ablaze as if they had been recently torched, or had gone up because they were too close to the others. There was no way to fight fire here, and in any event, Tara didn't see any movement in the village.

They watched for several minutes, the smoke rolling over them when the wind brought it their way. No one moved in the village.

The smell of burned flesh came with it.

Steve pointed.

There was a shape on the ground in front of the large building. A person. Tara couldn't tell if it was a man or a woman, but it appeared that the person was dead. The clothes on the person were burning from the heat of the fire.

He's got to be either unconscious or dead, Tara thought.

The person was not moving. Smoke from the huts behind the larger building blocked her view from the rest of the plateau.

Tara felt that she was watching this from directly above the village, not really here, a silent spectator to some outlandish video game. She stood behind Steve and no one said anything. A loud bang came from one of the huts and Tara jumped, and then except for the noise of the fire, it was quiet again.

"Steve."

"What?" He continued to watch the village.

"Where are our terrorists?"

"Don't know."

"There must have been forty or fifty people living in the village."

"Maybe they're just going 'round shopping," Delores said.

On the second day out from Lima they had stopped at a village with about ten huts, and there seemed to be a lot of people there, maybe fifty. Tara watched the quiet village and didn't see a dog, a chicken, a child.

Nothing moved.

They stood there behind the rocks and watched.

"Steve, where's Robert?" Tara whispered.

"He's looking at the camp from another place." Steve glanced at her quickly and then resumed his vigil from the relative safety of the rocks.

"Do you think we can get out of here?" Tara asked, still whispering.

"Maybe, but we don't have any food, or a map. Hopefully Robert will find some of what we need if the terrorists don't find him first. We've got to know where to go and how to get there."

Tara saw some movement at the edge of the clearing, over to her left. As she watched Robert left the brush behind the huts and walked toward the man on the ground in front of the large building. The burning man.

Robert glanced around the hut and then walked to the man and stood over him. He looked at him for several seconds and then continued around the building, walking toward the smoldering huts, looking first at the ground, then the burning huts, and finally at the brush surrounding the village. As Robert got to the side of the building, he stood away from the heat and he looked up toward Tara and Steve and shook his head slightly. Tara felt a sudden fear, as sharp as the sudden fear on the day before when they saw the woman with no feet. She reached out for Steve. She had been under a constant level of fear in the last twenty four hours, the fear of the unknown and not being in control, but now she thought that Robert should get out of there, that they should all hide and make plans to get the hell away from the village, this place of death.

*The killing is not done here, and I bring death.*

"Let's get out of here," she whispered to Steve. "More bad stuff is going to happen."

Steve nodded, and they both turned to look out over the village. Tara felt with a clarity, with a certainty of her heritage that for some reason she was where she was supposed to be, that she and Delores and Sabrina and Steve and Robert, and even Carl and those who were killed the day before were destined to be just exactly where they were now. They all had a purpose, and maybe it was just for her to get to see her parents again, to find out what she should do for the rest of her life.

In the village Robert found something on the ground and was bending down over it. He stood and looked at the brush and rocks where Tara and Steve were. Robert walked behind the burning remains of the building and went out of sight. He moved cautiously, deliberately, like an old man who didn't want to fall.

*Grandfather, help us, Tara prayed.*

*Please help us.*

*I don't want to bring more death.*

# Chapter 11

Robert appeared at the far edge of the clearing. He walked around the smoldering huts, carrying a large pack on his back. He held a lump in front of him, close to his body.

A child. Robert was holding a child. Tara started to walk out from the tree, and Steve put his hand on her arm.

"Wait," he said softly. "Let him come to us."

Robert looked like a street person with his entire belongings carried with him. He was holding a little girl. Her feet dangled down, flopping with each step he took. One arm fell toward the dirt as Robert increased his pace, walking fast the last twenty yards, his eyes bright under the soot on his face. He handed the girl to Tara as he entered the shade of the tree.

Tara held her arms out and clutched the girl, looking at Robert and then sat down behind the tree.

"She's breathing," Robert said. "I found her behind the huts, under a tree." He motioned to Steve and they walked a few feet away and began talking, his voice a low buzz. The girl was thin, with crude straw sandals, wearing a little white sleeveless shift. She was covered with soot and dirt. She had a nasty looking bump on her forehead and was bleeding from scratches on her arms. She looked to be about five or six years old. The girl moaned and stirred, blinked her eyes, looked at Tara, and began screaming, a high keening sound, saying something over and over, words Tara didn't understand.

Steve spoke to her softly in Spanish. Robert handed Steve a gourd of water and he poured some on her lips. The girl looked at him and then the others. Tara helped her sit up. Steve introduced them, pointed to each in turn as he told the girl their names. He pointed to her.

"Felicia," she mumbled, her eyes wide. She trembled and Tara gave her a slight hug. Steve handed the water gourd to Tara, and Felicia took two swallows, and then handed it to Tara. She seemed comfortable with Tara's arms around her, so they stayed like that.

"I don't think we can stay here long," Robert said, looking back at the village from under the tree.

"What'd you find?" Tara asked. Robert began talking as he

watched the village.

"It looks like the village was attacked from the air. There is no other place to land, and no signs of an attacking party being here, no footprints of army boots, no rifle brass. The huts and the main building look as if they were strafed or hit with rocket fire, maybe in an attempt to kill the terrorists if they were hiding there. The man in front of the main building is dead, I don't know what killed him, didn't get close enough, although his wounds are fatal from what I could see.

"In the back by the huts, there are three more bodies, at least one of them from our terrorist group, maybe more in the huts. Then I found the girl. She may have tripped and hit her head when she ran. I didn't see anyone else. I found the bags of water and some sacks of roots next to one of the huts."

"Except for the dead one, any sign of the terrorists?" Steve asked.

"None." He looked around. "But they can't be far away."

"Felicia," Steve said. He sat on the ground next to her and began talking quietly in Spanish. She told him that there had been about twenty people living in the village, her uncle and aunt, who lived in the largest hut behind the church, and four other families. The village also had a priest, but he was away, maybe down by the coast, at another village. They had visits sometimes by the terrorists, sometimes the soldiers with helicopters, and sometimes with the drug people. She said in a grave tone of voice that maybe most of the people in the village were dead or gone.

"Mamma y Pappa?" Steve asked quietly.

Felicia shook her head. "Vamos, dead," she said. Tara's heart stopped, and she kept her arms around the little girl.

"Okay," Steve said suddenly, as if he had been wondering what to do and it came to him. "Let's see if we can get out of here before the terrorists return. We need food and water, and I'm going to ask our new friend here where we might find some. We'll fashion packs as we go, and we should be only a day at the most from the village where the bus dropped us off. Let's get the hell out of here." He stood up.

"What about her?" Tara asked.

"Que..." Steve asked the girl. "Do you know the way to the coast? She shook her head. No.

"Food and water?"

"Si."

Tara got up on her knees and pulled Felicia up until the girl was standing, with Tara's arms still around her.

"Ask her if she can walk," Tara said to Steve, and before he could say anything, Felicia stepped away from Tara and walked under the tree, out into the open and into the village. Tara caught up with her and took her hand. Felicia looked up at her and squinted, but didn't pull her hand away. She tugged at Tara's hand and pulled her around the remains of the large building in the middle of the clearing. Tara let herself be led by the little girl, the small sandals sending up little puffs of dust as they walked away from the heat. Tara turned and looked at Steve and her two friends. They were leaving the shelter of the rocks and brush and starting out into the clearing. She didn't see Robert.

She led Tara past the remains of the huts, glancing once at the end hut, and then into the brush behind the clearing. They were on a path, wide enough for Tara to walk beside Felicia. The little girl didn't hesitate and continued down the path, winding now down a slope. Tara heard running water and they came to a small stream cutting across the path. Felicia walked down to the water and then turned to her left along the stream. Tara had to let go of her hand as the path narrowed. The stream was in a small ravine, the banks just higher than Tara's head.

The girl walked a few feet downstream, and then turned back uphill. She pointed. At first Tara didn't see anything. Felicia moved some grass aside, and there was a small cave the size of a car, and Tara could see baskets and gourds, and the others came up behind her.

"Who do you hide your food from?" Steve asked in Spanish.

"People who come with guns," she said. "The people with the army, the Shining Path, and the people with the coca leaf." She looked around at Steve, and then bent down to pull a water gourd out of it's hiding place.

"They'll be back."

"When?"

"Soon, I think, and they will not be nice to us."

"Where are the terrorists, then?" Tara asked.

"On the run, I guess," Steve said, looking around. "But where's the army?"

Robert pointed toward the horizon on the other side of the village. Three wasps rising up from the trees. Helicopters. "There, and we better not be around when they get here."

# **C**hapter **12**

Washington, D.C.
Senate Hearing Room

Fox News Reporter Tony Rodriguez brought the image in sharper, aiming the camera on the witness table. Except for his film crew, the room was empty. They were assigned to film the next two hours of testimony before this obscure committee, and Tony was bored to tears. He waved at Elaine at the second camera position, and she took a seat at the witness table so they could get the contrast right.

Tony stepped in front of the camera, holding an imaginary microphone, and in his best voice announced the boring events that were about to take place. I could be bigger than Geraldo, he thought, maybe as good as Greta or even O'Reilly. I just need a chance. And with Fox News, since I'm not blonde or cute, I need a fucking miracle.

The crew waited behind the camera as the committee members filed in, looking like a group of unhappy judges. It was a beautiful spring day outside and there was golf to be played. Tony looked with some interest at the delegation coming through the back doors. The senior senator from Oregon, his silver hair brushed back and flowing, was leading a small Indian man to the table.

The meeting was called to order by the chair, and there was some discussion at the table before the chairman looked up again.

"Senator Sterling, do you have some opening remarks?"

"Just an introduction, Mr. Chairman," Sterling said as he stood. "I would like to present Chairman Bluefeathers, the tribal council chairman of the Confederated Tribes of the Cold River Indian Reservation of Oregon. He has a short presentation to give to the committee before we work on the agenda of fishing rights."

Bluefeathers stood slowly and looked at the committee members on the bench in front of him. Only a quorum. Well, it didn't matter that the others were missing. What he had to say he was saying for the Great White Father's record. He looked down the table and prayed for the wisdom to say what needed to be said. He waited a full minute and then looked up at the senators and staffers, noting that some of them were already squirming, their attention wandering, beginning to talk with each other. He knew they were wondering if the old Indian knew how to talk. He waited a while longer before he spoke.

In his years of dealing with the Šiyápu he found that they had the patience of a hungry child.

And then he began, speaking in a strong voice, knowing as he spoke that his words would start events that might kill many people.

"On almost every Indian reservation today and for a long time, Veterans Day is a solemn and respected day. We have a special Veterans Day Pow Wow to celebrate this day. Indians have long been members of the armed forces, and we are proud of it. We are proud of our warrior heritage. It was our country first, and we fight for it, regardless of the temporary occupants of power. We have sought peace for many years, and we live in peace with all of our neighbors.

"And now, a neighbor to the United States in South America, the nation of Peru, has taken some of our children and has not returned them safely.

"We have asked for help with our children being held captive in Peru. We have asked the State Department to find our children, and we get delays and double talk.

"We have asked the President of the United States, the Great White Father, to help us, and he is too busy. And now I learn from my relatives, the Yakama Nation, that one of the students made it safely out of the mountains to the Great White Father's embassy in Lima, Peru, and that the Great White Father turned him over to the Peruvian Secret Police and he is most certainly dead."

The senators and staff began talking all at once, some staff members getting up and leaving the room. The people in the audience were talking and shifting in their seats.

"Even if our conquerors will not help us, we will find our children, wherever they may be." Bluefeathers paused, watching the senators, waiting for them to be quiet. They had the temperament of children at the beginning of summer - they didn't listen well. He waited until the room was quiet.

"We will fight Peru, the country, it's citizens, it's armies, to find our children, and you will not, not with your armies and your billions - and you should be ashamed of yourselves.

"Today, we, the Confederated Tribes of the Cold River Indian Reservation of Oregon, declare war on the nation of Peru."

There was a titter of laughter from the back, and then someone began yelling. The chairman of the committee banged his gavel and tried to bring order to the room. Bluefeathers stood, and waited, wondering how they ever got anything done here. Again, the room fell silent.

"We are a sovereign nation, the status given to us by the treaty of 1855, a treaty that recognized our sovereign status as an independent nation, a nation within a state, within a nation. A treaty that was ratified by this very legislative body." Bluefeathers stopped again and waited. This time, no one spoke.

"We believe in this treaty, and we have not broken it. We believe in it even if the Great White Father has a history of breaking his word on almost every treaty that he has entered into with the Indians. At the very least, he has not honored it. Together with our allies, the other Indian nations in this country, those who will help us, we will demand of Peru that our children be released, or we will fight to the death."

The senator from Oregon had a stricken look on his face. He started to rise and Bluefeathers held his hand out and motioned for him to remain seated. The senate staffers were now silent, and although they usually whispered amongst themselves when Bluefeathers had testified in the past, they had somehow amassed the collective wit to realize that this was not the time to gossip. The three senators assigned to the committee were not quite so bright, or respectful.

The chairman was talking to Senator Harkness. Bluefeathers cut them off with a look. He decided to teach more patience, and for thirty seconds there was complete silence.

"We know that you see us as a people incapable of fighting, as people living on handouts. Our treaties with you say that the Great White Father will take care of the Indian people's health and welfare in perpetuity. You may see some of us as a weak people, some of us as drunks. But you must know that we were here before you, before your numbers and your diseases and your promises overwhelmed us. This is our country, and now also yours, and again you have failed us. To the government of Peru, make no mistake - don't believe as the yellow hair Custer did, that we are weak. Some of our people have grown weak with alcohol, drugs, some of our young with gangs, as yours have, and we accept responsibility for growing weak with these distractions, but we are not weak, we are strong."

The senator from Oregon flinched at the last word. Bluefeathers began again.

"We ask the Great White Father no more for help in these things, for help with getting our children back. We see you spend millions and often billions on what amounts to frivolous things, and you don't even give us the time of day when we ask for help. Oh, I know you laugh, as the President of Peru will laugh, but we are warriors.

"And I say to my people and to the leaders of the Indian nations - we need your strength and leadership. To our elders, we need your wisdom and guidance. And then to our people who take up the drugs and booze, get off of it. We will show you the way, for we are the people." Bluefeathers looked at the panel in front of him.

"We know you will try to stop us.

"You can't.

"To our American friends of all races and countries who have come to this our native land - don't fight us.

"Watch us.

"We are warriors once again. We don't ask for help, just get out of the way. We will fight for our children, as you would do for yours. For too long we have stood by and watched our own decline. We may fail in our attempt to get our children back. It may already be too late. Even now, as I speak, we are trying. If the warriors we send to collect our children die while they are trying, we will send more. If we don't get our children back, we will exact a terrible vengeance upon the people of Peru.

"We have tried to live in peace with our neighbors, but time and again you come around, see what little we have left and try and make it yours.

"We still say, okay, white man come crying 'round and want more - we'll give a little until maybe we won't have so much and he won't bother with us. We see that the Great White Father is a generous person, helping people around the world with money and volunteers, and we wonder what we have done to be so neglected and miserable, as if we are now all dead and spirits.

"We go into towns and you scorn us, don't see us, make your jokes. We are the invisible people. We are the People.

"The great Nez Perce Chief Joseph said, 'From this day forward, I will fight no more forever.' I say to you, we will fight forever for our children. And to those Indian children who hear this, go back to your elders and ask...no go back and beg them to teach you the old ways, for they will keep us as a People.

"We are at war."

Tribal Council Chairman Bluefeathers of the Confederated Tribes of the Cold River Indian Reservation of Oregon folded his arms and stared at the senators on the bench. It would do them good, Bluefeathers thought, for the people here in Washington to learn patience. He considered standing there for several minutes, but saw no point in it. He slowly turned and began walking up the aisle behind him. He smiled as he wondered how long the Šiyápu's patience would hold before all hell broke loose, for everyone knew that Šiyápu didn't have the patience of a baby spilyay.

All hell broke loose as Chairman Bluefeathers reached the back door. Staffers began yelling, and the Fox News reporter leapt over a chair like a thirsty coyote going for water, holding his microphone up in front of the startled Senior Senator from Oregon.

A miracle.

At the back door, Bluefeathers sighed, and thought about where his Tara was. He said a quiet prayer for her and wondered how long it would be before the killing started.

# Chapter 13

Portland, Oregon

On their way to Portland Martin told Hawk about former DEA Agent Dennis Underwood, and why they needed to see him.

"We met when Dennis was working out of the Portland DEA office, working on a task force. You may not believe it, but at one time I had long stringy hair and a beard, looked like a strung out crank freak." Martin looked over at Hawk, sliding into the left lane as he passed a car. They were on I-84 between Gresham and Portland, coming up on I-5, going to meet Underwood at his condo in downtown Portland.

"In fact," Martin continued, "when I first met Dennis, we had a meeting in the federal building over on Pine, and they made me wait in the lobby until someone from the Portland Police Bureau came in and identified me."

"You looked that bad, huh?" Hawk said, smiling.

"I couldn't cash a check with my relatives, that's how bad I looked, and here I was in this meeting with the feds, DEA no less, but the DEA then were the cocaine cowboys, going after major smugglers from Columbia, looking like yuppies, successful business men, you know. Anyway, I had been working buying crank outta meth labs from these low life assholes, and all of a sudden I was thrust into this investigation where we were looking at yuppie low life assholes, driving Lexus and Mercedes and BMW's and going to the Arlene Schnitzer Concert Hall listening to the Oregon Symphony and such and it just wouldn't do to have some cranker like me getting into this investigation. We had a meeting in a conference room with a head honcho from the San Francisco office, seven or eight DEA agents, the FBI, IRS, and three people from my team, the Portland Interagency Team.

"The head DEA agent started the meeting by introducing himself, said he was SSAIC Warner, and told the rest of us to do the same."

Hawk looked at Martin, his eyebrows up.

"Oh, SSAIC is a federal thing for Supervisory Special Agent in

Charge. It's a big thing with them." Martin took the ramp for the I-5 south lane.

He smiled as he told Hawk about their first meeting. The pecking order for federal employees was everything. And those who aren't a part of the order were nothing. Martin had listened as the SSAIC had talked on about the mandate from their respective bosses that they should all work together to get the dopers in jail, dope off the street, and they would do that by going after the big kahuna, the person who got it "off the boat from Columbia." He also said that everything that was learned by one agency would be shared by all, and Martin had stared at him at that. One of the guys from the Sheriff's Office had laughed, causing the SSAIC's cheeks to take on a pink tinge as he said that everything would be shared.

When it came time for Martin to introduce himself, the others looked at him like he was a wino who had taken a wrong turn and found himself at the table. The only thing better was the man sitting next to him. He not only *looked* like a cranker biker, he smelled as if he had just been cooking meth the old fashioned way, with P2P that smelled like cat piss.

He introduced himself as Dennis Underwood from the DEA. Martin noticed that the others in the room treated Underwood as if he had just crawled out of a broken down trailer court and told them he was dating their daughters.

"Dennis took me aside after that meeting and said that we should shave, dress like an insurance salesman, and think about buying large amounts of cocaine. Yuppies. Own a vineyard maybe. Go to the Schnitzer Concert Hall. We were in the big time now with the SSAIC."

Hawk laughed. Martin took the Marquam Bridge and came into the downtown area from the south, looking for Front Street.

"Anyway, we worked these people who were getting a bunch of coke off the boat in the Columbia River, and they had all of the yuppie shit and a shit load of a tax free income. The dopers had a lot of property, cars and the like, and the DEA wanted to seize that stuff under the forfeiture laws. I don't think they even cared about getting the drugs off the street, just seizing the property.

"Dennis and I worked well together, made some busts, and then the last I heard he headed for Peru, working with the DEA contingency there to destroy the cash crop of the entire eastern side of the country.

Said it was pretty hairy. Anyway, he said that he needed to talk to us when I called him and told him that we were going down south to get the students. Said he wanted to talk us out of it."

Martin found Front Street, and then turned on a little short street that ended at the sea wall at the Willamette River, just a few blocks south of downtown. There was an upscale condo unit rising up on the banks of the river, red brick and terraced, with shops on the ground floor on the sidewalk by the sea wall. A marina was below, with a floating restaurant in the center of it. Martin parked on the street and they walked up the winding sidewalk, looking for the retired agent's address.

"You been here before?" Hawk asked.

"Yeah, there was a case a few years ago, a detective sergeant from Portland, a female, was accused of killing her sister. She lived here."

"Did she?"

"No, but she went through a lot before she was able to prove that she didn't. Ended here with the suspect in the river. I'll tell you about it sometime."

Martin looked out over the sparkling blue water of the river, the buildings of east Portland, the Rose Center gleaming at them from across the brightness of the water. They walked up the terraced steps to Underwood's apartment. Underwood answered the door and stood back, looking at Martin and then at Hawk. Underwood looked like a college professor who might teach chemistry or math, a large man with the beginnings of a stomach, gray flowing hair, a gray goatee. He was wearing a black sweater and jeans, holding a glass of milk.

"Martin..." Underwood said as he led them into his living room. "You must be Hawk." He shook hands with Hawk and waved toward the couch and chair. "Please have a seat." Martin stood and looked out the floor-to-ceiling windows, looking at a barge moving up the river.

"Nice view," Martin said.

"Yes, it isn't bad," Dennis Underwood said. "Can I get either of you anything? Drink? Coffee?" He looked at the glass in his hand. "Milk?"

"Coffee."

While Dennis was in the kitchen, Hawk stood with Martin and looked out over the river. "Will this Dennis go to Peru with us?" Hawk asked quietly.

"Not likely," Martin said, "but it won't hurt to ask." Dennis ground coffee and looked at Martin.

"You guys realize that you are in deep shit with the declaration of war thing. What the hell is that all about?"

Martin and Hawk looked at each other, and then back at Dennis.

"You mean you don't know?" he asked, incredulous.

"Know what?" Martin asked.

Underwood shook his head and turned on his television. They watched as the news clip replayed, a video of Bluefeathers talking to a panel of senators, the voice over saying that the Chairman of the Confederated Tribes of the Cold River Indians of Oregon had just declared war on the nation of Peru.

Martin's stomach churned. He looked at Hawk, who just shrugged. It was an Indian thing. Now the chances of them getting into and out of Peru were just about zero.

"Did I understand that you want to go to Peru to look for the students?" Dennis asked. "And, after this...this whatever he just did there in Washington?"

"It's not that we want to go," Hawk said. "We have to. When the chairman tells us to do something, as tribal members, we have to go." He looked from Dennis to Martin. "The Chief here, he doesn't have to, but he has volunteered."

Underwood laughed and took a sip of milk. He clucked his tongue. "Martin, a chief of police and working for a reservation. Who woulda thought. But you're not here to listen to my ideas of how the world should be run, you're here to pick my brain about Peru."

"Yes," Martin said. "What's left of it."

"I think we would be better off in the dining room around the table, with the maps," Underwood said, and he led them into the room and spread a map of Peru on the table.

"I went to Peru the first time 'cause a buddy of mine said that you get to whack people there," Dennis had told Martin. "I had been working for the DEA for about ten years, and thought it was time for something different. And I needed to get away from the rut I was in, working hundred plus hour weeks, living in a surveillance van, making the big bust, then winding down with a few beers and then doing the whole thing all over again. Didn't think we were ever going to stop the major dopers, but I needed to do something different."

He pointed to a place on the map on the Pacific coast of Peru.

"You'll fly into Lima, the capital city, and I hope you have a good reason to be there, because if the government doesn't want you there, you will be on the same plane going back to where you came from. The Peruvian Army, the "Iron Fist," is an extension of the worst of the government, and is one of the region's largest. When you land in Lima, I have a contact for you so you won't be so lost. He'll help you move around the city, rent cars, and maybe work as a guide. In fact, I have several names, the first two are the most reliable. From Lima you will need to travel north along the coast, and then directly east up into the Andes Mountains, and end up on foot. The area is inhabited by Quechua Indians, some scattered villages, occasional army patrols, and drug runners."

Underwood bent over the table, looking at the map, Hawk and Martin on either side of him.

"How long they been gone now?"

"Two days since the first kids were killed."

"When you going?"

"We leave tomorrow from Portland."

"Oh shit," Underwood muttered. He poured coffee and handed mugs to both of them. "Sure you wouldn't want something stronger?" Dennis Underwood looked at them. "Well, I need something, and you would too if you knew what I know about that place.

"From Lima you will go by road to Huaraz, here," Underwood pointed on the map. "It's up the coast about 250 klicks to the north of Lima. The road is paved and pretty good, although the army will have a presence on the road, roadblocks and such, and regardless of what you might think, they won't fuck around. You'd better be tourists, but I don't know what you are going to do with Hawk and whoever else goes with you. They're not stupid, and will be aware of who they have, or who the terrorists have, or just who the hell is in the country. They might think it was a joke, but did you have to declare war on Peru?"

"You gotta be on the reservation to believe it, Dennis," Martin said.

Hawk laughed.

"This is serious shit, Hawk," Dennis said, looking at him as if he were from another planet. "These guys in the army probably killed a lot more innocent people than the terrorists and the drug dealers combined. Let me tell you a story about just how the army fucks with people." He took a long drink from his glass, and then leaned back against the counter and crossed his arms. Martin thought again that he looked like a college professor, but he knew different.

"I was working out of a base camp in the friggin jungle, just east of Huanuco. We had camps set up in the main cocaine growing and processing regions. Most people think that Columbia is the cocaine capital of the world, but more coca leaf is grown in Peru than in any other country. Our camps consisted of tents with wooden floors, and we had about ten of us per tent. We had UH-1 Hueys on loan from the government, and worked with the army to eradicate processing labs, and generally fuck with the drug runners. We lived and worked as if we were a forward army base camp in a time of war.

"We wore camo fatigues in camp, carried M-16s anytime we were out of the tent, and I mean, man, that we were in a small clearing surrounded by a high, tropical jungle, and everything out there is hostile. When we got word of a processing plant, and these things were portable, we would load up and go look for it, but it was usually fucked up from the start. The Peruvian army liaison colonel would screw around until we were in a wait status from 7 in the morning until 10 or so, and then we would fly, three Hueys, sometimes shadowing a squad on the ground, and usually when we got to the clearing or village where the processing had been going on, we would find traces of the plant, but no plant. By then the plant was on a bunch of donkeys somewhere, going to the next location. The colonel would make a lot of noise and pretend to be pissed, but we knew that someone had paid him, and we were just making it look good. The ones we did take down I think were those who didn't pay him.

"We'd look for druggies and run into terrorists. When the army found a suspected terrorist location, the army troops would strafe, bomb, shoot, kill, pillage a village until there was nothing left. Hell, most of those people didn't know what hit them, were not part of the drug trade, not part of the terrorist organization . . .

"One morning we were on hold, waiting beside our helicopters for orders to fly. Three army copters had taken off a couple of hours earlier, and then we were told to load up, to look for a village where they had a suspected processing plant.

"When we got there we could see smoke on the approach, and landed in a field close to a medium sized village. Everything was on fire including what had remained of the people. The army people assigned to us said that the terrorists had invaded the village and killed all of the people. There were eleven of us in the DEA contingent, and we approached the village as if we were in combat, and we were. I led a six-man patrol through the village, most of the huts now just embers and ash. The grass was on fire as we came through a small grove of trees. There were three people huddled behind the first tree, a woman and two kids about ten or twelve. They all had been shot. One of my men signaled me and pointed to the brass on the ground. He picked up several and handed one to me, putting the rest in his pocket. They were M-16 rounds, and the terrorists carried AK 47's. The people had been killed by the army.

"This entire village was staged for us. A show. Most of my team wanted to shoot it out with the army right then and there, but we wouldn't have gotten out of the country alive, and our deaths would have been attributed to the terrorists, or maybe the druggies. The village had been assaulted from the air and the ground, and we quietly picked up a lot of M-16 brass, used exclusively by the government troops. Even if it was a show, a stage for our benefit, the army got a lot out of it. They showed the Indians, the terrorists, and the druggies that they were in charge, and would do anything they wanted. It may have been a show but the people were very dead.

"In fact, the cocksucker didn't even care what we believed, he knew that in our reports we could write about our suspicions, but we couldn't really prove anything, you see, so we looked at bodies of whole families butchered by the army.

"And you guys are going to a foreign country with a kick ass army that has probably already killed the students, and you are going to get them out?

"Bullshit," Dennis said angrily, staring at the river.

"You're gonna get dead, is what you're gonna get, and Hawk and everyone else who goes with you. I don't know why I'm doing this, cause it won't do any good. Just what makes you think you can succeed?"

"Ever been on a reservation?" Hawk asked.

Dennis shook his head.

"There would be some people would think that this is a good thing, Indians killed in Peru, Indians going to Peru to get killed. That's one thing we do so very well, white man come 'round and say, 'anybody want to die today?' We got third generation fetal alcohol syndrome babies, land that nobody wanted and put us on it, some crack houses, gangs, but we also got a spirit, and a generation of elders who will make a difference. 'Go back to the old ways,' they say. Hell, the 'old ways' was to die and be convenient for the white man. I appreciate your help, Dennis, I really do, and so do my people, and your concern. Martin here, he doesn't have to go with us. We're going. Then you can come 'round and say, 'what a buncha stupid fucking Indians.' Maybe we need to die honorably again. My cousin, my father, my friends, many of them die pukin' their guts out with alcohol. Pukin their bloody livers right out their throats. I've been there, I've seen that. Maybe happen to me someday, but I doubt it. We haven't been presented with a way to die with honor for a hundred years. Hell, we'll get volunteers from over a hundred tribes." Martin looked at Hawk with surprise.

"To die. . .in. . .Peru. My friend Martin," and Hawk touched Martin's shoulder, his first act of friendship, "he doesn't have to go, but Martin, he has some things to prove too, I know. Coming 'round dying, that ain't so bad, just not getting the chance to die. The old ones need new stories to tell our kids, something out of the twentieth century."

Martin looked at Hawk. That's the most Hawk has talked since I've known him, he thought.

Hawk smiled, uncomfortable, embarrassed now.

"Okay, I'll shut up and help you," Dennis said, grinning. "Didn't mean to get you going. But if you want to die honorably in Peru, I guess I can help you get there." He pointed at the map. "According to the news reports, the kids were killed and the others captured right here, above Huaraz.

"They would have been taken uphill, to this area, since if they went down, it would be easier for the army to find them. If they go over the top of the Andes and make it down to the jungle on the east side into the Amazon basin, it would be impossible to find them. I don't think the terrorists will take them that way. They want to make a statement where they can be found."

Martin studied the map, looking at the elevation markers. "Is that 6,000 meters?"

"Yes, and there are higher passes in the area. About 18,000 feet. Too high for them to go, but it can be done."

"How should we look for them?"

"Leave Lima in a truck or van," Dennis said. "I'll try to arrange for a van and a good driver to meet you at the airport. Go to Huaraz, but you must know that the army will have patrols and roadblocks all over the backcountry. The terrorists may have a leader in the brush with them who has his shit together, but don't count on it. It may be a bunch of kids with guns."

"What about guns?" Hawk asked.

"You can't get into the country with them," Dennis said. "If I try to locate someone to get some to you, you may be betrayed or compromised before you get there. Your best bet is to ask your driver and then be careful. If you get caught with a gun, you will be in prison or shot. Maybe you should pretend that you haven't heard what is going on, and hire your guide to take you to the ruins that the kids went to. You'll then be in the same area with a very plausible excuse.

"Last thing, if you become hunted, you might stand a better chance of getting to the embassy in Lima than any other place. There are six to eight million people in the metropolitan area around Lima and you might be able to get lost there for awhile.

He raised his glass to Martin, then to Hawk.

"Well, good luck, amigos. I'll make some calls for you, Martin, and have a contact to meet you at the airport. Once you leave Lima, you're pretty much on your own. And if there's a war going on –"

He rolled the map and gave it to Martin. He shook Martin's hand at the door and leaned close to him.

"This is about the school, isn't it?"

Martin looked out at the water. He waited a minute and then spoke.

"Maybe, I don't know."

"You think you have to do this?"

"Yeah, I guess I do."

Dennis Underwood nodded and extended his hand to Hawk.

"Take care of this fool...he's worth it."

As Underwood shut the door he shook his head again, knowing with a certainty that he would never see either one alive. He grimaced, thinking of things in South America that he didn't tell them, things about the drug runners, private armies, terrorists, the army, the secret police.

They didn't stand a fucking chance.

# **C**hapter **14**

Hawk deftly moved through traffic, letting Martin direct him to their destination. They had a shopping list from the chairman, and from the number of stops they had to make, it would take them most of the day. Their planning for the most part was finished. They would be in Cold River for a few hours and return to Portland to the airport.

"What was that about, the school?" Hawk asked.

Martin didn't respond.

"If we're in this together, I'd like to know."

Martin waited, and then spoke, softly at first, so Hawk had to lean over to hear.

"I think I'll give you the short version," Martin said. "The long version is just not something I want to relive." Martin started talking, and when he got to the part about his arrival at the school, Hawk pulled over and Martin finished the story.

"Underwood was leaning on my car as I came out of the school. He didn't say anything, he was just there. I guess I kinda lost it after that," he told Hawk. "I didn't go back to work for months, and then finally resigned. Oh, I know, I'd seen a lot of death working homicide, but I hadn't held a child who died in my arms." He looked at Hawk.

"This is my first job in four years."

"Well, someone must like you to recommend you to us."

Martin nodded.

*At night, I can still feel her breath*

They went over the plan as Hawk drove back to the rez. They were to take American Airlines to Miami, then on to Lima. Twenty-four hours of travel to get to Lima, then up to the countryside.

"We're going to pose as tourists," Martin said. Hawk laughed.

"Do I look like a tourist to you, Martin?"

"No, not really," Martin said, "but it's the best plan I can come up with in a short time, and it will work as well as any."

This is crazy, Martin thought. But then, Claire didn't make it to age seven. What am I afraid of?

# Chapter 15

Huascaran National Park
Peru

Delores carefully placed her swollen feet in the icy stream and moaned.

"I may never leave here, Tara Red Eagle," Delores said. "My feet haven't felt so good since we left home."

Felicia reached under the bank and pulled a basket from it's hiding place. The villagers must live in fear, Tara thought, to have a hidden supply.

Tara heard someone running along the path they had just used, running fast, and she looked for a place for them to hide when Robert flashed into view, coming from the direction of the camp, his face streaked with ash and sweat. He carried a rifle and a green pack.

"Soldiers," he panted and stopped, "in the village and they're coming this way."

"How far?" Tara asked. Steve jumped across the narrow stream to join them.

"Don't know, maybe a minute." Robert leaned over and put his hands on his knees, handing the rifle to Steve as he fought to recover. "Been . . . running . . . fast," he gasped. "I don't think they saw me, but I don't know."

Steve held the rifle and looked at Robert as the others crowded around him on the narrow trail.

"Where'd the rifle come from?"

"Tell . . . you later, when I . . . get my breath."

"I don't think they will chase you as fast," Steve said. "If they're army, I'm sure they have run after people in the hills before, with disastrous results. In fact, they may not follow you at all."

Tara heard a shout down the path toward the village, and any thoughts they had about them not following Robert were gone. She started to tell Steve that maybe they should trust the soldiers but before she could get it out, she heard someone firing a rifle, not far off, the sound loud. She felt rather than heard a bullet brush past her head, fluttering through the air as if it were a deadly, fast moving insect. The rocks and brush snapped and jumped around them. Robert snatched the rifle from Steve's outstretched hands and ran behind their little group and fired a long burst back at the soldiers, running toward them as they came out onto the trail a hundred yards back.

The sound was deafening. The soldiers disappeared from view, and Robert stopped firing and yelled.

"Let's go." Another burst of gunfire came from down the trail, and then it was silent.

Tara jumped at the sound of the close firing, her ears ringing, and as she turned to run she heard a cry behind her. Delores fell backward and sat heavily on the trail, her feet splayed out in front of her, looking down at her feet as if she had never seen them before, the dust of the trail turning to mud where her wet legs had landed. A red stain was spreading on the left side of her chest and she brushed at it absently, trance-like, as if it were a fly to chase away. Tara stood with her ears pounding, her feet rooted to the spot. Close by, Robert fired an answering burst of gunfire, and it was quiet again. Steve yelled something, and he dropped to the trail beside Delores.

"Nooo!" Tara yelled, and ran back to Delores, dropping her gourds, throwing herself on the ground beside her friend. Sabrina came up behind Delores and held her head, looking over Delores' shoulder at Tara. She shook her head, a small negative shake.

"Delores, can you hear me?" Tara said softly.

Delores nodded. "I–"

"Shhhhhh, don't try to talk," Tara said, fighting tears, knowing she couldn't sob in front of Delores. Tara saw movement behind Sabrina and Steve rocked forward on his knees, his face white, his right arm bleeding, the blood soaking through his shirt and starting to run down his fingers. Tara could sense that Robert was to her back, covering the trail.

Steve spoke to Felicia in rapid Spanish, telling her to lead them away from the troops and find a place where they could hide from them.

"Si, padre," she said, and turned and ran up the trail, following the river bank, carrying a basket and a water gourd, the gourd banging crazily on her back. Sabrina followed behind Felicia. Steve and Robert got on either side of Delores. Robert handed Tara the rifle and pack and they bent over and picked Delores up in a chair carry. He looked at Delores's wound and then up at Tara again. His eyes told her that he knew that Delores was a dead woman.

"Oh, God, leeeaaaaave me, pleeeze leave me here," Delores cried, and Steve and Robert ran with her, Delores's head banging against Steve's shoulder, both men running awkwardly, grunting.

Tara ran behind them. Delores cried out and Tara cried with her, tears making streaks in the dust on her face.

"Don't huh-" Tara sobbed.

"Don't hurt her, Steve." Tara cried as she saw blood from Delores's wound running down Steve's good arm. Up ahead, Felicia turned and plunged into the brush, and then Sabrina disappeared from sight. Steve and Robert stopped when they came to the place where Felicia left the trail, and Steve gathered Delores up in his arms and plunged into the brush, holding her as one might hold a child. Delores looked unconscious.

Or dead.

Robert followed Steve off the trail for several yards, and then touched his shoulder and Steve stopped. Tara came up behind them, numb. Robert took the rifle from her and reached over and wiped some blood from Steve's arm and looked closely at the wound. Steve said something to Robert that Tara couldn't hear and Robert walked back down the trail toward the stream. He didn't look back as he disappeared from view.

Tara put her arms around Delores and gave her a soft hug, and then looked up at Steve.

"I can't carry her anymore," Steve said. "I can't feel my right arm and the left one's gone. We need to get her further up away from the main trail."

Tara put her arm under Delores's legs and then slid her left arm under Steve's, getting a grip, feeling the weight settle and pull on her muscles. She wondered how Steve was able to carry Delores as far as he had. His arms were slippery with blood, his chest slick and glistening, as if he had been working out and was sweating blood. They started off, awkward at first, and Delores moaned, mercifully not awake.

Steve and Tara moved another hundred yards through the scrub brush and came upon Felicia and Sabrina. They gently laid Delores down, Steve taking most of her weight with him, and then slumped down beside her, his dark face a pasty gray. Tara looked back over their trail and couldn't see very far. They should be safe here for a while, especially since she didn't think Robert would be taken quietly. Sabrina got some water and was ripping up Delores's shirt and began cleaning around the wound, an ugly hole and bruise in the chest above Delores's left breast. Sabrina placed a patch of cloth on the bleeding hole in Delores's chest, and held it there until it stuck to the blood. They rolled Delores slightly to look at her back. Sabrina ripped the blood soaked shirt down to expose Delores's back, and drew her breath in sharply as she saw the exit wound. The bullet had blasted a part of her back away leaving a hole the size of a baseball. Sabrina packed cloth around it from her shirt. They sat there, looking at each other, Tara and Sabrina, knowing that their friend was dying, not wanting to say it out loud, not wanting to talk about it.

Tara sat there holding Delores and could hear Sabrina talking quietly with Steve, heard her rip his shirt to look at his wound. Sabrina came from the poorest of the poor on the reservation, and Tara knew that as she was growing up, Sabrina had to patch up a lot of people. They just didn't go to the hospital in those days. Tara wiped Delores's face with a corner of her shirt, wiping the dirt and a smudge of blood from her face. She bent down to listen to her friend's breathing, and thought that it wasn't there, but after a minute, Delores gave a little hitch and took in a deeper breath.

Steve and Sabrina were whispering, with Felicia joining in at the end. Tara watched as Sabrina and Felicia walked past her, down the trail. They returned a few minutes later, carrying two poles. They sat on the ground with the poles between them and began fashioning a stretcher with the baskets and thongs from the gourds. Felicia's hands flew fast, weaving the baskets over the ends of the poles. Tara watched, held Delores tightly and rocked with her, trying to elevate the wound. Once, she thought she heard voices, but she wasn't going anywhere, she was staying with Delores.

Robert came back quietly, not running this time, his face bright with the adrenalin of combat. He squatted at Delores's feet, facing back along the trail.

"I obscured our trail down the hill a ways," he said quietly. "I placed some evidence alongside the trail and then crossed the stream. They should be able see it even at a run."

"They gonna buy it?" Steve asked.

"Might, if they don't have a good tracker with them."

"What evidence?" Tara asked, stroking Delores's cheek.

"Drops of blood."

As Tara held Delores, Steve and Robert spread their possessions out on the trail. They had woefully little: Two water gourds, three baskets of food, containing what looked like ground root, and the AK47 assault rifle. Robert had several magazines of ammunition in the small green bag.

"We have no maps, sleeping bags, tents, phones, or even Taco Bell," Robert said.

"And at least two groups of people looking to kill us," Steve added. "What do you think about the army? Can we expect any help there if they know who we are?"

Robert shook his head.

"Why not?" Sabrina asked.

"They must have been following us when we were climbing up to the village," Robert said. "Not a bad tactic, hitting the village from the air, and that I'm sure of, and then dropping a squad off below us, a squad that could then come back into the village on foot, looking at the dead people as if the terrorists had hit the camp first. They might even have it on film.

"Anyway, when I went back into the village, they must have been resting, because one of their lookouts saw me, and that's what saved me. I had found the rifle and ammo bag under a mat at the edge of the village, and was carrying the rifle when the army guy saw me. I don't think he even saw the rifle, or they all would have opened up, but their lookout didn't want to go down the trail after me alone, so he had to wait for the rest of the squad to catch up. I got lucky." He looked at Steve and Delores.

"You guys didn't."

Tara looked up at him and held onto her friend. "What about Delores, we can't leave her."

"No," Steve said. "We don't leave anyone."

They talked quietly for several minutes. As Tara listened she couldn't help but think that this was not real, that she would wake up and be home or in her room in Eugene. Robert left again to look for the army, and when he came back, the lines of the trees in the afternoon sun meant that they didn't have much time before dark.

"They went back toward the village," Robert said. "No way of knowing if they left someone out there in a listening post though."

"Chance we'll have to take," Steve said. "We can't stay here long. We have to get Delores to a doctor and I have a hunch that the army will be back here in force in the morning." He said doctor without much conviction, but at least it was something, Tara thought. When they left, Tara and Sabrina carried the stretcher, moving slowly. Felicia followed, with Robert and Steve up ahead. They walked downhill until they came to the path by the stream again. As they turned onto the trail by the stream, Felicia tugged on Tara's arm. She said something that Tara didn't get, and they turned back down the trail.

"Steve," Tara said. He walked back toward her. Tara pointed at the little girl and Steve motioned for Felicia to join him. They talked, quietly, in Spanish. She waved at Tara, and they walked slowly back toward the village.

"She's going to wait for the army to leave, and then the villagers who are alive will come back. This is her home."

They walked slowly, and after what seemed like a mile (Tara knew it was more like a quarter of a mile) Tara called to Sabrina to put the stretcher down. They lowered it gently, and after a minute, with her muscles still screaming, Tara picked up the poles again. The sun was going down behind the mountain to the north of them as Robert came back and told them that they would stop for the night. They had covered what Tara thought was four miles, over a ridge and then part way down the other side. Delores cried out, and then was quiet.

As they moved off the trail behind Robert, Tara saw Delores was watching her, her eyes glistening with pain.

They moved into a circle of rocks and set up camp as best they could. Sabrina started to prepare the food they carried, mixing flour and water to make dough. Robert and Steve talked about making a fire, and in the end decided that they had to risk it, looking for root, brush, wood, anything that would burn.

Tara held Delores, knowing that her friend was dying, knowing with a bitter certainty that if she had picked Las Vegas for a vacation that her friend would not be dying in a strange land. She thought of her mother and father, dead these long years, and wondered what she should do.

Think of the message of the coyote, her father had said. She looked at Delores in the dark and didn't see any message there, only pain and death.

"Will you draw me?" Delores whispered, closing her eyes.

Tara nodded, not trusting herself to speak. She held Delores tighter.

"I'll draw you and all the little brown babies you'll have, every one," Tara managed to say, and a tear fell from her eye and rolled down her cheek. She traced Delores's face with her finger, trying hard not to break down.

*That should be me there on the stretcher. That should be me.*

# Chapter 16

Cold River Indian Reservation
Oregon

Hawk drove the Bronco up the canyon, the headlights sweeping across the sage brush and rock formations. He slowed and turned off the pavement and onto a dirt track. The lights of Cold River were far below. Martin saw the lights of a house ahead and they turned into a gravel driveway and stopped. A light on a pole lighted the area in front of the house.

Hawk's truck, a Ford diesel pickup with a camper crouched on the back, was parked in front of the house. His wife Susan's Honda Accord was on a cement pad in front of the garage. A typical western ranch style house, with Detroit and Japanese cars in the driveway. The grass in front of the house, the gravel driveway, all had a manicured quality to it, and Martin looked at Hawk as he got out. A fishing boat was parked on the side of the house, waiting patiently for summer.

"Hawk, this is . . ."

"What'd you expect, a tent?"

Martin shook his head.

"Well, I know you white guys call them 'teepees,' but mostly we call them tents."

Martin laughed.

Susan met them at the front door. "Chief Andrews," she said warmly. "Please come in."

Martin had met Hawk's wife on several occasions, usually when Hawk met her for lunch, but he met her often on the job, since Susan was an EMT assigned to one of the ambulance crews. Another enigma. She rode a motorcycle to work and chewed tobacco, had collar length dark hair (shorter than her husband's hair) was pretty, smiled a lot, liked to kid, and was substantially younger than Hawk. She was wearing jeans and a Seattle Seahawks football jersey. Martin looked back at Hawk, who stood there grinning.

"Chief thought maybe we lived in a teepee, one of them tents," Hawk said, and he laughed.

"Did not," Martin protested. He stepped past Susan and stopped just inside the living room and looked around. There was a large television in the corner, a couch, and on the wall above the television, a large dream catcher, a round hoop with beautiful white fur and feathers. On the opposite wall Martin saw a computer work station, with a child's buckskin dress thrown over a chair, an incongruous display of the past and present that didn't seem as strange as it was at first.

A home. That's what made it different from his rental place. The dining room had folded clothes on the table. A home. He didn't know what he thought he would find in Hawk's house and he was bothered that he was surprised. He knew that it was important to Hawk that Martin come to his house on their last night here.

A blur came down the hallway and ran past Martin, yelling "Daddeeee," and launched itself at Hawk. Martin had a glimpse of a little girl in a nightgown and bunny slippers run past him. Hawk scooped her up and brought her into the living room, the girl's arm tight around his neck.

"Martin, this is uh, this is Maya, our daughter."

"Hi Maya," Martin said.

Maya buried her face in Hawk's neck and then peeked at Martin.

"Maya is five, and definitely not shy," Susan said. "When she knows you, she won't ever stop talking."

A young boy wearing Star Wars pajamas came out of the hallway and looked at Martin. Susan made the introductions.

"Our son, Danny."

Danny walked past Martin and glanced at him and then walked to his dad's side and put his arms around Hawk's massive leg. Martin suddenly felt like an awful intruder, imposing on a family on their last night.

"Why are you still up?" Hawk asked.

"I said that they could get up to see you before you go to Peru," Susan said, holding her hands out to Maya. The girl shook her head. No. Susan walked to the kitchen and motioned for Martin to follow. Hawk led the kids to the couch and was growling at Maya when Martin followed Susan to the kitchen.

"They're going to miss him so much," Susan said as they watched Hawk growl, tickle, and laugh with the kids. "And today Maya said that she didn't want her daddy to go to Peru and find her Aunt Tara. She didn't want her daddy to get hurt."

"What do the kids know about what we are trying to do?" Martin asked.

"Everything. If they didn't hear it from us they would hear it at school. There are no secrets here. Some of the kids told Maya and Danny today that their dad was going to get killed in Peru. Danny and Maya are very proud of their dad, and they know he must go, but they don't want him to leave."

"What about you?"

"Hawk is the best thing that ever happened to me, but I...I wouldn't have it any other way. He has to go, and you don't. If he didn't go, he wouldn't be able to stay here. The Hawk I married would go and die in Peru trying to do the right thing, before he would even consider not going. Don't think he doesn't hurt at the thought of not being here to see his kids grow up, or with me, but he has to go. Don't you see that, you Šiyápu?" She said Šiyápu softly. Susan put her hand on Martin's arm.

"If you can," she said, "take care of him and see that he makes it back. I'd kinda like to have him come cryin' around me every now and then, telling me what he wants from his wife."

Susan walked to a sliding glass door in the dining room and opened it. "Come with me," she told Martin, and then louder, "Hawk, I'm going on the deck."

"Yeah, go ahead and do that smoking thing outside." He shook his head and Martin heard him muttering about his wife being a medic and smoking.

They stood looking out over the dark desert, the spring night air cool, the stars brilliant, more than Martin remembered from his childhood in the country.

He had been in the city for twenty years, and was still startled by the number of stars that you could see from the high desert. Martin could see the lights of the community of Cold River, just down the canyon.

Susan smoked in silence as they watched the stars and the distant lights. Martin felt like an imposter, the worst kind of intruder, but he couldn't refuse Hawk when he was invited out to his house. They had planning to do, things to pack, had to pick up Lori and head to Portland. When they went back in, he would tell Hawk that he needed to go, thank him, and then take the Bronco back to Cold River.

"I'm sure you've heard that Hawk is one of the best trackers in the country," Susan said softly.

Martin nodded.

"He learned as a child from his grandfather, and then his father. When he was twelve, he found a lost hunter when the men couldn't find him. The elders looked at Hawk differently after that. As far as they were concerned, he was a man. I think you know that Hawk is very proud of who he is, of what he is and his place here. This tribe needs him. He wants to be the police chief, be on the tribal council, be chairman someday. And he will be good at it.

"Last fall, before you got here, Hawk was called up to northern Idaho to track a little girl who had gotten separated from her family in an early snow storm. People there had tried to find her, thought all was lost, that she would never be found, and one of the deputies who had worked with Hawk up on the Umatilla Reservation told the search and rescue people to call Hawk.

"He left within ten minutes of getting the call. Told me that it could be Maya up there in the woods, freezing, wanting her mommy, her daddy, her brother. You see, he had to go, and there was never any question in my mind that he would find her. He can read sign where the best trackers can't find it, can follow a track in the snow where there isn't any. It's uncanny, it's . . . it's just Hawk.

"When Hawk got there the searchers were ready to go home, thinking that the little girl would never be found, and he made them stay, complete strangers, and he began looking at the area where she had last been seen, an area that was part of the Bitterroot Mountain chain, an area with steep canyons and large pine trees. Rock faces and escarpments. An area with ten inches of new snow.

"When Hawk started looking for the girl, he started in an area directly opposite from where the searchers had been concentrating their efforts. He knew that they had to find the girl that day, or they wouldn't find her alive. The search began over again, and Hawk organized teams to go down from the ridge line and look under trees, bushes, rock. They searched all day, and when it got dark, most of the searchers went home, except for the family and Hawk. But he knew that the girl couldn't survive another night alone in the woods, that she would die. It isn't that he knows how to track, he knows where to track, where to look. He knows just where people or animals will go, as if he could see for them, as if he somehow was them. He found that little girl just before eleven at night, her body shut down with hypothermia, and Hawk ran her down to the cars, carrying her, running, yelling."

Susan lit another cigarette, and shook her head and laughed softly. "Can you imagine Hawk running down hill, carrying a little girl? Wouldn't think he could run, would you? He told me later that he was going to find her, that he would still be there if he hadn't.

"He will find his cousin, Tara, those other people, and yes, he still believes they are alive. If he dies, he believes it was the right time for him to die. He is, without a doubt, the bravest man I know."

Susan looked at Martin and touched his arm. "He just gets too damned noble sometimes for his own good, Martin. Please make sure that he does his noble macho thing in Peru, and then bring his big ass back here to me. Okay?"

Martin nodded. He turned to look through the glass door into the house. Hawk was still on the couch, his head back, Maya and Danny sleeping in his arms, their heads on his chest. Hawk turned his head slowly and looked at Martin and Susan as they came in.

"What you two been cryin' around about without me?" he whispered.

"How handsome you look, Husband."

"Yeah, right. Let me put these two to bed and I'll show you handsome."

She smiled.

"Uh, look, I think I should go," Martin said, looking at the front door.

"Man, you're gonna stay right here, we'll make a bed for you on this couch. Then we'll get up in . . ." Hawk looked at his watch, "we'll get up in three hours, meet the others, and head for Peru." He grinned. "Then do battle with an army of a million, fight the terrorists that get in our way, and, uh, take care of the drug runners for good measure." He laughed and rocked forward, standing with his sleeping kids, and walked down the hallway.

Martin felt strangely at home for the first time since he had arrived on the rez. In the morning he was going to Peru with this large, gentle, wise man who was now calling him friend. Hawk and Susan came out into the hallway. Hawk headed for the kitchen.

"Oh, yeah, and we're gonna save the young women in distress while we're in-country, helping them with their other problems. Getting them home, they'll be properly grateful."

Hawk laughed, his large frame shaking as Susan started for him, telling him what she was gonna do if he even thought about "grateful."

Martin didn't know what they would find in Peru, who they would leave behind in shallow graves, but he knew it would be bad. Maybe they should call the whole thing off and urge the Indians to try the State Department again.

He thought of Claire as she died in his arms, and he thought of how he couldn't save her. He shivered and could feel her breath on his cheek.

Somehow he knew the killings would begin again before they arrived in Peru.

# Day Four

# Chapter 17

It was still dark when Hawk drove the Bronco down the hill to the agency past the red brick of the Bureau of Indian Affairs school as they passed. Ahead of them, down toward the police department and jail the street lights cut empty circles of light out of the black streets.

They entered the parking lot of the police department and saw several cars in the lot, some with parking lights on, motors running. Sgt. Lamebull had a patrol car parked in front, backed up to the building. The interior light was on and he was writing in a notebook. He looked up as they drove in and parked beside him. Martin saw Lori get out of her car and walk toward them, wearing jeans and tennis shoes, a brown leather jacket, her long brown hair swinging as she walked.

They assembled in front of the lobby, out on the sidewalk. Lori dropped a backpack.

"I can't believe I'm here," she said, shaking her head. "Especially with the chief and the captain. I must be crazy, going to Peru with the two people I have embarrassed. You guys must have wanted some comic relief."

"No, just an interpreter," Hawk growled. Martin watched the two of them looking at each other, and knew that Hawk didn't forgive her for her McGruff stunt, something that made him look bad, like he couldn't control his own people. Martin hadn't gotten used to the order of things here, and even though Lori's antics should have been an employee problem, he knew that with Hawk and Lori, it was more than an employee situation. Way more.

Dan Martinez and Sherman Tewee came up and waited by the Bronco. Tewee had been a police officer in the past, and was now the director of the Natural Resources Department. About thirty, he was fit, wore his hair long, wore Levis and a flannel shirt. Martin had heard that Tewee was an army vet and a good tracker. He knew his way around a city, having lived in San Francisco for several years.

Martinez was a medic and fire fighter. He too, had once been on the police department, but left as many tribal members did because they were not always well liked in the community. Here on the rez as well as the rest of the world, people may hate the police, but the damned fire fighters and medics were always loved.

"You bring the gear we asked for?" Hawk asked Tewee.

"In the bag," Tewee said. "The phones were guaranteed to work on the new satellites in that area. Guess we'll find out when we get there."

"Let's load the Bronco," Hawk said. "We'll be leaving in a couple of minutes." He looked at Tewee and Martinez. "You boys bring your passports?" Hawk looked at them and they both nodded.

Martin looked out toward the street as a car came into the parking lot. A new Dodge pickup pulled up and stopped. Chairman Bluefeathers got out and walked over to them.

"Hello Martin," he said. "You think you can bring them back with this bunch you have here?"

"We're gonna try," Martin said. "We'll be in Peru in about sixteen hours. Any word from the feds?"

Bluefeathers shook his head. "The Great White Father won't help us, doesn't want to get involved. Nothing, no word."

"How you gonna do here while we're gone?" Hawk asked.

Bluefeathers looked at his nephew. "For a youngster you sure have the idea I can't take care of things when you're gone. Well, I still can, and will. You'll see when you get to Bear Creek Springs."

"See what?"

"Just get going, bring them back. We'll have someone monitoring the phones and cell phones day and night." Bluefeathers gathered them together and gave them a blessing before sending them off. He walked up to Tewee and Martinez and Lori, saying a few words to each of them. He looked closely at Lori and said a few words to her. Hawk got in the driver's seat, with Tewee and Martinez in the back. Lori stood by the passenger side of the Bronco with Martin.

"I'm not sitting between those two testosterone-filled buttholes," she said evenly, as she eyed the two men in the back seat.

"Hey, Lori, I took a bath this week," Tewee said and laughed.

"Get in the car," Hawk said.

Bluefeathers sadly shook his head.

Lori got in and Martin slammed the door behind her, and they left the parking lot. They were taking a 7 a.m. flight to Denver, and then on to Miami and Lima. Hopefully, their contact would meet them there. Martin looked back at the parking lot and saw the morning watch officers looking on, standing in front of the building. He waved and one of them waved back. He wondered if any of them wished they had been chosen, or if they just wanted to go home after their shift was over. They were probably thinking that they would never see any of us again. Stupid Šiyápu, they were saying. Hawk stopped at the highway.

"Well, here goes nothing," he said, and turned left, accelerating up the grade and out of the town of Cold River. He kept his foot down and they rocketed up the three mile grade, Sgt. Lamebull following in his patrol car.

"Captain, I have to pee," Lori said in a small voice.

"Better find some way to hold it," Hawk said. "We're not stopping." Martin settled back and closed his eyes, the voices in back fading away. As he drifted off, he thought about what Dennis Underwood had said - that they would not be coming back. He wondered what others would think of his journey with the In-dins, especially if he didn't come back. He had a sudden thought that if he were killed he might get to meet Claire again. She had become, in a sad and frightening way, his kin, his adopted daughter who controlled his dreams and waking thought.

Maybe I will see her.

"Jesus Christ!" Hawk yelled, slamming on the brakes, throwing Martin forward against his shoulder harness. Martin jerked awake and looked out front. Up ahead, there were cars blocking the road, and further along, a line of headlights, backing up the hill, as if they were stopped. As they got closer, Martin could see the flashing lights of tribal police cars and barricades.

They had blocked the bridge.

The bridge over Bear Creek Springs was cement, with low cement railings. Only forty yards in length, it spanned a deep gorge, a slit in the basalt formation. With thick forest on either side of the road, there was no other way into the reservation, at least from the north, serving the cities of the Portland area, the tri-cities area of Washington State, Seattle, and points north. Bear Creek Springs Bridge was just inside the reservation, near the northern boundary. A barricade was at the north end of the bridge. Martin saw two police cars parked on the bridge, their flashers going. Cars and trucks were backed up as far as he could see on the other side. A man was waving the cars into a tight turn around. The truckers were stuck.

Hawk slowed and then stopped behind a patrol car. On the Cold River side of the bridge there were about twenty cars and trucks parked along the road. He rolled down his window and several people came up to the door. Charlie Winter Hawk, carrying his old 30.06 rifle, Vic Cramer, an off duty police officer, and behind them, Martha Coeur d'Alenes, Martin's nemesis.

Cramer was grinning.

Martin glanced at Hawk and then looked out at the mess.

They had closed the border.

There was a television news truck on the other side, moving slowly into position through the traffic jam. Martin got out and walked up to the bridge and looked over the span. They could see several police cars on the northern side. Someone walked up behind him, and he turned to see Martha Coeur d'Alenes.

"Never thought you'd get mixed up with crazy In-dins, did you Martin Andrews?" She said it softly, as if she were thinking of something to come. When she spoke his name it was not without kindness, and Martin took it that way.

"No, I guess not," he said. He pointed across the dark bridge at the lights.

"Who's over there?"

"Oh, troopers from the Oregon State Police and some Wasco County deputies. I think maybe the sheriff himself came over from The Dalles. Some news people. Heard the governor was supposed to come. Bluefeathers said to call him on the cell if the gov showed up."

"Any problems?"

"Had some truckers want to fight early on, little after two this morning, but the word must be out, cause traffic is down to a trickle. I told the OSP people that it might be better to put up a sign where the road to Hood River comes in about fifteen miles up, save everyone some trouble. Or block the highway in Portland."

"Who from OSP?"

"A sergeant, then a major, who told us to open the road, and I told him to check with the gov, that this was sovereign land and that the borders were closed. But the biggest problem in the bunch was a Department of Transportation guy. Thought he was gonna have a stroke, yelling around about how we can't close his highway, was gonna fight all of us."

"He still over there?"

"Yeah, him and a bunch more."

"I'm surprised that they didn't try to move the cars."

"I told him we'd blow the bridge if they came onto it." She smiled at Martin. He almost felt sorry for the people on the other side if Martha was after them.

"Can you do that, blow the bridge?"

"Yeah, Herald Runs Like Deer used to do demolition stuff in the army. Yesterday he rigged the supports to three bridges with dynamite . . . bridge down at the agency across the Deschutes River, too. We closed them down just after you and Hawk came through from Portland."

"Jesus."

"We're scared, Martin, but we aren't going back now. I guess you better bring the kids back."

Martin nodded, the seriousness of where he was, of what he was doing came over him. If he didn't get killed in Peru, he might just spend the rest of his life in prison.

"You take care, Šiyápu." Martha sang a song, a song to protect him, she told him. A blessing. And then she gave him an Eagle feather, telling him that it would protect him. Martin held the feather and watched as she walked forward, across the bridge to the cars where the other tribal members were waiting on the bridge.

Martin stood and looked out over the dark span, the lights from the many police cars and barricades flashing over the old bridge, the trees on the other side giving it a surreal look as if it had all been set up to film in Hollywood, and if he turned around he would see the cameras and the director ready to yell, "Action," or some such thing.

"This is real, isn't it?" Lori said, walking up behind Martin.

"Looks that way, and we haven't even started yet."

"Think we'll get back here?" She spoke softly, her voice a little husky, shaky at the end. This was the first Martin had seen of anything but confidence in Lori. He grinned, hoping to look more confident than he felt.

"Sure. We'll go down there and snatch them and then fly back here. No problem."

A young kid came running up and told them that it was time to go, the excitement in his face and eyes reminding Martin of the excitement and fear he felt when he went into battle for the first time. Excited and scared shitless, afraid of letting his buddies down.

No one spoke as Hawk started across the bridge toward the cars. When they approached the patrol car blockade, the car in their lane backed up and let them pass. Martin waved at Martha as they slowly moved from the bridge onto the pavement. A truck driver was yelling in the face of a trooper, the flashing lights making his body look jerky and out of sync as he waved at them, his face flushed and distorted. They all heard him yelling as they passed.

"Fuckin' wagon burners, fish clubbers, takes me four fucking hours to go around."

Camera lights washed out the darkness as a film crew moved in on the trucker. They were waved down by a trooper and deputy as they started to accelerate past the truck. Hawk stopped and rolled down his window. Sheriff Gardner of Wasco County leaned down to the open window.

"Sure hope you guys know what the hell you're doing, Hawk." He was a tall, thin man, completely bald, wearing the dark brown uniform of the Wasco County Sheriff's Office. Martin had never seen him in uniform before, but there was sure to be many photo opportunities before the day was over.

"It's outta my hands, Jim." Hawk shrugged.

"Yeah, maybe." Gardner bent down and looked into the Bronco at Martin. "Martin, can I talk to you for a minute, outside the car?"

Martin shook his head. He did want to talk with Gardner, but if he left the Bronco, he might never regain the trust he had built. "Jim, I guess anything you want to say to me can be said in front of all of us."

"Hope you know what you're doing."

"We all do, Jim. Can we pass? We have business with some feds in Portland."

Jim Gardner looked at Martin for a long few seconds, straightened up, patted Hawk on the arm, and then stood back, waving at the deputy in front of the truck to let them pass. Hawk drove fast, Martin thinking any minute that they were going to be stopped by the Oregon State Police. The OSP troopers, Martin knew, were the most cold blooded, ruthless, uncharitable collection of ticket writers in all of the fifty states. And with the news of the closing of the borders and the closing of the state highway that ran through Cold River (a highway that the OSP thought of as their own) they were certain to forget about professional courtesy for Hawk.

Hawk slid around a corner, accelerating through ninety, trees on both sides of the road a green blur, going up the slopes of Mount Hood.

"OSP gonna find you and write you, Hawk," Martin muttered.

"Fuck'em," Hawk said, and pushed the pedal down harder.

They approached the junction to Hood River and saw two sets of headlights approaching. As the vehicles passed, Martin saw that they were media trucks with the relay dish antennae on top.

"I just want to get there," Hawk said.

"Well we probably should have driven something besides this white Bronco, this car that looks like O. J.'s," Martin said.

"Why is that, Boss?" Lori asked.

"'Cause we're not in Portland yet. Got about eighty more miles of hostile territory before we make it to the airport."

Hawk hit the brakes as he came up behind a slower car and then accelerated past when the road straightened out. Martin wasn't too worried. He had ridden with Hawk before on "hot" calls, calls for help that demanded speed, like the wild ride yesterday. Hawk was a gifted driver. In fact, most of the Indians Martin had ridden with drove with remarkable skill.

Must be an Indian thing, Martin thought, a skill left over from hanging onto horses and all. Hell, now I'm starting to sound like Hawk. What the hell am I thinking of, and what am I doing here in Indin Country?

Some of us are gonna die with this crazy rescue. And he knew from hard lessons, from the school with Claire, that he couldn't save all of them.

# **C**hapter **18**

Huascaran National Park
Central Peru

In the dim light of the fire Robert and Steve drew a map of Central Peru in the dirt, using rocks and sticks as landmarks.

"When we were captured we should have been about here," Steve said, making an X in the dirt with his finger. Tara watched, hoping they would tell her that they were close to a town, something big enough to have a doctor, someone who could help Delores.

Sabrina held Delores's hand and sang quietly to her in Sahaptin. Tara listened to the song about a brave young man and a young Indian girl, and was trying to follow what Steve and Robert were talking about. She sketched Sabrina holding Delores. She tipped it up and showed it to Delores and was rewarded with a weak smile. They had made Delores as comfortable as they could, and while Tara wanted to push on, even if they had to go blindly in the dark, she knew that Delores wouldn't be able to do it. She looked down at her friend, the light from the fire making her face shine. Her eyes were open, bright and hard.

"Water," Delores said.

Tara gave her a sip from a gourd, and Delores nodded when she tried to swallow.

Had they been captured on their first or second day out, Tara supposed, it would not have been as bad as it was, but to be captured on the last day, the day when your brain had prepared you for your return it was worse. Since then she had been in a kind of inertia, in shock, and she knew now that her inertia and lethargy could and would kill her. The professor hadn't been a favorite of hers, but his death had affected her most of all. He was an elder, a figure of authority, and while he had been somewhat officious, he didn't mean any harm, and had been killed just for talking. And he had showed a fair amount of courage for doing that.

She had to take part in the discussions about where they would go and how they would get off the mountain and back to a town, but she couldn't, and left it up to Steve. On some level, Tara knew that she had to be part of whatever decision was made. She refused to believe that her dearest friend in the world would die.

*Grandfather, where are you now?*

Tara put her sketch aside and leaned over to look at the crude map that Steve and Robert were working on. She had studied maps of Peru when she had decided to go visit the pre-Columbian ruins, and she was familiar with the general layout of the country. Peru is situated on the west coast of South America, and Lima, the capital city, is on the Pacific coast, roughly in the middle of the country from north to south. They had flown to Lima and stayed a couple of days; from there they had taken a bus up the coast about 200 kilometers (120 miles) on the beautiful coast to Paramonga, then northeast approximately 130 kilometers, to the city of Huaraz, a mountain city with about 50,000 inhabitants. They stayed in Huaraz for two nights where they were outfitted and met their guides. From there they hiked up into the Cordillera Blanca Mountains to the village of Conococha, then straight north into the Huascaran National Park.

They had met Pedro and Mario in Huaraz, and by the day of the helicopter and killings, they were friends. Their first destination was the Inca ruins to the south of Nev Huandoy, a mountain peak of brilliant white snow. Tara loved the Parque, Reserva o Santuario Nacional, the national park. That first day, the hike was easy and they stopped early for dinner. They camped just outside the ancient city, and celebrated that first night, singing songs around a small fire. The professor told stories about the ancient inhabitants, and Tara sketched. Sabrina and Delores were used to her constant drawing, but the others would come over to look. Tara was surprised that the guides knew the words to the songs they sang, but why shouldn't they, her group was certainly not the first to go on the trek.

That first night in the mountains, Steve was again the comedian, mimicking the bus driver, the college students who were with them, often making fun of himself. Tara had thought then that he was like many of the professional students she had met - he hadn't figured out that you had to work at some point in your life and Steve sure acted like he never would.

Boy, has that idea changed.

"Okay, if this represents Huaraz," Steve said, "and this line is our route, and we were within a day of Huaraz and the bus, where the hell are we?"

"We're right here," Robert said. He placed his finger in the dirt, about six inches from Huaraz. "We have to go downhill from here, through the mountain pass we saw from the village, then down to Huaraz. Once we leave the park, we keep that big ass mountain, what is it, Nev Huandoy on our right to hit the road and go down to Huaraz.

"How long?" Tara asked.

"If there are no army patrols and we don't run into the terrorists again, it will take us a day to get back to the hills above Huaraz." They looked at the map.

"Maybe a day and an evening to get to the city," Steve said.

"What about a village somewhere?" Tara asked.

"There were no villages between us and Huaraz," Steve said. "Robert and I talked about it and we don't know if going east would help. We would still be in Peru and would be in a large rain forest in the Amazon basin and would still have to get out to another country somehow. Delores wouldn't make it, and we don't have our passports."

Their passports were divided between the army and the terrorists. Of the five of them left, only Robert had left the meadow with his. The rest of their passports had been in their packs. And the terrorists took Robert's the first night on the trail.

"Tara," Sabrina said softly, her voice urgent. Tara looked across the small fire at her.

"Delores wants to talk to you."

Tara crawled over to her friend and took her round face in her hands, trying not to cry. Steve and Robert moved over to where Delores lay, and Steve leaned in close, touching Sabrina and Tara. His face was slick with sweat. Sabrina started to say something, and he shook his head. There was nothing to be done for his pain.

"Tara," Delores said, her voice riding on a puff of air as she panted, the pain making her eyes glisten. Tara squeezed her hand, fighting tears.

"Don't talk, little one," Tara said in a husky whisper.

"You remember," she gasped, strained, and then started again, her words agonizing to hear, "you remember when we started the first grade, old Mrs. Baker from town used to talk around saying that you and me and Sabrina would never, never amount to anything?"

Tara nodded, the words from her best friend coming out so slowly.

"Well, she was wrong." Delores glanced up at Sabrina and then at Steve and Robert.

"These two, these two have so very much talent," and then she coughed, a bright spatter of blood spraying from her mouth, and she continued, her voice so weak they had to lean in to hear.

"These two, they are my friends."

Tara held herself with a will she didn't know she had, kept herself from sobbing, and she looked at Sabrina and was almost undone. The quiet, introspective Sabrina, who used to tease Delores about her weight, was holding Delores as tears streamed down her face and dropped on Delores's hair.

"All I ever wanted," Delores whispered, "all I ever wanted was to marry that boy, you know that Lorenzo boy who works at the lumber mill, just marry him and have a bunch of –" and she stopped and smiled, and then coughed again.

"He doesn't know," she whispered, "he doesn't know it yet but we were going to be married, have a girl, no a boy first, then another boy and a girl, little brown beautiful babies, and my girl would have been so beautiful, oh Tara she would have been so beautiful, wearing a white dress." Delores stopped and stared, back on the rez now, thinking about what could have been. Tara shook her head and looked away, the nausea of guilt rolling from her stomach up to her throat. Delores was here because of her. Tara wanted so much to tell Delores that she would be alright, that she would have a bunch of babies and they would be beautiful, but she couldn't bring herself to say that, and they would all know it would be a lie, and it was just so, so...unfair.

Delores began whispering again and Tara leaned close, her face inches away, Delores seeing something that wasn't there.

"Lorenzo, he doesn't know this, but I've been talking 'round about it and he'll know when you get back. Tell him, you both go and tell him that I would have made him very happy." She panted the last part, and then moaned.

"Delores, don't," Tara whispered, biting her lower lip until she tasted blood, trying to keep from breaking down. She reached for

Delores and stroked her face as she began to whisper.

"The kids would have played basketball in the Indian league, Lorenzo would have stayed out late with stick games and I'd be mad at him, and then he would go crazy trying to make it up to me. On Saturdays we would drive down there to Bend to Costco and shop, getting that pizza for lunch, a new jacket for Lorenzo...tell him, ummmh, tell him I could have made him very happy."

Sabrina sobbed, and held Delores. Robert and Steve looked on, Steve's face wet, Robert's tight with anger.

"If, if I had two daughters, I would have named them Sabrina and Tara, after the famous writer and the famous artist, my best friends, and I, uh, you would have –" Delores squeezed her eyes shut and moaned. She looked up and whispered again.

"I know that you will write, Sabrina, you, uh, will write scary books that scare people around like that Stephen King guy, and just, write something about me, what I wanted, what I uh, you know, and draw me, Tara sister, draw my little squiggly warm babies that I never, uh, oh I just wanted –" Delores sighed, and stopped talking, her breath just going away, quiet.

She died in the morning, an hour before first light.

"Delores," Tara whispered, holding her friend's face. Tara looked into the sightless eyes, and thought of Delores as she had been on that day when they were eight, Delores holding wilted flowers in her hand at the funeral for *ila* and *tuta*, holding the flowers and crying for Tara.

Tara sobbed, the tears coming now in a flood, dropping onto Delores, her voice rising into a wail, not caring who would hear, holding her friend, grabbing Sabrina, holding Delores between them and she sobbed until she couldn't breathe. Later, when she could breathe, she wanted to take the rifle and find the soldiers. She looked at it in Robert's hands and wanted to do that. But it would mean they would all go with her, and they all would die.

As the sky turned gray, Tara realized that Robert and Steve were moving around them, quietly busy with something. They were carrying something back and forth, rocks...for what, a fire?

Tara let Delores go and yelled.

"No!

She glared at Steve as he placed a rock on the pile with his good hand.

"We're not leaving her."

"We have to," Sabrina said firmly. "She would want us to, and you know it."

"Robert and I, we'll do what you say, Tara," Steve said. He looked at her and motioned to his bad arm. "I can't do much with this, but I can help with a stretcher."

Tara looked at each of them in turn. She nodded, and grabbed her sketch pad and ran from the camp. She ran blindly, stumbling on rocks, crying, the tears running down her face, her chin quivering. She stumbled and went down, her sketch book flying, and she fell heavily, throwing her hands out in front of her. She lay where she had fallen, sobbing until she thought she couldn't cry anymore, and then would start again, the unfairness of it all and the thought she would never see Delores again gave her a pain that she thought would kill her. After what must have been an hour, she opened her eyes and looked around, the sky grey and light in the east. She could feel them watching her, and knew that Sabrina wasn't far away, but she didn't care.

Tara pulled a stub of pencil from her pocket, retrieved her sketch pad, and began to draw. As she sketched, she knew what she must do.

She must prepare Delores's body, and she was not worthy. As she sketched she tried to remember what she had learned from her grandmother, but at the time she was told about the dressing, she was too young to care. Now, she thought bitterly, my best friend has died, and I don't know what to do. A person who prepares the body to go on to the next world must live in a certain way, live a clean life. To be a person who can touch the body, you must be a good person, for this is the last thing you can do for a person before they go on to the next world.

For the dressing she needed a burial dress of white buckskin, plain white, with white leggings and moccasins. She didn't have it, and she couldn't make it here. She didn't have otter furs to braid in Delores's hair, nor did she have a beaded headband, but she could braid her hair.

Tara sketched and thought of what she would do. She would get Sabrina to help her. When she finished the sketch, she looked at it, and knew that she would do more if she lived, and she would never forget her friend. Tara walked back to the camp and held her sketch up for the others to see.

The sketch was of Delores holding a baby, a baby with a small wreath of flowers, a baby with a miniature Delores face.

A beautiful baby girl.

Tara sat next to Delores and began to clean her face with the tail of her shirt. When she was done she held her friend's face in her lap and began to comb her hair with her fingers, humming as she worked. Sabrina came up and sat beside her and together they braided Delores's hair. Tara couldn't remember the words of the songs that needed to be sung, seven sets of seven songs, but she did remember the last one, and she began singing softly as she carefully placed Delores down.

Sabrina sang with her. Steve stood and looked on. Robert wasn't in sight.

"We must face Delores to the east," Tara said, and began to pull the body around. Sabrina helped until they had Delores facing east. They sang again, and then Tara placed the picture in Delores's folded hands on her stomach. She walked over and picked up a rock and set it on her friend's shoulder, and walked away, crying.

"I can't do this," she sobbed, and sensed Steve come up behind her. "No!" She waved him away. As she sobbed she tried to sing the seventh song again, and the words wouldn't come out.

"Please...puh...leeese," she sobbed, and turned to Steve and Sabrina, "please cover her."

Tara stood like that for some time, her arms crossed, hugging herself, and when she turned around, there was a pile of rocks where Delores lay. They stood in a little group beside the grave, now full light just before sunrise, the pile of rocks a futile age old attempt to keep animals from the body - and Tara found that she could no longer cry. She wasn't finished, but just for now she felt empty and alone. Robert came back and looked, and then walked off, holding two packs and the rifle.

Sabrina held Tara.

"I love you, Tara, and I love Delores," she whispered. For Sabrina, that was a speech. Tara nodded. Sabrina picked up her basket and stood there, her eyes down. She walked ahead to join Robert.

Tara knew that Steve was somewhere behind her, waiting. There was no sound that morning, and Tara was taken at the stillness of it all, a stillness that she had felt at her parents' funeral. Except then, it seemed like most of the tribal members had been there. Hundreds. On that winter day, it had snowed early, and the family burial plot beneath the rimrock was covered with six inches of snow. Her father's friends had been there early, as was the custom, and dug through the frozen ground to make a grave. And this time they had to dig two of them.

Tara stood with her grandparents as the tribal elders, Martha Coeur d'Alenes she thought, sang in Sahaptin a beautiful song about life, and then she had prayed, a mixture of Indian and Christian belief. Delores came over and held Tara's hand, her friend since they could each remember. They were in kindergarten together, first grade, and now the third grade. Delores, her eyes red from crying, held Tara's hand throughout the ceremony. Afterward at the church, they had sat and talked, while many elders came up and touched Tara, said nice things to her about her mother and father.

*Delores. And now she was on the ground in a stupid country because she wanted nothing more than to be with me, no matter where I went for spring break.*

*I couldn't help her, Grandfather. I didn't learn the lessons well enough to keep us safe.*

Tara wanted to cry again, but couldn't and she knew she had to leave, but to leave Delores like this, to run away and leave her body was harder in some ways than it could have been to leave Delores here alive. To leave her without proper dressing and burial, without going to a sweat lodge for five days after the dressing, it was, well it was not the way it would end.

Steve touched her arm and Tara turned to look at him, her chin trembling, her legs shaking, and he gently put his arm around her, holding his bloody arm awkwardly out of the way, and Tara threw her arms up around his neck and held on, her sobs coming fast, shaking her, and Tara Red Eagle of the Cold River Indian Reservation of Oregon, cried again.

They stood like that while she cried, tears running on Steve's neck, her face pressed against him, and he didn't say anything.

Tara finally let her arms slip and Steve held on, holding her up with his good arm until the sobbing slowed. She pulled back and he let her go.

"It's...it's just so...unfair," Tara whispered.

She started to cry again, a whimper, and she hugged herself and looked up at Steve.

He nodded.

She leaned into him and whispered.

"Thank you."

Tara looked at the grave and spoke, talking more to herself than to Steve. "What she wanted out of life was the best and cleanest and truest of all, the best of what any of us wanted -just to be a happy wife and oh, she would have made a great mother. The best of all of us. And in her way, she knew it, that what she wanted was good. She was happy for us, but Delores was very happy for her own dream." She looked over at Steve.

"Why did this happen, Steve? We're just a bunch of college kids, on vacation. Why is this happening?"

She bent over and picked up her pack and turned to follow the others. She looked up to give herself a sense of direction, focusing on the mountain peak of Nev Huaran. They were at the 13,000 feet level on the hillside around Nev Huaran, and Tara knew she would be back for Delores to take her body back to Cold River.

Sometime.

Somehow.

It just didn't matter how.

The sun was coming up when they left, and they set off with Robert in the lead, then Sabrina and Tara. Steve stayed a little back, watching, looking. They had a view that would have been stunning during any other circumstances. Bright blue sky, although cool this morning, the snow covered Nev Huaran to their right, and the coarse green grass of the high country. It reminded Tara of the rolling hills of Montana, except this was higher and steeper, with more rocks.

They saw the bright colors of the climbers just before noon.

# Chapter 19

Washington, D.C.
The Oval Office

"What the hell are they doing out there? Closing their borders as if we were at war with them." President Miller slammed his phone down and looked at his audience in the Oval Office. He didn't get an answer and didn't expect one. "Declaring war, what kind of stunt was that?" He looked at June Raul, the Secretary of State, and then at his National Security Advisor, Tom Steele.

"Mr. President," June said, "Mr. President, we didn't have much time to assist the students, and as far as the declaration of war goes, well, uh," and then she stopped, looking down at her notes, "it appears that it is a legal declaration of war, as far as international law is concerned."

"How the hell can that be, the reservation is in Oregon for Chrissakes!"

"Our treaty with the middle tribes of Oregon gives them the status of complete sovereignty, the status akin to a foreign nation."

President Miller looked at his Secretary of State as if she were a pure fool. The press was going to kill him over this, and he was already taking some heat. He pointed at Steele.

"Find out what happened in Peru," and then he stood up and looked out the window, the view distorted by the thick ballistic glass. With the fights in Congress, the press having degenerated years ago into a supermarket tabloid, and the constant Mid-East terror threat, he didn't need a damned incident with a foreign nation.

"Uh, there is one other thing, Mr. President," Steele said.

"Go ahead," the President said, and thought, did I really nominate him for this job?

"Uh, Mr. President, there seems to be an F.B.I. agent assigned to the reservation, who has uh, well, he's missing."

# **Chapter 20**

Portland, Oregon

Hawk got to Portland in under an hour and they didn't meet any OSP troopers along the way. Martin convinced Hawk to slow down through the town of Sandy where they would have certainly been stopped for five miles over the limit. They had been quiet on the way up, thinking about the unknown that awaited them in Peru. Martin had been involved in a lot of operations in the past, but even those with little planning had been conducted in the United States where he spoke the language, understood the customs and laws, and knew how to play the game.

Lori was probably right about him wearing a dress in a Peruvian jail, and it seemed less and less like a joke.

"We may re-define 'long term parking,'" Hawk said and he entered the economy lot at the Portland airport.

"Meaning what?" Lori asked, scooting forward in the seat, glaring first to her right and left.

"Meaning that none of us may come back from the land down south," Hawk said, throwing the shift lever into park and throwing open his door.

"That'd be too bad, Tribes can't find their car." Lori struggled to get out past Hawk.

"Oh, they'll find it alright," Hawk said. "Bluefeathers said to call him with the location of the car. He's sending someone for it today."

"Right," Lori said.

They took the shuttle bus from the lot through the construction to the terminal and checked their bags. As they walked through the concourse, Martin led them to a restaurant. Dennis Underwood was waiting for them at a corner table.

"Buenos dias," he said and waved to the chairs.

"Buenos dias," Lori said.

Dennis looked at her. "This is your interpreter?"

"Yes, and a police officer," Martin said.

Underwood gave her a long look. "I still won't go with you, but I have two contact names in Lima, and one in Huaraz, if you make it that far. From what I hear from people in Lima, the army has the country shut down pretty tight. What's your cover?"

"Large tour group from Miami. Peruvians don't want to cancel, give the impression that their country isn't safe and all. It may help us."

"Might work," Dennis said, "but you had better be prepared with something else when you split from the group."

They ordered breakfast and as they waited Dennis told them stories from Peru, the drug runners, the people in the Andes, the country.

"What about phones?" he asked.

"We have several cell phones, one for each of us, going to tell them if they question it that we have to keep in touch with our respective businesses each day. I hope that the batteries last, and that they don't get confiscated by customs, although the large tour group should help."

"Satellite uplink?"

"Yes, and we had people from the travel agency direct us to our cell phone provider and have them re-program them so they will work in Peru. We were told that it is routinely done without any problems."

"You better hope so. How you gonna find them?"

"Go to Huaraz and find your friend. Get a hotel room there in the Gran Hotel Hauscaran, the one where the students stayed and use that as our base of operations. We're gonna have to split from the tour group at the airport."

Dennis looked at Hawk, and then at Martin. "Good luck amigo, and keep your head down. If those phones work, call me. I might be able to think of something to keep you out of more trouble."

"Sure you won't come with us?"

Dennis grinned and shook his head. "I think that my name is probably on a list at the airport. Probably not be a good thing for me to do. My future travel plans don't include Peru." He laughed.

They boarded the plane at 7 a.m. for their flight to Miami. Hawk was snoring before they reached cruise altitude, his head against the window. Lori was next to Hawk in the middle, and Martin was on the aisle. The others were somewhere back in the plane. Martin leaned his head back and closed his eyes. He tried to relax and rest, but his brain felt as if it would explode, information flashing across faster than he could take the information in. He opened his eyes and looked over at Lori. She was staring at him.

"You should get some sleep," Martin said. "We might not get too much when we get there."

She shook her head. "Can't." She looked as if she wanted to say something, and then shook her head again. She stared at the seat in front of her.

"Why you going around with us?" she said suddenly, turning to Martin. "Especially since you're a Šiyápu?" She smiled as she said "white man," and she said it softly, with a current of feeling with it, a good feeling, Martin thought.

"Bluefeathers told me to."

"These aren't your people."

"Maybe they are now."

Lori looked ahead again, not replying, and after a minute, Martin thought she was through.

"I hear people talking around about you, saying that you had to leave your last agency, that you had some trouble, that maybe nobody wanted you. Oh, they say you're a good cop and all, but you had some trouble, say you didn't belong anywhere, and now we got you." She looked closely at Martin.

"What trouble?" she asked.

Martin stared at the seat in front of him and for some reason he wanted to talk to Lori about things he had never been able to tell anyone.

He told her about Claire and the trouble it gave him afterward - the emptiness, the futility of it all. His voice grew husky when he told of feeling Claire's breath on his cheek, of hearing her voice, of her death.

Lori put her hand on his arm and waited until he was finished. "I know about not belonging," she said. "I know how you feel. If you had belonged to something, maybe you wouldn't have come to us, to Cold River. If you have been looking for something, for someone, for a family to belong to, I understand that. I was born in Mexico to an American father and Cold River mother. I never really fit anywhere. Oh, I'm a tribal member, but I also get called the really bad things by people, and I tell myself that it doesn't matter, but it does." She looked at Martin.

"Maybe that's why I do the thing I do with McGruff. I want to hurt someone." She looked at him, twisting her hands in her lap.

"Well, one thing about it, they won't forget you."

"Maybe I'm going 'cause the chairman come 'round and told me to go, but I really don't have to, no one expected me to. I could have stayed on the rez and found a reason not to go. Maybe gone up to Portland for a few weeks until it blew over, something like that, maybe go to Bend for awhile."

"So why did you decide to go - or are you going?"

When Lori answered, she spoke so softly that Martin had to strain to hear.

"Maybe I'm coming round looking for something, just like you, Martin."

# Chapter 21

Cold River Indian Reservation

Chairman Bluefeathers sat in his office at the tribal administration building and looked out over the sagebrush hills and the mountains beyond. He'd found a way to get a couple hours of sleep, and would need to get a nap before the day was over.

He leaned back in his chair and thought about what he had done and where he was taking the tribes. He didn't know if he was doing the right thing at all, but he knew that they had to do something. He wasn't afraid of making decisions, hell he had been trying to run this multi-million dollar corporation for years, and the one thing he did know was that he had the power of a president, a governor, a king, all rolled into one.

The tribal council was a body with a lot of wisdom, but in times of war, all of their old ways of doing things would not work. Many of the people looked to him to fix their problems, and Indians weren't afraid of telling him what needed fixing.

Mabel Waits-for-Deer wanted him to have someone come over and fix her stove, again, and she didn't care if there were students in peril. All she knew was that her stove didn't work, and by God if one of those young men who worked for the tribal administration didn't come over to her house on Hollywood Drive and fix it she wouldn't vote for Bluefeathers again. And then Connie Roberts had been yelling around about her son in jail, saying he should be out, even after Chief Andrews sat with her and showed her the court documents that meant her son had another six months to serve.

Bluefeathers sometimes thought that the white man wasn't their problem, that they had turned into a bunch of whiners, and had evolved into precocious, cunning, complainers who didn't like anything that was done for them. There would be plenty of them to criticize him for what was going to happen next.

He got up from his desk and walked to the window, looking out over the hills. He was dressed in his usual dress: blue jeans, western shirt, large belt buckle, cowboy boots with a riding heel. To wear the clothes of the white man rancher may seem incongruous to some, but Bluefeathers had been wearing them for so long they were a part of him. Other Indians, especially those working in the tribal casino, wore traditional Indian dress.    That newcomer to the council, George Wewah, was coming around wearing a tie-dyed shirt and sandals. Bluefeathers shook his head.

In his boots he still was a small man, and to an outsider this may be taken for a person of diminished power.

The Indians on the reservation knew different.

Except for the artifacts from his tribe, his office could have been in any executive suite in any city in the country.  He had a large cherry wood desk with a computer station. The office had a round oak table and chairs for small meetings.  He had photos of his children and grandchildren and of his ranch on the Cold River Reservation, up in the mountains toward Mt. Jefferson.

Bluefeathers looked up on the knoll to the north of him, a bare knob of land.  The ground sloped down to Shitike Creek, and then on the other side, there was the old BIA school, police department and jail, fire and ambulance station, and the post office.  The knoll, appropriately named, "Soldiers Hill," had once had a troop of U.S. Calvary stationed there.  He had a picture of it somewhere, an old washed out black and white photo, showing the rows of white soldier tents gleaming in the sun. There had been a corral for the horses down on the other side, away from the creek.  As he stared it was as if he could see them now, walking around tending their horses, wearing their blue uniforms.

The blue coats had been here to keep the peace, primarily to defend the reservation against marauding bands of Snake Indians.

From 1859 to 1873, Cold River Indians had served as scouts for the U.S. Army, especially during the campaigns against the Snake Indians in 1868, and the Modocs in 1873.  They had a history of service with the Army.

Bluefeather's great great grandfather had served as a scout during many of the campaigns and had been wounded and received a pension for the rest of his life from the army.

If he squinted he could see the tents down by the river even now, the U.S. flag flying over the command tent. At one time, Bluefeathers knew, there were over a hundred Cold River Indians in service of the U.S. Army, and that the Cold River Indians had never been at war with the government of the United States. Indians, including his relatives, had always taken pride in their service in the armed services, including the ones lost in every war since World War II - Viet Nam, Korea, the Wa-Tetahm boy with the Marine Corps over there in Desert Storm, and then Afghanistan and Iraq.

His people had always done their part.

And they still did.

He had a list on his desk of the tribal members currently serving in the Armed Forces, and their occupation and skills in the military. In an hour he would have a similar list from most of the tribes in the country. For his plan to work, he needed some fighters. Indians who could make war.

He needed some pilots.

The problem was, and he knew it well, that no one could keep their mouths shut here on the reservation, not out of spite, but out of curiosity and the belief of the right to know if a decision affected a tribal member. For what he was planning, only a few people could know - Jimmy Hanson and Arlene Horse on the council; Sammy, the personnel director; Martha Coeur d'Alenes, a wise elder who was trusted by other elders and could keep her mouth shut; Josephine, his secretary; Joe Hall, the chief financial officer, on his way back from L.A.; and Sal Wahanna, the director of the hospital.

Bluefeathers knew that he couldn't politically survive outside the reservation without support from at least some of the other tribes, and he included in his inner circle the tribal council chairman from the Yakama Nation, and the chairman from the Mashantucket Pequot Tribe in Connecticut. Chairman Dennis Lenwya from Yakama was already here, and Charley Johnson from Connecticut was on his way.

So far the barricades at the bridges were holding, and the authorities from the State of Oregon were allowing people to cross if we let them in. He knew that it would really hurt if the blockade were two-sided. People had already cleaned out the store up by the post office, and were going to Madras and Portland to shop. They would have trouble in town if this weren't resolved. He had never been tested as a leader during war time, never had to make those hard decisions as to who would live and who would die, but then, many leaders around the world during the past fifty years had never been tested in war. He took this seriously, not a pretend war, as some people in Washington, D.C. thought it was.

People were going to die. In both countries.

The people he sent to Peru should be half way there by now, and he expected a call from them. Was this so different from the time the troops were camped here, over a hundred years ago? The world is still a dangerous place, and they would all find out just how dangerous.

"Phone call from the Senator, and Joe just arrived," Josephine said, standing at the door. Bluefeathers took one more look at the riverbank, the cavalry tents fading from view as he walked to his desk.

"Senator, how the hell are you?"

"Well, Chairman, I'm up here at the bridge across Bear Creek, and it appears that I can't come across."

"You've always been welcome here, Senator."

"I've got an escort of State troopers with me, two cars."

"Well, Jim, we don't have anything against the Oregon State Police, but this time you'll have to come alone. Walk across the bridge and we'll bring you on down to the agency. We'll have lunch, you and I and talk about how to get back to normal."

There was a silence on the line, and Bluefeathers could hear muted argument in the background.

"Trust me, Jim," he said.

"What do -?"

"You don't take any troopers with you when you come over for a salmon bake on the river. This isn't any different, we're still your friends." Bluefeathers paused. He needed the senator here, but that was part of his plan that he had spoken aloud.

"You know," Bluefeathers said, "you know this is most likely temporary, that this will work itself out, and we are not at war with the United States, only Peru. Come on across the bridge on foot, and we'll drive you down. Oh, and Senator, bring that Fox camera crew with you, that Rodriguez guy." There was another pause on the phone.

"Alright." The arguing increased in the background. He turned to his secretary.

"Have someone drive the Senator down here, give him our own police escort. I don't want to see him for an hour. Send Joe in, and I want to see Sammy as well."

He looked around his office. It was twenty-five miles from here to the northern boundary, the bridge at Bear Creek. He had an hour before the Senator got here and demanded to know what the hell the In-dins were going to do. Jim Sterling was an old friend, and the senior Senator from Oregon was an influential person in the U.S. Senate. Bluefeathers thought that it was too bad that he was going to have to lie to the Senator.

Joe came in and flopped in one of the chairs around the table, his tie undone, his white shirt wrinkled. Sammy followed and Bluefeathers watched them. Joe looked like a successful accountant, had an MBA from Stanford, and as CFO of the tribes, he followed the money. Took care of it. Understood it, and made it work for them. He was thirty-one, and good. Sammy, the personnel director, was short, wore a suit, and had long salt and pepper hair that was braided. Joe spoke without preamble.

"I've anticipated major interference from the government, especially if this thing goes for awhile, and the worst thing they could do, outside of an invasion for any reason, is to seize our assets outside of Cold River, or freeze our bank accounts."

"How long will it take for them to do that?" Bluefeathers asked, looking over at Joe. He liked it that the younger man didn't question the course of events. Joe just gave him what was needed.

"We still have a country to run," Bluefeathers said, "and a war to fight."

"Politically, who knows, but it can be done electronically or physically, with a writ from a federal judge. Once it becomes politically acceptable."

"Can they do it this week?"

"Doubtful, but next week . . ." He shrugged.

Bluefeathers remained standing. Sammy was writing on a legal pad at the table and had brought a stack of folders with him.

"Will we have any warning?" Bluefeathers asked.

"Call the bank," Joe said. "Steve French, president of the U.S. Bancorp of the Pacific." Bluefeathers called Josephine.

"If we have warning, what can we do?"

"I've established accounts in the Cayman Islands, a few dollars in each, and I believe if I have an hour or so I can transfer most of the cash out of the country. The bonds and longer term investments might be frozen, but we wouldn't necessarily use them anyway."

"Sammy, what about power?"

"Portland General Electric's getting about twenty million dollars of our hydroelectric generation annually, and we supply all of Cold River, parts of two counties, and –"

"Can we cut them off?" Bluefeathers asked. Sammy looked at him. "I'm told we can, not hard from what our engineers say."

"Let PGE know we're they're friends, we may want another player on our side. What about guarding the dams?"

"Already done," Sammy said. He made a note.

Bluefeathers walked to the window and looked out over the knoll where the bluecoats had camped. "At one time there were two troops of General Crook's soldiers there, getting ready for the final push against the Snakes." He suddenly wondered how they got to this point, and wondered what would happen to his country. To use sovereignty as a sword was one thing, but to lose may mean to lose the whole nation as well. He walked to his desk and pushed the intercom for his secretary. When she entered, he spoke without turning around. It calmed him to look at the place where the tents had been.

"Call a meeting in the council chambers in one hour, with the people on the list on my desk. Tell them to talk to no one."

Josephine left and was back within seconds.

"Pacific Bancorp is on the line."

Bluefeathers pushed the button for the speaker phone.

"Steve, thanks for callin' on us poor In-dins. I have Sammy and Joe here listening."

"What can I do for you, Mr. Chairman?" There was just the right amount of concern in his voice, Bluefeathers thought.

"Just give us a little notice when and if the government or any agency comes sniffing around our accounts. We do not want our liquid accounts seized."

"Well, Chairman Bluefeathers, you know that anything I can do for the tribes, I will, and –"

"That's not good enough!" Bluefeathers yelled. Sammy looked up from his pad. "We have a lot of money with you, and over the years we have made a lot for you, and you have used our support of you personally to get where you are. I want notice."

"Certainly, Mr. Chairman, as I said, I'll personally do anything I can do for you and for the tribes, certainly within the confines of our rules, and I can assure you that –"

Bluefeathers angrily stabbed the release button and the room was quiet. "You better get some operating capital the hell out of there, Joe," he said. "Today." He walked to the window and looked out at the knoll above the river. The cavalry tents were gone.

He felt the anger build, willing it to go away so he could think clearly. He started talking quietly, to the window, to himself, the others watching him and listening.

"Šiyápu come with plans to help the Indians with their money, to show them what to do with it, and these same men get rich and often powerful playing around with Indian money, then go crying around when there is something the Indians really need, fucking bankers, you need a loan they say, 'No, can't do that, you're an Indian on the old rez, aren't you?'"

Bluefeathers stopped, looking for the tents and not seeing them, his voice getting louder, struggling to control his anger.

"And when you have plenty of money they come 'round and say, 'Hey Indian, can I loan you plenty of money, maybe play with some of your money? Oh, can I go on that fishing trip on Indian lands so I can tell my family and my buddies at the country club what a friend I am to the blanket ass, wagon burner Indians?'" He realized that his fatigue was causing the control to slip away, his anger making his voice louder than he wanted it to come out. He suddenly felt foolish, and that was not how he needed to feel. Time to make some decisions. Joe and Sammy hadn't interrupted or said a word, and he hadn't expected them to. He turned back toward the table.

"Joe," he said quietly, the anger slipping away with his decision, "when this Peru thing is over, however it concludes, I want to see plans to move all of our money, bonds, stock funds, all assets, everything, away from U.S. Bancorp of the Pacific. Two weeks, Joe, after they return safely, we move everything."

Joe cleared his throat. "Just so you know we will lose some money by not going to maturity on some of the bond issues, and possibly some funds."

"Fuck'm. Do it." We're starting to see who our friends are, he thought. And he hadn't thought of Tara and the others for some time now, at least not in the front of his mind, but the worry was there, just below the surface.

Josephine came back in. "Senator's here. He's got a camera crew with him." She handed Bluefeathers a single sheet of paper.

"Tell him we'll be just a minute, and then come back in here." Bluefeathers glanced at the paper and then started to read it. "I'll be damned," he muttered. Sammy and Joe looked at each other and waited.

"This paper," Bluefeathers said, "contains a list of Indian Nations and reservations who have declared war on Peru, and are asking us if we need help. Good God, the Navajo, The Cheyenne River Sioux, The Cold Mountain Apache, The Oglala Sioux at Pine Ridge, The Blackfeet Nation, The Red Lake Band of Chippewa in Minnesota, and . . ." He put the paper down and wiped his eyes. The list contained other names, the Yakama Nation, the Nez Perce, Jicarilla Apache, White Mountain Apache. Other tribal councils who were not contemplating a declaration were pledging support. Sammy and Joe stood behind Bluefeathers and quietly exchanged high fives.

Bluefeathers turned and spoke, feeling for the first time old and afraid, knowing that they had to go forward now. *What the hell have I done?*

"I want to use the good Senator to be a spokesman for the Tribes, and although he may be an innocent spokesman, he will be a good one. He gets to tell the people in Washington that this is all a mistake, that we will let it go after we rattle some bones and feathers or something. We need to have people believe we are harmless, at least for the next twenty-four to forty-eight hours."

Sammy looked up. "What happens in the next twenty four hours?"

"You have a list of demolition experts here?"

Sammy handed a folder to Bluefeathers. "Tribal members on top. Some from the other tribes further down on the list."

"We gonna blow something up?" Joe asked.

"We're gonna hit Peru where they live in the United States." Bluefeathers spread a map out on the table.

"Embassies?" Sammy asked, his eyes large.

"Embassies and Consulates. Beginning with this one." Bluefeathers pointed to a spot on the map.

"Senator's gonna look like shit after this," Joe muttered.

"He's gotta do something for all the salmon he's been comin' 'round eating all these years," Bluefeathers said, and Joe and Sammy laughed. Bluefeathers folded the map and placed it in Sammy's folder. There was a knock on the door and Josephine ushered Senator Sterling in. Bluefeathers walked toward the sliver haired spokesman and held out his hand, smiling. The camera crew filed in and were directed to the corner to set up. Rodriguez adjusted his tie.

"Senator, sorry about yesterday." Bluefeathers warmly shook the senator's hand. "We're gonna include you in our plans, let you help us poor Indians through this misunderstanding. I want you to take word back to the Great White Father in Washington."

# Chapter 22

Peru

Tara saw a flash of yellow below her, yellow on the ground with other colors, the colors of the jackets of the climbers from England, she thought.  Tara stopped. Sabrina and Steve came up and stood beside her.  Robert was just ahead and off to the side, crouched down, studying the ravine ahead.

They looked down at the colors, the jumble of bodies, a careless discard of people in the wrong place at the wrong time, thrown carelessly on the ground a hundred yards down the hill from them.

"Steve, is it -?"

"Yeah, Charles and them."

She stared at the bodies and didn't want to go down the hill, with Delores behind them and more death in front.

A week before, when they had arrived in the mountain town of Huaraz, they met climbing and hiking groups from around the world. That first night, Steve had introduced himself to a group of young men and women who were standing on the sidewalk in front of their hotel.

There were six of them, and from listening to them talk, they were college students from England and like Tara and her friends, on holiday from their studies. Steve talked and waved his arms, and then pointed at Tara and her friends.

Why does he think he's our ambassador, Tara thought as they approached.

"Charles, these lovely ladies are Sabrina, Delores, and Tara," Steve said, introducing a slight dark haired man who was apparently the leader of the group.  He wore strange looking glasses that Tara found out later were designed for climbing, and had a bright yellow jacket tied around his waist.

Nerd.

"Very pleased to meet you," he said.  He introduced the others. Ted, a student in London, was the youngest of the group at eighteen; Bill and Elmore, getting ready to go into the military in the fall, Herbert, a student at Oxford, and Marilyn, the only woman, a climbing specialist and owner of a climbing shop in London. She looked to be Tara's age.

"Looks like it will be awhile before we can register," Charles said. "We were just going for a walk, check out the city, as it were, and Ted here

doesn't want to go. What say we all go and he'll watch our things."

"I don't really want -" Tara began.

"Let's do it," Delores said. "Anything's better than staying in the lobby." Tara looked at Sabrina and then decided to go. But she didn't want to join, she just wanted to hike. She got a small spiral sketch pad from her pack, a number two berrol black beauty pencil, and joined her friends.

They walked along Avenida Luzuriaga, a main thoroughfare, and passed hotels, travel agencies, a lot of climbing equipment shops with gear hanging in the windows, pizzerias, cafes, and bars. Tara didn't know what she expected, but she was unprepared for the liveliness of the city, the vitality and color of the shops. It was somehow more European than she had expected. She had thought that they were going to a sleepy Peruvian village, and she found herself in the center of a bustling commercial center that catered to the gringo with money.

She walked down the sidewalk with her friends, suddenly feeling good, listening to Steve and their new friends ahead, a slow and pleasant walk. This is why I came here, she thought. To experience new things with people I love. They caught up with the others in front of a hiking store.

"I'm hungry," Delores said, "but so far I haven't seen anything I could eat."

Charles laughed. "Actually, there are quite a few places here you would like, places you would find on your west coast, like that pizzeria across the street." He pointed to a store that looked as if it had once been a large storeroom. "Our chums who have been here before said it is a good one."

In the early evening the place was already crowded. The far wall was a climbing wall, and in the large room, Tara could see two video screens. Some kind of show was going on opposite the climbing wall, and throughout the room waiters were carrying trays of pasta and what looked like pizza. And pitchers of beer.

They were seated and Tara watched the activity, Charles encouraging them to get on the wall. He said something to Delores and

Sabrina, had them laughing, and Tara found herself relaxing in spite of her annoyance at Steve, their self-appointed entertainment director. They watched as a man in yellow climbing shorts and a blue shirt literally ran up the wall, pulling himself up and stepping on the rocks as if he were on a fast crawl on a horizontal surface. When he got to the top he did a half bow and rappelled down to the whistles and claps of the crowd. There were people standing in line to climb, Tara saw, and it reminded her of some of the pubs around the University of Oregon.

Delores and Sabrina were laughing at something, and Tara thought that she should join the group, but instead she opened her tablet and began

sketching the climbing wall. She sketched the climber as he reached for a handhold, his face intense with concentration. She heard Charles and the others ask about the reservation, about Sabrina and Delores. Tara saw Sabrina push her glasses up, her face serious as she talked about herself.

"Well, I write," she said, and then laughed.

"Indian stuff?" Charles asked. It seemed to Tara that he had a gift for getting people to talk. But then, he didn't know Sabrina.

"Maybe I'll be an Indian Stephen 'crazy Fox' King, here we come, scaaary Indians from that Micmac cemetery, and I'll show you real Indians, scary Indians, make you want to run back to England."

They all laughed, and Sabrina started again.

"Or be Dean 'Big Timber' Koontz, write scaaary stuff about people who get lost in the dark on the rez, or Johnny 'Little Snake' Grisham, write about famous Indian attorney, F. Lee 'Snake in Grass,' Bailey, who saves poor Indian maiden from being murdered by gang of ruthless litigators." She had them now, and Tara knew that this could go on all night. Sabrina not only liked to write stories, she loved to tell them. When Sabrina stopped, Tara saw Charles looking at her.

"Tara, what do you think of Peru so far?"

She turned when she heard her name, looking at Charles.

"I'm sorry, I -"

"I said, what are you drawing?"

She held up her pad and showed the group.

"An artist," Charles said with a grin. He leaned forward to look closer. "And, a good one. But I said, what do you think of Peru so far?"

Tara closed her sketch pad. "I thought it would be one large, primitive village, like the poor ones in southern Mexico."

"And now?"

"Well, this place is like Disneyland, with a climbing theme."

"And beer," Steve said, holding a mug up and laughing. Their pizza arrived and they ate, drank beer, and Tara thought they could have been anywhere: London, Manhattan, Kansas City, Los Angeles, or Seattle. The English climbers and Steve kept them laughing with stories about the world, climbing, and where they would go next.

Charles matched Steve with jokes, and seemed to know every one that Steve told. Tara listened absently, working on her next sketch. Charles and Steve were talking about flying, something they had apparently both done, although Steve said, "I have the takeoff down pat, it's the landings I have trouble with." Charles laughed. Tara shut her notebook.

"What will you do when you get back to England?" she asked, looking at Charles.

"Why, Tara, my beautiful aboriginal woman, I'm going to become the Prime Minister, like Churchill, and have you for my gorgeous wife." He laughed, and the others laughed with him. Even Sabrina and Delores were laughing.

"You'll become the Queen of England before we ever marry," Tara said, laughing at him. The rest of the group roared and the Englishmen pounded on the table.

"And you know what," Ted yelled, still pounding the table. "He will actually be the P.M." Charles laughed and adjusted his glasses, pulling his coat up over his shoulders. He turned and looked at Tara.

"Tara, you know what my cousin once said, one of his most famous quotes?"

"Who is your cousin?"

"Sir Winston Churchill."

"Yeah, right, you coming 'round here telling us poor In-dins that your cousin is Winston." Tara smiled, and added, "Besides, wasn't he impotent, like many of his relatives?"

Steve laughed and slapped Charles on the shoulder.

"Don't know any impotent Englishmen," Charles said, and grinned at Tara.

"Me either," Marilyn said, blushed, and took a drink of her beer. Charles slid over next to Tara.

"There is but one way to find out, my dear Tara," he said, still grinning at her.

"Ooooooohh," Sabrina laughed. "This one is a match for you, Tara girl."

"Yeah, a match made in Peru. What did your poor impotent cousin say, Charles the climber from England, Charles who's going to be the next P.M.?"

"He said, 'there's nothing quite so exhilarating as being shot at without result.'" He winked at her, and they all laughed.

He looked at Delores, who had been laughing and eating, but not doing much talking.

"Delores, is it?"

Delores nodded, and looked down at her pizza.

"Well Delores, your two companions have told us something about themselves. What about Delores?"

She looked down, and Tara thought for a moment that Delores wouldn't talk at all, and then she lifted eyes up and looked around. She was smiling.

"I'm not like my friends," she said. "I just want to get married and use my talent raising kids." She looked directly at Charles and grinned. "But from what I've learned tonight, I guess the father won't be an Englishman."

The roar of laughter from their table caused most people in the crowded place to stop and look at them. Tara laughed until tears came to her eyes. Charles was laughing as hard as anyone, saying, "Good one, boy that was a good one."

They finished their pizza and beer, talking and laughing, and in spite of her reluctance to go along, Tara found that she was enjoying herself immensely. She hadn't seen Delores and Sabrina laugh this way in a long time. Tara sat and sketched Charles, and then gave it to him as they left the restaurant.

He solemnly kissed her on the cheek, and then winked at her as the others laughed. He held it up and looked at it critically.

"I'll put this on my wall when I'm the Prime Minister."

"If you're ever the P.M., I'll come over and do a better one."

"Deal."

They walked the few blocks back to the hotel, talking quietly in groups. As they got to the courtyard they exchanged addresses, using Tara's sketch pad for note paper, talking about the reservation and

England, making plans to visit, Charles and the others wanting to come out the next summer to see more "real Indians."

"Almost be P.M. by then, Tara my dear," he said, and walked them to the lobby, his ridiculous yellow jacket tied up high around his waist. Steve shook hands with their group, got a hug from Marilyn, and they parted laughing. The climbers were leaving much earlier than Tara and her friends.

As she walked to her room that night she was smiling, feeling really good for the first time since she had decided to make the trip. This was what kids, college kids and people her age should be about before the grind of life caught up with them - meeting new friends and having fun. When Tara had awakened the next morning, the tents and the climbers were gone.

And now, standing on the hillside looking down at the jumble of bodies, she knew she didn't want to go on.

Well, Charles, you didn't get to be the P.M. and you didn't get to learn from your cousin. Whoever shot you didn't miss, and we are going to end up that way very soon. This isn't just about us, this is about a country going crazy, with people running 'round killing everything that moves.

In the early morning of the day they buried Delores, Tara, Sabrina, Steve and Robert started down the hill toward the bright yellow jacket.

# Chapter 23

From a distance the color was a bright splash against the green and brown grasses. Tara focused on the bright yellows and blues of the jackets as they walked closer.

"Steve...maybe it's not them."

Steve shook his head, as if to deny what was in front of them. Tara looked at him and then down at the ravine. She stopped, not wanting to go any closer. From where she stood she could see a yellow jacket on the form of a person sprawled at a crazy angle.

"I was hoping that they got away," she said softly.

Steve nodded.

They walked until they could look the full length of the ravine. The color of the clothing and gear made it look all the more out of place. She could see individual bodies now, the colors of the jackets splashing wildly on the grass.

Robert approached from uphill in the ravine, holding the rifle in front of his body, ready. He circled the jumble of bodies and tents, and at one point he knelt down and picked something up from the ground. Tara watched as Robert checked each body in turn, and then he shook his head. She willed her feet to move forward, and she walked down the slope. Steve and Sabrina followed. Tara had seen so much death in the last few days that she thought she would get used to it.

She came up and stood in front of the first body, looked at Charles, his body laying at an unnatural angle, in death his features twisted and dark. He appeared to have been shot in the back, his jacket black with dried blood.

You'll never be Prime Minister now, Charles, she thought, and the words of your cousin Sir Winston Churchill won't do much good.

There were six bodies in all: Charles, the four other young men that they had met in Huaraz that night, and a woman. Marilyn. Robert and Steve began to examine the bodies.

"How long since this happened?" Steve asked Robert.

"Don't know, really, since the coldness of the night will slow down rigor and decomposition. Maybe, two or three days, or only one day or so." He stood up and looked around at the bodies. He didn't speak for several minutes. Robert walked over to a body and looked at the wound.

"Judging by how close together they are, it looks as if they had no warning, or very little. Nobody had a chance to run." He walked to another body and turned it over, carefully, as if he didn't want to wake the person. When he turned the body, Tara saw that it was Marilyn, her blonde hair matted with blood. Robert looked at her hands and tried to flex the fingers. He shook his head.

"Charles still has his pack on," Tara said, and pointed. She didn't want to go closer.

Steve looked at Charles and then walked a short distance away and checked a body that had fallen away from the others, as if he had tried to run at the last minute. He turned the body over, and Tara noticed that the person was wearing a pack. Steve checked the pack and began laying items on the ground.

"Doesn't look as if any of the packs were gone through," he said, holding up a flashlight. He stood up and looked around the body on the ground, and then walked around in a circle, and then again, wider. He looked at Robert.

"You find any brass?"

Robert shook his head. No.

"Why not?" Sabrina asked. Tara looked around, and thought that if someone shot her, at least she wouldn't have to walk anymore.

"They were shot from a distance," Robert said, standing up and walking to them. He looked up. "And not from the air." He looked at the bodies, and then at the surrounding hills. "There," he pointed at a low hill a hundred yards uphill from the camp. Had they kept walking, they would have passed through the spot.

"That's where the brass will be." He held the rifle in his right hand and jogged up the hill. Steve followed, slowly, cradling his wounded arm.

"Get the packs," Steve said over his shoulder, and then tried to jog after Robert.

Removing a pack from a person who has fallen asleep was hard enough; trying to get a pack off a dead person with stiff limbs was almost impossible. Tara walked to Charles first and started there. If she didn't she knew she would lose her nerve and not continue. Sabrina joined her.

Tara said a prayer to protect herself from the dead, to protect

Sabrina and the others. She might not be able to protect them from the living, but she could at least try to protect herself from the dead. She mumbled the words faster, not wanting to look at Charles, praying that Charles and the other dead wouldn't hurt her. She prayed and said all she knew of the old words, and then stopped. She looked around at the bodies. Sabrina sat close by, sitting on her heels, staring.

Tara tried not to think about what she was doing to remove the pack from Charles. She looked up at the mountains and her skin tingled, thinking that someone could be aiming a shot at her at that moment.

There was a mountain lake down below and past the lake it was only a dozen miles to Huaraz. If they could just make it there they might have a chance. There were phones there, and people there who were not connected with the army or some terrorists. Sabrina joined her and tugged on the straps and Tara felt the pack move. Tara looked down at what she was doing.

Charles had been shot more than once and from the amount of blood on his head, he hadn't died right away, but had been left there, bleeding. His left arm was folded under him, his right arm pulled up as if he had tried to pull himself forward on his stomach. Tara pulled on the straps and she couldn't get them over his hands. He was too stiff, the blood matted on the straps of the pack and the jacket. His right arm came up, curling into a grotesque claw, and she looked away.

"Here, undo the straps," Sabrina said and unbuckled the "D" ring and pulled. Sabrina began to open pockets in the pack, pulling items out and laying them on the ground.

"Tara."

Tara looked at her friend. Sabrina was unfolding a piece of white paper, a piece of sketch book paper. Charles had kept it in a pocket in the top of his pack. Sabrina slowly folded the sketch and put it in the back pocket of her jeans. Tara looked over the grass of the hillside and watched it wave in the wind. She didn't look up as Sabrina left her and went to another body. As a child in Cold River, she used to sit with Delores and Sabrina and watch the wind blow the grasses in the high meadows, dreaming of what they would do when they grew up.

Well they weren't going to grow up any more, and after a while, she went to help Sabrina.

Don't look at the faces, she thought, and with cold and trembling fingers she was able to remove packs and go through pockets. She felt like a grave robber. Within minutes they had a pile of packs, tents, and clothing. Tara sat down and leaned on the pile of packs. She was in this position when Steve and Robert came over the crest of the hill they had climbed. They were carrying a pack they had found.

They spent the next ten minutes going through the packs, replacing what they needed in case they had to stay out longer, and discarding what they didn't need. Food. They all munched on energy bars as they sorted. Sleeping bags. A lightweight tent. Water.

Tara stood and shouldered her pack, heavier now, and waited for the others to do the same. Steve carried a small pack in his left hand.

"Which way?"

Steve pointed to the hill he and Robert had been on. "We pick up the trail again up on the crest."

"What about Charles and the others?" Tara asked, knowing the answer.

Steve shrugged, and started up the hill.

Tara took a last look at Charles. She mouthed the words to a prayer as she turned away.

When Tara and the others had started on the trek, they hadn't gone an hour or two without coming upon a campesino, a local Indian, usually with his family, and often, with other trekkers. They had stopped at two small Indian villages, and in one case, had camped outside the village. During the past two days, Tara hadn't seen any traffic in the hills at all. Not a local, a donkey, a horse, or another trekker or climbing party. In fact, Charles and his friends were the only people they had seen.

And they were dead.

They came over the last hill above Huaraz in the early evening, about six p.m., Tara thought. She sat down heavily and looked down on the town. Even at 9,000 feet, Huaraz was below them, about four miles down the valley. Below her she saw movement on the road that ran north and south through the valley, trucks and busses, but it was so far that she couldn't see people. The trail they were on continued down the hill and wound out of sight a mile down the hill. In the distance, Tara saw donkeys and people on the trail, headed for Huaraz.

"What's with all the people?" Tara asked.

"Market day tomorrow," Steve said. "And even with a war on,

market day doesn't wait for anything. The roads will be full of people tonight and tomorrow." He pointed at a spot further down the valley.

"Looks like a checkpoint down there, by that rock outcropping." Tara followed Steve's arm and saw a cluster of vehicles on the trail, but at this distance, she couldn't tell what they were.

"Maybe we shouldn't go down there tonight," Sabrina said.

"And maybe I need a hot shower," Tara said, "but we aren't going to make it around the army." She started off down the hill without waiting for the others. She was tired, wanted to call her grandfather, wanted a hot shower, for the killing and insanity to end.

Steve caught up with her a hundred yards down the slope.

"What's the hurry? They will close the town down when it gets dark."

Tara's shoulders slumped, and she kept walking, head down, just wanting for this nightmare to end. She wanted to see her grandfather, to think about her parents, her friend Delores.

It took them an hour to get within a mile of the checkpoint. What Tara saw caused her to slump down on her pack. There was an army squad on the trail, stopping campesinos as they made their way on the trail to town. Further to the north, Tara could see a second checkpoint, with men watching the hillside. Nothing like being expected.

They were done for.

Robert was lying on his stomach, the rifle out in front of him, looking at the units.

"They're looking for us," he said.

"How we gonna get by them?" Sabrina asked.

"By going east," Tara said, and the others looked at her.

"They expect us on the west side of town, maybe south or north, but we have to go in on the east side, and in the morning when the traffic is the heaviest." She slammed her fist into her pack. Another night in the hills, smelling like a transient.

Living with the dead.

# Chapter 24

Miami International Airport

Martin walked off the plane, groggy, his fatigue worsened by the early afternoon sun. During the flight from Portland to Denver he had talked quietly, first with Lori and then with Hawk. The turnaround at Denver had been quick, with an early morning flight to Miami. He had slept for maybe an hour, and the bright sunlight coming in the windows of the concourse didn't help.

Hawk came up beside Martin when they reached the boarding area.

"When we gonna meet the group?"

"An hour." Martin waited for Lori who came out of the jetway with a scowl, with Dan and Sherman trailing behind. If I look as tired as they do, Martin thought, we're in trouble. Peru is east of Miami, and the effect of the travel would only get worse. They were going to have to rest as much as they could on the next flight.

"Oh brother," Lori muttered, stopping in the concourse, giving an evil look to a man in a suit who went away talking to himself. She glared at Dan and Sherman. Dan scratched himself, looking sleepy.

"Put me with these two again, Boss, and I will give a new meaning to the term 'savage.'" She glared at Dan. He grinned and held his hand up to give her a high five, and she ignored it. They had stopped next to a tour group, each person with a yellow smiling face stuck on their tunics, a face with the logo, "Sun Country Tours."

"Alright, stay together, people," a woman shrieked. She pointed at a couple who looked as if they should be on oxygen and yelled again, "You there, come on, stay in line!" Lori looked at Martin, then at Hawk. They had walked into the meeting place where a group of about thirty people were pressed together, some elbowing for position so they could hear and see the group leader. They had located their tour group.

The group leader, a stocky woman with coiffed hair dyed a reddish brown, was bellowing into a handheld microphone, her eyes darting around to keep a count of her herd. She was wearing a brown suit with a yellow blouse, and the total effect on Martin was nauseous. And if she affects me like that, Martin thought, I don't want to think about Lori's reaction.

"That suit is justification for capital punishment," Lori muttered, rolling her eyes.

"Alright people, I need for each of you to put this yellow tag on your shirts, jackets, or blouses, and at NO time during our trip can we be without them." She grabbed the hand of the man standing in line in front of her and jammed a bunch of yellow tags into his hand."

"Alright, people, I need for you to get your passports out and have them ready for us to ..." She looked at Martin and the others standing just inside the seating area, watching her.

"Are you Martin Andrews, Elias Johnson, Dan Martinez, Sherman Tewee, and uh –" She looked at her list, flipping the page, her hair bouncing with it. "Lori Running, uh, Running Rox?"

"Fox," Lori said, starting forward.

"Yes, that's us," Martin said, walking up to the woman.

"Well, this is highly unusual," the woman said, loud enough for people to hear in the next concourse, "and you people are lucky to be admitted to this tour of the most famous –"

Martin thrust himself forward, pushing up to the woman, knowing that Lori was behind him, and he leaned forward until his face was inches from hers.

"In back of the line, I said ..."

Martin pushed forward again, and he thought he heard growling behind him.

"Please listen to me," he said quietly. "You let us in at the last minute because our organization paid a hefty bonus to your employer." He didn't know this for sure but he suspected that it was so, and in any event, he was sure that the guide didn't know for sure either. "A very hefty bonus, and there's one for you as well if we are not singled out from the rest of the group in any way."

Her eyes darted back and forth, the back of her legs up against a row of seats. Martin nodded at her, smiling. The things a chief of police in Indian country had to do.

She nodded, her throat making a clicking sound as she swallowed.

"We don't want to be treated any different from any other person here, and this is the last time you will mention to anyone that we were a last minute addition to the group."

166

She nodded again, and removed five tags from the clipboard and gave them to Martin. He smiled and moved back, bumping into Lori. He turned to look at his group, Lori giving him a thoughtful look. He motioned them to the back of the crowd. When they reached the end of the line, he put a yellow tag on his jacket, a tag that said, "Sun Country Tour Member."

He handed one to Hawk, who smiled and put it on his western shirt.

"I ain't coming 'round wearing one of them tags, Boss," Lori growled. "And if that woman with the ugliest hairdo in the country even speaks to me, I'll rip her fat, collagen-filled lips off her face."

"Stop, you're making my wiener hard," Dan muttered to her with a grin. Lori launched herself at Dan and Hawk caught her.

"Wear the tag," he said, his voice hard, void of humor, like a parent who has finally had it with a child.

Lori pouted and put the tag on.

Martin shook his head and walked to the back of the line, the others following, Hawk with his hand on Lori's arm. They boarded without incident, and after they were settled, Martin was able to sleep for the first couple of hours. Their tour guide, Shirley, had herded them onto the plane, giving them their seat assignments, barking out numbers to her aging charges. She was an officious person, and Martin was sure had never been in charge of anything important. There were a few moments of confrontation when Lori told Shirley that the five of them had to sit together, and Shirley must have been perceptive enough to make that happen.

Hawk, Lori, and Martin were in a row of seats in the rear of the Boeing 767.

As Martin drifted off to sleep, he thought of standing in the dark with Martha Coeur d'Alenes at the edge of the cliff, looking out across the dark span, learning that the bridge had been wired with explosives. Martha had told him that maybe he had found what he was looking for, a people, a place to be, a place to call home. Maybe he had. During the past two days, when they were planning for the trip to Peru, Martin knew that if he had told any of his old friends about what he was planning, they would have thought that he was crazy.

He slept, and the plane flew south across the Gulf, crossing Central America just south of Panama. Martin woke up to the hum of the airplane, quiet talking, and some laughter in the cabin in front of him. He looked over at Lori and she appeared to be sleeping. She opened one eye and looked at him and smiled.

"So, Boss got some sleep, huh?"

"Yeah." He looked at his watch. Hawk was not in his seat.

"Where's the big guy?"

"He's back in the galley, looking for something to eat, trying to get the attendants to feed him." She shook her head and laughed. "You never traveled with Hawk, did you, Boss?"

"Just to Portland, and don't call me Boss."

"One of our biggest problems in Peru is going to be keeping him fed." Lori leaned closer to Martin.

"Do you think we have a problem here with Ms. Shirley?"

Martin sat up in the seat and stretched. He looked at Lori and thought of how serious she looked now, not the Lori who tore down convention.

"We're planning to leave the tour in Lima, right?" She asked.

Martin nodded.

"When she's missing five of her most valuable, talented members, who do you think Big Lips will go crying 'round to?"

"Well, we're kinda making up the rules as we go, Lori, but I suspect she would at the very least alert the U.S. Embassy."

"Yeah, that's what I thought, so-"

"So, that's a potential problem," Martin said, "and we'll have to talk with her."

"Maybe I'd better talk with her, now," Lori said, grinning, getting up from her seat. Martin held his hand out, stopping her.

"If we tell her now, she'll freak out when we go through customs, probably think we're drug smugglers or something, and will still tell the embassy and the good old embassy people will tell –"

"The Peruvian police," Lori said.

Lori sat back down, leaning over to Martin again.

"Exactly."

"She's not that good of an actor," Lori said. "We might not even get through customs if she knows. I think we should tell her something after we get out of customs or she'll have the police or army looking for us and that will be worse yet."

"Well, in the next few hours we need to ease her doubts about us, maybe kiss up to her a little, get her to accept us."

"I'll leave the ass kissing part to you, Boss, being a chief and all you're probably coming around used to it." Lori laughed. She leaned in close and looked in his eyes. Her breath was warm on his face, and Martin realized then that he liked her laugh, her smile, and he secretly liked the way she had danced in the McGruff suit, and he knew he could never tell anyone. He shook his head and pulled back a few inches.

"I'll think of something to tell the woman," he said, not knowing what it was he said, aware of Lori's closeness.

"Martin," Lori whispered. He leaned forward until he was inches away again, their faces almost touching.

"Yeah."

"I like you."

"I like you too, Lori."

"I mean I like you more than a boss and an employee relationship."

"I, uh, don't know what to say about ... this, I, uh," and he stopped, not knowing what to say, knowing what he needed to say. He pulled back and spoke louder.

"This is awkward, Lori, and I am your boss."

Lori laughed. She moved closer and whispered. "Awkward is going to Peru with a bunch of Indians, or In-dins, as the chairman says. Maybe getting killed or thrown in jail, in Peru or when we get back. I just wanted to tell you how I felt before we got there and things turned busy, or turned ugly." She was quiet and kept her face inches from his, and for once she was not the witty, outgoing, confident person he had come to know.

"Martha Coeur d'Alenes told me that you, how did she put it, you 'liked' me."

"That old Martha goes crying 'round about a lot of things. You can't pay any attention to her." Lori suddenly grinned. "But in this case, she was right."

"Oh fine," Martin muttered. "How many people on the rez know this?"

"Just about everybody."

"That obvious?"

Lori nodded. She placed her hand on his knee and leaned forward and kissed Martin on the lips. She held the kiss for a few seconds and drew back. Martin didn't move.

"I wanted to do that a month ago when I first met you, but didn't think it would be the best thing to do."

For one of the few times in his life, Martin didn't know what to say. He tingled, and now was afraid to speak. It must be the fatigue, the tension, the closeness, the element of danger that is causing this, and it wasn't real. But it felt real, and for the first time in weeks, he didn't wonder what the hell he was doing with the Indians. Lori was beautiful, and different. Maybe that was the attraction, she was different. But there was more there. She was, well, she was Lori.

"So you played McGruff instead, thought that was a way to get noticed."

Lori laughed. "It worked, didn't it?" She reached over and took Martin's hand in hers.

"Lori."

She looked up at him.

"How old are you?"

"Twenty-eight."

"I'm -"

"Forty-nine," she said, finishing for him. "And it's fine, I don't go out much, and I'm tired of dating. I choose you."

Martin looked over his shoulder, looking down the aisle. "Hawk, what does he know?"

"That Hawk, he told me to leave you alone, that you were the boss, and I told him to mind his own business, and then Susan told him to mind his own business, and then he glared at me in that way he has and I glared back, but when Susan told him that, he knew it was finished."

"Everyone on the rez, even Chairman Bluefeathers?"

Lori nodded vigorously, and then grinned.

"What about me, didn't anyone think that I might object?"

"No, the people thought that it was a good thing, that we were supposed to be together, that if we were, you wouldn't let me do that McGruff dance again."

Martin laughed.

Lori slid out into the aisle, winked at Martin and walked forward. Hawk stood in the aisle and watched her, shook his head, and laughed, dropping into the seat. "You got a handful there, Boss."

Martin slowly nodded his head. He had to get his mind on the job.

"Tell me about your cousin, Tara. How will she act when she's captured, what will she do?"

Hawk sat and didn't speak for a minute. When he did, he stared at the seat in front of him. "She is a very determined person. Maybe it has to do with her mother and father dying, but she has always been determined to do something big. I expect that she will be running the tribal council in a few years if she doesn't become a famous artist first. Right now, well, she doesn't have the confidence in herself, she is afraid of making decisions for others."

"How will she act in this situation?"

"She will eventually take charge." Hawk looked out the window, and then at Martin.

"She will if she lives long enough."

# Chapter 25

Lima

Jorge Chavez Airport is north of downtown Lima, a mile and a half inland from the Pacific Ocean. They came in low over the water, the ocean a black nothingness below, suddenly replaced by the lights of Callao, a seaport city adjacent to Lima. A suburb, San Miguel was ahead, and beyond that, Lima. There were over eight million people in the metropolitan area, Martin knew, and he wondered how they were going to find their way in this country.

Hawk was sleeping with his head back, his mouth open, and twice Martin had to keep Lori from putting foreign objects in the big man's mouth.

"Do you think the customs people will know about Cold River, the declaration of war and all?" Lori asked.

"The whole world knows," Martin said. "The tribes on the Amazon probably watch FOX before the men go out to hunt for the day."

"My passport has a Cold River address on it," Lori said.

"Mine says Portland. Guess we won't go through Customs together." Martin smiled. "Maybe the average person working there won't put it together, but if they do, we go with the program. We can't fight our way out of the country."

"If Tara and the others are dead..." Lori began.

"We leave the country immediately and I mean all of us." As the plane landed Martin knew he needed to talk with his team. They either had too many people with them, or not nearly enough.

"Lori, how did the chairman pick Sherman and Dan? I mean why those two and not someone from the police department?"

"They had passports," she said. "He knows who has been traveling, who he can trust." She looked at Martin. "What, you have a better way to pick people who invade a country?"

He laughed, and stood up as they stopped at the gate. Lori pulled his arm, motioned to him to bend down, and she kissed him on the lips, a short kiss, but an electric one.

"Didn't know if I would get the chance again."

Jorge Chavez Airport is sixteen kilometers from downtown Lima, and Martin knew that tourists are required to show passports when entering and leaving the airport, and that was after leaving customs. Luggage was checked upon demand, and often several times before a person could leave the airport grounds. With the heightened state of alertness for the armed forces, the army might not even let them pass. The phones worried him. They must get the satellite cellular phones through customs for their plan to work.

When the plane stopped at the gate, Martin got up and stretched. They waited for the door to open and the passengers to begin crowding off, but no one moved toward the door.

"What do you think, Boss?" Hawk said, crouching and trying to stand.

"I think we wait with all of the others, and stay in the middle." He looked at his group and heard their tour guide yelling something.

"Alright, people, this way and stay together." She raised her clipboard and Martin saw that she actually had a whistle on a string around her neck. He looked over at Lori, who was standing in the aisle watching the guide with an amazed look.

"She whistles at me, Boss, I'm gonna shove that whistle-"

"Behave."

Lori shook her head and stepped back so Martin could enter the aisle in front of her. As they stood there, the door opened in front and the line started moving.

"Let's stay in the middle. Put some people between us, in the middle of the group when we go through customs." Martin knew that Peru averaged over a million tourists a year, and that most of them passed through Lima. He decided to have Lori behind all of them, the last person of their little group, so she could intercede with Spanish if she saw that one of them was in trouble. They walked off the plane into a large boarding area, where people were waiting for their flights. There were people in suits, soldiers in khaki, and campesinos with serapes and colorful shirts. In the corner a vendor sold a leafy plant, coca leaf, to be chewed.

They followed the tour guide down the concourse to a wide stairway and walked down, the press of people around them. Martin looked back and saw Lori and she gave him a nervous smile. The stairway took them down into a large room that Martin knew was the luggage hall. It looked as big as a football field, Martin thought, where hundreds of people waited beside large tables for their luggage to arrive. Others pulled bags from the tables and moved to the far end of the room for the customs booths. People pulled bags from the tables and shouted, argued. Martin walked around a family sitting on a luggage cart, a woman and child sleeping on the bags. In the middle of all of the bedlam, baggage handlers pushed carts through the room, picking out paths where none existed.

Their tour guide led them like chicks, weaving through the sea of bodies and bags of all description.

It took them an hour to locate their bags. Lori sat wearily on her backpack. Martin dropped his bag and sat beside her, the room still in constant motion around them. He nodded toward the exits. Even at this hour there were soldiers at the exits and lounging next to the customs tables. They looked young, mostly kids, from the suburbs or the Andes, joining up for a better life. Their youth didn't make Martin feel warm and fuzzy. In his experience, youth and guns and authority didn't make for a very good mixture. There was a line of people at the tables and it didn't look as if it was diminishing. Customs officials were going through every bag.

As Martin watched, a young man cleared the customs table, holding his bag together with clothing falling out, only to be stopped by the kid soldiers at the door and forced to go through the process again.

Great.

"You see those tables," Lori said, "we probably won't make it past there."

"Oh yes we will," Martin said. He looked for their guide and saw her holding up her arms, although he couldn't hear what she was saying. Behind her, the customs officer at the nearest table was a woman. She wore a green uniform blouse and skirt. She had short gray hair and the scowl of a pissed off attorney. What got Martin's attention was the .45 caliber pistol she had taken out of it's holster and slammed on the table, to make a point he thought, and if that was what she had intended, she had accomplished her task.

"She likes her gun," Lori said in his ear. "I'm impressed."

A young Peruvian man was waiting in front of the table and jumped as the customs officer slammed her gun down. He looked around wildly as she dumped his suitcase over on the table, his belongings there for all to see. She picked up her pistol and prodded the pile of clothes and magazines, said something with a snarl, and shoved the suitcase and clothing at the man, waving him on.

Jesus, Martin thought. Hawk came up beside him and said something Martin couldn't make out. Martin looked at him.

"Is this a sorry way to run a country or what?" Hawk said, looking at the customs tables. The next person in line at the gun toting customs official's table was waved on through, and the crowd seemed to collectively sigh.

"It's like out of a movie, isn't it Martin?" Lori asked. She shook her head as they watched the customs officers paw through suitcases, often yelling at the passengers.

Their tour guide was waving her arms again, and they stood up.

"Be cool," Martin said.

"Right," Lori said, looking at the tables.

They held their packs as the group was herded up to the customs tables by their guide. Ahead of them, a family Martin had seen on the plane was waiting for their luggage to be torn apart. At the next table over, a soldier led a man away.

If we can just get the cell phones through, Martin thought.

They approached the customs area, their guide in the lead, holding her clipboard. She placed her bag on the table, said something to the official, and then pointed back toward her group, speaking rapidly in Spanish. She scowled at them, and then looked bored. Terrorists or not, tourism was the country's life blood. The customs official motioned for Thick Lips to pass, and then waved all of them through.

If I look as guilty as I feel, Martin thought, then we're screwed. His pulse quickened as he passed the customs inspection area, tried not to look at the woman with the .45, and then walked on by. He heard Lori say something in Spanish as she walked by, and then they were outside. Thick Lips walked past him, counting her chicks.

The scene outside the terminal was, if anything, more disorganized than the scene inside. There were soldiers and people everywhere; collectivos, cars, taxis were pulling up and people threw luggage inside. The driver would yell at traffic, and then pull out without regard to oncoming vehicles.

"Where's our guy?" Lori asked.

"Said he'd meet us here," Martin said.

"How will he know us?"

"Dennis said he would find us."

Their tour guide walked up the line, and Martin stepped out of line to intercept her.

"I need to talk with you a moment," he said, blocking her way.

"I'm very busy now, we can chat when we reach our lodgings." She spoke as she looked at her list and moved to push on past, and Martin stepped into her.

"I don't want to make a scene," he said harshly, "but if I have to get your attention, we'll all be in trouble. We, my friends and I must leave your group. We have to return to the states tomorrow, and you will say nothing."

"But-" She looked past Martin at the row of army tanks on the outside of the drive, the soldiers lounging against the tracks, and then back at Martin.

"These are unusual times in this country, and I'm sure you can see that. We don't want any trouble. Don't say anything, or-" Martin pointed at the tanks and shook his head. "We will accompany the group to the hotel, and then," he shrugged. She turned and walked up to the front of her group, her hands shaking as she walked. As she walked away, a man approached Martin from the street. He looked to be about forty, was wearing a brown leather jacket, tan slacks, and had shoulder length black hair. He stood next to Martin, looked out over the sea of cars and busses, and asked, "Are you Martin Andrews?"

"Yes."

"I'm a friend, an amigo of Dennis Underwood. Go to your hotel, get your rooms, and I'll contact you there."

Martin nodded.

"Too many soldiers here, less in downtown Lima. I'll contact you after you get settled." He started to move away and Martin placed a hand on his arm.

"Any word on the students?"

"Yes," the man said, and then walked into the crowd.

# Chapter 26

Lima

The hotel in Lima was downtown on the Avenue Nidolas de Pierola, the Hotel Crillon, an old established hotel, a favorite with travelers. For Martin and the others, getting on the bus at the airport to the hotel was made easier by staying with their tour group. Their guide, a now somewhat subdued guide, Martin thought, avoided the touts who wanted to make some American dollars, the taxis, the private cars and cycles, and herded her charges through the unfamiliar sea of hustlers and onto the right bus.

Martin watched the landscape from the window of the bus, the dark city streets (now with a tank at most intersections) changing from the bustle of the airport to a shanty town that existed in a concentric ring around the city, the poorest of the poor. There were brown mud huts on ground that appeared to be an endless landfill. A gray pall hung over the city, probably from the fires in the shanty towns. As they got closer to the city, the shacks changed to small houses, then small walled courtyards, and in the city, the contrast was amazing. Wealth, proud and audacious, adorned the houses and streets. In the section before the river, the Rio Rimac, there were as many Mercedes as there were taxis and busses.

A city of contrasts and beauty.

The churches and mansions rivaled those in any city in the world. As they entered the modern downtown business district, a police car went screaming past, a Ford Crown Vic, Martin thought. They rode through the Jr de la Union, the main shopping street in the old downtown, and within three blocks they stopped at their hotel.

The Hotel Crillon was old, elegant in the architectural style of the Spanish conquest of South America - ornate designs, balconies, steep roofs and tile. Martin wearily shouldered his bag and waited to get off the bus. His group was quiet, tired and nervous. No one spoke as they entered the lobby. It reminded Martin of a Catholic cathedral, tall ceilings, dim, and with the echoes of train station marble.

Their guide for once didn't have anything to say as she handed them their room keys, one for Martin, Hawk, Ted and Sherman. One for Lori.

"Oh, goody," Lori muttered. "Ted and Dan can fart and fornicate with each other."

Thick Lips turned to Lori and grimaced.

"I mean bond, bond like the men they are." Lori glanced at Martin and then said, "Okay, I'll be good." She turned to Thick Lips and said something in Spanish, laughing, and their tour guide actually smiled. Lori said something else, and Martin caught the word "huevos," and Lori and the woman began laughing, Lori slapping her knee. She smiled at Martin, proud of herself. It might not be too bad of a trip after all.

# Chapter 27

Above Huaraz

Robert mixed the paint with a stick in three cups he had arranged on the ground in front of the small fire. Red, black, and green. Tara watched and thought he looked like a tragic figure, a warrior who was about to do battle against insurmountable odds, and she thought that he knew it. Robert wanted to be a warrior and somehow knew what was needed. She supposed it wouldn't do them any good if he was a warrior too late, or too early. It doesn't do anyone any good if they are a warrior without a war to prove their courage.

It was, she knew, an honorable profession.

An honorable thing to do.

She looked down the valley at the lights of Huaraz, the cooking fires of the Campesinos on the hillside too numerous to count. In the end they had decided to start a fire, since there were so many around them. They were sitting in front of it, Robert on his knees applying the stupid paint he had mixed. Steve was laying on his side, elevating his swollen arm, and Sabrina was sitting beside him, talking quietly.

Tara loved Robert then, loved him as she would a brother. Even though he was a few years younger than she was, she realized that she thought of him as the older brother she never had. As she watched this small wiry young man of the Apache nation while he painted his face - she loved him. She wanted to tell him, but somehow she knew that she didn't have to. Over the past two days, she and Robert had fought side by side, helping the others get through this killing and the threat of death. He had helped her protect and take care of Delores, and now he was going to fight for them again, and he believed he would be going to his death. She knew he was, and he seemed so calm, too calm, and it was crazy, he should be with his friends back home, with his parents, with his dog. He should be on a date somewhere.

Robert applied a streak of red across his forehead and then one down his right cheek, checking his work in the small mirror Tara held for him. She touched his arm.

"Robert-"

She stopped, not wanting to continue. She was tired, she wanted to cry and she knew it wouldn't help, that it wouldn't make it easier for him.

"Robert, you know that you don't have to do this, not now, not this way."

He took the mirror from her and held it up, looking critically at his chin. He looked over at Tara and grinned.

"You, Tara, you are the sister I never had, a good friend here in this country. But we both know that I have to do this, that you need to get the others out of here." He looked in the mirror again and continued as he applied a streak of black paint under the red line, highlighting it.

"This is what I was meant to do, and you know it. You call the white man the Šiyápu. We call them...we call them the conquerors." He looked at her, and then at Steve and Sabrina. Steve nodded. He handed the bowls to Tara and took off his shirt.

"Put some black stripes down my back, like my face," he said, and turned his back to her. Tara dipped her fingers into the black greasy substance and made a tentative stripe down his back. He laughed. "Steve, don't let her make it cute." They all laughed, something Tara thought she would never do again. Robert began speaking quietly, almost as if he were talking to himself.

"Mostly, the conqueror of today wouldn't understand this, at least not now. There are some people in the service who face death, some cops, but not most. Maybe we are a generation of people who rely on others to keep us safe. We hide in our houses. That professor, the one from California, the one they shot, I bet he thought he was safe, that as long as he went crying around about how much he liked them, he was okay.

"And then they shot him." Robert leaned over the fire and applied a black stripe to his chest, running it down his stomach.

"You ever think that the professor was there for us, that he was there for me, that the world might just need a mousy professor from Berkeley now and then to make us warriors look good?"

Tara shook her head. No.

Robert looked up at her and grinned.

"That he was born to be who he was."

"You still don't have to do this, Robert."

"Maybe I was born to do this." Robert's grin faded and he looked closer at Tara, the shadows cast by the flashlight making his face look like an old warrior, an old man, and more than a little unnerving to Tara.

"But," he continued, "those people will find out that I am not a professor from Berkeley. I am what I was born to be. I am a warrior."

Robert looked at his face again and stood, picked up the rifle and checked it, then let it hang down by his side.

"What do you think of my face?"

"Scares the hell out of me."

"Maybe Steve was right," Robert said. He looked at Steve, who gave him a thumbs up. Robert looked at each of them slowly, and then spoke.

"Steve said that once in a while, each of us should have the ability to paint our faces and go out and protect our families. Each of us should have the ability to do battle." He smiled again, looking down over the valley, looking out over the ground he had to cover.

He's looking for the bad spots, Tara thought, the soft ice, the ice in the road, the place where the ball might go out of bounds, and she loved him more then, the quiet kid warrior who was going to his death.

She walked to Steve and sat beside him. His legs were out straight, his face flushed. Robert walked over and stood above them, carrying the rifle and the small pack. He was wearing jeans, hiking boots, and no shirt. He carried a jacket on the pack. The paint was drying on his face and stomach, the slashes of paint making his body look grotesque, frightening.

"You look pretty grim, little brother," Steve said.

"I'm going to fight worse than I look," Robert said, and squatted down beside Steve. He reached down and took Steve's good hand in his.

"You take care of yourself. You're a brave person. You might not look like an Indian, but you fight like one, so you must be one. You have the heart."

"I'll go with you," Steve said, and sat up straighter, cradling his swollen arm, the veins standing out on his neck, the muscles in his face twisted with pain. Robert put his hand on Steve's shoulder and gently pushed him back down.

"This is something I have to do. You need to make sure that these two, Sabrina and Tara, get back to their homes. Who knows, if I had been the one to get shot, I would be here and you would be going out to do battle, to create the diversion we need so the rest can cross the road."

"You don't have to let them get you."

Robert looked out over the terrain, then at the place where he knew the army was camped on the road. He shook his head.

"We both know there isn't a lot of cover out there where I can hide and slip away. But if I can somehow make it to the city, they will never find me." He turned back to the fire. Tara stood and walked to Robert, with Sabrina behind her.

"When you hear the commotion," Robert said, "get him across the road and into Huaraz."

"You sure we'll hear it?" Tara asked quietly.

Robert grinned and nodded.

Sabrina gave him a hug and a long look, and then Tara hugged him fiercely, holding back tears for the umpteenth time tonight. She released him and kissed him on the cheek.

"Thanks," she whispered.

"Por nada," Robert said. He removed her arms and held her at arms length. He handed her a folded paper.

"A letter to my family and one for the tribal council. You have to survive, Tara Red Eagle of the Confederated Tribes of the Cold River Reservation, so my people will know what we have done here."

Tara nodded.

"So that my people will know what I have done." Robert walked away from the fire and sat on a rock, looking out over the battleground he would find in a few hours.

After a few minutes, Tara joined him on the rock.

# Chapter 28

Above Huaraz

Tara and Robert sat for an hour, neither talking, comfortable with each other, and for Tara it was as if she had known him for years, maybe all of her life. She knew it wouldn't do any good to talk to Robert about staying, so she didn't. She wanted to sketch, to draw him as he was now, but she knew that she could recreate him exactly, at any time in her life, even if she lived to be ninety. She started talking softly, just to Robert, in a very light voice, almost a soliloquy, a sing-song small voice.

"When I was little," Tara said, "sometime after my parents died, my grandparents would take me camping, and I know for some people how we live may seem like camping, but we lived in a one story ranch style house with electricity, indoor plumbing, and color television, and later on, computers. And all this on an Indian reservation. Can you believe it?"

Robert looked at Tara and nodded. He spoke quietly, remembering something from the past.

"When I was a kid," he said, "we had an old black and white TV that someone had thrown out, our first television, and we used to gather around it and try to figure out the picture from the snowy shadows on the tube, since we only had an antennae, an old rabbit ears at that, and the nearest TV relay was about twenty miles away, on Lookout Rock. Yeah, those were the days. Out in the desert of the Southwest, a little brown Indian kid, sitting in the corner watching reruns of Magnum, P.I., a dozen relatives in the room at noon, looking at Hawaii in black and fucking white."

Tara nodded. She had grown up on the rez.

"You said you went camping. We didn't go camping because growing up was so much like it, didn't have electricity much of the time."

Tara nodded. She knew that she was fortunate to have grown up on the Cold River Reservation, as far as reservations go. Many of the Indians in the South lived below the poverty level, and that the unemployment was over fifty percent for many Tribes.

She lay back and looked up at the stars, a crowded sky, but not the same stars that she had grown up with. During the late summer in Oregon, she would go up to the high meadows with her grandparents and go on the traditional food gathering trips. They would pick huckleberries, sleep under the stars, and Tara would lie there between her grandparents, sometimes Delores with her, and watch the sky. She often wondered which star her parents would be on, where their spirits were, and wish that her mom and dad were with her. In the mornings her grandmother would boil water in a can on the campfire, and throw coffee grounds in the water. It was a long time before Tara knew that you could also make coffee with filters and strainers. She and Delores would sit in the early morning cold in front of the fire, blankets wrapped around them, and watch as her grandmother prepared breakfast.

Shivering with cold, she and Delores would share a tin cup with coffee and would talk about what they might do that day. They must have been about ten, and at that time in her life, Tara never thought about life off the reservation.

Tara and Delores would help with the huckleberry picking, and then would be allowed to play in the stream, getting cooled off with their friends. The boys would be off with their fathers, checking out deer paths in the forests around Mt. Jefferson.

Tara shook her head and the images of the ten year old Delores faded. Robert was saying something.

"-and it was a long time before I knew that most people in the country had electricity. I thought everyone lived like us."

"On my reservation," Tara said, "we only lived about fifteen miles from Madras, the town with a high school, and the older Indian kids took the bus and went to school there, and we would go there to shop sometimes, even though we had a store on the rez, and we would go to restaurants in town, so I pretty much knew how people lived off the rez, but still, it was different. My grandmother would sometimes go for weeks and not go into town, but my grandfather would go in every week for something, parts for the tractor or something."

And it struck her that in many ways they had grown up in small, similar nations within a larger nation, and that experience of growing up on a rez wasn't one that other people could understand. Tara didn't understand that until she had gone away to college, where most of the kids came from upper middle class and upper class families, and fell all over themselves to show how culturally aware they were, and they didn't understand anything.

They hadn't grown up on the rez, and that was that.

And she knew then that the hope she had of the United States government coming to their rescue was a false hope, that if they were to get out of Peru alive, they would have to do it on their own, that her grandfather wouldn't let her down. It was going to be up to the Indians.

Like Robert.

And like Steve, even if he didn't know what an Indian was yet.

Robert left before morning, walking away from the camp without looking back.  Tara wouldn't call to him for fear that he might.

# Chapter 29

Cold River Indian Reservation

Chairman Bluefeathers stood and thrust his hand forward.

"Senator Sterling, thanks for coming to see us poor In-dins."

The Senator shook the chairman's hand and grinned, clapping Bluefeathers on the shoulder.

"Chairman, I must say that this has taken me, hell, all of us by surprise." The Senator looked confident, like a white haired grandfather, and that was his strongest asset. He was not particularly bright, but he was photogenic, and was a political veteran in his fourth term. Bluefeathers motioned for the senator to be seated at the small conference table.

"Senator, you know that we just want to get our kids back, and maybe we shouldn't have jumped the gun and declared war on Peru, but I wanted to get their attention."

"Well, you certainly did that, but why didn't you call me? You know that-"

Bluefeathers held his hand up. "You know, as an afterthought, we should have done that, and that's why we called for you to come see us. You have always been our friend," and at that, the Senator nodded several times, "and will be. I just wanted to tell you of our plans and, hopefully, this whole thing will help you in some small way."

"We want you to assist us," Bluefeathers continued, "assist us with the State Department and the rest of the government, maybe even with the governor, another friend of ours."

"You know I will do everything I can," the senator told them. He went on about how he had always been a friend, and Bluefeathers thought of how much this Šiyápu sounded like the banker, coming around to help us poor In-dins.

"Senator." Bluefeathers decided that the meeting had served it's purpose. The Senator continued to drone on about what a friend he was.

"Senator, have you considered how this little incident here could actually help you?"

"What do you mean?"

"I mean you have certainly been a prominent senator, but to work as a go-between for us with the United States government, maybe even Peru, will mean that every news agency in the world will be listening to you,

Smith

filming you, watching you work in the political arena. This could be a huge win win for us, Senator. Help us put an end to this. I'll bet that there are cameras right now at the Bear Creek Bridge. Let people know first of all that we are not at war with America, with our friends in town and in the state, or any state for that matter, and that we are Americans."

The senator beamed, and this time Bluefeathers was the one to clasp the senator on the shoulder. After all, the senior senator from Oregon had to do something to pay for all of that salmon he'd eaten over the years. The Senator stood and they shook hands. He left, saying that he would do anything possible to help his friends.

Bluefeathers knew that the next twenty-four hours would be the most hazardous for his nation. The course would be decided for their country and most likely for those in Peru. Would the diversion he created assist those in danger, or would he be creating a more dangerous role for his granddaughter and the others?

For the United States government to turn over the kid from Yakama was traitorous, and whether or not his granddaughter got out alive, it was time to show honor and courage to the rest of the world. He didn't want this role, but if he accepted the perks of leadership, then he must take what comes with it.

Who *was* this Ambassador to Peru who throws young kids to the wolves? Who do these people think they are that they can do this? We are, after all, citizens of the United States, never mind that we were the first here to establish civilizations and culture.

"Chairman?" Josephine was standing behind him.

"Yes."

"The others are ready, and Chairman Johnson is here from the Mashantucket Pequot."

"Give me a minute, and show him in."

He turned to Sammy, who had been making notes on a legal pad during the meeting with the senator.

"I need to see him alone, Sammy. I'll see you at the meeting, and Josephine, send the Yakama leader in as well."

He had to receive the leader from the east alone, and during the meeting, he had to show his leadership, not just to his own tribe, but to the Yakamas and the Mashantucket Pequots as well. Sometimes he thought that leadership was nothing more than looking good and saving face. More wars had been fought, more people had been killed over saving face than for any other reason, except for maybe religion. He shook his head. The door opened and Chairman Johnson stood there, wearing a tailored grey suit, white shirt, and power tie. Johnson was not much taller than

187

Bluefeathers, and had the dark characteristics of the Mashantucket Pequot tribe.

"Charley, come in, let us poor western cousins take care of you." He walked forward and shook Johnson's hand, and they both laughed. Johnson had visited Cold River on several occasions, and he and Bluefeathers had found that they genuinely liked each other, and their friendship had gone beyond their official duties.

"Poor western cousins, my ass," Johnson said. "Hell, you got a beautiful reservation, land, trees, a beautiful mountain, and a river. All we got is a dinky little patch of woods that doesn't amount to a few hundred acres."

"And the largest casino in the world," Bluefeathers said.

"Well, yeah, that."

Bluefeathers motioned to a chair at the small conference table and they both sat down.

"I am about to convene a meeting of the tribal council, some of our key people, and I want you to be there. Dennis Lenwya from Yakama is already here and in the meeting room. I'm going to talk about some things that will disturb some people, but my speech is not going to be as harsh as Dennis's speech - he has already lost a tribal member due to the treachery of the U.S. and Peru. He wants to wage all-out war on Peru, actually invade the country. You and I both know that we can't win that kind of war, and we would lose public support if that happened."

Charley nodded.

"We will, however, take some steps to up the ante a little bit, with the ability to back off. You have a tribal member somewhere in Peru with my granddaughter, Charley, and I need your support, but I don't know what that is yet. I don't expect every Indian nation to declare war on Peru. As it is now, we are a novelty, something of a joke, and I would like to keep it that way."

"Some of my tribal leaders think you are crazy," Charley said with a laugh. "I think you are very wise, and have the courage and wisdom to lead all of us. Some of them didn't want me to make this trip, but you know what, they have grown soft with casino money." Charley Johnson looked at Bluefeathers and smiled.

"They think I'm crazy, too, but until they replace me, we'll back you, in the open, loudly, or behind the scenes, whatever works. What the hell good is the casino money if we can't use it when we need to?"

"Just be prepared for a cat fight in the meeting," Bluefeathers said. Johnson laughed and stood up and laughed again. "Hell, I've been to tribal meetings before. Are they ever any other way?"

The meeting was held in the tribal council chambers - a large room with floor to ceiling windows on two sides, cedar walls and a rust colored carpet. The tribal council sat at a large horseshoe table, carved out of solid pine and lacquered to a brilliant shine. There were eleven positions around the table, with a voice activated microphone on the table in front of each position, with room enough beside each tribal council member for an aide to sit.

There was a table in the center of the horseshoe with two microphones, a table for those presenting evidence to the council. Chairman Bluefeathers had been in the witness seat before over the years, and he knew what the Christians in the old coliseum in Rome felt like when the lions were released.

As Chairman Bluefeathers entered he met Dennis Lenwya the chairman from Yakama just inside the doorway and shook his hand. Bluefeathers took his place at the table, the end of the table near the door, and placed the visiting chairmen on either side of him. At a table behind Bluefeathers were Sammy, Joe Hall, Sal Wahenna, and his secretary. All of the council members were present except for the Chief of the Cold River Tribe, and it was reported that he was sick.

The council was made up of eight representatives from the tribes, some from distinct areas of the reservation, and some elected from "at large" positions. The other three members were the chiefs (for life) from each of the three tribes on the reservation: Cold River, Wasco, and Paiute.

When Bluefeathers took his seat the noise in the room stopped.

"This is an important meeting so I want to get started right away. Before we start, it is traditional for us to start with a prayer, so I could ask council member Martha Coeur d'Alenes to say a prayer for us." He nodded at Coeur d'Alenes, who was sitting in the middle of the table.

Martha Coeur d'Alenes stood and looked over the room, looking much the same way as she had looked at Martin when she had first met him. Bluefeathers had heard about the meeting, and smiled. Teach young Martin a thing or two about In-dins. As Martha started her prayer, Bluefeathers thought about how different they were from the world around them, not just the cultural thing, but the fact that they didn't have to worry about such things as having a prayer to start a meeting of their government.

She sang a beautiful prayer in Sahaptin, asking God for guidance.

"Mr. Chairman," Jimmy Hanson said. "Can you tell us what you think we should do next? People up in my area don't like this at all. And people still want their stoves fixed." He smiled and the council members and guests broke up into laughter, a request from a tribal member that would be made if the reservation were engulfed in fire.

Bluefeathers held up his hand.

"We are going to make the world notice this terrible event, and we are going to get our kids back. Tomorrow, we will set into place a plan to capture the Peruvian Ambassador to the United States."

The room erupted into noisy pandemonium. Chairman Bluefeathers smiled as a parent might smile at his child, patiently, wisely. He would admonish the group to not say a word, that their plans must stay in the room, but within thirty minutes of the meeting, family members would be told, calls would be made to family members off the reservation, then friends, and the plan would be compromised. They might throw him out on his ass, but he would lead this nation.

He looked across the room and caught Martha Coeur d'Alenes looking at him, a thoughtful look, and then a little smile. Bluefeathers was sure that she was thinking the same thing he was - it was too bad that he had to lie to the council.

What he was planning made the kidnapping of an ambassador seem like an insignificant event. If he could see into the future and know of the death that was surely to come, he might just call it off - or go to Peru himself and find the kids. But as a leader, Bluefeathers knew that hindsight was always better, and perfect.

# Day Five

# Chapter 30

Lima, Peru

Martin Andrews opened the door to his hotel room and Lori stood there, holding her bags in one hand and her backpack in the other. She walked past him and dropped her bags on the nearest bed, smiling at Martin as she did so. Hawk and Ted were watching television.

"I thought I would never get rid of Thick Lips, our weird guide - seems I'm her friend since I speak Spanish." Lori sat on the edge of the bed and looked at Martin. She was wearing black slacks and a gray sweater. "Have you heard from our man here?"

Martin shook his head and was about to answer when he heard a soft knock on the door. Martin opened the door to the man who had contacted him at the airport. The man entered, carrying a small briefcase.

"I'm Martin Andrews."

"Mr. Salazar," the man said, and Martin made the introductions.

"I'm doing this for Dennis Underwood," Salazar said as he took a chair at the small table. "He may have told you that he once performed a great service for me and my family, and I owe him." He looked around the room.

"And you know why we are here?" Martin asked.

"I know that you have come to find some friends of yours."

Martin nodded.

"Let me say this to all of you." Salazar looked at each of them in turn and shook his head. "What you are trying to do is impossible, and foolish, and I told Dennis this and he said that he told you this. Peru is a beautiful, wonderful country, but it is run by the Presidente and the army. In fact, the army runs the departments and the provinces away from Peru. The Presidente, even though he is elected, is in power because he has the support of the army and he is the Commander in Chief. I don't know if it has happened already, but if the Presidente declares an emergency, no one will be able to travel unless you have the consent of the army."

"Can you get us to Huaraz?" Hawk asked.

"Maybe, if we leave before morning. I have booked us on a trek out of Huaraz, and have all the necessary papers for that, so it might work to get us there. Unless the army shuts the highway down, in which case there will be no way to get there. And, you don't even know where your friends are."

"When do we leave?" Martin asked.

"At three a.m.," Salazar said. "Be ready at 2:30 and I'll come up to get you." He turned and placed the briefcase on the bed and opened the lid. He handed Martin a large automatic pistol and motioned for Hawk to look inside the briefcase. Salazar walked to the door and looked at the group assembled around the bed.

"Dress warm," he said, and entered the hallway, closing the door softly behind him.

Martin didn't think that there was time for him to go to sleep, but he did drift off sometime before one. Hawk and Ted were on the other bed, sleeping with their clothes on, Sherman on the floor with a pillow, laying by the window. Lori was in sweats under the covers, and Martin was on the edge of the bed next to the door, also with his clothes on.

Martin's dream was a continuation of the nightmares of the daytime, that he and his group had been taken into custody by the army and were being held for questioning. In the daytime it was all too probable; at night, it happened. He was being led down a hallway with cement walls, and it appeared that they might be underground, a dampness in the air. The ceiling lights did not push back all of the darkness. There was a feeling, a gloom that accompanied this place.

The guard in front of him wore the army field uniform, khaki, with the stripes of a first lieutenant. Behind him were two non-commissioned officers, walking up close, making the idea of turning around a bad one. They came to the end of the hallway and stopped before a door, where the lieutenant knocked. The door opened and Martin was led inside.

"Alto!" The command came from a dark corner. He couldn't see the walls of the room, but it didn't feel too big. The door closed behind him and he stood there, looking at a circle of light in the middle of the room. There was a small table in the center of the room and someone was seated in a chair on the other side. It reminded Martin of the Charley Rose show, where the guests are seated at a table in a circle of light. But this show wasn't in New York like The Charley Rose Show. This was, he was sure, in Lima, Peru.

Martin walked forward to the table and sat down. Salazar was seated across from him, his suit gone, replaced by the green of a Peruvian army officer.

The door behind Martin was flung open and someone threw a body in the room and it crumpled beside the table, the limbs twisted and askew, as if the person were dead. Salazar grinned at Martin and he stood up, walking to stand before the body.

"You looking for her, Senor?"

Salazar turned the body over and Martin was staring at the face of a person he hadn't met, but had come to know well.

Tara the chairman's granddaughter.

Her sightless eyes accused Martin of failure. The door opened again, and he heard the sounds of grunting, men lifting something heavy, and Martin felt and heard the thud of a body hitting the floor.

"Perhaps you're looking for him, Senor, the one you call Hawk."

Martin came up then, going for Salazar, moving as if he were tied up, his arms not responding, when there was another knock on the door, someone knocking, and...

The knock came again, and Martin raised his arms up, trying for Salazar, trying to get his arms up-

"Martin," someone said, the voice sounding like Lori, and

"Martin, wake up," Lori said, shaking him gently, holding his arm, and Martin sat up in the dim room, looking around, seeing Lori sitting beside him, holding his arms. On the other bed Hawk and Ted were out, Hawk snoring, with a racket coming from the floor by the window. Martin looked at Lori.

"What, did I-?"

"It's okay Martin," Lori whispered. "You were dreaming I guess, and I just helped you awake." She smiled and nodded at the door. "And someone's here."

It was Salazar, wearing his same black suit, the image of the army uniform gone. Martin asked for five minutes and closed the door. He returned to the bed, rubbing his eyes. Lori was dressed in a sweatsuit, her dark hair wet and in a pony tail.

"I showered," she said. "I didn't know when that would happen again."

They woke the others up and they were ready in minutes, joining Salazar in the hallway. Martin felt like they were skipping out on something, like leaving without paying, this sneaking around in the middle of the night.

Out on the street it was cool, the air moist and foggy. They loaded their gear into a small bus, a collectivo, as Salazar called it, and drove through the nearly deserted streets of Lima.

Within a half hour they were clear of the city, and started along the Pan American Highway, north toward the city of Huaraz. To get there, they would have to go along the coast for a hundred fifty miles, and then to the east into the mountains, reaching altitudes of over 10,000 feet.

To find Tara and the others.

Dennis Underwood, the DEA agent safely retired in Portland had better be a good judge of character, because if Salazar couldn't be trusted, they were in prison, or worse.

Hawk sat up front in the van, Martin and Lori in the back. They had agreed to leave Ted and Sherman in Lima, to make their way to the embassy, so they wouldn't all be together.

Lori dozed with her head on Martin's shoulder.

# Chapter 31

Huaraz

Colonel Miguel Hernandez leaned back in his chair and waited for his aide to bring him coffee, and at four a.m. he needed it. He lit his first cigar of the day. He had established temporary headquarters in Huaraz and was in contact with units in the field and his commander in Lima. The leader of the terrorists, Eduardo, as he was now called (and he has been known as many things) cut off the Indian woman's feet in the meadow. What a nice touch. When Hernandez first met Eduardo, he didn't know that the man had the creativeness to do such a thing, but it sure had impressed the others there, including the Americans.

That Eduardo had to die was of little consequence. He had done what needed to be done, and then some. It was too bad that Eduardo couldn't be rewarded for his resourcefulness, but if anyone found out that Eduardo talks to me, Hernandez thought, then I will be looking at the inside of a prison cell with only one way out. He laughed silently then, thinking that the little war that Eduardo (and the foolish impressionable children he got to follow him) had created had spread. There were reports of fighting in Chimbote on the north coast, a fishing village and now the location of oil refineries. Eduardo couldn't possibly be responsible for all of them.

One thing I know for sure, Hernandez thought, is that in order to put down this "rebellion," I will use the Iron Fist to smash it, and will become a general in the process. And earn the president's undying gratitude.

Oh, yes, nothing like a little war to spice up an army career that was going nowhere.

Even if you had to start the war.

One thing, though, the rest of the students would have to be dealt with. They could not be allowed to leave Peru alive.

# **C**hapter **32**

Above Huaraz

Robert knew he would have to move down closer before first light, and if the guards had night vision binoculars or goggles, he was toast. During the daylight there had been guards at either end of the bridge. Soldiers were deployed along the road before dark, and he was sure there were listening posts out. That's how he would do it if he were in charge. He hadn't been in the army, but he had grown up on the rez, and had played war from his earliest memory. And stealth was his friend.

Robert shivered, thinking it was the cold and not the coming fight that was causing him to shake. He was working his way down to the riverbank, and decided to crawl the last hundred yards. He crawled a few feet more, the river now about 100 feet ahead, and stopped. He heard something above the murmur of the river and he froze, lifting his head up as an animal would, sniffing the air. He waited two minutes, then three, and started to move his hand forward and he heard it again, this time louder against the sound of the water, and it ended abruptly. He placed the palm of his hand down, carefully, looking around in the almost complete darkness, holding the AK-47 with his right hand, placing his left down. He moved forward this way, taking five minutes to advance ten feet.

He listened.

He started forward again and froze, his left hand up in the air, the sound suddenly right in front of him, a rumbling sound. He heard the sound stop and start, then catch, and he knew what it was. He was listening to someone snoring, and he was right on top of them. If it hadn't been for the sound of the river, he would have heard it fifty yards ago. He strained to see into the darkness. He looked ahead, waited, and placed his hand down. He didn't bring his rifle up into firing position, because if he fired now, he wouldn't help the others at all.

He waited.

Patience.

His stomach growled, louder than the snoring, a mean tight growl, and he thought that dying without a decent pizza to eat was the worst thing.

The snoring stopped.

*They must have heard my stomach.*

He slowly brought the rifle up without thinking about the consequences. If anyone shot, he or a soldier, the effect would be the same. He might as well be the first one to shoot.

He waited longer, and he thought that it was actually getting lighter, that they were not far from first light. He waited another five minutes, and could then make out the shapes on the ground in front of him.

Two, no, three soldiers, sent out here as a listening post, curled up on the ground in front of Robert, laying amidst the rocks of the riverbank, unseen from any passerby. Robert carefully moved around them and then stood between two boulders. He slowly worked his way down to the edge of the water. Across the river were the lights of Huaraz, subdued in the mist and spray, and only a few lights, the cities in the Peruvian countryside not using lights like a similar sized city in the United States.

The river was noisy here, the rocks down river from the bridge forming a natural chute of icy water. At the water's edge he stood between two dark boulders, taller than he was, and looked back up the bank.

Nothing.

He sat the AK-47 against a rock and stretched, trying to ignore the pain in his stomach. He couldn't remember the last time he had a full meal. He held his stomach, the pain not just the pain of hunger. His stomach was jumping, churning, and he suddenly didn't want to die. He didn't want to die here with none of his friends around him, and he didn't want to die alone in a strange land. It would be a lot better if there was another person with him, Steve, Sabrina, Tara - someone. But he knew that he was better than that, that he could be a warrior, and this was what there was for him to do.

To calm his nerves he tried to think of the things he had heard from his father, mother, and grandmother. The stories when he was growing up, stories of a powerful tribe, when the Apache were free to roam the south lands in New Mexico, Texas, Arizona, California, and Mexico.

I may have been born for this time, for this day. It seems right.

Robert eased down between the boulders, aware of the men sleeping just sixty feet above him. Maybe they would be the first to pay for their sleeping on duty. He thought about going up and quietly killing them, but he didn't think he could kill all three of them before they either sounded the alarm or got him. Maybe if he had a bigger knife. The thought of killing an enemy with a knife both scared the shit out of him and thrilled him at the same time. He had painted up, and it was time to do battle.

He wanted to wait as long as possible to start the fight, but that might not be left up to him. If he were discovered it would begin right then. He lifted the rifle and pushed on the magazine. It was in tight and he didn't want to eject it and check it again. It would make too much noise. He had two twenty round magazines, and if the fight went right, he should be able to cause quite a commotion.

The rocks around him grew into shapes, and then he could see the river. The riverbank on both sides was strewn with boulders. The water was churning past, throwing up mist and spray. Above him and twenty yards from the bank, a dirt road ran along the river, going downstream from the bridge. Another fifty yards further down, there were two roads or tracks adjoining, and yesterday there had been an army checkpoint there. The checkpoint consisted of an armored personnel carrier and five or six soldiers.

He would attack from here.

It was light enough now that Robert could see his hands, his rifle, and make out the buildings of Huaraz across the river. He turned to watch the bank above him. With the roar of the water, he wouldn't be able to hear if someone approached him from the bank. He turned in a crouch and started up the bank, quietly, slowly, his rifle out in front of him, a warrior of the Lipan Apache, with the great Chief Cochise. Or maybe Mangus Colorado. But Robert knew better. As a tribal member, Robert's lineage was written on paper, down from the great Chief Goyathlay, The One Who Yawns. The white man knew him as Geronimo.

Some of Robert's relatives didn't much like Geronimo now, thinking that because of the leader's exploits, he brought death to people on the reservation. The army withheld food and supplies while Geronimo was off the reservation, and many of the people died.

But he had courage, that one. And he had a desire to be free.

Robert was one of the few descendants of the Lipan Apache, a band that had been almost wiped out by 1900. The few survivors had been placed on the Mescalero Apache Reservation.

From the time of his earliest recollection, Robert and his friends played cowboys and Indians. Robert was one of Geronimo's men, and later, before he was ten, he played Geronimo himself. His friends would kid him and say that he was too small to be the great chief, but he would insist on playing the leader. They would sneak down through the rocks above his parents' house and attack the army, or the settlers who had stolen their land. Robert's sister and her friends were usually the unsuspecting settlers, and Robert liked to see how close they could get before his older sister yelled at them to leave her alone.

Robert took another step, a warrior of Geronimo, his face painted. He was wearing blue warm up pants taken from one of the climbers, his chest and face painted. He wished he could have been in the traditional deer skin leggings, loin cloth and knee-high moccasins. To die in the clothing of his people. He held his gun up in front of him, crouching, the barrel shaking. He stopped and leaned against a rock, holding the gun tightly, waiting for the shaking to stop.

*Some warrior you are, Robert, hands shaking and all.*

He started up again, the shaking still there, the rifle barrel wobbling, his thighs shaking with each step. He stopped and took a deep breath and then forced himself to relax. He started again, the shaking not so bad. As he approached the top of the bank, he crouched lower, the place where the guards were sleeping just above him. Because of the roar of the river to his back, he didn't hear the guard above him approach.

As Robert started to look up over the bank, he found himself staring at a soldier standing on the bank above him. The soldier, a young man about Robert's age, was fumbling with the buttons on his fly, his eyes half closed, and Robert raised the rifle up, three feet below the soldier, and as the soldier's eyes flew open and he half turned to run, screaming, the sight of Robert's painted face a view of the devil. Robert shot him twice in the chest, the body flying backwards and out of sight, the shots a loud explosion.

What happened next was automatic, responses long buried with his ancestors. Robert yelled a war cry, his ears ringing with the shots, and he leaped the rest of the way up the bank and saw the other two soldiers just feet from him, standing, one smoking and the other reaching for his rifle, and Robert shot the one closest to him once, and then shot at the soldier with the rifle, shot once and missed, the man bringing his rifle up and firing a burst at Robert, the rounds passing Robert's head with a buzz, just as Robert fired three more rounds, all of them hitting the soldier, and the man went down.

Robert stood and looked at them, holding his rifle at his side, the barrel smoking, and he yelled again, his stomach churning. But at least his hands had stopped shaking.

He looked to his right at the bridge. One of the guards was looking down at the road, as if he had heard something. There was traffic on the bridge, mostly foot traffic, people coming out of the villages in the hills to go to the market; a few donkeys, a bus.

To Robert's left, the reaction was immediate. The soldiers at the checkpoint were standing by the vehicle, looking at the river. One of them shouted and pointed at Robert, bringing his rifle up, and from a hundred feet Robert screamed and fired at the group of soldiers, pulling the trigger, forgetting about counting, seeing one of the soldiers go down in a cloud of dust, the bullets from the soldiers hitting the rocks all around him.

He fired again and the guards were gone, crouched behind the armored vehicle or on the ground. Robert yelled once more and dropped behind the rocks. He looked up toward the bridge and he could see the soldiers there running toward the checkpoint, a sergeant driving them on, yelling at them. People were still moving on the bridge, moving across toward the town.

*Move away from the bridge, you warrior, son of Cochise, son of Colorado, son of Geronimo.*

He swallowed, his mouth dry, wishing then he had taken more water, but knew that it wouldn't matter in the next few minutes.

*Cross the road.*

The thought entered his head and he was moving, and then he was moving up again. The soldiers from the bridge were moving toward him, slowly now, crouching, their weapons out and ready. They were on the road with no cover or concealment, walking slowly, four of them, their boots making little puffs of dust as they walked. Robert waited until they were twenty feet away, close enough for him to see the fear in their eyes, and he jumped up and fired, moving the barrel, trying to get all of them, and he pulled the trigger, screaming, and the gun clicked.

Empty.

*Christ, I forgot to change clips.*

He jerked the magazine out and reached for another one in his pocket as the soldiers fell, the one in the rear running past him toward the checkpoint, the dust rising up, and three of the men in the road were still and not moving as Robert slammed the new magazine into place and slapped the bolt forward to charge the rifle.

A bullet hit the rock next to Robert's head and he jerked back, chips of rock stinging his face. He felt blood run down his face, mixing with the paint, and he smiled. He knew what he must look like now. He resisted an urge to close on the Armored Personnel Carrier, to get closer to the soldiers so they could see his face, so he could scare his enemies to the point where they couldn't function, and he could kill them all.

He looked up at the bridge and saw that the traffic was moving fast, people running into the town, the bridge open for now. He believed that they must be across, that they were awake and got Steve across. And then he knew that they did, that Tara wouldn't let him die for nothing, and he believed that they would get home and tell his family.

He wished he was with them.

In the quiet he crawled to the men in the rocks, the soldiers who had been sleeping, and found two rifles. He grabbed them by the barrels and pulled them toward him, backing down over the bank of the river on his stomach, pulling the rifles after him. They were M-16 Colts from the United States. He checked the magazines and found one full, one almost full. He removed the partially full magazine and put it in his pocket. Two rifles were enough.

He thought then that if he could just get past the armored vehicle, and there were maybe five very scared soldiers there, he might have a chance to go into the back country and get away. Robert knew that if he could get away from these few men and into the countryside, that no one could find him. He rose up on his knees and started to move quickly through the rocks, moving toward the APC, now thirty feet away. He peeked up over the riverbank and didn't see anyone. They were either inside or on the other side.

Robert worked his way past the checkpoint, just below the bank, and he smiled.

*If you go over the bank you can kill them all.*

He resisted the thought and continued to crawl, and was twenty yards past the checkpoint when a dozen bullets hit the rocks around him, slapping the rocks like angry bees hitting a car windshield. He dropped down, as the bullets continued to storm over him, rock chips flying. He looked around the rock he was lying behind, and saw the soldiers on the opposite bank, at least a dozen, standing on the shore and firing directly across at Robert, close, maybe forty yards away. As he started to back away, he caught movement on the bridge, and saw an army truck race across from town, a truck carrying what looked to be thirty soldiers.

He was trapped, and he knew that there was no way out of this. If he moved, the soldiers on the bank would kill him. The truck with the soldiers would be on the bank above him in less than a minute, and there was no place to go.

*The river, go to the river.*

Robert was about ten feet from the water, slightly above water level, but if he moved he would be shot. Better to die moving than to stay here and be shot like a gopher in a trap. He could hear the truck on the road above him, hear the engine above the roar of the water.

He put the barrel of the AK-47 on top of the rock and fired a burst across the river. The reaction from the other side was automatic. The firing stopped. Robert poked his head up over the rock and looked across. The soldiers were scrambling for cover, firing as they dove behind rocks on the other side. The gun clicked empty and Robert dropped it, picking up the M-16. He rose, firing, and ran for the water, yelling, screaming at his enemies, the sight of him coming for the water causing the soldiers on the other side to look for a place to hide.

A bullet from above took Robert in the shoulder, spinning him around, and he caught sight of soldiers, lots of them, standing on the bank above him, firing down at him, and then he was hit in the leg and he dropped on the bank, half in and half out of the water, the bullets hitting the water.

A bullet hit his hand and he dropped the rifle, crying out, and he pushed himself into the water, the coldness shocking, more powerful than the bullets, and he slipped under water, choking, the water pink with his blood, the bullets hitting the water with loud thwack, another bullet hitting Robert, and he slipped under, watching his enemies shooting, and the current took him down, churning, and he couldn't breathe.

*I am a warrior, son of Cochise, of Colorado, Son of Geronimo.*

And then he was playing with his friends again, crawling through the rocks, the desert sun warm on his back, sneaking up on his sister as she played with her dolls, his sister the evil settler, the evil cavalry commander.

*He was the warrior Geronimo.*

# Chapter 33

Huaraz

When they crossed the bridge it was easier than Tara thought it would be. Most of the guards were gone, and the few left within sight of the bridge were distracted, standing in the road looking toward the area of the shots.

When the first few shots had gone off, Tara jumped. They were waiting just across the road from the bridge, and were ready. First there had been one shot, and then several, and then nothing. As they reached the bridge there were several more shots. Each time the shooting stopped her heart went up, thinking that Robert had been killed. She didn't want to think about Robert, about what was happening to him, and she knew then that they should have gone back around the city, looking for a way in for all of them.

*We should have looked for a way to not sacrifice Robert - there must have been another way.*

People had been moving past their hiding place before first light, leading donkeys carrying potatoes, produce, and crafts for the market. Tara didn't think that she would be able to sleep after Robert left, but she had dozed beside Steve, with Sabrina on the other side. They got up and looked out over the trail, watching as the traffic changed from shadows to shapes to people moving along to set up at the market.

"I think we should go," Steve said. He struggled to get up, his face gray with fatigue and pain. Sabrina grabbed his good arm and helped him to his feet, where he stood, swaying. He rewarded them with a grin.

"Hey, I look good, right?" He gave them a low laugh, and then his grin stopped.

"Robert gone, or did I just dream that?"

"He's gone, and I don't think we could have stopped him," Tara said. She leaned closer to Steve and peered up at him in the dim light. "Can you walk okay, maybe a half mile or less?"

"Piece of cake."

The bridge was a new cement bridge, the previous one having been taken away with the mudslides and flood of 1970. Although once they were on the bridge, it was less than forty yards to the other side and the town, it seemed longer looking at it from where they stood. The city of

Huaraz was on the other end of the bridge, the east side of the Rio Santa, and a few blocks east of the river was the market. If they could reach the market, they might just have a chance. The square and surrounding streets would be crowded with locals and with tourists, even with the recent terrorist activity. There hadn't been time for the country to rid itself of tourists.

Tara knew that they wouldn't stand any scrutiny at all, their clothes a collection of mountain climbing jackets and pants, blood stained, torn. They looked like what they were - refugees in the middle of a war zone.

The group of soldiers who had been on the end of the bridge were gone. When Tara glanced down the road, far down river, she saw what she thought were bodies in the road. She moved up close to the family they were following, pulling Steve and Sabrina with her, and she walked beside a campesino woman carrying a child. Maybe they would make it. She could hear Steve puffing behind her, and heard a groan as he stumbled. The campesino woman beside her looked around and then kept walking. Up ahead, Tara could see the buildings of Huaraz that lined the river. They were almost across the bridge and within three blocks they would be at the market. A horn blared up ahead, and to Tara's horror she saw a large army truck lurch around a corner and sway onto the bridge. The back of the truck was filled with soldiers.

The donkey in front of them was pulled to the side of the bridge and the truck swept past. After the truck passed they hurried off the bridge. Tara pulled Steve to one side and sat him on a bench in front of a small store that sold climbing equipment. People were walking to the market as if nothing had happened.

Steve was gasping, his face pale, gray with pain.

"I'm fine," he panted. "I just need to rest for a minute and...it's great to be back to civilization."

Tara looked around. They had left Huaraz just a few days ago, but it was different somehow. Maybe it was just that when they were here before, they had the expectation of a trip, of a new adventure. They were young and were exploring. A town that was not significant then, and now had become a much more deadly destination.

There was a different feeling to the town. A few people glanced at the three of them as they rested in front of the store, but most people went on by without a look. And then she knew what it was - the people were different. It was as if they were expecting something.

Fear.

They were afraid, and they were waiting for something bad to happen, but they tried to look like business as usual. And where had that army truck come from? When they were here before, Tara couldn't remember seeing anyone dressed in an army uniform. Now she had seen dozens, and in the last few minutes. She looked over at Sabrina. *Jesus, if I look that bad, we're in trouble.*

"Wait here a second," Tara said, and she stepped into the street. When she got to the other side, she looked back at Sabrina and Steve. They looked like two of the sorriest critters she had ever seen, Steve, drawn and gray, his climbing clothes dirty, torn and bloody. He certainly didn't look like he belonged here. If anyone saw them from a block away, they were finished.

Tara looked down at her clothes, and she knew that they had to get some clothes first, then something to eat. She walked back, as she reached the other side, she saw an army patrol walking toward them from a block away. There were three soldiers and an officer of some kind. They might have been walking to the bridge, but they certainly wouldn't miss the three of them when they got closer.

Tara stepped to the side of Steve and Sabrina and tried the door of the climbing shop. It was locked. She looked up and there was no other place to hide. The patrol had stopped a half block away and were talking to some people who had just crossed the bridge. Tara turned around and pounded on the door, the sign hanging inside shaking. She looked back down the street and saw that the soldiers were finished. She pounded again and saw a face in the window.

"Abierto, arriba," she said, and motioned for Steve and Sabrina to join her. They had seen the soldiers, and stood behind her.

The door opened, and they entered. The shopkeeper closed the door behind them, and then glanced out the door at the soldiers. He looked at Tara, then the other two, and turned the sign on the door to "Closed."

Steve spoke to him as he came back around the counter. There was climbing equipment on every surface and hanging from the walls and ceilings - tents, sleeping bags, ropes, ice axes, crampons, and stoves. "Amigo," Steve said in Spanish. "As you can see, my friends and I, we need your assistance."

The shopkeeper nodded.

"We are from the United States, have been trekking in the mountains, and, and uh, we ran into some trouble."

"Ah, Senor, there is trouble in town," the shopkeeper said in English. "We have had the army here for three days, and I've heard that they are looking for some gringos who have helped the terrorists." He introduced himself as Senor Robales.

"They're probably looking for us," Tara said. "But we didn't do anything, we were kidnapped by the terrorists, then shot at by the army."

"I make my living with people such as yourself. I will help you but you must come in the back."

Like most shops, there were living quarters in the shop. Tara helped Steve negotiate the counter, and walked behind a curtain, pulling him behind her. In the back, there was more gear piled on the floor, and some on a workbench to be repaired.

"My wife is gone to the market with our children, so I am here by myself."

Tara told him what they needed. Food. Clothing, and a doctor for Steve. A place for Steve to stay and rest. A phone.

"Food, clothing okay. I have a friend who is a doctor who will come to look at him tonight." He looked at Tara. "A phone is more difficult. If you call Lima, probably okay. If you call the United States, they may catch up with us."

"A pay phone then," Tara said.

"There is a phone company on the other side of the market, maybe a kilometer from here." He gave her directions.

Thirty minutes later, Sabrina and Tara had eaten their first full meal in three days, and were dressed in the colorful dresses of the women in Huaraz. Sabrina wore a bright red long sleeve blouse and long heavy skirt. Tara wore a dark serape and a skirt. Both wore the wide brimmed hat of the peasant women. From a distance, Tara was sure that they would blend in. Up close, they were sunk. Neither spoke Spanish.

Tara looked out the shop window at the street. There was a lot of traffic on the street, but she didn't see any soldiers. She opened the door and looked up and down the street, and then stepped out in front of the store. Sabrina followed.

They walked across the street and stopped in front of a small office. Sabrina started laughing and pointed at Tara.

"You should see yourself, Cousin."

Tara looked at her reflection in the window and grinned. She looked like a lump, her figure gone, her face hidden under the brim of the hat. "Maybe if I carried something from the market," she laughed.

They walked to the market, the street becoming more crowded now, the noise of the open air stalls rising above the traffic. On the corner of Fifth Street and the Avenue the market began, an open air tradition with the town since it was a small village, hundreds of years ago. They walked through the stalls and vendors, the smell of food making Tara hungry again. They had the money from the shop and it was hard to pass up the food. The stalls were filled with produce, with meat, baskets, clothing - an outdoor bazaar stretched for several blocks down Fifth Street. Tara found the phone and dialed the numbers for the long distance carrier for the United States. She picked up the phone and began to dial, and then stopped. It had been almost two weeks since she had talked to her grandfather. What would she say to him? That she had gotten Delores killed? That she was not to be trusted with the life of another. Would she tell him that she was responsible for the lives of her parents, that if she had somehow gone with them they would still be alive. She had always thought, that nagging thing in the back of her mind, that she was the reason her parents were killed.

If they hadn't been going Christmas shopping for *her*, if *she* hadn't begged for gifts, asking for dolls and things like that, then they would be here.

*Help me Grandfather, I don't want to get anyone else killed. It's just not fair, and it would be my fault.*

She started to dial, and looked over at Sabrina. They needed to get out of Huaraz, and soon.

But we are not out of Peru yet, and the army was here in force, looking for us.

Looking for me, Tara thought.

She glanced past Sabrina at the crowds of people, feeling like an imposter. She worried that the army would find them because of their otherness, their trying to pass for natives. We walk different, look different, she thought, like dressing up a dog in cat's clothing, we are aliens here and might as well have a neon sign hung around our necks.

She finished dialing.

"Hello, I'm trying to . . ."

"Ola, esta operatore."

"Hello," Tara said, feeling more and more conspicuous. "Hello, abla englese?"

"Uno momento."

Tara waited for what seemed like several minutes, with clicking and beeping on the line. She glanced around, nervously, willing the operator to come on the line.

"Hello, Operator." The voice was heavily accented, but Tara could understand it.

"Yes, operator, I want to place a collect call to the United States. Can you help me?"

"Possibly, what is the number?"

Tara gave her the number and her name, and then waited. She had no idea what time it was on the west coast, and didn't really care, as long as someone answered the phone. It was actually almost 7 a.m. in Cold River, but she had to try, to let them know that they were alive and needed help. When the voice came on, she didn't wait for the operator.

"Tribal Council."

"Jo, this is Tara," she blurted, and began to cry. She dimly heard the operator in the background, asking about the charges.

"Tara, are you there?"

It was such a relief to hear a familiar voice, she felt a dozen emotions all at once, and couldn't talk. She handed the phone to Sabrina and leaned against the phone booth and sobbed, hating herself for being such a baby at a time like this. It was just so unfair, for Delores not to be with them.

And Robert.

She heard Sabrina tell Jo about Delores, and where they were. Sabrina held the phone up to Tara.

"Tara."

"Grandfather," Tara said, her voice quavering. He sounded so old, so frail. She didn't know if she could find the strength to talk loud enough. She knew he would wait for her to speak. When she was able to, she began again. "Grandfather did you hear about Delores?"

She heard the love in his voice when he told her that he knew about Delores, and what they had done on the reservation. He told her that Hawk and others were in Huaraz. Tara bit her lip to keep from crying when she told her grandfather where they were.

"In front of the phone company. On fourth street."

"Stay there," her grandfather said. "They'll call me in the next few minutes."

"Grandfather, I . . .I'm sorry."

"Just stay there," he said, and the connection was broken.

Tara hung the phone up and leaned against the booth. Sabrina put her arm around her shoulder. As she straightened up, the phone rang, and Tara picked it up, looking at Sabrina.

"Yes."

"This is the operator. Did you wish to place another call?"

"No, thank you."

The operator disconnected the call and thought of the information she had just heard. The colonel would be interested in this, she thought. Maybe give her a free trip to Lima. She looked up a number and dialed, eager to trade her information.

# Chapter 34

The Foothills of the Cordillera Blanca
5 a.m.

The van slowed and Martin brought his head up, blinking his eyes against the glare of the headlights. He looked at his watch and saw that they had been on the road for almost two hours. He glanced over at the driver and then back out front. They had left the coast and were starting up into the mountains. The headlights picked out the sides of the canyon they were driving up into, rock formations and brush. The van was now almost stopped.

"Why are we stopping?" Martin asked. There was nothing in the road. Salazar pointed ahead.

"I saw a flash of light on the hillside, maybe coming from around the next corner."

Martin turned and looked into the back of the collectivo, the darkness making it hard to make out shapes.

"Hawk," Martin said.

"Right here."

The van continued, slowly, rounding the corner at an idle. Martin saw the flashing lights as soon as they got into the corner. There was some kind of barricade up ahead. Flashing yellow lights like the kind used for construction. It came to Martin all at once that this was a military checkpoint, placed in the canyon in such a way that it was unavoidable. You came around a corner and there it was. The army had probably used the same spot before.

Up ahead, an army truck blocked the road, the kind of vehicle with a khaki canvass top. A Humvee was parked on the side of the road. The Peruvian army had purchased vehicles from the United States during the last year, Martin knew, and this display of the modern tools of war made him feel warm and fuzzy all over. There was a small squad of soldiers in front of the truck, Martin could see four of them. Possibly a small squad under the command of a sergeant.

"You want me to drive up to them?" Salazar asked."Yes, we sure as hell can't outrun that Humvee."

"We couldn't outrun my grandmother," Lori said. "Confident little buggers, aren't they?" she muttered.

"They have every reason to be, it's their country," Martin said.

As they came to a stop, three soldiers detached themselves from the vehicles and walked to the center of the road. Martin felt something push into the small of his back, and reached behind him and felt the grip of a pistol. He leaned up slightly and placed it under his waistband in the small of his back and pulled his jacket down over it. His stomach churned as he realized that theirs was the only car at the roadblock, in the middle of the mountains, in the early hours of the morning. The soldier in the front held up his hand as the headlights swept over him. The other two flanked him, standing on either side of the road. Salazar pulled up close to the sergeant and stopped, rolling down his window.

"Let me do the talking, por favor," he whispered.

The sergeant came up and leaned in the window, his rifle held casually in his right hand. Martin felt clammy, and realized that he had done this very same thing hundreds of times in his career - approach a strange car and look into the window, searching for whatever was wrong with the occupants. And they must have felt as I do now, he thought.

The soldier looked to be in his thirties, and if anything, he looked bored. He must have pissed someone off to be stuck here on the dog shift in the middle of nowhere. Usually this was not a good sign, to have a pissed off officer in charge of your life. Shit does roll downhill, as Martin knew, and if this person were truly pissed off, he would make sure he got his pound of flesh and make people squirm before he let them go.

If he did let them go.

He said something that Martin didn't hear, and then spoke louder.

"Destination, and identification!" He passed the light over Martin, then Lori and Hawk.

"Huaraz," Salazar said without hesitation, sounding bored, and a little put out at being stopped. "Touristas," Salazar said.

The sergeant held out his hand. "Passports." He then curled his fingers toward his palm and straightened them, rapidly, a universal sign for "give it to me."

Martin dug into his pack, slowly, knowing all too well the drill and handed his passport to Salazar, who looked at him and then gave it to the sergeant. Lori gave two passports to Martin, and muttered, "mother fucker." The sergeant straightened and removed the light from Martin's eyes, flashing it on the documents. He took his time, looking at each page of the passports, thumbing through them with a maddening slowness. He looked at the pictures and then shined the light inside the car and compared the faces to the passports.

"Whaddya think, Boss?" Hawk asked in a murmur.

"I think we wait and see what they do," Martin said. A line of sweat trickled down Martin's side. This could be the end of their trip right here. Not only would the chairman's granddaughter be here, but so would a good part of his police force. Stuck here ... or worse.

"Get out of the car," the sergeant yelled at Salazar, and then yelled something at his men. The soldier on the right side closed in, leveling his rifle at Martin's window.

"What we gonna do?" Martin asked Salazar.

"I could take the two on this side," Hawk said quietly, his voice telling Martin that it was so.

"We just get out and talk to them," Salazar said with a smile. "Plenty time enough for cowboy John Wayne if we need to."

"Cowboy, shit," Lori muttered. "We're the Indians...and we're gonna win this one."

On the other side the sergeant had stepped away from the door and was yelling at Salazar, motioning for him to get out of the car.

"Get out slowly," Salazar said, and opened his door. Martin stepped out and stood by the passenger door, joined by Hawk and Lori. The sergeant shooed Salazar around the collectivo and had him stop in front of the headlights.

"Senors, Senorita, he wants you up here," Salazar told Martin.

The sergeant held up the passports in front of him and looked at them again, this time in the headlights.

"Martin Andrews," he said in passable English. Martin raised his hand. The sergeant called the others' names out, and when he got to Lori, he looked up and at her. The other soldiers seemed to crowd in closer.

"Tell him that our plane was delayed," Martin told Salazar, "and that is why we are out here in the middle of the night. That we're going to join our friends in Huaraz. Tell him."

Salazar started to speak, and the sergeant waved his hand. He walked closer to Lori and smiled.

"How does it happen that a pretty senorita like yourself is out in the middle of the night with these men?" He smiled again. Martin could smell alcohol then, and knew that this wasn't going to go down easy. These men knew that they weren't going to be disturbed by any senior officers. They were alone.

"We're going to Huaraz to join friends, like the driver said," Lori said. She held out her hand.

"Now, can I have my passport back?"

"Momento," the sergeant said, and held up his hand. He curled his index finger toward Lori and stepped back. "Come with me to the truck, we'll check on your passport."

"I don't think so," Lori said.

Martin looked at Hawk. Hawk gave him a slight nod.

The sergeant stopped smiling. He yelled something and another soldier jumped down from the truck and stood there, his arms folded, waiting for the sergeant.

"This was not a suggestion," the sergeant said. He jerked his head toward the truck.

"We gonna let her get raped, Boss?" Hawk whispered.

"No." The two soldiers were in front of Martin now, and to his right, their rifles pointed in the direction of the car. As Lori moved toward the sergeant, they both followed her with their eyes.

"Take the sergeant," Martin whispered to Hawk, and it seemed as if he were moving in slow motion, reaching for his back, thinking that the soldiers were relaxed, not expecting any trouble, and he found the handle of the pistol. He pulled his gun and fired at the nearest soldier, rapidly, three shots in succession, all within a second, the first and second bullet striking the soldier in the chest, the third at the base of his nose, the soldier falling backward in a spray of blood, and then Martin was firing at the second soldier, getting his shots off before the rifle of the first soldier hit the ground, firing four shots at the second, trying to get him before he could squeeze the trigger of his rifle, dimly hearing Hawk shooting and yelling at Lori to "Get down get down," and then the second soldier was falling, squeezing the trigger to his rifle as he fell, a long burst that sounded like a string of firecrackers, and then he was down, and Martin turned to look for the fourth soldier. Where the hell is he? He was right there and now he's gone, and then Martin was running for the truck, yelling at Hawk as he ran.

He was aware that Lori was down, not knowing if she had gone prone on her own or if she was hit, and Martin ran past the sergeant's body toward the headlights of the truck. As he reached the front bumper he was in the dark, his eyes blinded by the headlights, and he jerked the passenger door open and stared at the interior of the cab, the soft green light from the radio mounted between the seats giving Martin a view of the empty cab. He heard sounds of boots hitting pavement behind him and he ran for the back of the truck, the sounds way down the road, the fourth soldier getting away, and Martin fired at the sounds until his gun was empty.

"Well," Hawk said as he came up beside Martin, "at least he'll keep running for awhile, or hide. Probably not going to be a factor in the next couple of hours."

"Martin!" Lori yelled from the front of the collectivo.

"Check the truck and the Humvee, I don't want any more surprises." Martin jogged to the front of the truck and stopped, the scene in front of him a strange madness, a chilling picture of death, and the suddenness of it all hit him then and his knees shook.

The sergeant's flashlight was in the road, shining out at an odd angle, casting dark shadows on the pavement. There were four bodies on the road, the blood on the pavement black and glistening in the flashlight. Lori was standing over the fourth body. Their driver Salazar was face down in front of the collectivo. Lori looked up at Martin and shook her head.

Martin slumped in front of the truck and motioned for Lori to join him. He thought of his constant question, *what the hell am I doing here*? And now it seemed so contrived, so self important. He was in Peru and had just killed some men in a foreign country, soldiers no less, and now they probably wouldn't make it to the next town before they were hunted down and killed.

Or captured.

Martin thought about what Bluefeathers had said about leadership. That he would know what to do when the group needed a leader, but this was stupid. What we're doing is stupid, he thought. The others are surely dead and there's no way we can just traipse around and find them if we're running and hiding for our lives. What the hell are we gonna do now? He put his arm around Lori and thought of a line from the movie "Aliens," when a young Marine named Hudson said, "We're in some pretty shit now."

"We're in some pretty shit now," Martin muttered.

Lori nodded her head slowly, and they waited for Hawk.

# Chapter 35

Martin drove the truck off the road to a point where he hoped it couldn't be easily spotted from the air, the bodies of the dead soldiers and the barricades stacked inside. Hawk parked the Humvee behind it and got out as Lori drove up in the collectivo. They had driven without headlights, guided by starlight alone, and Hawk and Martin stood behind the Humvee as Lori turned the collectivo around on the narrow path.

Martin hoped that the Peruvian Army ran like some others he had known, that by the time the soldiers were discovered missing and were found, a long time would have passed. The fact that the soldiers were drinking gave Martin hope that they didn't expect to be relieved any time soon.

Lori got out and held the driver's door open for Martin.

"You drive," Martin said to her, and started around to the passenger side of the collectivo.

"I don't mind so much getting shot for a noble cause," Hawk said, "but I sure as hell don't want to be killed in a traffic accident in Peru when it could have been avoided."

Lori snorted and sat down in the driver's seat and slammed the door. Hawk grumbled and got in the back and Martin took up his position as a passenger in the front seat. Lori revved the engine and popped the clutch, throwing her passengers back into their seats. Martin thought that Hawk had a tremendous amount of self-control to remain quiet.

Lori left the headlights off as she followed the dim track. When she came to the pavement she stopped and waited.

Nothing. No one coming.

She turned on the headlights and entered the road, the sudden light blinding them, her face drawn and grim. She drove fast, as if the demons of the battle were following them (and maybe the demons of what might have happened to her, Martin thought) downshifting through curves, the engine groaning. After a few minutes, Hawk settled in the back and closed his eyes. Martin tried to stay awake, but soon he nodded off to the rocking of the collectivo.

When Lori was sure Martin was sleeping, she let the tears come, a silent flow that continued for some minutes. When the tears stopped, she began to shake, and thought that she would have to stop to control her hands. She got through it by telling herself that she didn't have all that much going on for her at the rez anyway. She had always been able to deflect unpleasantness with a smile, with a joke, and she knew that it just wouldn't work anymore. She felt such an overwhelming sadness that she didn't think she could keep her arms up on the steering wheel.

It just happened so fast, she thought. As a police officer she had been trained to react, and once she had been shot at in the dark by people in a passing car. But this, this was so quick, so brutal. She knew she would never be the same again. She slowed the van and started to cry again, until she was stopped in the middle of the road, sobbing.

The blood looks black in the light, she thought, and wondered how much longer in the day they would live.

Martin reached for her and held her and she let him, and thought of Hawk in the back seat, who was wiser than he looked, because he kept his mouth shut.

Martin drove for the next three hours, until well after sunup. Traffic had been increasing as the sun came up, cars, trucks, an occasional bus. They were high in the Andes now, the sun coming between two mountain peaks to the east of them. He stopped on the side of the road and quietly got out. Lori was sleeping in the front passenger seat; Hawk turned over in the back when Martin got out. Lori sat up and crawled over into the driver's seat.

"I'm sleeping for awhile, Lori," Martin said. He closed his eyes, and was instantly sleeping when the collectivo started.

"What do we do when we get to the next roadblock, Boss?"

Martin sat up, thinking that he had just closed his eyes. The sun was well up, and Lori was slowing the car. They were coming up behind a line of cars and trucks, people on foot, donkeys. He rubbed his eyes as the car stopped.

"Huaraz," Lori said. She nodded toward the front, "And the mother of all military checkpoints."

Martin rolled his window down and leaned out, the morning air fresh, chilly. A hundred yards ahead there was indeed a checkpoint. From where they were stopped on the road he could see a jumble of military vehicles, Humvees and trucks, a very large roadblock indeed. Even if the commander were drunk, they were sure to have people stationed behind them, and on the sides.

*At least that's what I would do.*

"Hawk."

He heard something, a mumble, and felt the collectivo rock.

"What?" The growl came from the backseat.

"Wake up, we have problems."

The van rocked again as Hawk shifted his massive bulk. He sat up and thrust his head up over the front seat.

"What's up?"

"The mother of all roadblocks," Lori said sarcastically. Her voice went up at the end and Martin could hear her fear.

Hawk looked through the windshield and looked around.

"We're ten minutes from the soldiers," he said. Like Martin, Hawk knew about roadblocks.

"What're we gonna do, Boss?" Lori asked.

"You're driving, just tell them that we're going to the market."

"Oh, right...what about the guns?"

"Give them to me," Hawk said, and Martin watched as Hawk placed the pistols in a bag at his feet. The line of cars, donkeys, trucks moved forward.

"They're looking for us, Boss," Lori said, her voice quavering.

"I don't think so. We're moving slowly, but they would have had us by now if they knew who we were. And," Martin said, looking out the driver's side window, "the outbound traffic has stopped and we're still moving."

He could see the town ahead, a building on the other side of the checkpoint with the Spanish architecture of the 1700's. They moved slowly past an army truck idling at the roadside. A soldier leaned against the tailgate of the truck. He held a rifle and had a bored expression on his face. He looked at Martin and then past him.

"That little rabbit who ran from the checkpoint this morning, you think he's been found?" Hawk asked quietly, looking at the soldiers.

"No," Martin said, his words more confident than he felt.

"Why not?" Lori's hands gripped the wheel so hard that her knuckles were white.

"Because several people have looked at us, and there's no recognition," Martin said. "Remember, what he may have seen at that checkpoint may have been very little, maybe our headlights, and nothing else. We could be from another planet and he wouldn't know which one. He was scared, and when the shooting started, he ran. If he was picked up, they still might not have found the truck, and he might have told his superiors that they were attacked by twenty or thirty terrorists."

"Still gonna have to get rid of this car," Hawk said.

They edged closer now, a truck and a collectivo in front of them. All Martin could see now was army khaki.

"We can't shoot our way out of this one, Boss," Lori said, looking at an armored personnel carrier parked beside the road.

"Maybe we won't have to." A car trying to come out of the city was stopped ahead of them, the soldiers' attention drawn to something. The driver was standing by his door, waving his hands, his face red. The truck ahead of them was waved through. Lori looked over at Martin again, smiled, then grinned and let the clutch out.

"What are you grinning about?"

"Just wondering what you're doing here, with Hawk and me, didn't you find enough ways to get killed up there in Portland?"

"What the hell am I doing-"

"Crying around with us Indians," Hawk said, and they all laughed, Hawk shaking the collectivo with his laugh.

"Put your face back where no one can see it," Martin said, and grinned out at a soldier who was watching them. They hadn't laughed since they entered the country, and it felt strange to be laughing when they were about to be killed. Martin tried to tell himself that they didn't know about the dead soldiers, they couldn't know what their car looked like, and as soon as he would think that they were going to be okay, he would suddenly grow cold with a certainty that the soldier who escaped had been found and had given his superiors a complete description of the collectivo and its occupants.

Lori rolled forward and a soldier put his hand out as they rolled past. Lori stopped, her leg shaking as she held the brake.

"I'm not going with them, Martin," she said softly. "No way, no matter what." She turned from Martin and looked up at the soldier at her window.

"Hola," she said with a smile.

He leaned over and looked inside, first at Martin and then at Hawk.

"Where are you going?"

"Restaurante," Lori said. The soldier stood up and looked at the line of cars behind them. He waved them on and Lori let the clutch out, stalling the car as her shaking foot jerked the car forward.

"Alto!"

Martin's stomach lurched as he looked up, catching Hawk's eye in the rear view mirror.

"If it turns to shit, Boss, I'll pass a gun around the side of the seat," Hawk muttered. "In the confusion of the shooting maybe one of us can get away."

"Lori," Martin said quietly, "if it goes badly, walk around the truck ahead, get out of sight, yelling at us, throwing your hands up in the air, as if we are causing the problem. Then get the hell out of here and to the market on foot." The soldier was back at her window.

"Women were never meant to drive," she told him in Spanish. He laughed.

"I just thought I'd better ask who you have here, Senorita."

"Just a fare," Lori said, and Martin was sure she was batting her eyes at him. Christ if she were wearing a skirt, she'd be pulling it up.

"I'll be dropping them off in a hour or so," Lori said, giving the soldier a look up and down. "When do you get through playing soldier?"

"In a few hours," he said, looking anxiously over his shoulder.

"Do you know of a restaurante where we could meet?"

"Si, the el Sombrero."

"I'll find it and be there," Lori said, and let the clutch out, her leg shaking. She managed to keep the car going. Martin looked back and saw the soldier standing there, looking at them, and finally he turned to wave the car behind them through.

Lori drove into town, her face white, her legs shaking.

"I thought we were going to have the mother of all firefights, Martin."

"Susan would be pissed if she had to raise your kids by herself."

"You saw her, Boss. She wouldn't raise them without a man, but I'd come back to haunt her if that happened."

"You haunt me now, just being in the back seat," Lori said.

The streets were crowded as they got into town, stores on each side, most of the traffic going up to the market ahead of them. Lori found a side street and pulled off the main highway and parked the collectivo by a small rock building. The van seemed to give a sigh as she turned it off, as if it didn't want to be involved with them any longer.

"We're not gonna get out of here quite so easy, Boss," Hawk said from the backseat. He pulled himself up and climbed out of the van.

"Probably not," Martin said. He pointed to the bag that Hawk removed from the van. "Call Cold River, see if they have heard anything." Martin stretched and looked down the street toward the main street they had just left. Lori walked around the front of the van and stood beside Martin and they waited as Hawk called.

"That Hawk, he's talking to the chairman," Lori said, smiling.

"How do you know that?"

"His voice changes, he has this whiney sound to him when he talks to the man."

Martin laughed. Hawk looked over at them and gave them a little grin. The grin faded and then he was somber, talking lower, pressing the phone against his ear. He pushed the power button on the phone and looked at Martin and Lori.

"They're here, maybe ten blocks away."

"It's about time something went right," Martin said.

"They alright?" Lori walked up to him.

"Tara and Sabrina are. Delores was killed."

Martin tried to picture Delores, and found he could not. He had met her during his first week on the job, but he didn't have an idea who she was.

"We grew up with her," Lori said, and then was quiet, as if that said it all.

"Can we take the van from here?" Lori asked.

Martin looked at the collectivo and then out at the street.

"It looks like all the others I've seen around here. Let's take it to meet them."

They got in the van for the last time. Martin knew they were living on borrowed time. They had to get rid of the van, and get the hell out of the country. They had to get out of the country right away. But at some level, he knew that their time was running out.

And he hated it when he was right.

# **Chapter 36**

Lori parked the collectivo a block down from the telephone building. As Martin watched, two campesino women left the front of the phone building and approached the van. One was pointing. The other one walked in front of the van and around to the driver's side. She was of medium height and wore a long skirt. Her face was shaded by the brim of the large hat she wore but there was something about the way she walked that was different from the other campesinos that Martin had seen. When he thought about it later, he realized that she walked in a way that was more direct. Western. North American.

When the van approached Tara had been sitting on a bench in front of the phone company, her head in her hands, with Sabrina beside her, watching traffic.

*You can't think of Delores now or you won't make it.*

She had been ready to cry since she had talked to her grandfather. Delores should be here, I should be hearing her funny voice now, her talking about having a half dozen squiggly babies, a husband who worked in the mill or in the admin center. Tara had heard it so many times and now it would never be.

And now it was for nothing. First her parents. Then her Delores. For the second time in her life, Tara felt alone, even more alone than when she had been a third grader.

I'm gonna die here, she thought.

She blinked back tears and Sabrina reached over and took her hand. Tara looked down the street, not seeing the cars and people, the movement around her.

Sabrina stood up, still holding Tara's hand, watching a van down the street. She pulled on Tara, saying something to her.

"Huh?"

"Tara, look, that van."

Tara stood and tried to follow Sabrina's finger.

"Tara, I think that Lori is in that van!"

Tara looked, shielding her eyes, and took a step closer. She could see two people, a man and maybe Lori. Her stomach lurched when she had the thought that she had seen the man before, maybe up in the hills when they were running from the terrorists and the army, but she had seen the man before. She stared at him.

"Who's the guy?" Sabrina asked.

"Grandfather said something about chief of police. Maybe that's him." They walked closer. Tara ran as she recognized Lori.

"Lori!" She yelled, causing people to stop and stare. She threw her arms up and waved.

*Ohmigod it's Lori*

Sabrina said something to Tara but she didn't hear it. She walked to the bumper and looked closely through the windshield as Lori got out with a surprised look on her face.

Tara threw her arms around her and began to cry.

Martin got out and heard the side door open and Hawk joined him in front of the van. Hawk brushed past Martin and grabbed the other campesino woman.

"Sabrina."

Martin looked around and saw that some people were watching them as they walked past. Most of the traffic was still moving toward the market. Two blocks down, toward the river, Martin could see the turret of an Armored Personnel Carrier as the APC turned on the street. The commander was up in the turret, wearing a green helmet and headset.

Martin grabbed Hawk's arm and pointed. The big man's eyes widened.

"Lori, Tara," Hawk said urgently, "we gotta go. Now!" He pointed at the approaching APC.

"We take the car, Martin?" Lori asked.

"Yes, you drive, let's get it off this street, be ready to jump out when I say." Martin and Lori got in the front, with Tara, Sabrina and Hawk in the back. They pulled away from the side of the building into the traffic, and Martin turned around in the seat to look for the soldiers. The armored vehicle was now a block behind them, the turret visible above the cars that separated them.

"Turn here," Tara said, pointing left toward the market. "We've got another of our group in the back room of a climbing shop. He's been shot and needs help."

Lori turned down the side street, the street jammed with people, donkeys, collectivos, and cars.

"We can't get through here, Boss," Lori said. She stopped on the side of the street.

"Pull in that alley there, we might have to use this again and if we can hide it..."

Martin walked with Tara and Lori, following Sabrina and Hawk through the market. The market looked like many Martin had visited in

Mexico and Central America. Stalls with all manner of merchandise, food, clothing, even a cellular booth at one end, advertising specials for visitors and residents. The open areas around the stalls were packed with people and they didn't draw much attention.

"I'm surprised to see you here, Chief," Tara said.

"It's an Indian thing," Martin said, and Lori laughed. Tara gave him a quick smile in return. "When your grandfather tells you to do something, you do it and then later think about what a fool you are."

Tara laughed and nodded her head.

"I keep thinking though, what the hell am I doing coming 'round here with you Indians." This brought more laughter from Tara and Lori. They had moved through the market and were now on a side street. Martin looked at the woman walking beside him. She looked as if she had been awake for days, and her eyes told him that she had seen things she didn't want to ever see again.

Sabrina stopped ahead and was peering through the front window of a small shop. The door opened and Sabrina entered the shop. Martin got to the door of the shop, looked up and down the street, and then he entered, followed by Hawk, Tara and Lori.

A small man closed the door immediately. He had short black hair and looked to Martin like many of the campesinos he had seen in Peru. He was the owner of the store, dressed in a bright red anorak, jeans and running shoes. Martin looked around the store and noticed the packs, sleeping bags, climbing gear covering the walls. Sabrina walked around a display counter and entered a back room.

Martin crowded with the others into the small room behind the counter. A young black man was on the couch, his face ashen, his right arm swollen and inflamed. If he doesn't get medical attention soon, Martin thought, he isn't going to make it . An odor of infection hung in the air. Tara introduced the man on the couch as Steve, said he was an Indian from an eastern tribe, and that he had saved their lives.

"I guess I should go first," Tara said, and she sat on the couch with Steve. She told of the events of the past three days. She told of their last day of the trek, the fight with the army and the terrorists, and the people killed on that first day. As Tara talked about Delores, Martin thought that she was going to stop, but she continued, telling them about Robert, the shooting, and then she stopped. Martin saw a tear roll down her cheek.

"And then, we, uh, Robert..." Tara said, and then she started to sob. Martin watched as Steve reached and put an arm around Tara, his other arm bloody, held across his body.

"Two days ago," Steve said, "when we were in the village, Robert said that it looked as if the village was hit from the air. The army had definitely been there. And then when we found the climbers, the same thing. If the army was responsible for most of the killing, they want to find us in the worst way. They know what we have seen."

"Join the club," Hawk said.

"And Robert, where is he now?" Martin asked.

"He went off to create a diversion," Steve said, "to get us into town. From the amount of firing we heard, I'd guess he was successful."

Martin looked around the room. "It looks as if between our two groups we have managed to become the most wanted people in the country." He told them of the roadblock, of the fight, the hiding of the truck.

"Can we get to Lima?" Steve asked.

"There were tanks surrounding the airport when we arrived last night," Martin said. "It isn't going to be easy."

"You guys are the rescuers, how do you propose we get out of here?" Steve asked.

"I don't know sweetie," Lori said, "but you three testosterone-filled cowboys and Indians better come up with something soon, or we're gonna have our pictures in every post office from here to Spain."

"The van's out...I don't think we'll make it very far," Martin said. "We need –"

"Senor," the shopkeeper said, pushing into the room, "Senor, we have a problem. The army-"

Steve swung his legs over the side of the couch and tried to stand. Tara helped him up.

"I'll go to the front," Lori said, and followed the shopkeeper to the front of the store. She was back in seconds.

"A squad of soldiers is coming down the street, checking the doors," she said.

"How did they -?" Sabrina asked.

"Probably the phone," Steve said. "That's how I would do it."

The knock on the front door made them jump.

Martin knew one thing.

He wasn't going to join the army.

# **C**hapter **37**

Huaraz

Colonel Hernandez put down the phone and leaned back in his chair. It wasn't an insurmountable problem, but a problem nevertheless. He knew that he could cover a lot of activity with the insurrection, and that he would most likely come out of this a hero, with a promotion to general a sure thing. The problem with the students and the climbers was easy enough to solve. He would blame the terrorists. If the U.S. Army Major thought differently, he still couldn't prove a thing.

Hernandez knew that he had just a few more students to round up. He didn't want to let them out of the country so they could make all kinds of outlandish accusations. He wasn't going to let them out of Huaraz, or at least out of the Department of Ancash. There was only one road out, and a fruit fly couldn't make it past the roadblocks, aerial patrols and roving patrols he had in place. It was just a matter of time.

God bless the terrorists. The only thing better for a military career would be a war with Ecuador, but he didn't think the Peruvian generals had the stomach for it. Well, one could always hope.

He picked up the report of the missing patrol, a roadblock on the highway south of Huaraz. He couldn't forget the terrorists in his haste to round up the students. He looked at another report, a shooting this morning with a lone man, a person his troops described as having his body painted. Who was this person? A new brand of terrorist? Certainly not a student. He had been in the United States, had been around college campuses, and he knew for a fact that students from the north weren't warriors. This was something else entirely. There was a knock on his door.

"Enter."

"Colonel." His aide entered and stood at attention.

"Colonel, we have located the terrorists posing as students from the United States."

Colonel Hernandez grabbed his hat and smiled.

"Lead on, Captain. We have work to do."

# **C**hapter **38**

Los Angeles

Senior Captain Leonard Mitchell shut the engine off and sat back in the seat. He had parked the car in the far corner of a long term parking lot at LAX. He sat there and thought about what he was doing, wondering why after all this time he had been called by Chairman Bluefeathers. Leonard Mitchell was Indian, a tribal member of the Cold River Tribe of Oregon.

*This must be payback for all of those years I didn't want to be Indian.*
With his eyes closed, he thought of one thing.
Weasel.
His name was Weasel.
Growing up on the reservation, everyone had a nickname. For Leonard Mitchell, the name was Weasel. He hated the name, and the negative suggestions it carried. He wanted a strong name like Elk, Hawk, Eagle, one of the nobler animals. Oh no, he was stuck with Weasel, and while the name Weasel didn't carry the same negative connotation in Tribal lore that it did in European culture, when his white friends in town found out about it, he was screwed.

Weasel left the reservation and was accepted at the Emory Riddle School of Aviation (using Tribal money). When he graduated he had a lot of twin time, a commercial ticket, an airline transport pilot license, and some jet time. He went to work flying corporate twins, and then moved up to a regional airline in Phoenix. Leonard Mitchell was now a captain for Freedom Air, flying the L.A. to Mexico City route in a Boeing 737. He had a white wife and three kids in the suburbs, and had successfully put Weasel and the reservation behind him. His wife and children had never been there.

When Chairman Bluefeathers had called, he was suddenly Weasel again. He knew he should have hung the phone up and quietly left the house for a beer. A lot of emotions came back to him during that phone call, and he found he couldn't refuse. He was Indian, and as hard as he had tried his past was going to catch him and hang on. Leonard had heard about the students in Peru, about the declaration of war by his tribe (it was still on the news) and he thought he could remain detached, but he had found himself thinking about the reservation, about his disappearance as a son. He hadn't talked to his mother in two years.

Bluefeathers, damned his wrinkled old hide, had said to him, "Weasel, your mother tells you to be careful flying around in those airplanes, and she tells me that God has been preparing you for this time, for this thing you will do for us." Weasel had remained silent on the phone (and he did think of himself as Weasel again, when he heard the voice of the chairman). What Bluefeathers had left unsaid, what he didn't need to say, was that Weasel had never returned anything to the tribe - respect, his presence, or the money. Weasel had just cut and run. Damn Bluefeathers and his sorry old ass. As for his mother, Weasel had nearly forgotten her belief that God determined everything. Her Shaker faith had always been a mystery to him, something he was ashamed of.

And now, sitting in the car at LAX, parking in the economy lot instead of his usual reserved place, he was Weasel again. Leonard Mitchell didn't exist. Weasel wore the white uniform of an airline captain. He looked at his passenger and nodded.

Weasel got out of the car and put on a dark blue jacket, looking like his passenger. The one thing that Weasel knew for sure this afternoon was that his passenger, who had introduced himself as John, was not a pilot, even though he wore a pilot's uniform. John was something else, and Leonard had some ideas about that, but he kept them to himself. John had introduced himself as a "friend" to the tribes, and Weasel let it go at that. Old Bluefeathers was crafty enough to employ some kind of special talent (or muscle) or worse to accompany good old Weasel.

The next part would be the hardest. Stealing a forty million dollar airplane from LAX, a plane that belonged to the U.S. Government, was insanity. The plane had security forces in place and a crew of four. They were going to steal (he couldn't bring himself to think the word 'hijack') a Grumman Gulfstream V, a fifteen passenger jet capable of flying a third of the way around the world without refueling.

It was insane. The old man on the reservation was insane, as well as the rest of those blanket-ass Indians he had left behind. His wife had been right. He didn't owe them anything.

Weasel, Leonard Mitchell, boarded the bus in the long-term parking lot and found a seat in the back. He rode in silence and looked at the red sun. He would probably be in jail by morning.

# Chapter 39

The Grumman Gulfstream V sat on the apron in front of a hanger owned by the California Air National Guard. The airplane was so gorgeous to Weasel that it seemed like a living, breathing thing. It gleamed in the fading light, the pilot and co-pilot visible up in the cockpit, going through pre-flight checks. The hanger doors were closed, and there was no activity on the ground around the plane.

There must be security somewhere, Weasel thought, as they got out of the airport shuttle. He looked across the runway at the activity around the main terminal. He had never tired of watching the pace of the airport, the pulse of activity quickening as the sun went down. People traveling at night to do business the next day. He sat his bag down on the apron, standing in front of the nose of the plane and off to the right, looking up at the pilot. He waved, knowing that the pilot would see his bag. It said "Grumman" on the side in large white letters.

Without talking to John he walked to the side of the plane where the air stairs were located. The plane was buttoned up, with the door closed. As he and John walked around, the door opened and the stairs unfolded. With a last look around, he entered the cabin of the plane.

Weasel had been told by Bluefeathers and then "John" that the arrangements had been made to get them on board the plane, and it looked as if the plan was working. They were on the plane and still alive. Weasel had visions of getting close to the plane and guards rushing out of the hanger and killing him in a furious burst of shots. The plan had been simple: the pilots had been told to expect two pilots from the Grumman factory to ride with them to evaluate the plane, and to evaluate the effectiveness of the training that a corporate pilot went through before a company could take delivery of the plane.

"Excuse me, Sir!" The voice came from the outside of the plane as Weasel ducked slightly to enter the cabin. He always ducked as a matter of course, with too many years spent in small commuters, though in the Gulfstream V he didn't have to. John was behind him and they both turned toward the voice. Below them on the ramp were three men in suits, and they didn't look like businessmen.

It had been too easy.

"Can I help you?" John asked pleasantly, and started back down, but not before he told Weasel, "stay inside, let me handle this."

Weasel stood on the top step and smiled down at the men. One of them had pulled his coat back to reveal a holster and a handgun. John walked down, talking to them as he went. He held his hands open, a gesture of friendliness. Weasel looked inside and forward, where the co-pilot was getting up from his seat, the cabin door open. Weasel waved, and waited for the man to join him. The co-pilot was young, dressed similar to Weasel - white short sleeve shirt, black tie, black slacks and shoes. He had red close cropped hair. Maybe former military.

"You the guys from Grumman?" The co-pilot held out his hand. "I'm Matthew Provost."

"Yeah, that's us, I'm Leonard Mitchell." Weasel jerked his head toward the men on the ground. "What's with the welcoming committee?"

"They tell you at Grumman who we're taking on this flight tonight?"

Weasel shook his head.

"Well, we're picking up some VIP's in a few minutes. Should be interesting. Hey, I thought there would only be one of you."

"Usually is," Weasel said. "The company just hired John there, and I'm taking him along to see how we do these."

"You do these on every one of the fives you sell?"

"We do this on every one we lease, and we lease most of them."

Weasel closed his eyes. He could fly anything with wings and an engine. Since Bluefeathers had browbeaten him into taking this ill-advised assignment, he had been studying everything he could find on the Grumman, going through the preflight, flight, and landing checklists.

He looked around the cabin. There were fifteen or so leather seats, seats appointed in the most luxurious leather, similar to an expensive sports car. The wood was trimmed in teak, and there were work stations and telephones at each seat. In the rear galley, he could see a flight attendant busy at a sink.

"Excuse me."

Weasel looked toward the sound of the voice, and saw the captain wave from the cabin. She had short brown hair and wrinkles around her eyes, wrinkles most pilots get from too much sun and trying to see through fog. For someone to be flying a V meant that they had a lot of jet time and were a very proficient pilot.

He guessed that she was about forty, and had an air about her, professional, businesslike. She stuck out her hand.

"Lydia Barnes."

I'm Wea...uh, Leonard Mitchell." As he shook her hand he wondered why he didn't just say Weasel. Habit, he thought.

"We've started the checklist," she said, turning back toward the instruments. Weasel set his flight bag next to the bulkhead that separated the cockpit from the cabin. He then leaned forward and thrust his head into the doorway and looked out over the cockpit.

"Do you want the right seat, left seat, what?" The captain continued with her checklist.

"No, you go ahead. I'll just observe."

Weasel heard voices outside, louder now, and then John entered the cabin. Weasel had a sudden wild thought that John was really an F.B.I. agent and that the entire situation had been concocted to put Weasel in prison, to get his flight status taken away. John looked around and walked to the rear of the plane and said something to the flight attendant and she laughed. He then walked up front and stood behind Weasel.

"Going through the pre-flight checklists," Weasel said. He introduced John to the pilot and co-pilot.

"How is it that we never met the two of you before?" Lydia asked, turning to look at John.

"They just hired us," John said. "Leonard here," and he put his hand on Weasel's shoulder, "Leonard here we hired away from the airlines. Wanted to see his family more, and all of that."

"Checklist complete," Provost said.

Behind them, Weasel looked at John, and then at the cabin. Two men in suits and a woman entered the cabin. One of them, a large man with white hair glanced forward and then sat down heavily in a leather seat.

"Let's get this thing going," he said to the flight attendant as she came forward. She walked back to the galley and picked up a phone and spoke to the captain. Weasel watched and wasn't so sure that the corporate pilot life would be so good after all, being a chauffeur, a waiter, a porter all in one.

"Starting the right engine," Lydia said, and Weasel watched as she began the starting procedure. Behind them a third man entered the cabin and Weasel watched as the flight attendant closed the door. Lydia handed Weasel a headset and he listened to the ATC as they were given almost immediate clearance to a taxi-way.

The plan was for them to let the plane get out of U.S. airspace before they announced that they were in command. As they taxied toward their assigned runway, Lydia announced the flight.

The takeoff was smooth, the jet accelerating quickly and evenly, reaching rotation speed in what seemed like seconds. Once they were in the air, the cockpit door opened and John entered, crouched into the cabin, and closed the door behind him.

"It's time," he said to Weasel with a slight smile on his face.

He's enjoying this, Weasel thought, and then he had another more dangerous thought - that John didn't care if he lived or died, that John was one of those people who always wanted to be tested in life or death situations.

No family.

No ties.

Just the ultimate thrill.

*What the hell did you get me into, Mr. Chairman Bluefeathers?*

"Time for what?" Lydia asked, half turning to look at Weasel.

"For us to take your plane," John said. He removed a small automatic pistol from his jacket. Lydia's eyes widened and Provost tensed, his eyes going very small and focused, as if he wanted to take the gun from John.

"I don't understand," Lydia said. "You are not from Grumman?"

"Never been there," John said. "We are, however, going to Peru, and Leonard here is a pilot. He turned quickly to Provost, who was glaring at John.

"Don't try to jump us or do anything funny." He looked at the co-pilot until he got a nod in return. "If you do, I'm gonna shoot one of your passengers, then maybe Lydia, then you. I don't want to hurt anyone, and don't plan to, but please understand. I know how to and I will."

"What are you going to do in Peru?" Lydia asked. "That country is like an armed camp sometimes."

"Rescue someone," Weasel said.

"Oh shit, the Indian thing," Lydia said, looking at Weasel. "And you're-"

"My name is Weasel. And I can fly this if I have to. Like you, there probably isn't much that I haven't flown. My job as of this morning was as a captain for Freedom Airlines." Weasel thought for a moment, and then spoke again.

"As of today, I fly for the sovereign nation of the Cold River Indians of Oregon."

# Chapter 40

Huaraz

Now that they were in a town, Tara just wanted to be left alone, she wanted to sleep for days. She sat on the bed with Steve and Sabrina, while Hawk, Lori and Martin stood in the small back room of the shop.

Hawk stood and looked at the front door, and then at the women on the bed. Tara and Lori were about the same size.

"Tara, quick, take off your clothes," he said.

"He's been trying to get me to do that since we left," Lori said dryly. "I suggest you don't do it." And then to Hawk, "Don't you men ever think of anything else, and with your cousin, no less? I'm gonna tell Susan."

"I mean for you two to change clothes," Hawk said, his face reddening. "I mean Now!"

Lori glared at him and took off her jacket.

"Look," Hawk said, "if Lori wears your clothes she can fit in out there, and she speaks Spanish. She can-"

"Find out what's happening," Martin said.

Lori looked at them and pushed her jeans down and threw them to Tara, daring any of them to look at her. They swapped clothes in silence, the room close, and no one said a word. Lori fastened the skirt and then stood up and held her hand out to Hawk.

"Gun," she said, glaring at him.

Hawk rummaged in his bag and gave her a pistol. She tucked the pistol in the waistband of her skirt and pulled her blouse over it. "If you hear shooting, just get out of here, okay?" She looked at Tara and then at each of them, and then at Martin.

"I'm gonna check the alley behind, and if it is clear, walk up to the end and see if there are soldiers there. Better be ready to go. And maybe you great big men can figure out where to go next, how we're gonna get the hell out of here."

Hawk opened the door, and with one last look, Lori slipped into the alley.

Tara shook her head, trying to shake the fatigue, to fight the desire to let the others take over. She had to do something. She knew that the people looking for them would not just let them wander down the mountain to Lima.

"Do you have a map?" Steve asked Senor Robales. Pedro walked to the front display and came back with a map. Steve spread it out on the bed.

"Why do we have to go to Lima?" Martin asked.

"Chairman said to go back to the airport," Hawk said. "He must have a plane there for us, telling us to meet at the airport." Hawk removed a cell phone from his pocket and dialed.

"Look at the map," Steve said. He pointed to a spot on the coast, directly west of Huaraz. "There's an airport at Chimbote."

"Where's that?" Tara asked.

"Here, maybe fifty air miles down hill from us. Maybe a hundred to a hundred fifty by road. According to the map, there is a commercial air service there, a long runway." Steve looked over at the shop owner. "Pedro, what's here?" He pointed to the coast of Peru on the map.

"Chimbote, a large city, Senor, maybe two hundred thousand people. Very dirty - oil wells and industry, thieves, very bad reputation." He smiled. "No tourists there, Senor Steve."

"What about the airport?" Steve asked.

"I don't know Senor, but I know you can fly out of there, in a jet plane."

Tara had been thinking of something Steve had told her during their time in the mountain. Steve had taken flying lessons (unless, of course, he was kidding) and if they could find a plane, he could fly them out of here.

"Pedro, are there planes here in Huaraz?" She asked, excited now. Maybe this could be over soon.

"Yes, of course, Senorita, we have a few planes here."

"Where are they, how far?" Tara asked. Pedro looked at her as if she were a pure fool.

"At the airport, Senorita."

"Well, right, of course, but how far is the airport?"

"Maybe a kilometer or one and a half kilometers. Not far, you can walk there in maybe ten minutes."

"What good is that gonna do us?" Sabrina asked. "We just gonna walk out there and rent one?"

Tara pointed to Steve.

"He can fly. Steve is a pilot." Steve didn't respond.

"You are a pilot, aren't you Steve?" Tara needed to believe that he could fly. She looked up as Hawk walked over to their group on the bed. He held the cell phone to his ear and held his finger up, said something into the phone, and then addressed the group.

"We have a plane on the way to Peru, Bluefeathers has talked to them and they say they can land at Chimbote. They'll be there in, uh, two hours."

"Two hours, how we gonna -"

"Steal a plane," Steve said, and he clutched the end of the bed and stood up, his face white, a silly grin on his face.

Lori walked to the end of the alley, feeling conspicuous, and at the same time, foolish. No wonder they fight all the time, she thought. Wearing clothes like these. We haven't worn this stuff on the Rez since about 1900. The alley was a jumble of cans, wooden boxes stacked up against the back of the building, and litter - paper, plastic bags, old tires in a pile. The alley was narrow, the backs of houses and other businesses there. It reminded Lori of riding a train in the States, seeing the back yards of houses, the areas where people hide things from their customers, from their front yards. She stood by the back door of the shop, amidst old packs, torn sleeping bags, and looked to her left.

Nothing.

She looked to her right and saw a little girl playing in the alley, up about thirty feet. She started that way. It was unreal being in an alley in a mountain town in Peru when just yesterday morning she had been in the relative safety of the rez at home. She knew what Tara must have felt like for the past few days. It was early afternoon and the sun was shining, but the temperature was cool. She wished that she had kept her jacket, but it sure didn't look like this old peasant stuff. She walked slowly, looking at the end of the alley. A green jeep drove slowly down the street at the end of the alley, crossing in front of Lori as she approached the street, the occupants looking at her and then driving on.

Great, how the hell we gonna get out of here when the army is prowling around, looking for someone to shoot? The little girl she had seen from the store was playing near the end of the alley, ducking in and out of boxes, playing with a kitten. She stood up when Lori approached, a girl of about eight, with a grimy face and shoulder length black hair, wearing a long tan cotton dress that was dirty on the bottom.

"Hola," Lori said quietly.

The little girl stood there and didn't say anything, and then pointed at the kitten.

"Yes, I see your kitty," Lori said in Spanish. "What is your name?"

"Maria."

"That's a pretty name. Maria, can you do something for me?"

Maria's head bobbed up and down once.

Lori walked closer. "Maria, can you look and see if the army is out in the street in front of these buildings?" She pointed to the row of buildings where the climbing shop was.

"Si," Maria said, and ran to the end of the alley. She looked up and down, both ways, solemnly, and then disappeared around the corner. Lori walked to the corner and looked at the side street where the jeep had gone. Maria was just going around the corner to the front of the store. What the hell are we gonna do if the army is in front. Lori walked down the street, keeping to the side, until she was at the corner. She stood beside a building made of gray brick, and looked out at the front of climbing store. The little girl, Maria, was talking to a group of soldiers down the street, almost in front of the store.

Great, an eight year old spy. As Lori watched, Maria pointed in her direction and the soldiers looked that way. She saw them laugh, and then Maria came skipping back toward her, the girl's hair bouncing as she moved. She looked over her shoulder at the soldiers, and then rounded the corner where Lori waited.

"Maria, what -"

"I asked them if they had seen my kitty," Maria said. "They told me to go away, as I knew they would. I heard some of them talking, and they said that they were looking for some people, some terrorists, and that I should go home."

Lori looked out over the street again, and saw that the soldiers had been joined by yet another group. One of them pointed to the end where Lori was, and they started down that way. They were maybe fifty yards away, coming toward the corner where Lori was.

*Time to get the hell out of here.*

Lori turned the corner and walked briskly down the alley toward the back door of the shop.  When she got halfway there, she started to jog, the
gun in her waistband banging against her side.  She stood at the back door, her breath coming in sharp gasps, her shoulders heaving, and looked back over her shoulder and saw a jeep pull into the alley from the direction she had come.

*Sure hope all that testosterone inside has some answers.*

*As the jeep came down the alley, the soldiers looking on either side, she took one more look, opened the door, and went inside.*

# **C**hapter **41**

Aboard the Gulfstream V

The Gulfstream was at 37,000 feet, flying two hundred miles off the west coast of Mexico, out from the state of Sinaloa, where the resort city of Mazatlan was located. Weasel stretched his right leg out as far as he could, trying to ease the cramping. He had looked back in the cabin once since they started, a quick peek that told him that John had established control there. When the announcement was first made, there had been shouting from the cabin, and then it was quiet. He had learned from Captain Lydia Barnes and the co-pilot that the ambassador to Peru was on board, the man who came up last. At some point, he guessed it didn't make any difference - to hijack an airplane, let alone an ambassador, would mean a long time in prison. He must have been insane to agree to this.

His cell phone chirped and he flipped it open. When it made connection, he didn't have time for greetings.

"Weasel, this is Bluefeathers," the voice said without slowing for pleasantries. "You need to land in a place called Chimbote."

"Where the hell's -"

"North of your original location I think."

"Hold on." He didn't like telling the chairman to wait, but he had no choice. He turned to Lydia.

"Chimbote, you know it?"

"Yeah, been there once," she said. "An hour's flight time north of Lima up the coast. Long enough runway for a heavy."

"Uh, Mr. Chairman, we can do that, but-"

"Good...I told them to be there in two hours. From the sounds of it, they don't know if they can do it or not. You need to refuel and wait for them there."

"We're on our way," Weasel said. The phone clicked off and he sat there holding it, feeling like a little kid, like when he was truly Weasel. Just Weasel. He looked over at Lydia Barnes. So far, they had made all of their course heading changes by the book, and their mid-course check-in with the air traffic control. It was comforting here in the cockpit, a place where he had spent a good portion of his adult life. When he wasn't in the cockpit flying, he was thinking about it. Yes, comforting. He looked at their heading.

"Do we need to change for Chimbote before our next ATC check?" he asked Lydia.

"No, we will approach from approximately the same heading, just let down an hour earlier. We may have to fine tune it as we get closer."

"When we change, call and get permission to land there for refueling. Say we burned more than usual or something. See if they can have something ready."

"Okay, but I sure hope you guys know what you're doing," Lydia said. "It was either a stroke of gutsy genius to declare war on a country with millions of people, or it was political and physical suicide." She shook her head. "Declare war my ass. Like I said, I sure hope you guys know what the hell you're doing."

"So do I, Lydia Barnes." He looked out over the haze of thin clouds covering the Pacific Ocean. From this height, he should be able to see the curvature of the earth on the ocean, but the water was covered today. The afternoon sun was to his right and slightly behind him, leaving the cockpit in a shadow. It was easy to sink into the familiar routine of the flight deck, and not think about what the hell they were doing. He had to agree with Captain Lydia Barnes.

*I hope we know what the hell we're doing as well, Lydia Barnes. Boy, so do I.*

Huaraz

"Don't look now," Lori said as she entered the back door to the shop, "but there are some army guys cruising the alley."

"How many?" Martin asked. They were all standing in the back room of the shop.

"A jeep, maybe three guys."

"We're getting out of here," Tara said, "and it has to be now. The army must know we're here somewhere, and it won't be long before they come for us."

"How, walk?"

"Pedro, do you have a car?" Steve asked.

"No, Senor, but why don't you call for a collectivo?"

"You mean, call a cab?" Lori asked, her voice going up at the end, astonished that it might be so simple.

"I don't have a telephone, Senor."

Hawk held the cell phone up and asked for the number. He dialed and handed the phone to Pedro.

"Have them bring the collectivo around back," Steve said.

When the collectivo arrived, they filed out the back door, Tara looking up and down the alley for any sign of the army. It can't be this easy, she thought, and entered the van, an old round Toyota that had once been white, now covered with dirt and rust spots. She sat in back and nodded, the rocking of the van lulling her to sleep, and she didn't even open her eyes when the others commented on the army vehicles they were passing. The van wound its way through the downtown, still a lot of people there for the market day. As they made their way to the edge of town, the driver picked up speed, telling Steve that the airport was only another mile up the hill. Tara drifted off to sleep, knowing somehow that she would need all of her energy in the next few hours.

She was not disappointed.

# Chapter 42

As Tara and the others made their way out of town a helicopter from Colonel Hernandez command found the truck that Martin, Hawk and Lori had hidden. The word reached Colonel Hernandez within minutes.

"What do you mean you don't know who did it?" His face was red, twisted. He yelled at the lieutenant who brought the news.

"It was the terrorists, and that's the evidence you'll find, maybe with some help from some students, some foreigners." He waved the lieutenant away. This might work out after all, he thought, no matter what the students said. After all, they had no proof.

"Bring the truck in," Hernandez said, and gave the radio to his executive officer. He didn't think the assault on the truck was the work of the Norte Americanos, but it didn't matter. He would find a way to blame it on them. Three blocks to go to find the students. He looked forward to this, and he had some troops with him who would be able to keep their mouths shut. His Humvee was the third in line, having learned from other skirmishes, other wars with the terrorists that to be in the lead car often meant sacrifice for one's country.

One block.

He would blame them for everything before he killed them.

# **C**hapter **43**

The van stopped at the crest of a small rise and they looked down at the airport. Tara opened her eyes and looked out at the runway and buildings below.

Ohmigod, that's the airport.

The runway was on the side of a mountain, with higher mountains on three sides. The runway was sloped down and ended in a sheer drop, the end of the runway a cliff of unknown height. Down below them the road wound down the mountainside, and ended at a group of hangers, the corrugated tin on the roofs stained with rust. There was a small shack next to the nearest hanger.

Hawk crossed himself, moving his hand from his forehead to his chest, muttering. Hawk was a member of the Shaker Church, and one of the things they borrowed from Catholicism was the sign of the cross. If he lived through this, he promised himself that he would tell Martin that he was a Shaker, that he could have warned the chief about this. In spite of the situation and the little bitty airport, he smiled.

Šiyápu

Who did Martin think he was, coming 'round to Peru with a bunch of Indians on a suicide mission? But what a good Šiyápu he turned out to be, and what a good friend he had become. Too bad they were all gonna die here.

Martin looked at the runway and he thought it looked awfully small. So did the others.

"I'm not flying in a plane outta that," Lori said, pointing to the runway. "My driveway's bigger than that, no sir, no way. The army would be coming with a basket and tweezers to pick us up at the bottom of that cliff. I didn't sign up for an extreme trip, one a them extreme games. See ya. I'm leaving before someone talks me into going in a plane off that thing."

"Sit down," Martin said. He turned to Steve. Steve's face was drawn and gray. Martin put his hand on Steve's arm.

"Can you fly?"

"If there's something there that will take all of us, yeah, I can get us there." Steve looked down at the runway. "I may not have much

241

left after we get to Chimbote," he added.

The van eased down the slope and crossed the runway at the upper end and pulled up in front of the nearest hanger. There was no one in sight, and it looked to Martin as if the office was deserted as well. When the van came to a stop, Martin and Hawk got out, followed by Sabrina and Lori. Martin watched as Tara held Steve's arm and helped him out. Martin saw the pain in Steve's face as he moved.

A forlorn Cessna was sitting in front of the nearest hanger, and Martin stood by the van, swaying, looking it over. There were several other planes tied down in front of the other hangers, but this one was probably big enough to carry all of them. If they stuffed themselves into it and it could get off the ground with them. It was a 206 he thought, and looked like one of the first ones Cessna built. Red and white, dirty, with an alarming stain on the cowling below the engine. At least the tires were up.

"Martin!" Lori pointed to the hill they just came down.

A vehicle was parked at the crest of the hill. It looked like an army Humvee, and he couldn't tell how many people there were inside. Time to find a plane and get the hell out of here.

"How long to fly?" Martin asked.

"If I find a plane with gas, and it starts, and it's a single engine, like this 206 here, I think ten minutes. Maybe longer. I need someone to help me go through a fast pre-flight."

"Take Sabrina and Tara with you," Martin said, "and get the plane ready. If this doesn't work we're toast anyway, so we might as well get ready to go. Hawk and Lori and I will find a way to take care of the Humvee, and hope to God it's the only one they sent out here." Martin started to turn away and said, "We've done this before, you know."

Steve smiled and nodded at Martin, feeling dizzy, and he looked for a place to lay down before he shook his head and pushed himself to focus on the plane. He was weak and nauseous, and thought for a minute that he might fall.

"Tara, Sabrina ...help me walk around this plane, will you?"

They came up on either side of him and Tara took his good left arm and draped it over her shoulder, while Sabrina put her arm around Steve's waist.

"Play your cards right big guy and . . ."

"I might get lucky?" Steve finished for Tara, smiling at her.

"And I might not drop you on the way around the plane."

"Sabrina," Steve said, resisting the urge to look around at the jeep that must be coming down the hill by now. "Sabrina, let go of me and open the door to the plane."

She walked under the wing and tried the door handle on the left side of the plane, or what she thought would be the driver's side of a car and the door swung open.

"Is there a key in the ignition, about where a key would go in a car?" Sabrina leaned over the seat and shook her head.

"No."

"Shit! Okay, look in the pocket on the door." Steve waited impatiently as she began pulling items from the pocket, and then she pulled out a key with a large piece of plastic attached.

"This it?"

Relief came over Steve even though he didn't know if it would start, if he could fly it, or if they could take care of the army. One thing at a time.

"Yeah, throw it on the seat and look for a plastic tube, like a syringe, in the pocket."

Sabrina proudly produced the plastic tube.

"Okay, bring it here," and he walked under the wing, with Tara holding onto his arm. Steve gave Sabrina instructions on how to push the needle into the fuel bladder opening under the wing, to test for water in the gas, and to tell him if there was any gas at all. Sabrina held the plastic tube up, looked at Steve to see if she was doing it the right way, and filled it with a couple of ounces of gas. It was clear, no water. Steve walked around the plane, looking for obvious dents and damage, wiggled the flaps, the rudder, and then had Sabrina repeat the procedure on the right wing. Checked the cowling for birds, nests, obstructions. Sabrina removed the tie down chains and the wheel blocks as Steve watched. The pre-flight was coming back to him.

"Help me inside, Tara, and Sabrina, stay outside, by the door." He sat slowly in the left seat, his right arm on fire, and risked a glance at the others. Martin was standing by the van. Lori and Hawk were nowhere in sight. The van driver was sitting in the van, behind the wheel with a worried look on his face. More like scared shitless, Steve thought. The jeep was about halfway down the hill. He looked over the instruments and for a moment his mind went blank.

Checklist. Gotta find the checklist. It was in the pocket where the key was. Steve had flown in a 206 before, but he had never operated one, only a 172, and he thought he could fly this one, if only for a short distance.

"I didn't have time to climb on a ladder and look at the fuel in the tanks," he told Tara. "We'll just have to trust the gauges."

He ran down the checklist, looking for the master switch for the electrical system. Hope to God the battery works, he thought, as he found the master switch. It was in the off position, and at least there had been a pilot who followed the rules. Radios...off.

A wave of pain hit him and he gripped the wheel to hang on. His right arm was now swollen from the shoulder to the elbow, and he could *feel* the infection spreading. The swelling against his elbow limited the movement of his arm. Checklist. Fuel selector, both tanks.

Carburetor heat - off

Mixture control - full rich

Steve looked at the mixture control, something alien to him, as the planes he had flown didn't have mixture controls. He left the settings alone, full rich. He'd worry about changing it later, during the run up, if they made it that far.

He turned the master switch on, and could hear the power come on as he prepared to start the engine. He reached for the key when he caught movement out the front of the plane.

The Humvee had stopped ten yards in front of the van and soldiers were getting out. One of them was yelling at Lori as he got out the passenger side and was bringing a rifle with him.

"Sabrina, get in," Steve yelled, and slammed his door. Sabrina climbed up on the right side and dove into the middle seat behind Tara. In the 206 there was a smaller third seat behind Sabrina. It would be a tight fit, but it was the weight of the passengers, the fuel, and the plane that was the problem. They might just drop off the end of the runway.

Steve turned the key to the on position and watched as the fuel gauges came up. Both the right and left tanks were half full, more than enough for the flight down the mountain to Chimbote.

As Steve checked the plane, Martin tried to think of a plan that would work against soldiers who now would be very cautious. He looked across the runway at the jeep, and saw it move forward, starting down the hill toward the airport. Hawk and Lori were watching it also.

"Senor."

The driver called from the van.

"Senor, don't worry about the money, I need to go now." He glanced up the hill toward the army jeep, and licked his lips.

"We need him here," Martin said, and Lori walked around the van and approached the driver, speaking rapidly in Spanish, holding her hand out. The driver sat there and looked at her. Lori looked up across the runway, pulled the gun from the band in her skirt and pointed it at the driver. He carefully put the keys in her outstretched hand and she returned to the passenger side. The driver sat still, his face drawn, his hand shaking as he gripped the steering wheel.

"We need to have them stop here in front of the van," Hawk said. He pointed to a spot about thirty feet in front of the van, and the same distance out from the hanger.

"How do we do that?" Martin asked, looking at the jeep.

"I stand in front of the van," Lori said. "When they approach, I will walk out and greet them, and they'll stop right there." Martin and Hawk looked at her, Martin not sure that he wanted her to be exposed like that. Hell, they all were, so it just didn't matter.

"Okay, you walk out, then what?"

"You wait here by the van, Hawk inside the hanger door where it's dark and they can't see him. Then you have an "L" shaped kill zone."

"God," Hawk muttered. He handed Martin a pistol and a spare magazine.

"The first guy out of the jeep will be on the passenger side, agreed?" Lori looked at them.

"Probably," Martin said.

"I'll take him, as soon as he gets out, and I mean the second his first foot hits the ground, and then I'll go flat on the ground. Boss here," and she looked up at Martin and gave him a light punch on the arm, "will take the left side, and Brother Hawk will do all on the driver's side, from his little hidey spot in the hanger."

"I should be out here instead of you," Hawk growled.

"Oh, yeah, that makes sense," Lori said sarcastically. "When those soldiers see your bulk, their necks will swell up, and it will be testosterone against testosterone. If anything swells up, I want it to be that itty bitty brain, and then they won't be able to think with the other one. Maybe we'll have a chance."

"Who's gonna come around and make their little brain swell up?"

Hawk said with a grin.

Lori stuck her tongue out at him and he laughed. He watched the jeep from the opposite side of the van.

"Good plan except for one thing," Martin said as he watched the jeep negotiate the last turn on the hillside road and head for the runway.

"What's that, Boss?" Hawk asked.

"Look at the top of the hill." Martin pointed to the crest of the hill where the road cut through, a half mile away. Even from this distance they could see several vehicles there, including what looked to be a large tracked vehicle.

"Shall we negotiate, give up?" Martin asked.

"No!" Lori screamed. She shook her head violently. "We stay with the plan and fly out of here or be shot." She looked at Martin and he saw the look of a scared, cornered, wounded woman. A very dangerous one.

"Game time, Hawk," Martin said. The big man grabbed Martin and gave him a gruff hug, put his arm around Lori, and then nodded.

"For a Šiyápu you're a good man, Boss." He looked at Lori and said softly, "You hug the ground when the shooting starts, cousin." Lori nodded and walked toward the hanger, keeping the van and the plane between him and the approaching jeep.

"Good plan except..." Martin said, as he watched the jeep negotiate the last turn and head for the runway.

"What's that?"

"That damned plane better start."

As the Humvee drove up and stopped in front of the van, Steve reached over with his left hand to turn the ignition key. He couldn't raise his right arm up high enough to grip the key. It was pretty much useless now, unless he needed something to keep him awake. He hoped that this old 206 had been used regularly, and that might mean it would start.

"Tara," he said, looking at the scene outside the plane.

"What?" She sat there frozen as well, watching the soldiers approach.

"Push that lever several times, the primer." He pointed with his left hand to the primer. She reached across and pushed it in until he told her to stop. Outside, the soldier in the passenger seat of the Humvee had opened the door and was pulling his rifle with him.

Steve turned the key and the propeller spun, slowly at first, then faster, and the movement froze the soldiers and Lori, catching all of them by surprise, and then the engine fired and Steve jammed on the toe brakes as the plane rocked forward a few inches, and as Steve and Tara watched through the propeller blade, Lori drew a pistol from the rear waistband of her skirt, holding the pistol down by her leg on the right side so the soldiers couldn't see it, and Tara remembered Lori like that for years, Lori holding the gun by her leg with her right hand, waving with her left, smiling at the soldiers, almost provocatively.

Lori walked a few steps in front of the van and moved to her left a little, in front of the driver of the van, hoping to give Martin a better shot at the soldiers. The plan, as she had outlined it, really sucked, a plan that should have someone else out here instead of her.

Like Hawk or Martin. Those two had been in police work a lot longer than she had, and had been in shooting situations before, but she knew that she had been right. If Hawk had been out front with his massive body, the soldiers might feel sufficiently threatened to park out on the runway, be out of effective pistol range, at least effective range for a pistol in a gunfight.

Lori forced a smile on her face and waved with her left hand, resisting the urge to look over at the hanger and see if Hawk was in position, or look behind her and see just where the hell Martin was. The Humvee stopped, about twenty feet away, and Lori turned her left side to the soldiers, as if she were going to say something to the driver, holding her pistol tightly behind her back, hidden from the soldiers.

*Sight picture, Lori, sight picture and squeeze, should be able to put them in an area the size of a coffee cup from this range*

"Hola," she yelled, smiling at the soldier on the passenger side, and then the plane engine whined, the noise loud just a few feet behind her, and everyone stopped, the soldiers looking up and behind Lori, and then the soldier opened the door all the way and started out, pulling his rifle with him, and as his right foot hit the ground, Lori brought her pistol up fast

*Sight picture, Lori*
*Squeeze the trigger*
and fired two rounds, both hitting the soldier in the chest through the window

*breathe*
and then a third round up higher through his head and he was

falling, the look of surprise on his face a curious mixture of blood and shock and then the driver ground the gears, trying to get back away and Hawk came out from the hanger firing fast, the bullets hitting the Humvee.

*Do something you're supposed to be doing something Lori*
and someone was screaming her name and two soldiers fired at her from behind the Humvee.

*They must have been riding in the back*
"Lori Get down getdowngetdown!"

Martin came up beside the van, yelling, firing at the soldiers, hitting one of them, and Hawk was yelling, firing, running at the Humvee from the hanger, his boots sending up little clouds of dust from the dirt, funny little clouds of dust, and then Lori was falling, something had pushed her, how could Martin push her over when he was to the side of her, the windshield of the van exploding behind her, and she didn't feel the ground as she slammed down on it.

Tara pushed the door open and kicked it away from her and jumped out of the plane as Steve yelled something at her. She leaned back in and he screamed at her.

"The prop, stay away from the prop." He pointed with his good arm at the spinning blade.

Tara nodded and waved at him, turned and ran out from the wing. She jumped when she heard a shot from behind the Humvee and then Hawk emerged. She sprinted around to the front of the collectivo and kneeled down beside Martin. He was holding Lori's head, pressing on her abdomen, his hand slick with blood.

"Let's go," Hawk shouted as he ran up, pointed at the runway. Tara looked up and froze. The trucks and armored vehicles were halfway down the hill.

"Get her in the plane," Tara said, and Hawk and Martin put their arms under Lori and lifted, walking bent over, holding her body as her arms dragged on the ground, as Tara led them around the prop to the door. Sabrina got out and then Hawk turned and pushed the front seat forward and worked his way into the middle seat, pulling Lori with him. He leaned her against the side and wormed his way into the small back seat area. Sabrina and Martin got in and Tara clamored into the front seat, the plane bouncing over the ground as Steve reached over and pushed the throttle in with his good hand.

Tara closed the door as the plane swung around the van, picking up speed, the wing missing the Humvee by inches, bouncing now as it hit the runway.

"Tara, push the throttle in all the way, now!" Steve yelled as they picked up speed, the wheels kicking up dust. Steve must have dispensed with the runup and whatever the hell else he should be doing on a takeoff, Tara thought.

"Tara, give me twenty degrees of flaps, now, that lever there," Steve yelled again. Tara glanced over at the hillside, and saw that the army jeeps had almost reached the runway, about fifty yards ahead of them. The plane picked up speed as Tara looked down to the lever between the seats. She pulled the lever up to the twenty mark and looked out again. They flashed by the lead jeep as it entered the runway. Tara jerked her head around and caught a glimpse of the army vehicles swinging onto the runway behind them. The plane picked up speed and the end of the runway raced toward them.

"Are we going to make it?" Tara yelled at Steve over the noise of the engine.

"I don't know, I don't even know the rotation speed of this thing, but we're going too fast to stop now even if we wanted to." He flew with his left hand, his feet balanced on the pedals. The plane suddenly swerved to the left and shuddered, Steve fighting the pedals and moving the yoke with his left hand to keep the plane straight.

"They're shooting at us!" Hawk yelled.

"I think they hit a tire," Steve yelled, fighting to keep it straight. A warning buzzer came on, a stall warning Tara thought, although she didn't know how she knew that, and as they hit the end of the runway Steve pulled the yoke back slightly and they were flying over the drop-off, the plane bouncing up sharply as Steve fought the controls.

Something hit the fuselage with a thunk and then it was quiet except for the wind and engine noise. Tara looked at Steve and if she had thought he couldn't look any worse, she was wrong. The skin on his face was drawn tight, and he looked as if he was going to pass out at any minute.

No one cheered as they lifted off. There had been no other choice - either get away or die. The afternoon sun winked at them between the peaks to their right and behind them, and they flew down through the rough mountain air.

"Tara, pull the power back, a little, slowly," Steve said. Tara put her hands on the throttle and looked at him and he nodded, and she pulled, slowly, and the engine was not as loud, and they headed down.

"We're going downhill all the way from Huaraz to Chimbote," Steve said with a grimace. "We could almost glide there, going from 10,000 feet to sea level in fifty miles, and we sure don't need much power."

"What's that down there?" Tara pointed ahead and below them. Steve looked.

"Fog."

"Can we land in it, if it is on the coast?"

"Uh, sure, but I've never done it before." He looked ahead and shook his head. "But, I've never landed with a wheel shot out either."

Tara looked at Steve for a long time, and then looked behind her. Martin and Sabrina sat in the middle seat with Lori sprawled out on top of them, Martin's arms slick with blood, his hands holding the wounds. Sabrina reached up and brushed Lori's hair away from her face, stroking her cheek. Tara looked at Martin and held his gaze.

Martin held his face down to Lori's lips, trying to feel air. He thought she was still breathing, but he knew she needed to be on an operating table immediately. Oh, God, but she has lost a lot of blood. As he watched, Lori opened her eyes and tried to move her head, moving her legs and tried to sit up. Martin held her.

"Lori, it's okay," he said, his face inches from hers. "Just lay still and . . ."

"Wh...where are we?" She looked around at Sabrina and then at Tara up front. Her head was directly behind the high back seat where Steve was sitting, on the left side of the plane.

"Only way you got me in this thing was to shoot me," Lori said.

"Yeah, and you forgot to duck," Martin said. "Remember our talk before the jeep got there?" Lori shook her head slowly.

"The last thing I remember was looking at the plane and telling you that I wasn't going in it." She stopped and looked at Martin. "It hurts," she said, and shut her eyes. "I'm *cold*."

Hawk moved around in the small back seat, trying to get his jacket off. After a lot of grunting and swearing, he pushed it forward to Sabrina, and they covered Lori. There was nothing more they could do for her.

Tara began singing softly, too soft to be heard above the noise of the engine. She sang words from her grandmother, and then sang them louder.

Sabrina joined in, and then Hawk, his deep voice covering them from the back of the plane.

They flew on, a group of survivors, battered and wounded, in a plane that might come apart during the landing, with a pilot who might not be able to land with an arm swollen up twice its size, with a tribal member almost dead. The plane bounced and Lori cried out as the sun suddenly dropped behind the mountain peaks and the cabin was dark, and Tara had a sudden thought.

We're not even out of Peru yet.

# **C**hapter **44**

Colonel Hernandez beat his fist on the window of the Humvee as the driver stopped at the end of the runway.

"Shoot!" He screamed and jumped out of the Humvee. He pulled his pistol and emptied the magazine at the disappearing airplane, and at his disappearing chances to eliminate any witnesses to his private war in the mountains.

"Get down on the ground!" Hernandez screamed at his driver, holding his pistol over him, pointing it at his head. His finger tightened on the trigger and he almost lost control there, but instead, he slowly placed his pistol in his holster. He kicked his driver in the ribs and stalked off toward the end of the runway.

Maybe he could make it across the border and into Ecuador.

# Chapter 45

Washington, D.C.

"We ever find that agent, the one that's missing on the reservation?" President Miller was in a good mood. He had just won a major victory on his budget proposal, and if it passed, he knew he had a chance to make history. He made decisions based on what he thought the country needed, not political expediency. It was his second term, and he could afford to.

"No, he's still missing. The Indians say they don't know where he is," June said, looking at her notes.

"Mr. President." F.B.I. Director Chilson spoke from his seat in the corner.

"Mr. President, we can't find agent Larry Morrow, and because of this, we have every reason to believe that he has met with foul play. The borders of Cold River are closed, we haven't been allowed access and in my opinion, we should have a plan to find him. We've got what amounts to a group of people practicing war on a nation that's a friend of the United States. At some point, we need to take control of the reservation."

The President nodded. He didn't want to allow a situation to get completely out of control. It appeared that order had broken down. Borders closed, F.B.I. man missing, and that crazy declaration of war. Terrorists probably involved.

"Can we get enough F.B.I. personnel to do the job?"

"Probably," the director said, "but this is most likely a job for the military, some unit close by, call in the National Guard, restore order for the good of the reservation, all that."

The President looked up from his desk. "I don't want another Waco," he said.

They assured him it wouldn't be another Waco or another Ruby Ridge. They were going to do this one right.

# Chapter 46

Aboard Gulfstream V, 200 miles west of Ecuador

"You understand what's going to happen to you all when you get to Lima, don't you boy?" Ambassador Roberts sat in the leather seat, his face jiggling as the plane bounced. He had remained in his seat during the flight, calling the flight attendant often to bring drinks and food.

"Of course," John said, and smiled.

"You better hope we can get you away from the Peruvian security forces, or as they say in Arkansas, your ass is grass. Them good ol' boys don't fuck around with hijackers and the like. They might just shoot you full a holes in fronta us." The ambassador leaned back and laughed, his jowls shaking as he moved.

"Well, Ambassador, you might just as well hope we don't get shot 'full a holes' too soon, as you put it."

"Why is that?" The ambassador was enjoying himself as they got to the end of the flight.

"Do the Peruvians like you?"

"What do you mean, 'course they do."

"Because when we get there, y'all will be my prisoner."

The ambassador's face grew dark. He started to say something, and then sat back and glared at John.

John looked around the cabin. The ambassador and his assistant were on the lounge seat; the attendant, Mary, was in a jump seat at the rear of the cabin by the galley, reading a magazine. She looked up and caught John's eye and gave him a smile and then went back to reading her magazine. It was as if she was used to such happenings when she flew. She probably enjoyed seeing someone shut the ambassador up, since he was such an insufferable prick. The agricultural attaches, both the U.S. and Peruvian, were talking softly in a row of seats at mid-point in the cabin. At least as far as the cabin of the plane was concerned, John had things under control. The ambassador was a pain in the ass, but that was expected. The ambassador's aide kept looking at John as if he wanted to jump him, but John thought that it was more out of impressing the boss than it was out of the aide really having the cajones to do it. He would bear watching though. John knocked softly on the door to the flight deck and Weasel opened it part way.

"How much longer?" John asked, glancing inside the cockpit and then back to the cabin at the ambassador.

"We're going to give the announcement and begin our descent for a landing in Chimbote in about five minutes," Lydia said.

"Keep it to yourselves about the new landing site," John said. "Might as well keep the ambassador happy until the last minute." He looked at Weasel. "You drivin' this thing on the landing?"

"No," Weasel said. "I have a deal with the crew - they perform flawlessly, don't be cowboys, and they can continue to fly their plane. Otherwise, if I have to, yeah, I can fly it. They're gonna contact Peruvian ATC for a flight change now. Let them know we're coming, get gas lined up, whatever we need. We're gonna tell them that the Ambassador has a meeting with an official in Chimbote, call came in at the last minute, and so forth. Once we land, hopefully our people will be there and we can turn around."

John nodded. "Let me know when we're on final, five minutes from touchdown, just tell me 'turning on final' or something like that on the intercom.

"Okay," Weasel said, and didn't ask. He had decided hours ago that he didn't want to know everything there was to know about "John."

The sun was just over the water, going down behind them, throwing a reddish glow over the sea when they began their descent into Chimbote.

Lydia made the announcement, and then they were busy. Landing after dark in a strange airport, made for a busy time for the crew.

"Patches of ground fog ahead," co-pilot said.

"Yeah, but we're gonna fly by wire on this one," Lydia said. They had dialed in the airport's coordinates in their computers, and the auto pilot would take them to within feet of touchdown, and then Lydia would land the plane. The plane slowed further, their descent rate of 5,000 feet per minute meant that they would be at sea level in minutes. At 10,000 feet they slowed their rate of descent and continued to drop. Matthew tried to contact the control tower in Chimbote again, without success.

"Maybe they're out for dinner," he suggested, uneasy now, and they all looked again at the radar. The radar said that they were the only plane out there.

# Chapter 47

Cold River Indian Reservation

Chairman Bluefeathers looked at the picture of his son-in-law, daughter, and granddaughter, Tara, taken at Thanksgiving almost twenty years ago, just a week before his daughter was killed. How differently things turned out, to raise a granddaughter, to lose a family. If possible, he loved Tara more than he had loved his daughter. She was made more precious by the accident, and now he was going to lose her. He no longer had a good feeling about this. He had to keep going, to try to salvage something for the reservation, for the Tribes.

Chairman Bluefeathers sat at his desk and looked at the picture again. In the next room, members of the tribal council, community leaders, and tribal leaders, were arguing. Now the argument had turned ugly as to how to proceed. Bluefeathers knew that he had at the most, a day and possibly as little as a few hours, to have some kind of successful resolution to his declaration of war, and acts of what amounted to treason against the Unites States.

He knew that he also may have a day or less before the federal government or the State of Oregon decided to "restore order," as they put it, and do so by force. The lessons of Waco were not lost on him. If the government could show, however thin the case, that there was a need to go onto the reservation to restore order, they would invade a sovereign nation.

Bluefeathers also knew that he was playing with fire when he brought up the issue of sovereignty and slammed the glove down in Congress. If the issues of sovereignty and the idea of sovereignty were weakened, then Bluefeathers would not be welcome on the Cold River Reservation where he had lived all of life. He would also not be welcome in any Indian nation. He knew what most other leaders of countries knew, and that was that you could go from being a visionary great leader in a matter of hours to a villain. History would write what happened in the end, not what happened in the middle or the courage behind decisions.

It's not necessarily how you attain office, he thought, but how you leave it. He pushed the thoughts from his mind that he hadn't done the right thing. He knew that if he crumbled now, there would never be any chance to assist his granddaughter and the others, nor would there be any opportunity to help those people who had put their lives out there for their people. The only thing that might be averted would be a shooting war with the federal government.

The intercom line on his phone chirped.

"Yes."

"I think you better take line one," Josephine said. "It's Turtle, and he needs to talk to you right away." Turtle was Richard Smith, a tribal member who worked for the casino.

The caller was excited.

"I'm up here...this is Turtle, and I'm up here in Gresham, driving around the Safeway store with my kids, and we was coming to Portland, and there's a whole bunch of army trucks and tanks headed towards the rez, and there's a bunch of them, and..."

*Well, so much for my time line*

This might work to solidify his position *within* the reservation, but Bluefeathers knew that he didn't have much time. He had known from the start that his granddaughter and the others might not get out of Peru, but as a leader he had to do something. Most of the tribal members knew that he would have done the same thing whether or not it was his granddaughter, and most of those who didn't believe it just didn't count.

He shook his head, missing what Turtle said next.

"...and I think there's maybe ten big lowboys carrying them Abrahms tanks, a whole shitload of Humvees and staff cars, maybe, uh, two or three platoons, in a buncha six-bys. They's all wearing helmets and camo uniforms, and -"

"Okay, uh, I get the picture," Bluefeathers said. "But Turtle, can you follow them, see if they actually hit the upper end of the rez, maybe they're going to Hood River or the Dalles, on some kind of maneuver."

"On a Wednesday night?" Turtle asked, incredulous.

"Well, you have a point there, but can you follow them at least to the border of the rez, so we can see what their intentions are, and all?"

"Sure, yeah." Turtle hung up.

*Christ, Bluefeathers thought, what the hell were they going to do, invade? He got Josephine on the intercom.*

"Get someone to run down south to Redmond and watch the armory. I want to see if there is any activity." He knew that Josephine had listened in on the conversation with Turtle, and most of the time that was a good thing. It saved a lot of time explaining what he wanted her to do, but it also made her a defacto ruler of the tribes. With her knowledge she could influence people. She sometimes had as much power as a tribal council member.

The Redmond armory was thirty five miles south of the reservation. A mechanized cavalry unit was there with at least a dozen M1A1 Tanks and support vehicles and at least one platoon of pretty well trained soldiers.

Bluefeathers had received periodic updates from the people in touch with the groups in Peru on their cell phones. He knew that the Grumman Gulfstream was approaching Peru and that his granddaughter and the rescue team were in an airplane somewhere by the coast. Josephine stuck her head in the door.

"We talked to both planes again. The Gulfstream is about to land, and the plane that Tara is in, the small plane, is on its way there, but they said that Lori had been shot, that she was pretty bad."

Bluefeathers got up and opened the door to the front office.

"I'm going to the chambers." Josephine raised her eyebrows and Bluefeathers grimaced in return. "I want to know immediately of any conversations from our people in Peru. I also want to know if we hear from any of our people watching the National Guard. Get the senator on the phone."

He stepped inside the tribal council chambers and the heated conversations died. Most of the council leaders and others were standing. This was no different from other serious issues that faced the tribe on sometimes a weekly basis. Bluefeathers thought about how this may seem different to outsiders, but until recently, fistfights were a common event on the floor of the U.S. House of Representatives in Washington. They just pretended to be more civilized.

Bluefeathers reached his chair at the head of the U-shaped table and sat down heavily behind his microphone.

"Please, be seated." He called Josephine, and when she appeared he told her what he wanted - two police cars at the council chambers in one minute.

"Army tanks are on the way to the reservation from the Portland area. We should know in a few minutes if they are mobilizing to the south. The last I heard, they were only twenty miles from the northern boundary."

"No!" The shout came from the back of the room. The room was filled with angry shouts, chairs scraping as the members in the room jumped up, some of the chairs going over backward. Bluefeathers waited a full minute, and then held up his hand.

"I'm going to take Sal, we're going to the bridge at Bear Creek Springs. I've already given orders for them to blow it." He didn't ask for a consensus, he just told them what he was going to do, and the room was quiet.

"What about them tanks firing onto the rez?" someone asked.

"They won't," Joe said. "At least not for a day or two, and then it's unlikely. For one thing, they don't keep the ammunition for the big guns in Portland. Nearest place is probably somewhere around Mountain Home Airbase in Idaho. At this point, we have a show of force and some soldiers with M-16's."

Bluefeathers knew that he would have their support if anyone tried to come on the reservation, and that support would last as long as the food and electricity did. He held up his hands.

"Before we leave, I'm going to give the order for our people to clear the bridge. We're going to give a warning to the state troopers and people congregated on the other side of the bridge, we'll give them a couple of warnings, get our people back to a safe distance, and then blow the bridge. I want to be there and watch this. We're leaving now. If the army stages on the other side of the bridge, they will not be a factor."

He stood up. The noise started again and he stopped.

"Martha, I want you to go to the bridge on the south and wait for my order."

The northern boundary was thirty-five miles from the agency; the southern boundary, formed by the Deschutes River, was a mile from the town of Cold River. The rest of the reservation was protected, at least from mechanized assault by mountains and deep gorges. They might have to blow a bridge in the northeast on a little used route, but they would watch that route and take it out if they needed to.

They were about to become an island.

# Chapter 48

Aboard Cessna 206, outside Chimbote

Tara's head snapped up as the Cessna hit a pocket of rough air. Lori cried out in pain as she hit the roof of the plane. Tara looked over at Steve. His head bobbed down on his chest, his face white, his eyes barely open.

"Your arm," Tara said quietly.

"It's at the point where it feels like someone chopped it off with an ax. I think it's swollen about twice the normal size. I had to split the shirt and release the bandage when you were in the alley."

"How far are we?"

"You're supposed to be the navigator," Steve said, with his teeth clenched against the pain. "But, we aren't far." He pointed ahead. "The haze and smoke and glow up ahead should be Chimbote. There's ah, there should be a lot of lights coming on now as it's getting dark, and the airport is on the southeast part of the city, inland about a mile from the beach. I'm gonna center on the left side of the lights, and I want you to look for a rotating beacon of some kind, a rotating light that will flash. There should be a beacon, the tower there is not operated on a twenty four hour basis. Everything in and out of there is covered by radar from Lima."

"Military radar?" Martin asked.

"Yeah, most likely."

They flew on, dropping down the side of the Andes mountain range into warmer, denser air. The lights grew brighter in the distance, and Tara strained her eyes to look down into the gloom for the beacon.

"Tara," Steve said. He nodded to the instrument panel. "This knob up here almost to the top on the right side...no...to the right, yes that one." Her hands stopped at the radio knob and he nodded.

"In the chart for this plane, in the map, it showed a frequency for this airport. Dial it there now. We should receive a broadcast from the airport with wind direction and temperature, hopefully it has been updated in the last hour. The lights should come on."

The announcement came over the headphones as soon as Tara got the frequency dialed in. A recorded voice told about wind direction, runway use, and landing sequences.

"There it is!" Tara said excitedly, pointing across the console, out of the left front quarter of the windshield.

"Maybe five miles," Steve said. He checked his altimeter and had Tara pull the throttle back. She looked over at him. His right arm lay in his lap with his left hand on the yoke, and he winced at every bounce. Many of the controls Steve needed were on his right side, and she would have to help him land.

"We're gonna get one shot at this," Steve said. "I can maybe fly around again if Tara hits the throttle at the right time, but the plane might not. The exhaust gas temperature is way too hot. I didn't set the mixture controls when we took off, and don't really know how anyway, but this engine is about gone."

"Let me know when it goes," Hawk said from the back. "I want to get off just before the engine quits."

"Steve," Tara said, "Tell me when you want me to work the throttle and flap things."

"Pull the throttle out more now, there, that's it," and the plane slowed, and descended faster. Tara felt a lurch in her stomach as the plane dropped.

"What the hell!" Tara watched as a sudden explosion and fire lit up the horizon on the north side of town.

"Looks like our friends are back," she said. She turned on the landing lights for Steve, the lights on the wings bathing the interior of the plane in light.

Hawk was talking on the cell phone again, and then he looked up at them.

"The Gulfstream is on the runway, at the north end, looking for fuel. They said to land to the north and taxi to them."

"Tell them we are three or four minutes from the airport," Steve said, "and that we can't taxi, we probably don't have a wheel. I'll come over north and then swing back around to land."

Another brilliant flash of light came from the north of town as Steve made the turn to line up with the runway. Tara keyed the microphone and the runway lights came on. No one said a word as they made a slow turn to line up with the runway.

# Chapter 49

Situation Room, White House

"Mr. President." Director Sherryl French of the CIA stood in front of a screen and pointed to a map of South America. "Mr. President, I would like to direct your attention to the northwestern part of South America, to the common border between Peru and Ecuador."

"We have received word from our field sources that the Ecuadoran Army is sending units to the border, specifically here, and-"

"We already have that information," President Miller said. The director of the CIA looked bewildered. "But, Mr. President, we just received this word within the hour, and I came directly here."

"While you were driving here, we watched it live on Fox," President Miller said sarcastically. "But continue, tell us why they are doing this now, and if it has anything to do with these students getting killed."

"Well, the two appear to be connected, as least the General of the Army of Ecuador has mentioned what he called the slaughter of students in Peru. But this may just be a war of opportunity as well. Peru and Ecuador have been at war in 1941, 1981, and 1995. In October of 1997, Ecuadoran soldiers reportedly launched some mortars at a post in Loreto, Peru. That border has been disputed for over sixty years. In fact, Ecuador claims a large part of the Amazon jungle, as large as the current country of Ecuador."

"What's our position?"

"I'd like to answer that, Mr. President." June raised her hand.

"Go ahead."

"We have a position of neutrality, of course, but we have sold weaponry and supplied the military organizations of both countries, with most of our support going to Peru."

"Wonderful," the President said.

"During the war in 1995," French said, "Ecuadorans claimed victory, and essentially defeated Peru for the first time ever, so this is something that was waiting to happen. The declaration of war by Cold River may have been a catalyst, but we believe this event was inevitable."

"Mr. President," June said softly, looking at a small television in the corner. She pointed. They watched as an aide turned up the volume.

"Put it on the big screen," President Miller said.

"...is Lisa White from Fox, a report just in from Guayaquil, Ecuador's largest city." The background graphics showed a map of South America, and then a blow up to Ecuador. "President Leonaras, in a speech this evening, announced that they were joining the brave fighters from the Cold River Indian Reservation of Oregon, and were mobilizing against the territorial invaders, the Peruvian Army. Peru and Ecuador have been..."

President Miller waved to his aide to turn the volume down, leaving the picture on. He was about to make a decision that he was sure was the right one, but one nevertheless that could go wrong.

"Let's get some people down there in both embassies and stop this thing if we can," he said. He stood, a signal that the meeting was over.

"One more thing." The assembled group stopped, frozen, waiting for their instructions.

"Let's take care of our end of this thing. Take control of the reservation. Any way you have to."

# **C**hapter **50**

Chimbote

"Wha-, where the hell are we?" The ambassador yelled as he turned in his seat to look out the window. The thump of the landing gear being lowered could be felt in the cabin. The plane increased speed slightly to compensate. "This isn't Lima!" He turned further around and was staring out the window.

"Hell, the lights from Lima and Miliflores should be all around us, there's six million people down there." He turned to face John, who was seated by the cockpit door.

"Chimbote."

"What the hell, what the hell we doing in God forsaken Cheem-BOO-Tay?" He drew each syllable out, as if it were distasteful to say them.

"We're landing here to take on fuel and some passengers."

"We are NOT taking on passengers in this plane...belongs to the U.S. Gov'mint."

"Relax, ambassador, or we'll leave you here. From the looks of the fires outside," John looked across to the window, "you won't want to be here long."

In the cockpit, Lydia and Matt were making final checks for landing with Weasel looking on. They were still trying the tower with no response other than the recording. Matt pressed his headset against his right ear, listening intently.

"You been following that channel?" he asked Lydia.

"If you mean, the airport advisory, about the massing of troops on the border?" She didn't wait for an answer to her question. She depressed the microphone switch and the runway lights came on, about ten miles ahead, Weasel thought.

"Runway in sight," Lydia said.

"Radar shows no other traffic," Matt said. Lydia hit the intercom switch and told the passengers to prepare for landing.

Other than not having an active control tower, and no other planes in the vicinity, it was a textbook landing. Weasel was as relaxed as he could be considering that they were about to land in a foreign nation that his reservation had declared war on, and they were landing with what amounted to a hijacked airplane. Lydia was executing a "short field" approach and landing procedure, just in case the chart was wrong and the runway was not as long as it was supposed to be. They flew over the numbers on the runway and landed, the wheels touching softly. The plane settled, Lydia pulled the power back and hit the reverse thrusters and began to brake. They came to a stop across from the terminal, a dark building that showed no signs of life. She turned to Weasel.

"What now?"

"Now we get off the active runway, find fuel and wait for our friends. They're about ten minutes out. They have wounded so we had better hurry. Judging from the fires out there it might not be too healthy here for too long. Lydia, if you can get ready for takeoff, I'll take Matt here and find a fuel truck. They have commercial 737's flying out of here so there should be some appropriate gas." He got up as Lydia taxied and opened the door, talking on the phone to Hawk.

Lydia pulled up out from the terminal and turned the plane so they were headed back to the end of the runway. If the wind held, they would have to taxi back and take off in the same direction as they landed. From where she was she could see the end of the runway.

Weasel ducked through the cockpit door and Matt followed him into the cabin. He nodded to John and walked to the cabin door. Matt pulled the release and the door swung down to the apron.

"I want off this plane, right now," the ambassador said, glaring at John.

"Nobody leaves this plane," John said, "except for the two pilots there, especially you, Mr. Ambassador. Nobody." John looked at the flight attendant. "When they leave, would you shut this door?" Weasel and Matt walked down the steps, and the door shut behind them.

Weasel stood on the cement apron him and looked around. Even in the dark, he was able to see the airport. The runway lights and the glow of the city lights gave the area an eerie twilight incandescence. A large fire to the north was reflected in the windows of the terminal.

The airport appeared abandoned.

Weasel could hear popping in the distance. Rifle fire. He looked at a row of trucks parked at the north end of the terminal.

"There," he pointed, and started across the apron at a jog. Matt ran up beside him and matched his jog.

"How long to fuel the Gulfstream?" Weasel asked.

"About ten minutes to fill it," Matt said, "if we work together and get two lines going. Let's find a truck with enough jet fuel and get moving." They slowed as they neared the line of trucks. A loud explosion in the city center caused Weasel to stop.

"I don't think we should stay here too long or order pizza or take out," Matt said. He sprinted toward a truck. Weasel watched as Matt looked inside the cab.

"No keys," he said and jumped down from the cab.

"Let me," Weasel said, and pushed his head and shoulders up into the floor area beneath the steering wheel. He reached up and turned on the interior lights of the cab and began pulling wires from the ignition. When he found the ones he wanted, he crossed them and the truck started. He turned to look at Matt. The co-pilot ran around the truck and got in the passenger side as Weasel put it in gear and they lurched forward. Weasel looked over at him. He shrugged his shoulders.

"You just learn these things when you grow up and need to get somewhere." He grinned and Matt grinned back. Weasel drove to the Gulfstream, positioning the truck next to it according to Matt's instructions. They got out and walked around to get the hoses.

Weasel saw the Cessna before he heard it. The engine was shut down to an idle. It came in over the numbers high and drifted down the runway toward them, still too high, the plane then nosing up and drifting to the side, then centering again, the landing lights blinding as Weasel looked at the plane. He shielded his eyes as the plane approached and then flew by them, slowing, dropping down, now just feet off the runway. As the red and white Cessna flashed by their position, Weasel felt a tightening in his stomach when he saw the landing gear. Matt saw it at the same time.

"Fuck me, the left main's shredded," Weasel said, and jumped down. "Start fueling," he yelled at Matt, and ran after the plane, running toward the runway just as the plane touched down.

Steve brought the Cessna in high over the end of the runway. He knew he didn't want to be short, and that the runway was long enough to land the Cessna practically anywhere on it. He came over high and stayed high, not wanting to set down. He hadn't flown much, and he didn't even know if a professional pilot could land the Cessna in one piece.

"When we come to a stop, get everyone out as soon as you can," Steve said. "The landing won't be pretty. I think we lost a wheel when we took off, and we might spin off the runway."

"We gonna flip?" Tara asked quietly as they flew down the runway, dropping lower.

"Hope not," Steve said, and flashed her a smile that was more of a grimace. Martin, Sabrina, Lori, Hawk - they were all quiet, waiting.

A few feet off the ground, Steve turned the yoke slightly to the right. The stall warning screamed at them as he tried to hit the good right wheel first to slow down. The plane hit on the right wheel, and then miraculously hit on the nose wheel as Steve pushed the yoke forward, and then settled on the left main. The plane jerked to the left as the metal hit the ground with a screech and a shower of sparks. Steve jammed the right rudder to the floor and jerked the yoke all the way to the right in an attempt to keep the plane straight. He reached forward with his swollen right arm and screamed in pain as he shut the engine off. He hit the fuel switches, the pain making him light headed, and his vision flashed black and then came back. They flashed past the line of trucks and on down the runway, drifted to the left, past the maintenance buildings, and slid off the runway, the left main hitting the gravel between the runway and the taxiway. The plane jerked around and they hit the taxiway sideways, still moving at thirty knots. They tipped over to the right as the good tire hit the pavement, the damaged main coming off the ground as the plane went over on the right wing and then slammed down on the left main,. They came to a stop on the taxiway, facing back down the way they had come from, tilting to the left, the end of the left wing inches from the ground.

Steve sat there for a few seconds, the plane silent, smoke coming from somewhere below the plane.

"Outeveryoneout!" Steve screamed, and he punched the handle to the left door as Tara did the same to the right. Tara swung out and dropped down out of sight. Steve sat there, too tired, too much in pain to move. He heard Tara swear as she jumped up and pulled Sabrina out. They both grabbed Lori's legs as Martin and Hawk started to slide the wounded woman out the opening. Martin held Lori's shoulders and tried to ease her out, Lori whimpering as they moved her.

They worked Lori out of the plane and onto the ground. Martin and Hawk pushed out of the cabin, Hawk falling on his back outside as he caught his foot in the sill.

"Get her away from the plane, now!" Steve yelled, and slid out to the ground, swaying. He saw a small finger of flame reaching out from under the engine cowling. Hawk and Martin were kneeling beside Lori to pick her up. Steve watched as the flame flickered and then came back, as if caressing the paint on the cowling in front of the windshield.

"When that reaches the fuel lines," Steve said, and didn't finish, all of them moving backward, now ten yards away, then twenty, when the left tank of the plane blew with a loud BANG, the shrapnel flying past them, the plane shielding them from most of the metal, and then someone was running toward them on the taxiway, yelling.

"Get down!"

A man in a pilot's uniform ran up and pushed Tara to the ground as she stood transfixed, watching the burning plane. She huddled beside Steve and Lori as the right wing tank exploded in a bright flash, and shrapnel shrieking over them, small pieces falling on them, and then she stood up, looking at the man in the pilot's uniform.

"Weasel?"

He grinned and stuck out his hand.

"His name's Leonard Mitchell," Hawk explained to the others, smiling as he grabbed the pilot. "But, on the rez, we just call him Weasel."

Martin and Sabrina left, and returned within minutes with a baggage handler and carefully loaded Lori on it. Weasel drove it slowly toward the terminal, and as they got closer, Tara saw the Gulfstream.

"Weasel, the airline pilot," Tara said, shaking her head. "Is it Leonard Mitchell the pilot, or Weasel the pilot? Seems to me that Weasel had escaped the Rez for good, became Leonard Mitchell the pilot. What you doing coming 'round here with us In-dins, us Indians who are trying quite hard to get killed?"

"Bluefeathers reminded me that my real name is Weasel." The stairs came down on the Gulfstream as they stopped. Tara walked up the steps behind Sabrina and Steve and entered the cabin. She sat quietly in a leather seat by the door. The look on the faces of the people inside was one of shock. Steve sat heavily in the nearest seat. Sabrina was covered with dirt, soot, had a bloody gash in her forehead, and her campesnio clothing was in tatters. The front of her white blouse was soaked in blood.

Tara knew that Steve looked worse. She saw Hawk enter the cabin, ducking in the doorway, backing in, carrying Lori by the shoulders. He looked over his shoulder at the leather-covered couch.

"Get off the couch," he said to the two men, still moving backward with Lori, Martin following with her legs.

"I am a United States Ambassador, and I want these people off my plane," the man sputtered, and then his eyes went wide as a strange man in a pilot's uniform reached the couch. The pilot reached down and jerked the ambassador up by his shirt, spun him around and shoved him back down the aisle, the ambassador going down on his hands and knees as he hit the first seat.

Hawk and Martin gently placed Lori on the couch.

Outside the plane Weasel watched as Matt disconnected the hose and pulled it over to the truck.

"We're done," he told Weasel. "This thing is full." Weasel heard a burst of small arms fire coming from somewhere behind the terminal, and he and Matt paused to look that way. The glow from the fires gave the deserted terminal an eerie presence as if it were somehow alive and watching them.

They ran to the side of the plane as the engines spooled up. Weasel ran up the stairway with the co-pilot and as they reached the cabin, Matt turned and hit the button to bring the stairway/door up. As the stairs left the ground, the large jet began to move, the increased power to the engines screaming in the cabin with the door open. When the door closed, Matt joined the captain in the cockpit.

Weasel stood and looked at Lori in the light of the cabin. Her face was gray, the color of dirty water. She looked as if she was breathing her last breath. He entered the cockpit and took up his place behind the captain and sat on the floor.

Tara's weariness overcame her as the plane started. She looked at Lori and couldn't tell if she was alive or not. Steve sat behind her and leaned back, closing his eyes. Sabrina was further back in the cabin, sitting by a man in a suit. The stark cleanliness and plush interior of the Gulfstream made her suddenly realize just how close to the edge, how ragged they were, and how close to dying they had all come.

The plane was taxiing, fast, the undercarriage shaking as they hit bumps in the taxiway. Tara looked through the window to her right and saw an explosion off to the side of the terminal. A jet of fire flashed up and then died down, and then they were past it.

*The terrorists and the army must be still at it. Well they can have it.*

She found that she didn't even care.

The plane slowed, turned, and then the sound of the engines increased and the plane began to move down the runway, and the cabin lights dimmed. Within seconds the plane was rocketing toward the wreckage of the red and white Cessna, the terminal flashed by, and the plane lifted from the runway, turning almost immediately to the west, out toward the ocean, the flight path taking them over the city of Chimbote. Tara watched the dark line of separation, of blackness that was the ocean. Below them she could see oil well riggings on fire, the lights of the town, black smoke, and a series of explosions coming from the center of the lights.

*The fires of hell.*

They were over the ocean and the lights were gone.

It was Tara's last view of Peru.

She had left her best friend there, her childhood friend Delores, and she didn't know if she had the strength to make good on her promise, to return for Delores's body, and the brave young Apache Robert. She sat there, quiet, the tears rolling down her cheeks.

Tara saw a man give Lori a shot, and then tend to Steve. She sat there, numb. The death of Delores was like something that had happened in another life, unreal. Delores. Robert. Lori dying just inches from her. All because she wanted to go to Peru on her spring break.

In the cockpit, Matt was speaking to Lima control.

"Lima control, this is Gulfstream 9528. This is a U.S. government aircraft, filing a flight plan for Los Angeles. Uh, be advised Lima, there is a serious problem in Chimbote. I would guess that the airport is closed." Matt looked at Lydia and Weasel.

"Lima control, this is Gulfstream 9528 -"

"Gulfstream 9528, this is Lima control. The army commander for that department is requesting that your aircraft return to Chimbote for a brief customs inspection."

Weasel shook his head. No.

"Lima control, we can't on this trip. As I said, we carry embassy personnel, and we have been recalled to the United States."

There was no response.

"They're thinking, probably checking with a supervisor on what to do," Weasel said.

"Another fifteen minutes we'll be over two hundred miles out from the coast of Ecuador," Matt said.

"Can they scramble anything that fast?" Weasel looked out at the darkness, and then leaned forward to look at the radar.

"Probably already have some Mirages in the air," Matt said. "But I'll just bet they're busy."

Colonel Hernandez read the dispatch from Lima for a second time. He was to take troops from his Department of Ancash and join up with forces on the Ecuadoran border. It pays to be proactive, he thought. He smiled, and then yelled for his executive officer to get his helicopter ready.

He had places to go, and a war to fight.

# Day Six

# Chapter 51

The Gulfstream climbed into the dark sky over the Pacific Ocean, heading northwest, reached a cruising altitude of 41,000 feet off the coast of Ecuador, paralleled Panama, and then continued north off the west coast of Mexico. In the cockpit, Lydia and Matt had dialed in a course for L.A. with a flight time of six hours and thirty minutes. Weasel rechecked the fuel load with Matt, and calculated that they had enough fuel to fly to Alaska if they had to.

The Gulfstream was a plane that had set many records, including a first ever non-stop flight from New York to Tokyo, a flight that had the Gulfstream Galaxy in the air for thirteen hours. Yeah, Weasel thought, they had enough fuel to go where they needed to go.

Cold River Indian Reservation

Bluefeathers stood on the highway and shrugged his shoulders in his sheepskin coat. A cold wind blew across the high desert. He looked across the bridge to the lights of the vehicles on the other side, the barricades throwing their yellow strobes on the sides of the canyon. When they blew the bridge a span of sixty yards would be impossible to cross with a vehicle. The canyon couldn't be seen from either side unless you stood right on the edge and looked down. It was a two hundred foot slit through basalt rock to the river below. From where Bluefeathers stood, he could see the darkness of the tree line going up the slopes of Mt. Hood.

Once they dropped the bridge, he knew that there was no turning back. He had decided that he would negotiate when he saw his granddaughter and the others. Behind him in the dark he could hear people walking on the road. His people. Talking in low voices. He smelled pipe tobacco and knew that George Cruz was there behind him.

Someone handed Bluefeathers a cup of coffee. He sipped on it and waited. The area where he stood, a high desert meadow in the mountains, was twenty miles long, in the northern center of the reservation, ringed with mountains, timber, and rivers. Yes, they would be on an island if he dropped the northern and southern bridges. There were mountains to the north, the tallest Mt. Hood, and to the west, Mt. Jefferson and Mt. Wilson. Yes, they would be an island, but he never kidded himself about their ability to be self-sufficient. He drove his new pickup to town once a week and bought food at the supermarket, sometimes more than once a week.

He had friends in town. Still, he had maybe a day to get things to the negotiating stage before he was thrown out of office and things went from bad to worse. He saw lights coming down the hill across the bridge. He had a sudden thought of just letting them come, but he knew he couldn't weaken. To do so would be a disaster, and his own tribe would disown him.

"Those lights, they army?" Bluefeathers asked Sgt. Lamebull.

"Looks like it, convoy formation and all."

"Give the order to blow the bridge in one minute. Did you warn the troopers on the other side?"

"They've been told. They moved back a ways."

When it blew there was a series of sharp cracks, a lot of dust and smoke. Not as loud as Bluefeathers had thought it would be. A ragged cheer went up behind him and then quickly died out when he turned around to look. The wind cleared the smoke away quickly, and they heard pieces falling into the sides of the canyon. There was a black emptiness where the bridge had been, and Bluefeathers suddenly felt the same way, black and empty inside. His shoulders slumped as the enormity of what he had done struck home. A quick fix didn't exist for what they were doing. He had just cut the main east-west route to the central, southern, and eastern part of the state.

The new high bridge to the south of the reservation, the one over the Crooked River Canyon, had taken the State of Oregon over four years to build. This would change the way that people did business with the reservation for years. There were tribal members here, and a lot of people in the town who didn't realize that the casino Kah-Nee-Ta was finished. They had just dropped the bridge on the only highway from Portland. He knew there would be a lot of people in the United States who would see this as a way to take back the little that the Indians now have. Get rid of the casinos. It will either destroy us or strengthen us. He hoped that they would survive, and he didn't want to lose sight of Tara and the others.

What a waste if they didn't make it.

"Chairman Bluefeathers." Sgt. Lamebull stood at his side, excited. Bluefeathers looked at him, thinking that he had lost.

"Tara, Hawk and the others, they're out of Peru, heading this way."

Bluefeathers smiled. He had known that Weasel would come through. Hadn't Weasel's mother told him that she had prayed at the Shaker Church for them? He stood without moving for several minutes.

"Blow the southern bridge," he told Lamebull. The sergeant gave him a quizzical look, as if he thought it was all over, and then spoke quietly into his radio, relaying the order.

Aboard the Gulfstream

Tara sketched, the image on the paper taking form and perspective. She couldn't tell what it was, something in the desert, pieces of shiny metal . . . pieces of a plane, with only the tail section left intact. She tore the sketch from the pad and carefully folded the paper and put it in her pants pocket. Steve looked at her with drugged eyes.

Tara leaned back and tried to sleep. She dreamed.

*Death follows me.*

In Tara's dream she sat on the rock with her legs crossed under her, looking down through the sagebrush at the huge federal fire management complex spread out below her. The facility had several beige buildings surrounded by a sea of green trucks that looked like a carpet of unhealthy grass. The complex was used to coordinate fire suppression teams throughout the west, and during the summer and fall, tribal members fought forest fires and wildfires all over the Unites States.

The morning sun had been over the ridge an hour, and there were just a few patches of low fog in the bottom of the valleys where the sun hadn't reached. As Tara stretched, she could feel the heat on her shoulders.

A man walked across the compound far below and made his way to a gate in the perimeter fence. At the distance of a half mile, he looked like a stick figure with no features. Even though she couldn't see his face, Tara knew who it was, and she began to sketch him as he had last appeared to her. That she could sketch him now didn't seem odd - she *knew*, just *knew* now what his face looked like. She sketched the lines on his face, around his eyes, his strong nose, his hair.

The Tara troll was quiet now, even though Tara knew her old enemy was still there, sitting on her shoulder just out of sight, waiting for her to make a mistake.

Tara's father walked slowly up the hill, picking his way around rocks and sagebrush. He was wearing what he wore when she thought about him - blue jeans, boots, a flannel shirt, and a vest.

"Tara."

He stood in front of her, smiling, and held out his hand. Tara stood and turned her sketch up so he could see it.

"You're good, but I've always known that." He seemed to have more wrinkles than she remembered, something easy to fix on the sketch. She handed her sketch to her father. He looked at it, held it up to the light and then carefully rolled it, holding the sketch in his right hand lightly, as if it were a treasure of ineffable value. With his left hand he took hers and walked up the hill, pulling her with him. Tara put her Berol pencil in her back pocket.

She remembered how she would follow him when she was a child, he so large and imposing, so large that he would block out the sun. Since her birth, he *was* the sun. He led her to the top of the hill where they looked down on the highway that ran through the rez to Mount Hood and on to Portland. The highway was a dark pencil lead running straight through the high plateau for miles. As they watched, a coyote broke from cover and ran to the road. When it reached the shoulder it ran up the road, parallel to the centerline until it disappeared over a small crest.

"Don't see spilyay that often in the daytime," her father said matter of factly.

Tara shook her head. No. She continued to hold her father's hand.

"I saw spilyay in my dream," he said softly, "and he talked to me." He looked at Tara, his eyes bright with love. "The spilyay told me that you were going to land in a jet airplane here, on this road." He pointed when spilyay appeared further down the highway, trotting up out of a dip in the road.

"He's going to the spot now, to wait for you."

"But Father, the plane, it's going to crash, and it's all my fault, I drew it." She looked up at him. "I can see the future, you know." A tear rolled down her cheek.

"Show me." Tara removed the sketch from her jeans and slowly unfolded it, as if it were a fragile thing. Her father looked at it carefully and handed the sketch back to her.

"I have seen that you are a person who can see into the future, and sometimes this is a good thing, and sometimes it is a bad thing. But you have the power to change it."

"Change – ?"

"If you can see it, you can change it."

"But Father, how can I?" She whined, as if she were eight again.

"You will know when the time comes."

"Father I –"

He was gone.

"Father, I love you."

He was gone.

As quickly as the spilyay had disappeared in the dip in the road, her father was gone. She stood there and looked down at the highway running straight for miles through the high meadow. She looked around for her father and knew she wouldn't find him. The desert faded and was replaced with a dim light. There was a faint humming in her ears and a gentle rocking. Tara opened her eyes and looked at the seat in front of her.

Hawk was talking to Martin.

Plane.

She was on the Gulfstream flying home.

"Gulfstream Flight 9528, this is L.A. Control, what is your status?" The radio had been silent since they left the coast of Peru, and the sudden direct call startled Weasel.

"Gulfstream 9528, we're just off the coast of Baja, looking to be in your area in two hours," Matt said.

"Status in cockpit, 9528?"

Matt looked at Weasel.

"Tell them," Weasel said.

"L.A. Control, this is Gulfstream Flight 9528, we, uh, we are in control and expect to touch down at the scheduled time. Why do you ask, Control?"

"We have reason to believe that your aircraft has been taken over and that you are not in control of your aircraft."

"Negative, L.A. Control. We just had to get out of Peru, and filed this flight plan kinda late."

A new voice came over their headsets. "Gulfstream Flight 9528, this is Supervisory Special Agent Roberts of the F.B.I., and I need to talk to the ambassador. Right away."

"Stand by," Matt said, and looked at Weasel. Weasel opened the door from the cockpit and looked back into the cabin. The lights were low and most of the passengers were sleeping. He caught John's eye and the man moved toward the cockpit. Weasel quickly explained what was needed.

"Tell them that John from the Confederated Tribes of the Cold River Indian Reservation of Oregon is in control of this aircraft, and that I don't want to talk to them."

The first two interceptors came up to meet them off the coast of Baja, California. Weasel checked the map. They were just south of Guerro Negro.

"We have company coming," Lydia said, tapping the radar.

"Who do you think?" Weasel asked, leaning forward, looking at the scope.

"Fast movers, probably out of Miramar Naval Air Station," Matt said, "Top Gun folks." Then he muttered, "Been there, done that."

Martin looked around in the dim light of the cabin. Steve moaned softly behind him in his sleep. John and the Peruvian agricultural attache were tending to Lori. The attache was a veterinarian and was doing what he could for her. The American attache had declined, saying that he really didn't know that much about animals, or agriculture for that matter. Lori was breathing in shallow little pants, her eyes closed, and to Martin, she looked bad.

Hawk came up the aisle and sat beside Martin.

"She'll make it."

Martin turned away and looked at his reflection in the window. A grimy face stared back at him, a face with a streak of blood on one side that would make him look frightening to anyone else.

John sat on the seat across from them.

"We need to talk," Martin said. "We're all gonna be in a federal prison for a long time, including Weasel up there. Or they might even send us back to Peru. We could land in L.A. or San Francisco, but I think we should go on to Portland, get Lori and Steve to a hospital that would be an hour and a half from home for Lori." Lori mumbled something and Martin bent forward to listen.

279

"No way...I want to go home." She whispered, her eyes tightly closed.

Tara sat up straight.

"We need to land on the rez," she said.

"We can't just make an airfield on the rez in a couple of hours," Hawk said.

"No, we don't have to. We can land on the highway, between Bear Creek and the agency. On the upper plateau." She thought of her father, feeling his love for her.

"Let's get the captain back here, and Weasel," Martin said. "They could tell us if we could do it."

"I wanna go home," Lori muttered.

When Captain Lydia Barnes and Weasel entered the cabin, Martin started.

"Captain Barnes," Martin said, "if we land in L.A. we could get medical attention for Lori and Steve right away. But we've been talking, and we think we should land on the rez."

Weasel jerked his head up and looked at Martin.

"Can we make Portland, nonstop?" Martin asked.

Captain Barnes nodded. "We could probably make Anchorage Alaska, but we just can't land on a little strip, we need a runway a mile plus long and the runways we land on are usually a couple hundred feet wide or wider."

"Don't know about how wide, but a least three lanes of highway, two miles level and straight, no trees, no rocks, no power poles or road signs. At least there won't be when we get there."

Martin waited while the captain thought over what was being said, knowing that such a landing had to pose grave risks for all of them.

"How far from Portland International is it?" Lydia Barnes asked.

"Ten minutes in the air," Martin said. "You could almost make it look like part of the pattern."

"As captain of this airplane, I'm not going to set it down anywhere but a decent airport, and I don't care who's in charge." She looked at John.

"Captain Barnes," Martin said, "we appreciate your cooperation, and your help in getting us out of Peru. We'll land in Portland. Please, you're in charge of the plane."

Lydia Barnes returned to the cockpit, and Martin continued.

"Why don't we land in Portland, have Weasel take off, and then land on the rez?"

Weasel shook his head. "I've never flown this plane before, and you want me to land on a road?"

Tara nodded her head.

"This plane lands at a hundred sixty miles an hour, and I've never flown it before, and you want me to land on the rez?" He looked around at the others, and Martin knew what he was thinking: that it couldn't be done.

"Can't be done," Weasel said, and walked back up to the cockpit.

"Call Bluefeathers," Martin said, and Hawk reached for his cell phone.

Weasel stopped at the cabin door and looked back at the group. They were all watching him, Hawk glaring at him as he spoke into his cell phone. Hell, even the wounded girl, Lori, was looking at him, her eyes bright with pain.

*There was a time when I would have tried to land this on an aircraft carrier and probably could have pulled it off...I would have tried to land this on old Bluefeather's ranch, but what good am I now if I don't land this on the rez? Can you do it, Weasel, one last landing?*

*Yeah, I can do it.*

He walked slowly back to Tara and the others and sat down across the aisle from Tara.

"I've got an idea," he heard himself say. "Here's what we'll do."

Cold River Reservation

The buzzing of chain saws came floating on the wind, through the open window of the pickup. Bluefeathers sat sipping bitter coffee, watching the first light come to the high desert, the sun hitting the snow covered peak of Mt. Jefferson, rising above the forest to his left. He was just ten miles southeast of the northern boundary of the reservation where he had ordered the bridge dropped. The section of road in front of him had a passing lane for two miles, and that was where the airport for the Cold River Indian Tribe was being built.

What he had just ordered - the cutting down of the power poles along the road was going to cause him more grief than all of the other stuff put together. If the electricity went out, then the elders would really get a piece of him. They complained enough during the year if their stoves didn't work. A small army of tribal members attacked road signs and power poles with chain saws. At one point, half mile away, a pole had fallen across the road, and some people were hooking up a pickup to pull it out of the way.

He had already received a flurry of complaints about the power being out, and it would swell to an angry chorus within an hour. He had given the order to put the damned power lines back on line as soon as possible, and he didn't care how.

"How you gonna explain this?" Martha asked.

"I don't think I'll even try."

"Plane's thirty minutes out now," Josephine said from the rear seat. "Still got the Air Force."

"Tell those people on the road to get the rest of the poles down now," Bluefeathers said. "Our people are coming home."

The Gulfstream was still being shadowed by the Air Force. In fact, Weasel could see two F-111 fighters flying just to the left of the large business jet. Probably from Kingsley Field in Klamath Falls. In the cockpit of the Gulfstream they were busy. Lydia Barnes had begun her descent while they were over the Pacific, and came over the Oregon Coast at 30,000 feet just north of Newport, on a course that would take them over the capital city of Salem. From Salem they would fly in a Northeast direction toward Mt. Hood, and would then be in the landing pattern for Portland International.

"Fifteen minutes to touchdown," Matt said.

"20,000 feet," he called again. "Looks like we're going to have good visibility for landing."

The sun came up and flashed over the mountains to the east. Up ahead, Weasel could see Mt. Hood, a snow covered mountain that thrust up out of the green carpet of forest. Wisps of clouds hung around the summit. Hood was home, just a few miles north of the reservation. To his right he could see Mt. Jefferson, the next volcano south of Hood. Jefferson was on the reservation. He felt a lump rise in his throat when he realized how long it had been since he'd been back.

"Fighters?" Lydia asked.

"They went east a minute ago, hanging around about ten miles out, probably to let us set up for landing," Matt said.

Mt. Hood changed in the windshield from dead ahead to being slightly on the right, and then was dead ahead again, filling the windshield, then slowly slid by on the right of the aircraft. They were over the Mt. Hood National Forest now, with nothing but trees in sight. Lydia was going over emergency landing procedures with Matt as Weasel looked on, Weasel watching the procedures, knowing that he could take off and land anything with wings. He wanted to be ready.

"Lydia," Weasel said, leaning forward between the seats, "prepare for a short field landing - leave as much runway in front of us as you can."

"Why?" She looked up sharply at Weasel.

"Lydia, we're landing in Portland, what you said you would do. Come in over the numbers and land short, stand on the brakes and stop."

She glanced at Matt.

"Look, Lydia, I can get John up here with his gun if that's what you want."

She blew air out of her cheeks. "Okay, if that's how you have to have it."

They were down over the Columbia River now, landing to the west.

"Three thousand feet," Matt called. Weasel could see the airport in the distance.

"Fifteen hundred feet."

Lydia had the flaps down, slowing the big jet, the rate of descent higher than normal. Not a great idea for everyday landings, but necessary for a short field landing. They came in over the numbers and hit hard, the landing gear coming up to the stops and then Lydia stood on the brakes as the reverse thrusters deployed, slowing fast. Up ahead, Weasel could see crash trucks on both sides of the runway, and beyond that, a SERT Team vehicle belonging to the Portland Police Bureau's Swat Team. Oh, yeah, they're ready for us.

"When you stop, brakes on and do not taxi - stay on the runway."

"Weasel, I can't leave this plane on an active runway, and I won't," Lydia said as rapid deceleration pushed Weasel forward. The tires howled and a cloud of gray smoke streamed from the main wheels under the wings. The plane came to a stop, and Lydia sat there and looked at Weasel.

"My aircraft," Weasel said. John opened the cockpit door behind them and motioned for Lydia and Matt to get up. Lydia shook her head and threw her headset on the seat and glared at them. Weasel knew she had a lot to say, but she slipped past him without saying a word.

"Good luck, Weasel," Matt said softly as he moved past and into the cabin. Weasel sat in the left seat and buckled in. He picked up the headset out of habit and put it on his head and adjusted the microphone. He didn't think he would be talking to anyone. He set the flaps for takeoff and hoped like hell there was enough runway ahead. If they ran out of runway, they would do so at somewhere between one and two hundred miles an hour. It looked far enough from here, but the distance would shrink fast as they hurtled down toward the end, urging more speed out of the plane. The terminal was on the left side of the Gulfstream.

"They're out," John said. Lydia, Matt, and the flight attendant were on the side of the runway. Weasel ran through a quick mental checklist, looking up from the gauges at movement outside. A crash truck was approaching from down the runway, with the SERT van behind it. Weasel stood on the brakes and eased the throttles all the way forward until they stopped, the plane vibrating, shaking. Before the first truck reached them, Weasel released the brakes and the plane seemed to jump forward. They had a lot less fuel now and the plane was much lighter than when they had taken off from Peru.

The SERT van raced toward them, paralleled them, and was gone as the Gulfstream rapidly increased speed. Weasel had never taken off in a jet with this short of a runway, and he urged the jet to go faster. He had a wild thought that they should have left the ambassador on the ground to lessen the weight, and shook it off, watching the airspeed indicator. He gripped the yoke harder than he ever had, even when he had started flying, waiting for the moment when he could pull back and they were flying.

The earphones crackled with warnings and commands from the control tower. He ignored the voices and watched the airspeed indicator move as the end of the runway screamed toward them. He had decided to lift up as they hit the numbers if they were close to rotating, that moment when the airplane would fly.

*We're not going to make it*

The end of the runway streaked toward Weasel, and as he hit the numbers he pulled back on the yoke gently, waiting for the gear to hit the barrier at the end of the runway and the plane to slam into the grass at over a hundred fifty miles an hour.

The numbers flashed under the plane and they were flying!

He kept the nose down slightly to increase speed and retracted the landing gear. Weasel pulled the yoke back and the Gulfstream shot upward. He turned slightly to the left and began a wide circle to the south, to take them back to the east toward Mt. Hood. He depressed the intercom to speak to the cabin.

"Well, we're up folks, next stop Cold River in about ten minutes. I want everyone to keep buckled, but I need someone up here right away." He had to talk to the tower, to let them know where he was going. Weasel knew that by now they were alerting other planes about his take-off and there were some worried and pissed off pilots out there.

"Portland tower, this is Gulfstream 9528, just leaving PDX at two thousand feet."

"Gulfstream 9528, Portland tower, maintain altitude and heading so we can get you back here safely."

"Negative, Portland, we're heading for Cold River. I'm going to turn to the east and climb to five thousand feet."

There was silence for a moment. "Uh, Gulfstream 9528, you are clear to turn east and climb to five thousand, then we'll vector you back. There's a Delta heavy at two thousand feet, just east of you."

"Gulfstream 9528."

They cleared him out of the traffic, but that didn't mean there weren't other planes around. He sensed movement behind him and saw Martin crouching in the cockpit.

"Martin, take the right seat and buckle in," Weasel said.

"Now what?" Martin asked. He felt as if he were facing a firing squad.

"Look for planes, look all around and yell out if you see one, I don't care how far away. I'm gonna be busy here."

They flew toward the snow covered slopes of Mt. Hood, the mountain looming larger in the windshield. They would follow the road, just to the west of Hood. The summit for the pass was just under five thousand feet. Weasel told Martin that he planned to come in just over the pass, and then start letting down, as the landing area was at three thousand five hundred feet, just miles from the southern slope of Hood. The high desert plateau on the rez, where the terrain went from a carpet of trees to sagebrush and juniper.

Martin pointed to a flashing light on the panel, and Weasel handed him a headset.

"Weasel...Leonard, please listen," Lydia said, "if you hear me listen and please acknowledge."

They didn't answer.

"Weasel, this is Lydia, please-"

"Weasel here."

"Please return to Portland and let your passengers off."

"Negative, my orders are to land on the road."

As they approached Mt. Hood, Martin saw the highway, and they made a turn to the southeast, following the road. He saw movement to his left and saw an F-111 just yards off his wingtip.

"Lydia, are you there?" Weasel asked.

"Lydia here."

"Get those fast movers off me, this will be hard enough to do without distractions." She didn't answer.

"What are they going to do, shoot us down?"

She depressed the microphone button and Martin could hear voices in the background. "Okay, Weasel, they're going away."

"Anything I need to know, Lydia, to help with the landing?"

"Keep the speed up higher than you might think, Weasel, so you can go around if you have to."

"Okay, well I'll talk to you after."

They flew over the pass at a thousand feet above ground level, and when the highway started to straighten out, Weasel started to let down. Martin listened as Weasel mumbled his landing procedure.

"Gear down.

"Flaps 30 degrees.

"Airspeed 200 knots."

They came over the trees at a thousand feet and were suddenly over the meadow. They flashed over the army convoy, his mind dimly registering the hole where the bridge had been, and then he saw the "airstrip." Damn, that road looks narrow. Three miles ahead he saw the flashing lights of a police car, and down the road another three miles or so, another police car. Bluefeathers said that he would mark the runway with cars, so this must be it. Martin glanced over at Weasel.

His face was white, drawn, and he was sweating.

The sweat rolled off Weasel's face. A drop hit the yoke and rolled off. He shook his head. Concentrate. He glanced at the altimeter.

*Three hundred feet. Airspeed 180 knots. Flying straight and steady, hand on the throttles, ready to hit it and declare a missed approach, save some lives and go back to Portland.*

*Christ the whole reservation must be here, what the hell? On both sides of the runway (and to Weasel it was now a runway) cars, trucks, pickups, vehicles of all descriptions were parked off the runway in the sagebrush. Ohmigod, there's even the bus for the Elders of Cold River parked down there, probably old Mrs. Wanapata selling fry bread, and then Weasel was busy, scanning airspeed, sink rate, lined up, Christ what are they thinking, and then he knew that his mother, his family would be there.*

Rodriquez had his camera crew set up where the tribal representative had pointed out to them, on the road by the police car at the end of the "runway." He had tried to interview Bluefeathers, the little old guy who started this whole thing, and with his braided gray hair, western shirt, jeans, and cowboy boots he certainly made good material, but Bluefeathers wouldn't talk with him. There was a lot of background material here to photo though, and he was going live in thirty seconds.

Rodriguez positioned himself so the camera took in the tribal police car, the "runway," the crowds of people and the almost festive atmosphere. He got his cues. Five seconds. He turned to face the camera.

"This is Tony Rodriguez for Fox, live from the Cold River Reservation in Oregon. We are here, with what must be most of the tribal members along a roadway in the upper part of the reservation. Fox has learned that a plane is approaching, possibly to land on this road behind me, and that the plane is carrying the students from Peru, students who have been-"

The camera operator in front of Rodriguez leaned forward, his eyes widening, and Rodriguez saw people around him pointing, some running past him. He turned and looked behind him and saw the Gulfstream coming over the trees, back toward the gorge. The size of the plane jolted him, even at over three miles the thing was huge for a landing on the road. He signaled for his operator to keep rolling.

"Behind me, as you can see, a plane is approaching, a large jet, planning to land on this road, coming to you live and exclusive on Fox."

Rodriguez waited, knowing that the visual impact of the plane landing was more of an impact than his words. He had a sudden thought: What if it didn't stop, and Tony looked around for a place to run. Rocks, juniper, and sagebrush. It didn't look too promising. The camera operator better hold in there though. Shots like this just didn't happen.

Tara placed the napkin on her leg and stared at the emblem of the Gulfstream embossed in gold and silver on the cloth. She started a sketch, quickly penciling in the road, the rocks, the brush and trees. She sketched an outline of the plane stopped on the road, intact. *Father please let this work.*

In the Oval Office, the President and his staff were watching the events from Cold River on the large screen. No one spoke, the scene far too strange, too dramatic for talk. The President felt a strange thrill, a feeling he associated with the need to pull for the underdog, the disenfranchised, and he knew then that much of the country would feel the same way.

"The ambassador's on board," the Secretary of State said quietly, leaning forward in his chair. "What do we do if they make this landing?"

"We negotiate," the President said. "We negotiate."

Tara's black pencil flew over the sketch paper, hoping she had enough detail, feeling Steve's eyes on her, wanting to get this right, wanting to deny death that might come in seconds.

*Weasel flew over the police car at a hundred feet, the high desert landscape flashing by, and kept his eyes fixed on the center line of the highway, his goal to have the mains hit on either side of the line, knowing that he had maybe a dozen feet of drift before the main wheels hit the shoulder, and then they would cartwheel and explode at a hundred fifty knots, the burning remnants of the plane blasting through the crowd, and he shook his head, throwing off the image, and let the speed bleed off, bringing the nose up, flaring, his hand on the throttles, ready to slam them forward and go around, and he knew then if he missed the approach he would land in Portland, and then the main gear hit the roadway, the landing solid, the nose coming down, and when the nose wheel touched he hit the reverse thrusters and waited for a second, and then applied the brakes, the Gulfstream holding*

*steady, the airspeed bleeding off, the pickups and cars flashing by,*
*people holding up rifles, flags, cheering, Hawk with a silly grin on his*
*face.*

*And then they came to a stop. On the rez.*

An Air Life helicopter was on the road just ahead of the police
car. Weasel shook his head and grinned. How that old man had
convinced Air Life to come on the reservation was amazing. Nothing
would surprise me now. Hawk was clubbing him on the shoulder,
yelling. Weasel grinned wildly. He felt like yelling and crying at the
same time. He was home. He wanted more than anything to see his
mother. His family. And then that old man, Bluefeathers.

Maybe they needed a pilot on the rez.

Tara sat in her seat, not moving as the plane came to a stop. John
opened the cabin door and stepped outside. Tara heard voices, excited.
She watched as two medics came aboard and kneeled down by Lori,
Jimmy Dhanisho flashing her a grin as they checked Lori and started
an IV. As they worked on Lori, Tara looked out the window. There
were people and cars all around the plane, watching, most of them
quiet now. Lori was carefully loaded on a gurney and as she went by,
she weakly gave Tara a thumbs up, tears running down her cheeks. She
said something to Tara, her lips working.

"Atauwisa." *Love.*

"Atauwisa," Tara said, and then Lori was gone. A cheer went up
from outside. Steve was next, and Tara reached out and touched him
as he went by. Tara closed her eyes and then opened them to see her
grandfather in front of her, looking at her in that way of his. She
reached out and grabbed him and cried his name, sobbing as she tried
to tell him about Delores, about Robert. He held her and stroked her
head.

"Grandfather, De-," and she shook. People went by her and
outside until just the two of them were there. Hawk stood by the
ambassador in the back, watching. Bluefeathers looked up and saw
them, nodding to Hawk.

"Who the hell's in charge here," Ambassador Roberts said. He
looked at the little Indian with gray braided hair. "I'm Ambassador
Roberts and I -"

"Take him outside, Hawk," Bluefeathers commanded. "Give him
to the leaders of the Yakama Nation. They have some things to
discuss."

Tara was home.

# Epilogue

Three Months Later

Cold River Reservation

Martin walked slowly up the dirt road, his boots making little puffs of dust that hung suspended in the still morning air. At 10 a.m. it was already eighty-five degrees. He shielded his eyes and looked ahead, walking east into the morning sun. The road below the basalt rim rock formation was nothing more than a trail going uphill through the sagebrush and juniper trees. The town of Cold River spread out in the valley far below him, the faded red brick of the BIA school looking out of place in the tans and brown of the high desert sand.

He stopped to wipe the sweat from his forehead. The boots and jeans were going to be too hot. His t-shirt with the faded SERT logo was dark with sweat by the time he got to the first burial plot. Martin resumed his walk, the drone of insects loud now as the air heated up. The road twisted toward the towering rock columns and he walked into the shade, noticing Tara for the first time. She sat with her back to the rock, sketching.

"Hello, Martin."

He sat beside her and looked over the valley.

"Hello."

She was wearing cut off jeans, tennis shoes, a tank top, her hair coming out of the back of a baseball cap in a braid.

"What're you doing up here, you Šiyápu?" She said it softly, and put her hand on his arm.

"Looking for you." Her face was clean, the grime and blood and pain of their first meeting gone. He looked over at her sketch and saw it was of him, walking up the road beside the burial plots, under the rimrock.

"Help me with something for a while?" She got up and walked up the road into the sunlight. At the next burial plot her Honda was parked off the road, the hatch open. In the back she had cartons of flowers, watering cans, gardening tools.

"You carry, I'll plant," she said.

They worked quietly on Delores's grave, Tara digging holes, watering, Martin breaking apart flowers and handing them to her. Pansies. Reds, whites, yellows, purples...brilliant oranges.

"Steve going back for the body...that was something, wasn't it," Tara said at last. She sat up and looked at Martin, her eyes shining.

"Yes, it was," he said, "but one of you had to get her body, and...and he knew where it was." Steve had gone back with a delegation from the State Department ten days after they flew out, his arm mending, going back to recover Delores, and that certainly wasn't without risk. Delores was flown home and her body received a proper dressing in Cold River. The entire tribe and hundreds of others came for the funeral.

"These will die in the sun," Tara said, "but Delores knows that we planted them and they'll be pretty for a day or so." She pushed the dirt around her arrangement.

"What about you two, Steve and you?" Martin asked.

"He's a good man, isn't he?" She said it as a statement. She rocked back on her heels and looked at Martin, wiping dirt from her face with the back of her hand. "I don't know, we're a country apart, him in Connecticut and me here." She played with the trowel in the dirt. "We're just going to see what happens," she said at last.

"Your grandfather, he wants me to stay on here," Martin said, getting to his reason for walking up the hill.

"What about it, you going to?"

He didn't answer.

"You should, you know, and what about Lori?" Tara grinned at him.

"She's still having some problems, walks with a cane, won't let anyone help her. Said to say hello."

"People been talking around how you carried her at the funeral. Looks pretty good to me." Tara dug more holes and pointed at a carton of marigolds. Martin broke apart the individual planting boxes and they worked for another few minutes in silence.

"Lori and I, well, she and I are going to be permanent. Whatever I decide to do here is alright with her."

Tara sat back on her heels. "Lori told me about you...your incident, your..."

"Claire, the little girl."

"Yes."

"Claire doesn't visit me as often," Martin said softly, "and I guess that's good." They planted flowers for the next several minutes. He had walked up here to discuss two things: his job and Lori. He didn't know if he should stay, if it was the right thing for him to be here. He'd had the talk with Bluefeathers, and the man wouldn't hear of him leaving. But that was because of the rescue, as people had taken to calling their trip to Peru, and it didn't answer the questions Martin had about himself.

When they had landed, Bluefeathers had immediately declared an end to hostilities, had negotiated with the U.S. Government to not bring charges against anyone connected with the rescue, had a press conference, the script already printed. "When we send soldiers out," he had said, "out to do battle for the United States, you don't return them to a trial. We did your job for you," he told the President. And the President went along with him, riding a wave of public support for Cold River. The F.B.I. agent hadn't been harmed after all - just out fishing in his secluded cabin.

Martin thought that Bluefeathers was amazing. In the past three months, the Tribal leader had managed to have a temporary bridge constructed across the Deschutes River, and the casino and resort was bulging with people who wanted to be able to say how they had been on the Rez. He had even managed to get Weasel's flight status cleared up. Quite a man. But Martin and Bluefeathers and not just a few others knew how close it had been to going the other way.

"Delores always liked flowers," Tara was saying. Martin nodded. He hoped that he had someone who loved him this much when he was in his grave. Delores was, in a small way, more fortunate than some.

"I'm staying," Martin said suddenly, the sun hot on his shoulders. He blinked back a thought of Claire, of the school, the cries of the children. Maybe they wouldn't haunt him so much now, here on the rez. Maybe they wouldn't.

Tara stood and handed Martin a canteen. "What're you gonna do, you Šiyápu, be a wanna be In-din?" She grinned.

Martin returned her grin.

"No. Working on the reservation is plenty for me...but I need for you to tell me how to ask Lori, to ask her to marry me."

"Well, that I can do, Wanna Be," Tara said as she threw an arm

293

around his shoulder.  Help me load this stuff and I'll give you a ride back to town."


San Carlos Indian Reservation
Arizona

The slight figure limped, dragging his left foot, walking up the road past the store at Whitesilver, thinking he would be at his mother's house before dark.  His face was hidden by a straw hat, the dirty clothes he wore hung loosely on his shoulders, his sleeves flapping gently as if on an uncertain scarecrow.  He had been waiting for this day since he was pulled from the icy water in Peru, unconscious and bleeding from a half-dozen wounds, tended to by campesinos and kept alive.

His family would tell stories about him, next to Mangas Colorado, Cochise, Geronimo.  They would sing stories about him.

Robert was home.

## Author Enes Smith

Enes Smith relied upon his experience as a homicide detective to write his first novel, *Fatal Flowers* (Berkley, 1992). Crime author Ann Rule wrote, "*Fatal Flowers* is a chillingly authentic look into the blackest depths of a psychopath's fantasies. Not for the fainthearted . . . Smith is a cop who's been there and a writer on his way straight up. Read this on a night when you don't need to sleep, you won't . . ."

*Fatal Flowers* was followed by *Dear Departed* (Berkley, 1994). "You might want to lock the doors before starting this one," author Ken Goddard wrote, "Enes Smith possesses a gut-level understanding of the word 'evil,' and it shows." Ken Goddard is the author of *The Alchemist*, *Prey*, and *Outer Perimeter*, and Director of the National Wildlife Forensic Laboratory.

Smith's work as a Tribal Police Chief for the Confederated Tribes of the Warm Springs Indians of Oregon led to his first novel in Indian Country, *Cold River Rising*. *Cold River Resurrection* is the second novel in the Cold River series. He has been one of the few Šiyápu to hold that position in Indian Country. He worked as police chief in 1994 and 1995, and even though he is a Šiyápu, he was asked back as tribal police chief in 2005.

He has been a college instructor and adjunct professor, teaching a vast array of courses including Criminology, Sociology, Social Deviance, and Race, Class, and Ethnicity. He trains casino employees in the art of nonverbal cues to deception. He is a frequent keynote speaker at regional and national events, and has been a panelist at The Bouchercon, the World Mystery Convention.

14241609R00167

Made in the USA
San Bernardino, CA
21 August 2014